BE CAREFUL WHAT YOU WISH FOR

by

Krystal Lawrence

Cover designed by Telemachus Press, LLC

Cover art:
Copyright © iStockPhoto/7218904/ChuckSchugPhotography
Copyright © iStockPhoto/9193473/eyewave
Copyright © iStockPhoto/10066023/Milous
Copyright © iStockPhoto/11245838/By_Nicholas
Copyright © iStockPhoto/24435527/Juanmonino
Copyright © iStockPhoto/5414434/dibbler2
Copyright © iStockPhoto./eszawa (MoonBats)
Copyright © iStockPhoto/13228172/blackjake

Published by Telemachus Press, LLC
http://www.telemachuspress.com

Visit the author website:
http://www.darksidestories.com

ISBN: 978-1-939927-44-6 (eBook)
ISBN: 978-1-939927-45-3 (Hardcover)

Version 2013.11.14

Printed in the United States of America

10 9 8 7 6 5 4 3 2 1

For Linden—
Forever in my heart.

BE CAREFUL WHAT YOU WISH FOR

PART I
What Elizabeth McGwire Did For Love

When a man loves a woman he'll sleep out in the rain.
–Percy Sledge, 1966

When a woman loves a man she'll kill for him.
–Elizabeth McGwire, 2002

Chapter 1

The building was old and drafty. The stench of decaying wood and mold clung to it with a tentacle-like grip. Thick layers of cobwebs festooning the rafters were graphic evidence of generations of spiders that had lived and died in this antiquated, moldering relic of years gone by. What one noticed upon entering the store was the multitude of well-worn books lining the dusty shelves and piled haphazardly along the walls.

Belda locked her small apartment on the upper floor and carefully negotiated the creaking staircase, her black cat at her heels. Her swollen, red-knuckled hands clenched a steaming mug of pungent tea. She was old certainly, but it was impossible to tell exactly how old she might be. Her gray hair was pulled back severely from her brow and coiled atop her head in a tight knot, which was held together with a large, ornate silver clip. She wore a wildly patterned flowing dress that fell just below her thick ankles, and flat black moccasins. A large silver medallion hung about her neck. Several bangles dangled from her wrists and earlobes. Her olive skin was smooth and nearly unlined, her eyes a disturbing pale gray. Her clients, who paid well for her special talents, often wondered why she did not cure her own terrible arthritis. They knew Belda most certainly had the power. If they had asked her, she would have told them that some things were better left in the hands of God. But of course, they never asked.

Belda had been in that same corner shop on Magnolia Boulevard for decades. She rented the gloomy building with the living quarters above when she arrived from Romania. When the building's owner died sixteen years ago, his son inherited the dusty old edifice. The son wanted to sell it. He lived in another state and didn't wish to be anyone's landlord. He put the building up for sale, then abruptly changed his mind and pulled it off the market the following week. No one ever knew why, not even his wife. But Belda knew.

Shortly after listing the building for sale, the new owner met a fellow named Nick at a bar. Nick bought him a drink. After he finished that libation, he had a sudden and inexplicable urge to keep the building and allow the tenant to remain. He received a rent check on the third of every month. The same amount his father received, on the exact same day, and business continued as usual.

The weather-beaten sign held by rusted chains read *Bella Luna Bookstore and Metaphysical Shop.* But books and psychic paraphernalia were not the primary business that brought desperate people from all walks of life to Belda seeking her services. She was far more than just the proprietor of a bookshop. She earned her true income from her other talents. She never advertised, but her business thrived. There were always those who needed her services and were willing to pay for it. Some paid dearly.

There were times when things didn't turn out very well for those who enlisted Belda's services. Such as the case of Elizabeth McGwire, a woman currently standing trial for first degree murder. But still they came, and unlimbered their checkbooks to gratefully pay whatever the asking price.

Once, long ago, a particularly annoying policeman started asking too many questions, looking into areas that Belda felt were none of his business. He vanished one cold November day, leaving a wife and two young daughters. He was never seen again.

~~~~

The sound of the bell above the door alerted Belda to someone entering the shop.

Gabriella Cruz strode in carrying a large canvas tote-bag filled with school books. She was a beautiful, raven-haired girl of seventeen and a senior in high school. She had been one of Belda's assistants for four years. Ever since her stepfather encountered a rather nasty accident, courtesy of Belda.

Before the *accident* Gabriella used to spend long afternoons hidden between the rows of dusty shelves reading book after book, waiting until evening when her mother would be home from work and it was safe for her to go home. Shortly after the girl confided in Belda about the abuse she was subjected to at the hands of her stepfather, the man fell victim to an explosion at the paper mill where he worked.

Though Belda never told her, Gabriella knew the old woman had caused the accident. This knowledge didn't inspire any shock or fear; only gratitude. Her life had been a living hell until that explosion. The woman rescued her from a hellish life of rape and abuse at the hands of her mother's second husband. In Gabriella's heart the end firmly justified the means.

Belda's other assistant, Nicholas, was on an errand this morning.
~~~~

Belda glanced at the cuckoo clock hanging above the sales desk and nodded to the girl as she came in. “Nicholas should be concluding his errand now,” she said.

The girl breezed by the woman, planting a quick kiss on her cheek and bent down to pet Eros, the black cat. “Yes, I saw on the news that the trial is starting this morning. You don’t think the woman will say anything, do you?” Gabriella asked, a worried frown creasing her lovely brow.

“It would be quite unfortunate for her if she did, my dear.” Belda appeared unconcerned.

Gabriella unlocked a drawer below the ancient cash register and withdrew an equally ancient leather-bound appointment book.

“You have Martin Reynolds, that businessman from New York at ten.”

A ghost of a smile crossed the woman’s face. “Ah, yes, Mr. Reynolds. His purchase is not quite completed. I just have a few things to add and it will be ready. I best go upstairs and finish it before he arrives.” Belda turned toward the staircase. “Come along, Eros, help me with Mr. Reynolds’s brew,” she called to the black cat sitting on the sales counter grooming his face.

The cat looked up at her, meowed briefly at Gabriella, and trotted off to follow his mistress up the stairs.

Chapter 2

A lone figure in a Polo shirt and khakis sat on a brick retaining wall, apart from the crowd clustered in front of the King County courthouse. He was a clean-cut man in his late twenties, unremarkable except for a twisted scar running from just under the left side of his jawline and disappearing into the hair at his temple. He smoked a cigarette and observed the chaos before him with little interest. He was here to deliver a message to Elizabeth McGwire—sole heir of well known, well respected, unfathomably wealthy, and now-deceased art collector Theodore McGwire.

Anyone else might have thought the task impossible given the media swarm, the police, and the extra security sure to be surrounding the defendant when she arrived, but Nicholas Aguilar was unconcerned with the task before him. His past was filled with far more dangerous and difficult errands than this one.

Nicholas possessed an amazing ability to enter a crowd unobserved and disappear like a wisp of smoke in the wind. He flipped the butt of his cigarette into the nearby bushes and rose to his feet as a sleek black limousine rolled to a stop at the curb.

~~~~

A sea of reporters, cameras, microphones, and onlookers blanketed the courthouse steps. The curb was lined with news vans from all the major networks, cable and local TV stations. The police were there for crowd control. Everyone waited impatiently for a glimpse of the pretty and petite redhead accused of such an unspeakable crime.

A blonde TV reporter looked intently into the hand-held camera perched on her assistant's shoulder, and announced, "The tension at the King County courthouse is mounting as the most sensational murder trial of the decade gets underway. Murder suspect, Elizabeth McGwire, is expected to arrive any moment with her attorney Richard Cohen. Followers of this scandalous case were stunned when McGwire met an astronomical bail amount and was released on bond two weeks ago. There was speculation she was a flight risk. Her trial begins in just over an hour and Channel 5 Eyewitness News will be live in the courtroom to bring you up to the minute details of this disturbing case. From Seattle, Fawn Turner, Channel 5 Eyewitness News."

Similar reports were being broadcast on other networks as this long, hot morning dragged on.

The reporters rushed forward engulfing the rear door of the limo as it opened. Dozens of questions were shouted at the small huddle of men in dark suits that surrounded the pale but composed woman. The defendant wore a powder blue skirt and cream colored silk blouse, with a Chantilly lace collar. Her auburn hair fell loose to her shoulders, and large dark glasses hid cat-green eyes.

Two of the men draped protective arms about her narrow shoulders, as the others held off the crowd with outstretched hands. They hustled her quickly up the steps into the courthouse. The media frenzy followed them down the long corridor toward the
~~~~

courtroom where Elizabeth McGwire's fate would be decided. They peppered her with a barrage of questions.

The defendant looked back over her shoulder and peered through the crowd to see if she could spot Darrin among the thick horde of people following her. Countless flashbulbs exploded in her eyes as she turned, momentarily blinding her. Elizabeth remained silent and in control as she allowed her defenders to lead her away from the pack of wolves nipping at her heels.

As they pushed the courtroom doors open and ushered the woman inside, she stopped and scanned the crowd again for any sign of Darrin. Her eyes, hidden behind the dark glasses, betrayed her nervousness. He promised he'd be here.

Elizabeth was released from jail on bond three weeks before, and though she had spent little time with her lover since her release, she was confident Darrin still cared for her and would support her through this nightmare. Elizabeth was not sure she would be able to endure this hellish experience without him. She wished she could have caught a glimpse of him somewhere in the crowd of people mobbing the halls. Because of the public interest and the media frenzy the case created, the courtroom would be packed. There would be few seats available, so she had told him to arrive early. His failure to phone her last night as he'd promised only increased her anxiety.

Elizabeth was temporarily distracted by someone thrusting a folded scrap of paper into her hand. As she looked up she saw the back of a retreating figure in a green Polo shirt disappearing into the mass of people that huddled outside the door. She looked to her attorney, but he was deep in conversation with Olin, one of the other lawyers assigned to her case.

They took their seats at the large, well-worn wooden table and she unfolded the small piece of paper the man had pushed into her palm. When she read it, an involuntary shudder racked her slender frame and she gasped.

Cohen looked at her questioningly and placed a reassuring hand on her arm. "What is it?" he whispered.

Elizabeth quickly refolded the note before he could see it and dropped it into her handbag. "Nothing. Just nerves." She attempted a smile that felt forced and insincere.

Cohen patted her arm again and told her to remove her sunglasses. He then turned back to the notes for his opening statement.

~~~~

While Elizabeth McGwire was scanning the crowd for her boyfriend Darrin Perkins, he was nudging the girl that lay in bed next to him awake. She began to stir and slowly awaken. He couldn't exactly remember her name. What the hell was it? Debra or Deirdre—something like that. He wasn't sure. They met last night while he was bar-hopping with some buddies and the bimbo ended up at his place. She finally opened one groggy eye, and he was reminded of the words from an old Willie Nelson song: *At two I came home with a ten and at ten I woke up with a two.*

"Come on, darlin'," Darrin said as he lit a cigarette and threw the blankets off the bed. "The party is over, and I gotta get down to the courthouse."

"What time is it?" she yawned.

Darrin grimaced as he was bathed in warm, stale breath, the ghost of old tequila blown into his face.

Startled by the sudden chill from having the blankets pulled off her naked body, the girl grabbed for the covers and Darrin yanked them out of her grasp.
~~~~

"It's show time, that's what time it is. Now get your ass up, will you?" Darrin climbed from the bed and zipped into a pair of Levi's, ignoring the girl's insolent stare as she padded naked into the bathroom.

Chapter 3

The courtroom was called to order with the Honorable Judge Rudolph Westerfield presiding. The defendant glanced at the jury. She looked nervously at the packed courtroom.

Olin squeezed her arm and whispered out of the corner of his mouth, "Liz, pay attention to the proceedings and stop looking around."

She shot him an ill-tempered glare, but kept her eyes straight ahead. *Damn Darrin anyway. I should have known,* she fumed to herself.

Patricia Camden, the county's deputy prosecutor and media darling, rose from her seat to face the jury. She wore a no-nonsense beige suit. Her short brown hair framed a plain but pretty face, nearly devoid of makeup.

"Good morning," she began, a small, polite smile on her lips. "On behalf of King County, I appreciate your time and willingness to help bring justice in the wake of an atrocious crime that was committed by the defendant, Elizabeth Gwendolyn McGwire."

She paused briefly to make eye contact with each juror individually before continuing. "The prosecution intends to prove beyond a reasonable doubt that on the night of August twenty-second, Theodore McGwire was murdered in cold blood by his only living relative."

Camden paused once again for effect, standing directly in front of Elizabeth, boring holes into her with her eyes. Elizabeth returned the prosecutor's stare without flinching.

When the silence that followed became rather awkward, Patricia Camden, realizing this ploy was ineffective, turned and walked back toward the jury.

"We have motive, ladies and gentlemen," she went on unperturbed. "The oldest motive in the book. Greed and lust for money. Money that Miss McGwire couldn't touch until her grandfather was dead. We have means. Because of Theodore McGwire's concern for the welfare of his granddaughter, Elizabeth, he invited her to live in his house until she could get back on her feet financially. And we also have opportunity. A dark hallway, and a strong young woman lying in wait. He was an elderly man, but in reasonably good health. He could have lived for many more years. But Elizabeth McGwire couldn't wait that long. She was out of time. She had just lost her job and been evicted from her apartment, she had creditors hounding her, trying to collect the thousands of dollars she had amassed in credit card debt, and her leased Mercedes was being repossessed. The accused needed money and she needed it fast. It wasn't enough that her grandfather allowed her to live in his home after she was evicted from her apartment. It wasn't enough that he offered food and shelter. Elizabeth McGwire wanted more. She wanted her grandfather to pay the mountain of debt she accumulated, and to all intents and purposes, subsidize her rather loose life style. Theodore McGwire refused to do this. He wanted his adult granddaughter to take some responsibility for her own life. So, on the night of August twenty-second, believing she was above the law, defendant, Elizabeth McGwire, coldly stood in the dimly lit hall until her grandfather rose from his bed. In the dark she brutally pushed him down the long wooden staircase, ending his life and ending her wait for his fortune. How many nights had she crouched in that darkened hallway waiting for her grandfather to rise in the middle of the night? How many days did she plot this horrendous crime before the opportunity arose to finally rid herself of her hated grandfather, Theodore McGwire, and gain access to his wealth?"

Patricia Camden shook her head in disgust. "These are questions we may never be able to answer. But one thing you will know by the end of this trial, ladies and gentlemen, is that regardless of how long she waited, Elizabeth McGwire realized her wish and ruthlessly ended an innocent man's life. The defendant is not exempt from the laws that govern the rest of us because she comes from a family of means. Being born into wealth and privilege does not give one the right to believe they are above the law. The laws of this state, and indeed of this country, are equitable to both rich and poor alike. No one, I may remind you, is a law unto themselves. The defendant, Elizabeth McGwire, must pay for her heinous crime. She must be found guilty. Thank you, ladies and gentlemen."

With that abrupt conclusion, Patricia Camden walked briskly back to the prosecutor's table and busied herself looking at papers, as if the defending attorney's opening statement didn't warrant her attention.

"Thank you, Ms. Camden. Mr. Cohen, your opening remarks." Judge Westerfield gestured to Richard Cohen with his hand.

Cohen rose from the defense table, buttoning his jacket.

Just as Cohen rose, a disheveled Darrin Perkins slunk in the rear doors of the courtroom. He was stopped by a guard turning away late-coming gawkers from the already overflowing courtroom. Darrin fished a crumpled piece of paper from his jeans. He handed it to the guard, who read it and allowed him to enter. Seeing no chairs available, Darrin leaned against a side wall trying to get Elizabeth's attention by a loud, obnoxious whisper of, "Pssssst, hey, Lizzie."

After three unsuccessful attempts to gain her attention, he was told to keep it down by the uniformed guard. Darrin sulked in his corner until the recess was called.

"Good morning, ladies and gentlemen," Richard Cohen began in a polite, soft-spoken tone. He leaned his tall, lean frame against the railing separating the jurors from the court stenographer's table and tapped one long, slender finger repeatedly against his mouth, staring off in the distance, as if lost in thought.

After a few moments, he commented, "You know, it's interesting to me that the prosecution seems to have everything but proof." He raised his voice on the last word and looked at the jury. Shrugging his shoulders, and in a soft, conversational tone—a tone much more suited to a friendly lunch than to a courtroom, he asked the jury, "Did you notice that? Ms. Camden says they have motive. Motive? A woman who was struggling financially and moved in with her only living relative until she could find a job and get back on her feet? That's motive?"

Shaking his head, as if dismissing the idea as ludicrous, Cohen continued, "Ms. Camden says they have opportunity. Opportunity? Elizabeth happened to be in the house the night her elderly grandfather misjudged his step and fell down the stairs? That's opportunity?"

Shaking his head again, Cohen went on, "No, ladies and gentlemen, that's only wishful thinking on the part of an overzealous prosecution, with absolutely nothing concrete on which to base their ridiculous accusations. I'm sorry, but it will take a lot more than just the fact that my client had the misfortune of being in the house on the same night Theodore McGwire accidentally fell to his death to prove their allegations."

Cohen walked behind Elizabeth and laid both hands on her slender shoulders. He was pleased to see Pat Camden glaring at him from the prosecution table, her papers now entirely forgotten.

"The prosecution's case is based solely on smoke and mirrors. There is not a shred of hard evidence that points the finger of guilt at my client. The prosecution's argument is pure fantasy. They have no murder weapon, they have no motive, no opportunity." He glared at the jury for emphasis. "My client did not murder her grandfather. The death of Theodore McGwire was an unfortunate accident. The county lost a benefactor. I myself attended the Seattle Art Museum charity auction just last year when Mr. McGwire donated an original Edward Hopper painting from his prized collection. We all feel the loss of this great man. But none more than my client, who lost not a benefactor, but her beloved grandfather."

Cohen shook his head, and swiped at his eyes with the back of his hand, as though wiping away imaginary tears. He inhaled a deep, sorrowful breath that could be heard all through the packed courtroom, "And now, as if Elizabeth hasn't suffered enough, the prosecution wants this innocent woman to be sentenced to a life within prison walls."

Cohen shook his head and looked earnestly at the jury. He concluded his opening statement with, "I know you good people won't let them do that. I know you won't let them turn a sad and unfortunate accident into a witch hunt. There can be no conviction of guilt, because there simply was no crime. Thank you, ladies and gentlemen."

He unbuttoned his jacket and sat down beside his client.

The judge, barely able to conceal his amusement at Richard Cohen's emotional opening statement, grumbled, "Thank you, counselor," and called for a fifteen minute recess. He loved Cohen's legendary opening remarks. Judges across the state had commented on many occasions that Cohen was wasting his talents as an attorney and should be writing movie scripts in Hollywood.

As the jury was led out, Elizabeth stood up and looked around for Darrin. She spotted him making his way through the rush of reporters charging into the hallway to record clips for the afternoon news.

"Hey, baby!" Perkins cried, as he deftly leapt over the wooden partition separating the defense table from the observers.

Elizabeth rose from her chair and threw her arms around his neck. He smacked a noisy kiss on her lips, neither one seeing the grimace of distaste pass over Richard Cohen's face.

"Where have you been?" Elizabeth buried her face in his neck. "I didn't think you were going to show up."

"Of course I showed up. I mean it's not like I had much choice," Perkins laughed. He pulled the piece of paper that had caused the guard to grant him entry into the courtroom from his pocket and waved it in front of Elizabeth.

She took it from his outstretched hand, and with dawning alarm cried, "What the hell is this?"

"A summons, Liz. Didn't Clarence Darrow here tell you the prosecution called me as a witness?" He shot a dirty look at Richard Cohen.

Elizabeth spun around and grabbed Cohen's arm, sending his Mark Cross pen skittering across the desk. "Richard, what's going on? Why didn't you tell me they called Darrin?" Her eyes were two huge saucers of fear.

"Calm down, Elizabeth. I just found out about it last night. He was on the list of potentials they gave us early on, but my office wasn't notified he'd been summoned until late yesterday." His tone was soothing, but he averted his eyes from her critical gaze. The truth was he just didn't feel like dealing with another one of his client's outbursts this morning. He had hoped the scumball she was dating would have told her about it himself.

"And you couldn't tell me this earlier?" Elizabeth demanded, her eyes blazing.

"Well, I assumed your boyfriend would have mentioned it to you," Cohen retorted, and immediately regretted his words. Her emerald green eyes burned with ever increasing fury.

Darrin was saved from any explanation to Elizabeth when the bailiff called the court to order. He beat a hasty retreat to the rear of the courtroom, where he stole one of the chairs from a late returning member of the press.

Chapter 4

Gabriella was putting away a fresh shipment of books when the melodic little bell over the door jangled. She looked over her shoulder to catch a stereotypical yuppy eyeballing the heart-stopping few inches of smooth, tanned flesh revealed by her blouse riding up from her stretch to reach the top shelf of the bookcase. In no particular hurry, she lowered her arm and adjusted her top.

"Good Morning, Mr. Reynolds," Gabriella smiled.

The newcomer cast a nervous glance around the shop. Barely above a whisper, he declared, "I have an appointment."

Eros trotted down the staircase and began winding himself between Martin Reynolds's feet. The man kicked at the cat with a look of disgust and bent down to pick the few stray cat hairs clinging to the leg of his slacks.

Gabriella narrowed her eyes. With a look that would have made a man much stronger than Martin Reynolds crumble, she responded, "Yes, we've been expecting you." She swooped down to pick up the offended Eros, never taking her murderous gaze from the quivering man's eyes.

"I… I'm sorry." He took an involuntary step backwards, "I'm allergic to them."

"Really?" Gabriella replied in a voice cold enough to turn boiling water to ice, one eyebrow arched in appraisal. Stroking the cat with long, graceful fingers, and never dropping her gaze, she asked, "And have you ever wondered what creature might be allergic to you, Mr. Reynolds?"

The man opened his mouth to answer, but before he could say anything further Gabriella dismissed him with, "I will let Belda know you are here. Have a seat in the office." She offered a small, chilly smile and pointed to a doorway nestled into the corner of the store.

Martin Reynolds, clearly relieved to be out from under Gabriella's torturous eyes, walked with quick steps into the small room. He dropped heavily into one of two chairs that dominated most of the room's cramped space. Martin took in the surroundings, and not for the first time wondered what the hell he was doing. There were the two chairs separated by a small, round claw-foot table adorned with burning candles. A high shelf on the wall held an incense burner, and musky smoke made his eyes water. The lighting was so dim that it took his eyes several minutes to adjust.

Martin was shaken by the eerie encounter with the striking shop girl, but even more so by the reason for his visit. If his wife hadn't insisted he go through with this when he told her about Belda and the unusual service she offered, he never would have been here in the first place. His hands were shaking as he extracted a handkerchief from his pocket. Mopping his sweating brow, he reminded himself that he could stop at anytime—even after he purchased what he had come for. Taking the item didn't mean he would ever actually use it.

He was jerked from his thoughts as the old woman entered the cramped office. She smelled of cinnamon and some other bitter herb that Martin couldn't identify. Mixed with the smell of the incense and candles in the stifling room, he felt his stomach lurch when she leaned over him and set her bulk into the opposite chair.

With no preamble, Belda set a small vial on the table between them. "Are you sure you wish to complete our transaction, Mr. Reynolds?"

He nodded once, his gaze riveted to the cloudy glass bottle on the table.

"Very well then," she sighed. "And you understand the terms of your purchase?"

"Yes," he answered, his voice a dry, dusty croak.

"Repeat them to me and we shall conclude our dealings," Belda stated.

"I am to tell no one about this. You are not responsible for the outcome. And there is no refund," Martin replied like a child reciting a spelling bee answer.

"And what are the consequences should you not withhold your end of our transaction, Mr. Reynolds?" Belda queried, in her brusk, businesslike manner.

"I die," Martin Reynolds barked in a choked sob.

"One last time, Mr. Reynolds. Are you sure you wish to complete this sale?"

Once more, he nodded.

"Very well then," Belda sighed, "You have the cash?"

He withdrew an envelope from the inside pocket of his jacket and slid it across the small glass table. Belda didn't even glance at it. She lifted the small vial in one old, withered hand and placed it into Martin Reynolds's sweaty palm, then closed his fingers over the smooth glass.

He rose from his seat on shaking legs. "Do you want me to wait while you count it," he stuttered, and hastily added, "It's all there."

Belda looked at him with her disturbing pale eyes. "I know it is, Mr. Reynolds. You needn't wait."

He mumbled a quick thank you, and stuffing the little bottle deep into the pocket of his slacks, he bolted out the front door. He nearly screamed from fright when the bell jingled overhead. He stumbled out into the harsh September sunlight and fought an urge to run as fast as he could from the peculiar bookstore. Stomach churning, breath coming in harsh little gasps, he fumbled keys from his pocket and climbed into a rented Lincoln Continental.

With shaking hands, Reynolds started the ignition and pulled away from the curb. As he disappeared around the corner in search of the freeway, he felt his upper thigh grow hot enough to burn. He felt the ominous weight of the small glass cylinder in his pocket resting against his leg. An unexpected, sharp cramp struck his lower belly. He pulled the searing vial from his pocket, slamming it into the glove compartment with a cry of pain and fright. His fingers immediately began to blister where they made contact with the small glass bottle. The cramp passed almost as quickly as it had come. Mopping sweat from his brow, attorney, Martin Reynolds, drove his big, fancy rental car to the airport a full three hours early for his flight back home.

Chapter 5

The first witness called by the prosecution was the medical examiner, Dr. Conrad Link, a weary, disheveled man in his late fifties.

Patricia Camden walked to the witness box. "Good morning, Doctor Link."

The doctor nodded and glanced at his notes.

"When did you first see the body of Theodore McGwire?"

"The night of August twenty-second. I was called to the crime scene to examine the body."

Cohen shot up from his chair. "Objection! What crime scene? The prosecution hasn't established that there was a crime," he fumed.

"Sustained," the judge grumbled, "Jury will disregard the use of the term crime scene."

Pat Camden bristled. "And what were your initial findings?"

Cohen rose from his chair once again. "Objection! Initial findings are inconclusive and speculative. Doctor Link shouldn't offer testimony on any findings except those discovered during the post-mortem."

Camden smiled sweetly, "Well, counselor, you did stipulate that Doctor Link is an expert witness, so surely his initial findings at the scene must have some merit."

She arched an eyebrow at the judge, who nodded, "Overruled, I'll allow it."

"When I entered the house I found the deceased lying on the floor at the bottom of the staircase."

Next to the witness box was an easel with a drawing of an outline of a twisted body lying at the base of a steep stairwell.

The medical examiner picked up a pointer and gestured to the drawing. "I could tell from the angle of the body that bones were broken, and from traces of blood on his lips I was sure internal injuries had been sustained." His tone was matter of fact.

"Did you immediately know the cause of death?" Camden continued.

Glancing at Cohen, the doctor replied, "I had some thoughts on the matter, but couldn't confirm it until the autopsy the next morning."

"And what was the cause of death, Doctor Link?"

"Theodore McGwire died from internal injuries. The spleen was crushed, one kidney lacerated, three ribs broken, and fragments of bone were lodged in both lungs. Additionally, he had sustained a concussion."

Cohen glanced at the jury box, and winced at the twelve identical horrified expressions he saw there.

The prosecution avoided the question of whether it was determined during the autopsy if Theodore McGwire's plunge down the staircase was accidental or intentional. Camden knew this was the one aspect of her case that was entirely speculative, and the doctor would not be able to answer with certainty. She had no doubt that the defense would point this out to the jury during the course of Doctor Link's cross examination.

On cross, Cohen opened with, "Doctor Link, the prosecution's argument is that my client—all 105 pounds of her—pushed Theodore McGwire down the stairs."

Cohen picked up the pointer beside the easel and pointed at the outline of the body. "Were you able to determine from the angle of the body whether he was pushed?"

"I was able to tell that he had fallen down the flight of stairs," the doctor answered neutrally.

"Is it possible he could have tripped, or lost his balance?" Cohen badgered.

"Yes, that's possible."

"So, you have no way of knowing how his body ended up at the base of those stairs. Is that correct?"

"Yes, that's correct," a resigned Link replied.

"It would take a great deal of strength to push a large man like that down a staircase wouldn't it? You'd need to be a pretty strong person to accomplish that, wouldn't you say, Doctor?" Cohen asked.

He knew instantly, even before the question was fully out of his mouth, he should have quit while he was ahead.

Camden's eyes flashed with victory as the medical examiner responded, "No, not necessarily. If someone came up behind him as he started to descend the stairs even a child could have pushed him. The element of surprise takes away any need for strength. I certainly saw no indication that there had been a struggle."

In a valiant effort to recover from his error, Cohen asked, "Well, could you tell from the position of his body if, in fact, he had been pushed from behind?"

"No, I could not." Doctor Link responded in an annoyed voice.

"Could you tell whether he had been pushed at all?"

"Objection! Asked and answered," Camden snarled.

"Sustained." Judge Westerfield shot a warning glance in Cohen's direction.

"Thank you, Doctor," Cohen finished, "Nothing further."

~~~~

The conclusion of the first day of trial was not a good one for the defense. Cohen's sixth sense told him he had not convinced the jury of Elizabeth's innocence, nor of the fact that she was on trial only because of the prosecution's zeal to bring in a guilty verdict in the over-publicized murder of Theodore McGwire, a Seattle icon and pillar of the community. This wasn't about justice; it was about becoming heroes to a public obsessed by the case. And of course, the county prosecutor's burning desire for reelection this coming fall.

The testimony elicited so far by the prosecution focused on the scant amount of circumstantial evidence they had to offer linking Elizabeth to her grandfather's death. There wasn't much—just enough to paint a very ugly picture of Cohen's client in the eyes of the jury.

Even though the defense was able to extract from the medical examiner that the fatal injuries Theodore McGwire sustained could have been caused just as easily from an accidental fall, on re-direct, the prosecution hammered home the point that it was equally as plausible that he had been tripped or pushed by his 105 pound granddaughter.
~~~~

Dr. Link's graphic testimony seemed to mesmerize the jury, leaving them with the image of the dead man's broken and twisted body imprinted in their minds as court adjourned for the day.

~~~~

As they exited the courthouse, the media followed Elizabeth and her entourage out to the big car with the tinted windows, firing a barrage of questions.

Cohen answered, "No comment," to the horde of reporters mobbing them as they entered the limo.

Elizabeth was sullen and silent in the back of the car, still angry with Richard for not telling her Darrin was called as a witness.

"Are you hungry?" Cohen asked, as they pulled away from the curb.

Elizabeth shook her head. "No, I just want to go home."

"Liz, we should probably go over what Darrin's testimony might be." Cohen was uncomfortable bringing it up, knowing how strong Liz's feelings were for this loser, but it had to be done. He couldn't, for the life of him, see why she was so head over heels for the guy. In Richard's opinion, Darrin Perkins was a scumbag and a barfly who'd done nothing to support Elizabeth through the nightmare she was embroiled in.

Richard Cohen had fallen pretty hard for his client, and it galled him that she shot him down because of the torch she carried for an unemployed low-life like Darrin Perkins. As is usually the case, her rejection of him made Elizabeth that much more desirable.

"What's there to go over?" she snapped. "What can they possibly want from him anyway?"
~~~~

"Liz, did you ever say anything to Darrin about wanting your grandfather out of the way? Ever make any jokes about killing him? Anything like that?"

"N… no," she faltered.

"Are you sure?"

"Well, I don't know," she replied. A piece of lint on her skirt became very interesting all of a sudden, as she began fidgeting.

Cohen placed a reassuring hand on her arm, "Liz, if there is anything you might have said that could incriminate you, I need to know about it."

She sighed. "We talked about a lot of things, and it may have been mentioned that things would be easier for us if the old man wasn't around. That's all."

"Easier how?"

"How do you think, Richard? I would have had money. Something neither Darrin or myself have much of these days."

Cohen shook his head. "That's what the prosecution is going to ask him, Liz."

"It's just that Darrin won't marry me while we are both broke… So, I may have said something about us being able to get married if Grandfather died. I didn't mean anything by it. It was just, you know, pillow-talk."

Richard winced as an uninvited image of a naked and lovely Elizabeth, flushed and rosy from sex, lying beside Darrin Perkins flashed across his mind.

"Any other pillow-talk along those lines, Liz? Did you ever tell him you thought about killing your grandfather?"

Again, the imaginary lint consumed her attention, as Elizabeth thought of the ominous message on the folded note that had been stuffed into her palm that morning.

She remembered with vivid clarity the night she told Darrin that her grandfather's money was going to be hers much sooner than he thought.

With a puzzled expression, Darrin had asked her what she meant.

The pact she entered into with the old witch-like woman in the eerie bookstore kept her from saying anything more. She desperately wanted to tell Darrin about the woman and what was in the little glass bottle she purchased, but the price Liz would have paid for disclosing this would have been her life.

"No. I didn't say I was going to do anything like that myself," she replied to her attorney firmly.

They spent the remainder of the ride in silence.

"Get some rest," Richard advised when the driver pulled into the mansion's circular driveway.

"Will they call Darrin tomorrow?"

Cohen shrugged, "It depends on how long Mrs. Renfrew's testimony takes."

An annoyed frown furrowed Liz's brow. "Well, I'm sure she will try to put as many nails in my coffin as she can, so that should take awhile."

Gertrude Renfrew was her grandfather's housekeeper and companion for the last thirty years of his life. She was the only other person in the house on the night he fell to his death, and she was a key witness for the prosecution. She was also no great fan of Elizabeth McGwire.

~~~~

When Elizabeth let herself into the big, lonely house, Mrs. Renfrew and her dog were nowhere to be seen. This wasn't unusual. The old woman avoided Elizabeth as much as possible.
~~~~

Liz would have seen to it that the housekeeper and her mutt were out of the house by now, had it not been for the eccentric old bastard's will. Her grandfather willed the house, its contents, and the bulk of his substantial fortune to Liz, with the stipulation that she not only remain living in the house, but that Mrs. Renfrew and the dog be given lifelong residency there as well.

Should Elizabeth try to sell the house, the estate would revert to Mrs. Renfrew, and Liz would be left with nothing. Elizabeth believed this was her senile grandfather's way of maintaining control of her life from beyond the grave.

The truth was the man was in no way senile, or even all that eccentric. The worst thing he could be accused of was being overly sentimental. The stipulation that Elizabeth remain in the house was born of Theodore McGwire's desire that his cherished home remain in the family. He hoped someday his granddaughter would settle down and marry, and future generations of the McGwire clan would be raised in the house he so adored.

Elizabeth dropped her Prada handbag on a chair in the living room and poured a glass of wine. She plopped down on the velvet sofa and glanced longingly at the telephone. She thought about calling Darrin, but the truth was, she was as pissed off at him as she was at her lawyer for not telling her about the damn summons.

Tears of frustration filled Elizabeth's eyes as she looked up at the paintings lining the walls of the room. A Picasso, named *Seated Woman,* seemed to stare back at her with hauntingly real, yet distorted eyes. Paintings valued at millions to collectors, protected by an intricate security system, hung in dusty frames all around the spacious house.

Elizabeth wasn't allowed to sell a single one; yet another condition of her grandfather's will. All the artwork in the house was to remain as is. She could redecorate, she could do anything she chose with the furniture or the rooms, except Mrs. Renfrew's quarters. But the damn paintings—every last one, must remain untouched.

With bitterness, Liz thought, *Just one of the paintings would cover all my legal fees and support Darrin and I for a hell of a long time.*

She drained her wine glass, then reached over and picked up the phone. She dialed Darrin's number and slammed down the receiver in frustration when the answering machine picked up.

"Bastard," she spat to the empty room, and rose to refill her wineglass

~~~~

Gertrude Renfrew sat finishing a lonely supper in her small kitchen. She lived in a private apartment Theodore McGwire added to the west wing of the house for her occupancy over twenty years before.

She was a homely, overweight woman, whose adoration of Theodore McGwire was due not only to his kindness, but also to the fact that he was the only man to ever tell her she was beautiful.

Theodore McGwire also had the rare distinction of being the only man she had ever taken as a lover since her abusive husband's passing.

Mr. Renfrew was an ill-tempered man with a fondness for strong drink and after-hours gambling on the docks where he worked as a longshoreman. He met a violent, but not terribly surprising end, in a drunken confrontation with the business end of a broken bottle after a poker game went bad.

Childless and lonely, Gertrude spent a decade in solitude and sadness before coming into Theodore McGwire's employ. What
~~~~

brought them closer was a shared love of art and good Cabernet Sauvignon; the latter responsible for the unexpected, but delightful transformation in their relationship one stormy November evening during a power outage.

With Elizabeth now living in the mansion, Mrs. Renfrew rarely ventured into the main house except to dust and tidy up. She felt closest to Theodore in her own private quarters. She missed him terribly, and spent much of her time grieving over his death.

Throughout the small apartment were gifts he had given her over the years. A silver hairbrush and comb set engraved with her initials, the framed print by her favorite artist, Andrew Wyeth, entitled *Master Bedroom.* Theodore somehow managed to get the print personally signed by Wyeth. On her coffee table sat the book, *Christina's World,* her Valentine's Day gift five years before.

When Gertrude finished her meal, she washed the dishes and donned a sweater. She put the leash on Rembrandt, her Boston Terrier, the best present of all. Theodore gave her Rembrandt for her birthday four years before. She took him out the back way to avoid seeing Elizabeth.

It made Mrs. Renfrew nervous, knowing that woman was in the house after being released from jail on bond. She hadn't had a restful night's sleep since Elizabeth's return to the estate. Mrs. Renfrew was as convinced of Elizabeth McGwire's guilt as the prosecution was. She hoped with all her heart that the evil woman would be found guilty and made to pay for what she had done to her beloved Theodore.

Rembrandt and Mrs. Renfrew cut across the back lawn of the grounds and circled the pool. They walked along the tall flowering shrubs and made their way toward the front of the house.

Elizabeth was standing looking out the front window as they walked by. The woman and her dog walked the same route at the same time every night. They ended their outing crossing in front of the living room windows at exactly seven-thirty p.m. The routine never changed and was never off by even a minute. Liz checked her watch—seven-thirty on the money—Renfrew was as accurate as the Greenwich Observatory!

Elizabeth, drunk, and with a sneer on her lips, knew the routine. *Now the dog takes a dump, and the old bat picks it up in her fancy pooper-scooper that Grandfather gave her. He gave Renfrew, the goddamn maid, the best of everything. Me? It was take care of yourself, baby. You old bastard, I hope you are rotting in hell!*

She shook her head in disgust and turned from the window, allowing the heavy damask drape to fall across the glass and cut off her view of the hated old woman. She poured another glass of wine. She tried Darrin's number again, cursed his answering machine, and slammed the phone down hard enough to crack the casing on the receiver.

She grabbed the nearly empty wine bottle from the bar and took it upstairs to her bedroom.

Chapter 6

The alarm clock began its shrill braying at five-thirty Tuesday morning. Richard Cohen, with a curse, silenced it with his fist.

He stayed up until one-thirty the night before trying to figure out how to offset the damage Elizabeth's boyfriend was surely going to do to their case once he took the stand.

With a yawn and a stretch, he climbed from bed and went into the kitchen to brew a pot of coffee. He threw on a pair of gray sweatpants and a t-shirt for his two mile jog around Lake Washington. No matter how late he stayed up working on a case, Richard never missed his run. It cleared his head and gave him his best perspective on a defense.

At forty-two, Richard Cohen looked like he was in his early thirties. He was tall and trim, with just the first hint of gray peppering his temples. He had never married, though women found him attractive, and he was listed among Seattle's most eligible bachelors.

He had seen a therapist after one particularly bad break-up. The analyst threw the word *co-dependent* around a lot. Cohen wasn't entirely sure what that meant, but one day over beers with a lawyer friend, she told him he had a *Rapunzel Complex.* When he asked what the hell that meant, she told him he was only attracted to women he could rescue from high towers. The higher the tower the harder Richard fell.

Cohen found the idea ludicrous and told her so, but in the privacy of his own mind, he thought his lawyer friend may be right.

In a brief reflection on his past relationships, he couldn't think of one woman he had ever fallen for that wasn't in some kind of trouble.

When Cohen returned from his jog, he sat on the deck overlooking the lake, munching wheat toast and thinking about his client, Elizabeth McGwire.

Cohen rarely lost a case. He was somewhat of a local celebrity who lived in the pricey Seattle suburb of Medina. Bill Gates was a neighbor.

Richard was the first attorney called for every high-profile murder case which took place in Western Washington. There were some cases he accepted pro bono because he liked the publicity. His set fee was two-hundred-fifty dollars an hour for trial prep, and three-hundred-fifty dollars for each hour actually spent in a courtroom.

It was a well-kept secret he used his own money to post Elizabeth's bond. She couldn't touch a dime of her grandfather's estate until the trial was over, and then, only if the verdict was not guilty.

Richard convinced himself he would have done the same for any client. Well, any female client. He didn't like to think of women in jail; least of all one as lovely or fragile as Liz. In fifteen years of practice Cohen had never fallen in love with a client. Elizabeth insisted on her innocence. Cohen believed she did not murder her grandfather, but he felt in his gut she was keeping secrets from him. This made him uncomfortable. Not because he might be defending someone guilty—it wasn't the first time he'd done that—but because the torch he carried for his client seemed to grow brighter and stronger with each passing day.

A client's guilt or innocence was of little consequence to Cohen when he tried a case. All that mattered was winning. The track record mattered, staying in the spotlight mattered. His last twelve cases all returned not guilty verdicts. It did not escape him that thirteen was an unlucky number.

~~~~

When her alarm clock sounded at seven-fifteen, Elizabeth McGwire awoke suffering from a miserable hangover. Head pounding, she tottered to the bathroom and threw up last night's wine supper. Pale and shaky, she took a shower and brewed a pot of strong coffee.

While getting dressed, her phone rang. "Hello," she answered breathlessly, expecting to hear Darrin's voice on the other end.

"Good morning, Elizabeth, how did you sleep?" her lawyer asked.

She sighed, "Oh, hello, Richard."

He couldn't mistake the disappointment in her voice and knew she was hoping it was Darrin calling. "I'm calling from the car. Just wanted to let you know I'm on my way over to pick you up."

"Okay. Do you think Darrin will be there this morning?" Her voice sounded forlorn.

"I have no idea, Liz. Didn't you talk to him last night?" His irritation was evident.

"No."
~~~~

"He must show up until called to testify," Cohen answered.

"Will I have a chance to talk to him before the trial starts?"

"If he's there early you can probably talk for a couple of minutes."

Cohen knew the scum-bag would not show up early. Darrin hadn't rolled into the courtroom before eleven o'clock the day before. Richard would stake his reputation on the fact that today would be no exception.

~~~~

The ringing of the telephone woke Darrin just after nine-thirty. He fumbled for the phone, and mumbled, "H'lo."

The female on the other end of the line sounded far too bubbly for this early in the morning, in Darrin's humble opinion.

"Hi, it's Darla," she squeaked.

"Who?"

"Darla." The happy voice turned instantly chilly. "Remember me? I fucked you night before last."

Darrin cringed. "Right. Hey sorry, I was asleep. So, uh, how are you?"

"I left an earring at your apartment. It's a little gold heart. If you find it will you let me know?" She was clearly still offended at his memory lapse.

"Yeah, sure." Darrin hung up the phone and glanced at the bedside clock. Seeing how late it was, he jumped from the bed. Not bothering to take a shower, he raked his fingers through his hair, donned the clothes he wore the previous day, and sped to the courthouse.

~~~~

When the chime above the door of Bella Luna bookshop sounded, Gabriella put away the biology book she was studying. She smiled as Nicholas Aguilar walked in.

He handed her a Starbucks cup and grinned. "Good morning, sunshine. Tall nonfat latte, half shot of vanilla."

"Thanks, honey."

"Where is the grand dame?" Nicholas asked, not seeing Belda.

A ghost of unease passed over Gabriella's face. "Lying down. She isn't feeling very well today."

"Oh? The McGwire thing?"

"She says not, but I think so," Gabriella replied. "I'm worried too. That McGwire woman is too emotional for her own good. She could let something slip."

Nicholas shook his head. "No, hon. No way. She's been warned, and she knows what happens if she talks. They never talk, you know that."

"Well, we've never had a client on trial for murder before either. Things don't usually go quite this wrong."

Nicholas looked at her for a long moment. His voice turned quiet. "Gabby, things always go wrong. It just doesn't usually make the front page of the newspapers or the eleven o'clock news. Most of the time it just makes a small headline lost somewhere on page eight of a local rag, and forgotten the next day."

"What do you mean?" she gasped, disturbed.

"Gabby, don't you get it?" Nicholas gestured upstairs. "She plays with people's lives. The natural order of things is messed up and life is rewritten. You can't do that without there being consequences, you just can't."

"Well, when she played with my life, she saved me from years of being raped by my stepfather. When she played with yours, she stopped you from going to prison for the rest of your life for something you didn't even do." Gabriella's voice was rising. "Things do not always go wrong, Nicholas. She helps people. She certainly helped us."

"Yes. Some get help, but others die. Your stepfather died, the bastard that cut the deal with the prosecution to send me up the river also died."

"They were evil people, not worth living. Who cares that they died," Gabriella spat, her eyes shining with tears. "Don't ever speak against Belda. I won't stand for it."

"I'm sorry, baby. I didn't mean to upset you," Nicholas soothed.

They heard Belda's creaking, slow progress coming down the stairs, as Eros bounded down in front of her and jumped on the counter. Nicholas scratched the cat behind the ears and went to assist Belda.

She smiled a warm greeting as he took the tea from her gnarled hand and placed one arm around her shoulders to guide her down the stairs.

"Thank you, Nicholas dear," Belda said, "My arthritis is acting up today."

"Can I get you anything?" he asked, concerned.

"No. I just need to rest a bit today. Will you be able to watch the store when Gabriella attends her classes this afternoon?"

Nicholas nodded, "Yes, of course."

"Thank you, dear." She saw the troubled look on Gabriella's face, and turned to Nicholas. "You haven't upset Gabriella have you?"

Before he could answer, Gabriella shook her head, "Of course not, Belda."

The old woman peered into the girl's eyes, then nodded, and turned her attention back to Nicholas. "Mr. Reynolds was here yesterday for his purchase." She pulled an envelope from the pocket of her dress and handed it to him.

He stuffed it into his shirt pocket without opening it. "Thanks. I'm surprised he went through with it."

"Are you?" Belda asked. "I am not. He does whatever his wife tells him to," she smiled.

Nicholas looked at her alarmed. "He told his wife about this? He told you that?"

"Oh, no, he didn't say he confided this to her, but he did."

Gabriella looked terrified. "But, Belda what if she—"

"Shhhh, girl. Hush now," Belda interrupted. "The wife won't say anything."

"How can you be so sure?" Nicholas wondered. "Maybe I should go to New York and—"

Again, Belda cut in, "Stop it both of you. I said there is nothing to worry about. Leave it be." Her tone stifled any further argument from her assistants. They trusted her, and were well-compensated for their work.

"Now then," Belda asked, "Gabriella, do I have any appointments today?"

Gabriella shook her head. "Nope. You had that actress scheduled for tomorrow, but she cancelled again."

"Very well. I'm going to go back upstairs and rest a bit more. Have a good day at school, Gabriella dear."

"I will. If you need anything call me later, okay, Belda?"

"Thank you, dear. That won't be necessary, I'm sure. I will have Nicholas with me."

He nodded, and took her elbow to help lead her back up the stairs. Eros trotted behind them.

Chapter 7

As the morning of day two of the trial drew to a close, Elizabeth was pale and shaking. The first half of Mrs. Renfrew's testimony had been grueling. She portrayed Elizabeth McGwire as a thoroughly unsavory character with absolutely no conscience.

When the lunch break was called, Elizabeth asked Richard to take her out a side door and get her something to eat. She felt faint. Cohen took her arm, and they both ignored Darrin's frantic waving as he tried to get their attention.

Liz couldn't bear the public scrutiny any longer. Cohen had the driver pick up hamburgers from a drive-thru, and they sat in the back of the air-conditioned car eating in silence at a nearby park.

When they finished their lunch and were headed back to the courthouse, Cohen asked, "Is there some reason you didn't want to talk to Darrin? He was trying to get your attention when we left the courthouse. Surely you saw him."

Liz nodded her head and looked out the window. "I was too tired to listen to his excuses about why he was late… Or why he didn't call me last night," she said in a soft voice.

Cohen suppressed a smile and gave her a nod of understanding. He wisely didn't say anything negative about the bum to her. *Let him dig his own grave,* Richard thought.

~~~~

"The prosecution re-calls Gertrude Renfrew to the stand," Patricia Camden announced.

The plump, elderly woman wore a simple white blouse over black slacks and flat-heeled sensible shoes. She settled her wide rear-end into the witness chair and the judge advised her she was still under oath. Gertrude nodded, and looked expectantly at the prosecutor.

"Mrs. Renfrew, were you aware of any animosity between the defendant and Theodore McGwire?" The DA asked.

Before the question was out of her mouth, Cohen shot to his feet, yelling, "Objection! Calls for speculation."

Camden shot an exasperated look at Cohen. "I'm not asking the witness to speculate. I'm asking her if she *knew* of any arguments between them."

Judge Westerfield looked at both attorneys for a long moment. "Why don't you rephrase that question, counselor."

Richard sat down, and Camden asked in a pointed tone, "Mrs. Renfrew, did you ever witness an argument between the defendant and the deceased?"

Again, Richard was on his feet shouting, "Objection! Relevance, Your Honor? Family members argue all the time."

Camden turned red with fury. Through gritted teeth, she spat, "Goes to motive."

The judge cast a level gaze at Cohen, admonishing him for not allowing the prosecutor to follow through with her line of questioning.
~~~~

"Overruled, I'll allow it." He then turned a friendly eye to the witness, "You may answer the question."

Mrs. Renfrew nodded her head, "Yes, they argued all the time during those last few weeks."

"And what were they arguing about?" Camden asked.

Richard started to rise. The judge shot him a look that dropped him back into his seat without uttering a word.

"Well, mostly about money. Elizabeth was in a mountain of debt and she wanted Theo to bail her out."

"And he didn't want to help her?" Camden continued.

Mrs. Renfrew laced her fingers together over her thick middle and thought about her answer. After a moment, she replied, "It isn't that he didn't want to. He loved Elizabeth dearly, and he had already paid the back payments on her car so she wouldn't lose it, but he wanted her to get a job, and try to take some responsibility for the mess she had gotten herself into. Theo thought it would be better for Elizabeth in the long run if she got back on her feet on her own."

"Did Ms. McGwire try to find work?"

"No. At least not that I'm aware of."

"Did you ever hear the defendant threaten Mr. McGwire?" Camden asked, bracing for an objection from Cohen.

Mrs. Renfrew hesitated also, expecting another outburst. When none came, she answered, "Not in so many words, but she was acting awful strange during that last week."

Mrs. Renfrew cringed as Cohen roared, "OBJECTION!"

The judge bent down toward Mrs. Renfrew, "Madam, please confine your answers to the questions asked. Your observations of the defendant's behavior have nothing to do with whether or not you heard her threaten Theodore McGwire. So, for the record, your answer to that question is no, you did not hear the defendant make any threats. Is that correct?"

"Yes, sir," the witness answered humbly, and lowered her eyes in embarrassment.

Pat Camden gave her an encouraging smile, "Mrs. Renfrew, when you say the defendant was acting strangely, what did you witness that you found out of the ordinary?"

"Objection! Calls for speculation," Richard yelled.

"No! Calls for observation, which goes to state of mind, which goes to motive," Camden said in a weary voice.

It was obvious the last half of this witness's questioning was going to be as brutal as the first half had been, and she was going to have to put up with Cohen's never ending objections. She hoped he would let up a little when the questioning of Mrs. Renfrew resumed after the lunch break, but no such luck.

"I'll allow it," the judge replied, also resigned to Cohen's tactics.

"She was whispering on the phone and kind of slinking around the house," Mrs. Renfrew replied. "I mean it wasn't one specific thing, she... she was just acting nervous, like she was waiting for something to happen. It's very hard to explain."

She glanced at Elizabeth. Seeing the look of naked hatred on her face, Mrs. Renfrew quickly turned away.

Camden studied the notes before her. "Mrs. Renfrew, let's talk about the night Theodore McGwire died. Tell us what you saw or heard that night."

"Well, I was asleep, and I was woken up by Rembrandt. That's my dog. He was barking and carrying on, so I got up to see what the fuss was about. When I came into the main part of the house I heard Elizabeth screaming and... and..." her voice broke and she couldn't go on for a moment.

The judge bent over, and said not unkindly, "Take your time."

Mrs. Renfrew dabbed at her eyes with a tissue from a box produced by the bailiff.

"Thank you, young man." She drew in a hitching breath and continued, "He… Theo… was on the floor at the bottom of the steps."

"And where was Elizabeth McGwire?" the DA asked.

"She was standing on the stairs. About five or six steps up."

"And what did you do?"

"I tried to ask Elizabeth if she called 911, but she was screaming, and I couldn't get her to listen to me. So I ran to the phone and I called, but it was too late. He… he was gone."

"Did you ask the defendant if she saw what happened?" Camden prodded.

"I tried, but she kept repeating 'it was an accident.' Every time I tried to ask her what happened, she would just say the same thing—'it was an accident.'"

"Did she say anything else?"

"Well, only one thing… I didn't know what she meant." Gertrude Renfrew plucked nervously at the wadded tissue in her fist.

"And what was that, Mrs. Renfrew?"

"She said, 'It wasn't supposed to happen this way.'"

Elizabeth clutched the defense table.

Camden's eyes shot up from her notes, and her lips thinned to a line, "She said 'It wasn't supposed to happen this way?' What did she mean?"

"I… I don't know. I asked her what she was talking about and she just started screaming that it was an accident again."

Camden shuffled her notes again. After a long moment, she finally said, "I have no further questions of this witness."

Cohen rose for his cross-examination and buttoned his jacket.

"Good afternoon, Mrs. Renfrew," he began.

She nodded indifferently and looked at him with wary eyes.

"Your testimony was that Ms. McGwire was screaming. She was clearly upset, is that correct?"

"She appeared to be upset, yes," Mrs. Renfrew nodded.

"Did she seem surprised?"

"She was hysterical."

"If she had just carried out a well-planned and well thought out murder, why would she be hysterical? Why would she be screaming like that?"

"Objection. Calls for speculation," Camden half rose from her seat.

"Sustained," replied Judge Westerfield.

Cohen continued without missing a beat—"Did you think my client pushed Mr. McGwire down the staircase when you first arrived and saw him lying there?"

"I didn't know what to think," the old woman shrugged. "I—"

Cohen cut her off with, "You never actually saw Ms. McGwire push him did you?"

"No. I told you he was lying at the foot of the stairs when I got there."

"Was there anyone else in the house at the time?" Cohen queried.

"Just my dog."

"So, no one actually saw my client push her grandfather."

"No, but she was standing halfway up the staircase," the housekeeper blurted out.

Cohen looked thoughtful for a moment. "I see. Well, where is her bedroom located? Isn't it upstairs?"

"Y… yes," Mrs. Renfrew faltered.

"So, isn't it possible that my client was coming downstairs for a drink of water or a nightcap, and when she saw her grandfather lying at the bottom of the stairs she started screaming?"

Pat Camden threw a ballpoint pen across the table and snorted in derision. She couldn't call for an objection when the witness had walked right into this line of questioning.

Mrs. Renfrew glared at Cohen through narrowed eyes. "Yes. I guess that could have been what happened." It was clear she wanted to say more, but she didn't want Judge Westerfield to admonish her again.

"Isn't it also possible she heard Mr. McGwire fall, and rushed out of her room to find out what happened, but did not see him until she was half way down the staircase, where you saw her standing and screaming when you came in?"

"I guess anything's possible, Mr. Cohen," the witness responded in a small voice.

Cohen smiled politely, "Thank you, Mrs. Renfrew. I have nothing further."

~~~~

Day two of the sensational trial closed. Television screens that evening across America were filled with commentary, pro and con, regarding the innocence or guilt of Elizabeth McGwire.

Jane Velez Mitchell held a heated and lively debate with Joey Jackson and Linda Kenney-Bodin regarding the trial, each offering their opinions, but arriving at no definite conclusions.

A weary Richard Cohen watched, felt his gorge rise, and with a particularly foul oath, hurled the remote control at the TV set.

~~~~

Elizabeth lay in bed reading a book—a bodice-ripper she valiantly plunged into to forget about the trial for awhile.

Though she had little appetite, she forced herself to eat a grilled cheese sandwich for dinner and stay away from the wine. She didn't call Darrin, and doubted that he would call her after the cold shoulder she turned in his direction that morning.

It was after ten o'clock and she was just dozing off, when she heard a motorcycle pull into the circular drive that fronted the house. She rose from bed and pulled the curtain aside just as Darrin was jumping from his bike and pulling off his helmet. She ran down the staircase and opened the front door.

"Hi, babe," he cooed as he walked in, squeezing her waist through the thin cotton of her nightgown.

Liz didn't reply. She offered him a cheek to kiss and closed the door behind him.

"Aren't you happy to see me?" Darrin pouted, his face crest-fallen at her less than enthusiastic greeting.

"I guess that depends on why you came." She turned and walked into the living room and sat on the couch.

Darrin plopped down next to her. Running his hand up her slender thigh, he purred, "I missed you."

Elizabeth softened instantly. "Really? Did you really miss me?"

Darrin took her hand and kissed the palm, "Yeah, baby, of course I did."

She sighed and allowed him to take her into his arms. His hands went immediately to her breasts and began caressing them.

"I missed you too," she moaned, as he pushed her back on the couch. Elizabeth tried to stop him long enough to get them upstairs to the privacy of her bedroom, but Darrin was not to be denied. She allowed him to make love to her on her grandfather's ancient velvet sofa, under the watchful and distorted eyes of *Seated Woman.* She sincerely hoped Mrs. Renfrew would not decide at that moment to come into the main house. Pablo Picasso might have approved of this tryst, but Gertrude Renfrew definitely would not.

When they both lay panting and bathed in sweat, Elizabeth murmured, "Let's go upstairs and go to sleep."

Darrin disentangled himself from her and rose from the sofa. "No, babe. You need your sleep and we both have to be up early tomorrow, so I am going home."

"No, Darrin. Please stay with me tonight. I don't want to be alone."

He sat down on the corner of the couch and took her hand, "I know, Liz, but I can't tonight. I'm sorry."

"Why?" she cried, tears springing to her eyes.

He shook her hand away. "Oh don't start, Liz. I hate it when you get all whiny and clingy. You know that. We had a good time, and I'll see you tomorrow, okay? Just don't hassle me about sleeping in the castle tonight."

She turned her head away. Darrin reached under her chin and turned her face toward him. With a leering grin, and a tweak of her left breast, he said, "You should sleep good tonight, right, baby?"

She couldn't keep the smile off her face. She never could stay mad at him. Liz put her arms around his neck and hugged him hard. "Yeah, I will sleep good tonight, Darrin."

"That's my girl." He handed her the nightgown he had carelessly thrown behind the couch.

She walked him to the door and watched with forlorn and miserable eyes, as his motorcycle disappeared down the street.

Chapter 8

"The prosecution calls Darrin Perkins to the stand," Camden announced, in a voice slightly tinged with regret.

Darrin sauntered from the rear of the courtroom and took his seat in the witness box. He wore his leather Harley Davidson vest for the occasion. The vest had been a gift from Elizabeth.

"Do you swear to tell the whole truth and nothing but the truth so help you God?" The bailiff asked.

"You bet," Darrin smiled and took his hand off the bible.

No one looked very convinced.

"Good morning, Mr. Perkins." Camden offered the witness a small smile. She was nervous putting Perkins on the stand. He was too unpredictable.

"How long have you been acquainted with the defendant?" she began.

"I don't know, a year or so."

"And what is the nature of your relationship?"

Darrin looked at Liz and winked. "We are friends… Uh, close friends."

"Are you lovers?" Camden pressed.

"Yeah, you could say that," he answered with a smirk.

Patricia Camden closed her eyes for a moment and decided to change her line of questioning.

"Were you aware of any..." she began, then remembering yesterday's barrage of objections, she quickly said, "Strike that." With a brisk shake of her head she started over. "Did you ever hear Elizabeth McGwire express any anger toward her grandfather?"

Cohen shifted uncomfortably in his chair. The objection he was preparing to shout died on his lips.

Darrin looked at the judge. He whispered, "Do I have to answer that?"

Judge Westerfield glared at Darrin with incredulous eyes. In a tone that barely masked his annoyance, he replied, "Yes, Mr. Perkins, you do."

Darrin shrugged. "Well, yeah, she was kind of pissed off at him after she lost her job."

"I see," the prosecutor responded, "And what was she angry about?"

"He wouldn't help her out," Darrin mumbled.

"She wanted money?"

"Well, she got fired and lost her apartment. Then they were gonna repossess the Benz. The dude had more money than God, so why wouldn't she ask him for help?"

"And what was the defendant's reaction when her grandfather refused to help her?"

"Objection!" Cohen thundered, "Asked and answered, the witness already said she was angry."

"Sustained. Ask another question, Ms. Camden," the judge sighed.

Camden nodded. "So, Mr. Perkins, did the defendant ever imply she was going to harm her grandfather?"

"No, she never said nothing about that. I think she just said, 'The problem is gonna go away,' or something like that. I don't remember exactly."

Both Elizabeth and Cohen shut their eyes and lowered their heads. Their faces bore identical pained expressions. There was an audible gasp, and a faint undercurrent of whispering ran through the courtroom.

Judge Westerfield rapped his gavel sharply.

Camden latched onto Darrin's answer with pit-bull tenacity, "What do you think Elizabeth McGwire meant by saying the problem will go away, Mr. Perkins?"

"Objection. Calls for speculation," Cohen called out, but his voice has lost some of its former bravado.

"Sustained," the Judge answered wearily.

"Did you question her about what she meant by that statement, Mr. Perkins?" Camden continued.

"Naw... Liz always talked. She was so mad at the old man by then, that I figured she was just, you know, spewing shi… er, stuff."

"Did she ever indicate that she had some type of a plan in mind to make the problem go away?"

Cohen knew Camden was going to milk that damning statement for everything she could. He wished he could strangle Darrin Perkins.

"A plan? No. She just thought he wasn't going to be a problem much longer. That's all Liz said."

Richard Cohen shook his head as Olin muttered, "Christ! He's crucifying us."

Liz was staring at Darrin openmouthed, unable to believe what she was hearing.

"And do you know what she meant by that?" Camden purred.

"Objection! Speculation again. Your honor, please," Richard grumbled.

"Of course," Judge Westerfield soothed. "Counselor, confine your questions to those that do not call for the witness to guess or surmise."

"Yes, your honor," Camden demurred. "Mr. Perkins," she resumed, "Did you ever ask the defendant what she meant when she said her grandfather wouldn't be a problem much longer?"

"Objection. Asked and answered," Cohen cried, slamming his hand on the defense table.

Camden smiled sweetly, "No, actually it wasn't. Care to check the steno tape?"

"Overruled," Westerfield ordered. He was counting the minutes until he could call a recess. A migraine was forming at his temples.

"So, am I supposed to answer, or what?" Darrin looked confused.

"Yes, Mr. Perkins, answer the question," the judge replied, rolling his eyes.

"What was it again?" Darrin's brow furrowed in confusion.

Cohen closed his eyes and pinched the bridge of his nose. The judge wasn't the only one with a headache.

The prosecutor told the court reporter to read back the question. Darrin admitted he had not asked Elizabeth what she meant by the comment, and she never told him. The judge advised Camden to move on.

The long morning's questioning dragged on. Camden forced Perkins to admit that Elizabeth's grandfather had taken her in. After much badgering from Liz, he did pay the back payments on her Mercedes, and received very little in the way of gratitude for his generosity. Perkins said Liz became angry and surly when her grandfather refused to pay any of her other debts.

Having elicited this information from the witness, Camden completed her questioning with, "I have nothing further."

Seeing Liz's pale face and her lawyer's stony stare, Darrin sensed the irreparable harm he had done. He turned to the prosecutor and hissed, "You had nothing to start with, lady." The courtroom tittered.

That remark would be aired on the evening news by practically every television station across America.

By the time Judge Westerfield called the lunch break, Darrin was sweating, Elizabeth was sobbing openly, and Pat Camden's gray suit had lost its crispness.

Westerfield called for a two-hour break instead of the customary one and a half taken at lunchtime. Everyone needed the extra time to regroup.

It had been a painful morning for the defense, and a nerve-wracking one for the prosecution, having to question a live-wire like Darrin Perkins. The media was in a frenzy of live reports and telephone calls to editors, as Elizabeth McGwire and Richard Cohen made a swift and silent exit through the side door.

The next morning's newspaper headlines would scream:

MCGWIRE'S LOVER
ADMITS SHE PLANNED IT!

Nancy Grace would begin her show that evening with, "Bombshell tonight! McGwire's boyfriend sells her out on the stand!" And every news station across the country would mirror that sentiment.

Cohen tried to talk to Liz about what should be done to repair the damage caused by Perkins incriminating testimony. She told him to do what he had to do, but to go as easy on Darrin as he could.

Richard slammed his palm against his forehead, and hollered, "Liz, he just dug your grave! Why the hell do you want me to go easy on him?"

Liz lowered her eyes. "Because I love him. He didn't do that on purpose, Richard. He really just doesn't know any better."

Cohen's jaw dropped in disbelief. *Go easy, hell,* he thought, *I'm gonna rip the guy a new one, that's what I'm gonna do.*

"No promises, Liz," he muttered, and turned away in disgust.

~~~~

The courtroom was still buzzing as everyone filed back in after the long lunch. Judge Westerfield pounded his gavel several times to restore order.

Cohen stormed to the witness stand and began his cross-examination of Darrin Perkins with no preamble and no pleasantries. He didn't even button his jacket.

"Mr. Perkins, are you currently employed?"

"I'm between jobs right now," Darrin replied, his expression turning insolent.

"When you aren't between jobs what do you do to earn a living?"

"Construction." Perkins couldn't keep a defensive tone from creeping into his voice.

"I see. And what's the highest grade you completed in school?"

"Objection," Camden called. "Relevance?"

"Background," is all Cohen responded.
~~~~

The judge shrugged, "I'll allow it."

"I dropped out in the ninth grade," Perkins growled.

"Who usually paid for dates when you and Ms. McGwire went out?"

Camden rose. "Your honor, I object to this whole line of questioning. What does it have to do with this case?" she cried in disgust.

"Yes, counselor, we are all wondering that?" the judge queried.

Richard sighed. "I will withdraw the question." He had created the image of an uneducated, unemployed buffoon in the minds of the jurors, and that was all he intended to do with that line of questioning. He knew he had been damn lucky to get away with it as long as he did.

"Mr. Perkins, your testimony was that my client made a statement to the effect that 'he won't be a problem much longer,' referring to her grandfather, is that correct?"

"Yeah."

"Is it possible *you* were complaining about her grandfather having all that money, and not helping *both* of you out? Is it possible Ms. McGwire made that statement because she was trying to appease *you?*"

"Me? What do you mean appease me?" Perkins asked, honestly puzzled.

"I'm sorry, I guess appease is kind of a big word for a ninth grade dropout. Let me rephrase that." Cohen's voice dripped sarcasm.

Everyone in the packed courtroom gasped, and before the DA could rise to her feet to object to Cohen's badgering, Darrin retorted, "Hey, I got the word okay. I just don't know what you're implying."

"Did you ever complain about Theodore McGwire's attitude to Liz?"

"Well, I agreed with her that the old man should have helped her out."

"Did you ever tell her, 'Hey, maybe we should knock the old guy off?' Even in jest?"

"Objection! This witness is not on trial, your honor," Camden yelled.

"Withdrawn," Cohen muttered, his bitterness toward this witness far too evident.

The judge thought, *Cohen really has it bad for his client.* He briefly contemplated threatening the lawyer with contempt, but let it go.

Cohen became aware he was losing control of his emotions, and immediately changed the line of questioning. He cleared his throat, "Mr. Perkins, when Elizabeth McGwire told you her grandfather was not going to be a problem much longer, isn't it possible she could have been implying that due to his advanced age she didn't expect him to live many more years?"

"Objection. Calls for speculation." Camden wore a smug look on her face.

"Your honor, the prosecution brought up this line of questioning. Surely, I should be allowed to explore what my client's intent might have been when she made that statement. It wasn't necessarily as sinister as the prosecution would have us believe."

The judge considered it for a moment, and then nodded. "Overruled. Go ahead and answer, Mr. Perkins."

Darrin's retention skills had not improved since lunch, and the court reporter had to repeat the question.

"Yeah," he nodded his head eagerly. "I'm sure that's what she meant. Absolutely. No question. The guy was old—real old."

Camden suppressed her smile behind a cough. In Perkins enthusiasm to undo the damage his damning testimony had caused, he was just making matters worse for Elizabeth by overcompensating.

The jury sat stone-faced, a few looking at Elizabeth McGwire with open contempt.

Cohen wrapped up his questioning in a hurry, fearing even more damage from Darrin's runaway mouth. Day three adjourned early.

~~~~

Richard drove Liz home, neither speaking. He made a few vain attempts at conversation, but Liz only grunted responses to his questions.

Later that evening, when Darrin stood pounding at the front door calling her name, Liz was sprawled on her bed. She lay oblivious to Perkins pounding and yelling, oblivious to her surroundings, oblivious to her troubles. Elizabeth McGwire was in a drunken stupor, which at least temporarily, brought her forgetfulness.

An irate Mrs. Renfrew stormed downstairs, warning Perkins if he did not leave immediately, she would call the police.

He decided to console himself with his new friend Darla, but when he called her Debra by mistake, she hung up on him. He felt a little better after flushing her recovered earring down the toilet and heading to the bars.
~~~~

Chapter 9

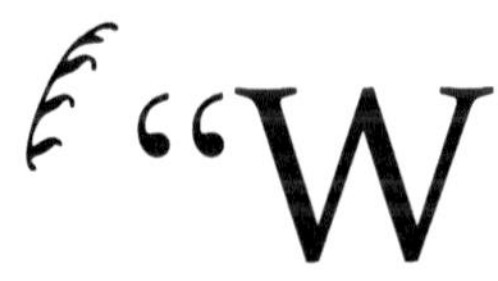

“Why do you hate that woman so much?” Mark Camden asked his wife as they washed the dinner dishes.

Pat looked up at him, startled. “I don’t hate her. I just think she is guilty as sin.”

“Well, you sure seem to be taking a lot of joy from the fact that her boyfriend tore apart her case today,” Mark commented. He’d listened to his wife gloat all through dinner.

Pat dropped the pan she was scrubbing back into the sink, sending warm soapy water sloshing onto the floor. She turned on her husband. “The hell I am!” she yelled. “What I am taking satisfaction from is the fact that he didn’t ruin *my* case, Mark. He very easily could have. What’s wrong with you? That woman is a cold-blooded killer. Don’t you want to see her punished for what she did to that poor old man?”

Mark Camden, well accustomed to his wife’s outbursts, shrugged his shoulders. “I’m not sure she’s a killer, Pat. The whole case is circumstantial. No one knows for sure she even did it. What if you are prosecuting an innocent woman?”

"What is this, Mark? Why are you defending her? You don't even know her!"

Mark sighed. "I listen to you give me a blow by blow description of what happens in that courtroom every day. And like everybody else in America, I read the headlines. I watched a little of the trial on Court TV today. That lady sure doesn't look like a killer. Hell, she looks like a strong wind would knock her over."

Pat turned her back on her husband. With stubborn finality, she said, "She did it."

Pat spent a restless night wondering if the male jurors were echoing her husband's thoughts. She secretly wished Elizabeth McGwire were a little less pretty and a little less petite. It would help her get a conviction.

~~~~

Belda was closing for the night when the bell above the door to Bella Luna jingled.

Though she had just come off of a darkened street, the woman who entered the deserted shop wore large sunglasses and a big floppy hat. Belda looked appraisingly at her from behind the counter. "May I help you?"

The woman removed her sunglasses. "Good evening, Belda." Her eyes were bloodshot and her words a bit slurred.

"Good evening, Elizabeth," Belda answered, her calm gray eyes looking kindly at her visitor. "I understand today wasn't a very good day for you in court."

Tears brimmed over Liz's eyes, as she sobbed, "No, not a very good day at all."
~~~~

Belda came around the counter with Eros at her heels and led Elizabeth into the shop. She locked the door behind her and turned the sign to *Closed.*

"Come, let's sit down." The old woman guided Liz by the elbow to the small room in the corner of the store. She settled her into a chair then went to make tea.

When Bleda returned with two steaming mugs, Liz had removed her hat and appeared to have gotten her tears under control.

Liz took a sip from the brimming cup. "Mmm, this is good. What kind of tea is it?"

Belda smiled, "Oh, just my personal blend. It will help to clear your mind a little tonight, and I think you will find in the morning, you will be lacking the usual symptoms that follow a night of imbibing spirits."

Elizabeth nodded and slowly sipped the tea. She wasn't surprised that Belda knew she had been drinking. When she entered the shop, it seemed as if the old woman had been expecting her.

After a few minutes, Belda said mildly, "Dear, why don't you tell me what happened the night your grandfather died. That's why you're here, isn't it?"

Elizabeth sighed and continued drinking from the steaming mug for a moment longer. She wiped her lips with a trembling hand. "I did just what you said. I made him a drink—a hot toddy, and I poured the potion in there. I brought it up to his room. I made sure he was in bed for the night, just like you told me. I… I didn't think he would get up in the night. He never does. He takes pills to help him sleep, and once he's in bed that's it, he doesn't usually get up. Not even to use the bathroom." Liz inhaled a shaking breath and gulped down the rest of her tea.

Belda waited patiently for her to go on.

"Can I have some more tea please?" Elizabeth asked, holding out her cup in unsteady fingers.

"Of course," Belda answered warmly. She took the empty cup from Elizabeth's shaking hand and left the room.

When she returned with the tea, Elizabeth took a sip, then set the mug on the table and looked off in the distance. She spoke like a woman in a trance. "I stayed awake. I know you said he wouldn't feel any pain, and he would just... just pass away in his sleep. But, I couldn't fall asleep, I was too nervous." Here Liz lapsed into silence and returned to her tea.

Belda again waited silently for the young woman to continue her narrative.

A few moments later, Elizabeth continued speaking as though there had been no pause. "About a half hour later I heard his bedroom door open. My room is just across the hall. It scared the hell out of me! I ran out of my room and saw him standing on the stairs. He was only two or three steps down when I came out. He was just standing there holding on to the railing. I... I said, 'Grandfather what's wrong?' He didn't answer... didn't even look at me. I don't think he heard me. He just stood there for a couple of seconds and then fell down the stairs. It was like his legs just went out from under him. I think he was dead before he hit the ground. I started screaming, and then that old bat Mrs. Renfrew and her mutt showed up.

"The next thing I knew, the police and the ambulance were there. They put Grandfather onto a stretcher, then covered him with a sheet and took him away. The police asked me what happened. I told them I got up to get something to drink and found him at the bottom of the staircase. They didn't believe me—I could tell they didn't." Her voice cracked and she grabbed the mug gulping greedily at the tea. "They kept asking me the same questions over and over. They called the next day and told me to come down to the police station. I was there for hours. They wanted me to take a lie detector test. I said I wanted to call a lawyer, and then Richard came down and they backed off. He said I didn't have to take the polygraph because they aren't admissible or something.

"When I left, I saw Mrs. Renfrew walking into an office with one of the detectives that had been asking me all the questions. They arrested me three days later, after an autopsy showed Grandfather had all these internal injuries. That staircase is really long and the steps are all wood; there isn't any carpeting to break a fall. But I think... I think he was dead before he fell down." She paused for a few seconds, biting her lip, and then looked at Belda with haunted eyes. In a soft, scared voice, she asked, "He *was* dead before he fell, wasn't he?"

Belda took Elizabeth's cold hand in her own gnarled fist. "Yes, he was. It was just very bad luck for you that he got up before your potion completed its work. It sounds like it was just seconds before the end."

My potion, Liz thought ruefully, not *the* potion. *My potion. All mine.* Elizabeth raised the mug to her lips. Suddenly, a disturbing thought forced its way into her mind. *What the hell have I been drinking here? How do I know she isn't trying to get rid of me with one of her potions?*

Belda, seeming to read her thoughts, said in a dreamy voice, "I wouldn't harm you, dear, unless I had a very good reason to. And even then, I would think twice about it. I really do like you. You remind me of myself in my youth." She squeezed Elizabeth's hand. "You know, Elizabeth, they are really nothing but plant leaves. Some of them are rather hard to come by, but individually, they are quite harmless. It's when you know the right combinations that you can get almost any desired effect on a human body. And, sometimes any desired effect on a circumstance." Here Belda chuckled, as if at a private joke. "Although, I must admit it takes a little more than plant leaves to change circumstances." She dropped a secretive wink. "You can make people love, make them leave, and yes, even make them die, Elizabeth. You know, your grandfather was quite lucky. Many people that seek my services to have someone eliminated don't always choose the most painless and humane method as you did, my dear. Sometimes they want them to suffer. Sometimes they want them to bleed. Your grandfather was fortunate that your choice was as gentle as it was."

Elizabeth thought the woman was utterly insane, and she shuddered. She thought, *Dear God, I made a pact with the devil when I bought whatever was stuffed in that vial.*

Wanting to change the subject, and needing some answers to questions that plagued her, she asked, "So, why didn't his autopsy show a heart attack. That's what it was, wasn't it?"

"Not at all," Belda replied. "The herbs you purchased simply make the heart beat slower and slower until it stops completely. There is nothing so forceful to the body as what the word *attack* implies. A heart attack is accompanied by symptoms. Left arm or chest pain; nausea or dizziness. Your grandfather experienced none of these things. The only discomfort I believe he encountered was a parched tongue. Unfortunately, that one minor side-effect caused you disastrous consequences, I'm afraid." Belda breathed a small, sad sigh.

They sat quietly for a few minutes. Liz swallowed hard and asked, "Did you send that guy to give me a note the first day of my trial?"

Belda nodded. "Yes, Elizabeth, that was Nicholas, one of my assistants. Sometimes when a person is under great duress they are moved to say things—admit things. Perhaps shift the blame somewhere else. I just wanted to remind you that wouldn't be a good idea."

"I wouldn't have! You already told me when I paid for the potion that I would die if I told anybody. I didn't think that rule had changed just because I got arrested."

"No, it didn't," Belda agreed in a bland, but somehow eerily menacing tone of voice.

"So, what's going to happen to me? What if they find me guilty?" Liz agonized.

"I believe all will turn out okay for you, Elizabeth. You just need to keep your head together, and always think before you speak," Belda responded. "Sometimes you have a little trouble in that department. A bit of a runaway tongue, no?"

"My lawyer doesn't want me to take the stand in my own defense. He's afraid I won't appear sympathetic enough to the jury."

Belda advised, "You should tell your lawyer that you wish to testify, Elizabeth. Insist on it, if you must."

Producing a small vial from her pocket, she folded it into the younger woman's palm. "Put this in your coffee the day you are to take the stand. It will make your testimony a little softer, a little more moving perhaps."

Elizabeth looked at the tiny vial with frightened eyes, "What is it?"

Belda's tone sharpened. "Yours is not to ask questions, Elizabeth. I am trying to help you because I feel, in some small part, responsible that things didn't work out exactly as you planned them. And as I mentioned, I like you. I can't say that about many of my clients unfortunately. You can take this or not, it's entirely up to you. Remember, Elizabeth, we always have free will. Just as you did when you chose to pour the potion you purchased into your grandfather's drink the night he died."

"I… I'm sorry," Elizabeth stammered. "It won't hurt me will it?"

Belda's tone softened once more. "Quite the contrary, my dear." The old woman rose, signaling that their meeting was over.

Elizabeth put the vial in her handbag. "How much do I owe you for this? I don't have much. Until the trial is over they won't let me—"

Belda interrupted, "No charge, dear. This one is on the house."

As Belda ushered her out the door, she sounded amused, as she remarked, "Elizabeth, dear, I am not insane; nor am I the devil. Not at all."

Liz stared at her open-mouthed for a second, feeling goose-flesh prickle her arms. She stammered her thanks and slunk out the door.

Once outside, Elizabeth donned the big floppy hat and glasses again. She thought with bitter irony, *I just said thank you to the woman that got me into the mess that ruined my life.*

Belda's voice exploded next to her, "You have no one to blame for this mess but yourself, Elizabeth McGwire!"

Liz jumped, and spun around, expecting to see the old woman standing right behind her. She was surprised to see she was alone on the empty street. She looked at the shop and saw all the windows dark. With an involuntary shudder, she climbed into the waiting taxi idling at the curb.

Chapter 10

True to Belda's word, Elizabeth awoke the next morning without a hangover. No headache, no nausea. In fact, she felt well rested and refreshed. She was pleasantly surprised when she looked in the mirror and saw her complexion looking rosy, her eyes clear and bright. Last night had been the first good night's sleep she had experienced since the trial began. She wondered if Belda would be willing to sell her some of her *personal blend.*

Liz had gone to see the old woman on impulse, partly because she was drunk, and partly from desperation. Who else was she going to talk to? She needed some reassurance that she wasn't going to spend the rest of her life in a prison cell. If things continued to go as badly in court as they had gone yesterday, surely that's where she was headed.

She wondered if Darrin was going to show up in the courtroom today, or if he would go off to sulk until she forgave him for his damaging testimony on the witness stand. She knew he didn't have anywhere else to be today. He was, after all, unemployed. She didn't believe his wounded pride would allow him to show his face in court today and offer support, but she really wanted him there. Liz's anger over his testimony was already beginning to fade. Her love for this man was not easily shaken, no matter what he did.

She sat down on the edge of the bed and dialed Darrin's number. The machine picked up. "Hi, honey, it's me," Elizabeth said after the beep. "I'm not mad anymore, so please come to the courthouse today, okay? I… I really need you. And Darrin, I love you. Bye."

~~~~

Having no access to Belda's personal blend, Richard Cohen did wake up with a hangover. His client wasn't the only one depressed over the day's proceedings. He too turned to a bottle for comfort the night before.

Richard skipped his run and downed four aspirin with half a pot of coffee. Bleary eyed and exhausted, he called Elizabeth. He was worried about her after her boyfriend's performance in court yesterday. He had never seen Elizabeth as despondent as she was last night when he took her home. He secretly hoped Darrin's testimony yesterday would be enough to open Liz's eyes to what a complete moron the guy was. Maybe she would dump him.

When she answered the phone in a somewhat cheerful voice, Richard felt an answering smile on his own lips—until he identified himself.

Elizabeth exhaled a disappointed sigh. "Oh, it's you."

"Yeah, only me. The guy defending your life. Who were you expecting?" he asked, annoyed.

"Never mind. Are you on your way?"

"Liz, who were you expecting to call?" Richard demanded.
~~~~

When she didn't respond, he barked, "Don't tell me you were hoping it was Darrin Perkins calling. Don't tell me you are even speaking to that bastard after what he did to you yesterday. Hell, after what he did to both of us!"

"I said never mind, Richard. Are you on your way over to get me now or not?"

Now she was angry and the morning was off to a miserable start.

Richard pinched the bridge of his nose and bit back a nasty retort. "Yeah. I'll be there soon." He sincerely hoped that Perkins wouldn't have the gall to attend the trial proceedings today. He couldn't stand the sight of that son of a bitch. Liz's anger might be rapidly evaporating, but her attorney's was only just beginning.

~~~~

When Cohen swung his Lexus into the circular driveway of the mansion, Liz was standing outside waiting for him. He was surprised to see how good she looked. He wondered if she had gone to a doctor for sleeping pills or something for her nerves. He also wondered if she truly understood the magnitude of the damage Darrin Perkins' testimony had inflicted upon her case.

Elizabeth climbed into the car and cast a critical eye at her lawyer. "Good morning, Richard. Are you sick? You look pale."

"I didn't sleep very well. What about you? You look fresh as a daisy."

Liz shrugged, "I slept fine. Great, in fact. So who's Camden calling to the stand to crucify me today?"

"Fortunately, no one that can do nearly as much damage as your boyfriend did," Cohen answered, his loathing of Darrin evident.
~~~~

"Richard, don't blame Darrin. He really didn't mean to do any harm. He just doesn't think before he speaks. You say the same thing about me, you know, so don't be so hard on him. Besides, he told the truth. What other choice did he have?"

Richard shook his head in frustration. "You know, Liz, if I live to be a hundred, I will never understand what it is you see in a loser like Darrin Perkins. You have no idea how badly his big mouth damaged your chances at freedom yesterday."

Elizabeth, losing her temper, shouted, "Shut up, Richard. You were hired to defend me, not to offer your unsolicited advice on my love life."

Cohen said no more. He drove on in silence, fuming at the stupidity of this woman.

After awhile, Liz said in a softer voice, "If you knew him better you would understand what I see in him. I don't know why everyone hates him so much. Hell, they don't even know him. He tries to do his best, just like we all do. Why can't anyone see that?"

"Elizabeth, have you ever heard the saying *love is blind?*" he asked.

She shot him a dirty look, and replied in an icy tone, "You don't know him. I do."

Richard didn't answer. There was nothing to say. He had fallen in love with his client, and he knew he would do well to quit wearing his heart on his sleeve. He suspected, after his cross-examination of Perkins yesterday, that his feelings for Elizabeth McGwire were probably evident to everyone in the courtroom. And anyone in the country that caught the trial on CNN or Court TV for that matter.

~~~~
~~~~

Court had been in session for two and a half hours when Darrin Perkins finally rolled out of bed and lit a cigarette. He saw the message lamp blinking on his answering machine. Hearing Liz's apology on his recorder, he laughed, "That's my girl. Never could stay mad at me." A half hour later, he wedged himself into the packed courtroom.

~~~~

Liz spent the morning stealing glances at the sea of faces in the overcrowded courtroom. Her lawyers scolded her about not paying attention to the proceedings, in her never-ending search for the wayward Darrin each morning.

At the first recess, Richard snapped, "He's not here, Liz. Probably for once in his life he had the good sense to stay away, so quit looking around the courtroom like you are bored. It doesn't sit well with the jury when they think you don't even care enough to pay attention at your own murder trial."

Liz glared at him for a moment, clearly irritated, but kept her eyes trained ahead for the rest of the morning. She would have missed Darrin's late arrival had her attorney not bristled as he caught sight of Perkins entrance out of the corner of his eye.

When Liz saw her boyfriend, her face lit up in a glowing smile. She raised her hand in a wave.

This blatant interruption came as the paramedic was describing his evaluation of her grandfather's twisted body lying at the base of the stairs to the jury.

One of the jurors, an elderly woman who looked like everyone's favorite grandma, gave the defendant a look of shocked disgust. Liz's cheeks reddened in embarrassment and she hastily turned around.
~~~~

She felt Richard's hot breath against her ear, as he whispered, "Knock it off, Liz. You are doing more damage to your own case than lover boy over there did."

She began to protest, but Olin put a restraining hand on her wrist and silenced her.

With the completion of Cohen's cross-examination of the paramedic, the prosecution rested their long and drawn out case. It was a flimsy case at best, based entirely on circumstantial evidence.

Cohen knew his real challenge was in persuading the jury to feel sympathy for his client. If he could convince them to regard Elizabeth as a fragile young woman, completely incapable of the hideous crime she was accused of, he would win this case. His biggest obstacle in this challenge was Elizabeth herself, and of course Darrin Perkins. The moony-eyed look his client's face dissolved into every time the jerk entered the courtroom was scoring her no points with the jury—nor any in the court of public opinion.

The man she was so in love with, had single handedly made Liz look like a cold, selfish opportunist. He portrayed her as a temperamental shrew; one so callous, she would happily knock off her grandfather without a second thought if she could gain ownership of his fortune.

The fact that Elizabeth lit up like a Christmas tree every time she saw Darrin enter a room wasn't lost on the jury. The obvious conclusion was, if the defendant wasn't angry at him for saying what he did on the stand yesterday, it must have all been true. But that didn't seem to faze Elizabeth McGwire at all.

Cohen didn't know how to make his client understand she must ignore Perkins if he continued to have the stupidity and the bad taste to show up in court everyday. When they broke for lunch, Cohen tried to tell her that her boyfriend should stay away for her sake.

Elizabeth accused him of being jealous, and insisted she needed Darrin there for moral support.

Finally, in complete exasperation, he threw up his hands. "Then, I hope you will find his support helpful during visiting hours at the penitentiary. Because if you keep this up, that's the only place you will be seeing him, Liz."

Elizabeth's face visibly paled. She pushed her salad away, her lunch only half eaten. "I'm not going to prison, Richard. If you let me testify, I can make the jury see that I am not the monster that Camden bitch has led them to believe I am."

Cohen shook his head. "Bad idea, Liz. I'm not worried about what you might say on direct examination. I think I can definitely evoke some sympathy from the jury for you. What I worry about is how you will react when Camden starts ripping into you on cross."

Elizabeth rolled her eyes, "Geez, Richard, what are you afraid of? You think I will jump from the witness chair and claw her eyes out?"

"That's not funny, Liz. Let's face it, you stare daggers at the woman every time you look at her. Your hatred for her is very apparent to the jury, and I think it might seal your fate."

"You really have no faith in me at all, Richard. Don't you think I can control myself?"

"To be honest, no. I'm not sure you can."

"I want to testify. You are my lawyer, so don't you have to do what I ask?"

"You want to testify even if it hurts our case?" he asked her, frustrated.

"It won't. Trust me."

Cohen sighed in exasperation and drummed his fingers restlessly on the table. "Fine, Liz. You want to testify, then go ahead and testify, but just remember I advised against it. I'll begin preparing your appeal tonight."

Liz reached across the table and squeezed Cohen's arm. "You won't think it's a bad idea after the jury hears my testimony. I promise."

"We will need to run through what you are going to say. Practice your testimony, so you will be prepared for whatever Pat Camden throws at you," he said, accepting his defeat.

"Oh, brother. Is that really necessary?"

"Of course it is! Don't you want to be ready for what she might ask you up there? Liz, have you forgotten this is your life we are fighting for? I cannot believe how cavalier you have become about this. You would do well to remember you are not out of the woods by a long shot. The jury doesn't like you, in case you haven't noticed," Richard cried out.

Liz took a deep breath. "Oh, calm down, Richard. Fine, we'll practice. How about tonight?"

Her attorney nodded. "Okay, we'll see how it goes. If you are ready to testify by tomorrow then I will call you to the stand. If we still think your testimony needs work then I can just fill the day with your character witnesses."

"I'll be ready by tomorrow, don't worry. I really want to get this over with."

"I wish I felt as confident as you do about this, Liz," Cohen grumbled.

"Trust me," she replied, a knowing little ghost of a smile crossing her lips.

Chapter 11

In Richard Cohen's opinion, the practice session which took place in his office that evening was a complete disaster. It only served to further his conviction that putting Elizabeth McGwire on the stand was a mistake of colossal proportions.

He and Olin spent several hours patiently trying to coach their client in demeanor and the proper tone of voice, as well as prepare her for the thrashing Patricia Camden would subject her to. Through it all Liz remained bored and uninterested. Every fifteen minutes she insisted on interrupting what they were doing to check her voicemail messages. Cohen knew she was hoping for a message from that scumbag boyfriend of hers.

When they finally quit for the night it was well after eleven o'clock. Cohen was packing his briefcase while Liz again dialed her voicemail from the phone in the lobby.

Olin slapped Cohen on the back. "Looks like your winning streak is finally over, buddy. In fact, we might have to go back to chasing ambulances after this one," he laughed.

Cohen bristled. He thought again of unlucky number thirteen.

~~~~

The next morning Richard Cohen sat at his kitchen table feeling sick. He knew that taking more time to coach Liz on her testimony was a waste of time. It wasn't going to change anything. What needed fixing was her attitude, and try as he may, she wasn't going to take things any more seriously or heed his advice.

He made one final attempt to dissuade his client from testifying in her own defense, stating the countless reasons it was a dangerous idea. His protests were futile and fell on deaf ears. She refused to budge. So, with a heavy heart and a churning stomach, Cohen cancelled the numerous character witnesses he had scheduled to appear on Liz's behalf, except for the two most vital to his case. He planned to call Elizabeth to the stand later that day as his final witness. Then the defense would wrap up its case and turn Elizabeth's life over to the jury for deliberation.

~~~~

Elizabeth's sleep was restless and fitful, punctuated by nightmares of being led away in handcuffs, while Darrin looked on smiling and waving at her.

She awoke with a start at two-thirty in the morning and climbed out of bed to rummage through her handbag. She found the vial the old woman had given her during her last visit to the bookstore. She carried it with her downstairs to the living room, where she sat on the couch with a snifter of Courvoisier VSOP—a leftover from the days her grandfather stocked a small but select bar.

She held the little bottle of strange herbs clenched in her left hand, while she sipped the expensive amber liquid. Her stomach was soon warmed by the cognac, her hand by the old woman's weird concoction. She opened her fist and looked at the small cylinder. It appeared to have come alive in her grasp. It glowed with a dull ruby color. The herbs packed within appeared to be moving, churning restlessly through their small glass confines.

This didn't frighten Elizabeth. In fact, she felt oddly comforted by the glowing red herbs stirring agitatedly in the vial as she watched.

She fell into a dreamless sleep, still holding the bottle loosely in one hand.

When she awoke to the alarm at seven-fifteen, the vial was beside her on the coverlet. On her palm were two small blisters, and beside her on the sheet, where the bottle came to rest, a round hole. It was no larger than a cigarette burn. Liz looked at it thoughtfully while running a finger over the singed cloth.

After showering, she made coffee and sat eating a piece of dry toast at the kitchen table. When the phone rang she ignored it. The potion sat on the table next to her coffee cup. The contents had returned to its original green color.

Liz wondered if her overtaxed mind, in the predawn hours, hadn't played tricks on her when she saw the contents turn a glowing scarlet and dance beneath the glass. Was it a fantasy brought about by the cognac? She knew the burned sheet and her blistered palm were no illusion. Therefore, the color change and the herb's restless stirring surely must have been real.

Glancing at the clock, she was shocked to see how late it had become while she was lost in thought. She knew Richard must be rushing through traffic, worried when she didn't answer the phone.

Elizabeth pried the cork out of the tiny bottle with one manicured fingernail. She watched mesmerized, as a slender plume of smoke escaped, drifting from the narrow opening in a graceful arc. A faint bitter odor enveloped the thin tendril of smoke.

With no further thought, Elizabeth picked up the vial and poured the contents into the remainder of her cream-laced coffee. The beverage instantly began to bubble and turn an obscene, repellent scarlet—the color of drying blood. The scent wafting up was repulsive. It lasted only a few seconds before the coffee returned to its creamy toffee-color and the bitter odor disappeared. Without allowing herself to think about what she was doing, Liz quickly swallowed the liquid and gagged. Her throat burned and she doubled over in a coughing jag. She grew lightheaded and grabbed the edge of the table to keep from falling to the floor. Eyes stinging, throat searing, she heard through spasms of pain, the sound of Cohen's car pulling into the driveway.

Richard knocked on the door for a full five minutes before turning back to his car to retrieve his cellphone so he could call inside. Liz opened the door just as he was retreating down the steps.

When she threw open the door, the relief on his face was unmistakable.

"Where have you been? You had me worried sick!"

Elizabeth could no longer feel the effects of the potion, except for a fiery heat in her chest and belly that was gradually subsiding. Her cheeks were rosier than usual, and her brow moist with perspiration.

"Sorry, I was running late this morning," she smiled.

"I tried to call you, why didn't you answer?" Cohen looked at her closely to make sure she was really okay.

"I must have been in the shower. I didn't hear the phone," Liz replied, avoiding eye contact.

He took her by the elbow and led her to the passenger side of his car. When they were on their way to the courthouse, Richard made one more attempt to talk Elizabeth out of testifying.

Instead of the vehement argument he expected, she responded in a soft voice, "You know, Richard, I love you for worrying about me so much. I really do. Why can't all men be as wonderful and protective as you are? If I hadn't met Darrin first, I really think you and I could have had something. Maybe someday we still can, who knows." She gazed at him, eyes shining.

Cohen was rendered utterly speechless by this uncharacteristic display of affection from the object of his unrequited love. His cheeks turned a dull brick color, and he fought back tears as Liz stroked his cheek with a gentle hand. Not another word was spoken during the remainder of the ride to the courthouse. Her attorney did not trust himself to speak at that point.

~~~~

Once they were seated and the noisy courtroom had been called to order, Olin leaned toward their client. He reminded her not to look around. "Just pay attention to the proceedings, and don't worry if your boyfriend is here or not. Today is especially important, Liz. We have to look good."

She smiled warmly at him and whispered back, "Don't worry, Olin. I don't care if Darrin shows up or not."

He leaned back in his chair. A disbelieving grunt escaped his lips, but he was satisfied she would behave.

Elizabeth took his arm and leaned toward him. "Olin, I never thanked you for what you have done for me. I just want to tell you how much it has meant to me. You know, I will never forget you no matter how this turns out."

Olin stammered a thank you, his eyes betraying his surprise at her words. At that moment he would have gladly traded places
~~~~

with her to spare her even one more second of this hellacious trial. Strangely, he felt sudden affection toward this woman who he had secretly held in contempt since the day she retained them.

Up until that very second, as the last day of trial was just about to commence, Olin knew in his heart that Elizabeth McGwire was guilty. The only person he ever told this heartfelt truth to was his wife. He worked diligently for Liz because she was their client—and when Richard Cohen won a case, so did he. He was successful by association, and he wanted it to stay that way. But, in those few moments, with Liz whispering those kind words to him, Olin completely changed his mind about her guilt. He wanted to scream at the jury to find this poor, frail woman not guilty and set her free.

Chapter 12

Elizabeth's two character witnesses were questioned, cross-examined, and then questioned on redirect before the lunch break. The women jurors looked doubtfully at Elizabeth's friend, Tiffany Sims. She was a woman with model good looks, who spoke in glowing terms of Elizabeth McGwire's many virtues. The male jurors just gawked.

Pat Camden could barely keep the smirk off her face as this Barbie-Doll of a woman, in bright red lip gloss, took the stand and spoke of the extensive charity work she and Elizabeth had been involved in together over the years.

Camden's cross examination was cursory, so convinced was she that none of the men in the courtroom even heard the woman's testimony. She was sure they were all too lost in their fantasies of this beautiful creature to pay attention to a word she said. The women present, obviously green with jealousy, did not seem to absorb it either.

Pat Camden, however, did manage to extract from the divine Ms. Sims that she could not remember the cause or name of a single one of the alleged charities she and Elizabeth had worked so tirelessly side by side to support over the years.

The testimony of Tiffany Sims was the most uninteresting of the entire trial, but that night on the TV news, it was her face, her huge mane of honey-blonde hair, and her ample bosom that graced most of the major networks.

~~~~

Richard Cohen's stomach churned, as he announced, "The defense calls Elizabeth McGwire to the stand," and waited for the wave of whispering in the courtroom to subside.

He had spent his lunch hour chomping Rolaids and going over his questions, while Olin took Elizabeth to a nearby coffee shop.

When Elizabeth rose to take the stand a hush fell over the courtroom. She looked small and fragile, as breakable as a crystal vase perched precariously on the edge of a desk. Wearing a demure, high-collared dress of pale yellow silk, she appeared the epitome of innocence, Cohen thought.

As Elizabeth McGwire gave her testimony, there was not a dry eye in the courtroom. The only person who was unmoved by the waves of despair pouring from Elizabeth's tortured soul was the prosecutor.

Patricia Camden, sensing defeat, and stunned that Cohen was able to elicit such moving testimony from his callous client, tried relentlessly to portray Elizabeth as a cold, calculating killer on cross-examination.

Every barb-sharp question she volleyed at Elizabeth was met with quiet and sorrowful dignity. A dignity and sorrow that no one, least of all Pat Camden, would have ever suspected this indifferent woman capable of. The more she tried to bait Elizabeth and
~~~~

provoke a violent reaction, the more she enraged the jury, who felt she was badgering what now appeared to be a frail, helpless orphan.

Camden knew her case was hopeless when Elizabeth McGwire, with tears streaming down her pale cheeks, sobbed, "Ms. Camden, I know you are just doing your job, and I know that we all wish there was someone to blame for my grandfather's death. You will never know how many nights I have lain awake asking God if I was to blame because I didn't wake up soon enough that night to stop him from falling. Asking God why he took the only family I had left. I don't blame you for wanting to see someone pay. I want to blame someone too. But, if anyone should be standing trial because my grandfather is gone, it isn't me. It's God. I didn't push him. I loved him."

And then, between tear-choked sobs, her slight shoulders wracked with shudders, Elizabeth wailed, "I still love him, and not a moment passes that I don't miss him."

~~~~

Closing arguments were brief, and then began the long hours of waiting, while the jury deliberated and tried to reach a verdict regarding Elizabeth McGwire's fate.

~~~~

Pat Camden bit her fingernails to the quick. She told her husband repeatedly that it seemed the jury was under some kind of a spell when Elizabeth testified.

"It was like the whole damn courthouse was mesmerized!" she hollered during dinner. "The bitch turned into Rebecca of fucking Sunnybrook Farm right before everyone's eyes."

"Who was her friend?" Mark Camden asked around a mouthful of mashed potatoes.

Pat threw a loaf of French bread at him.

~~~~

Cohen spent the evening with Olin and his family munching popcorn and watching videos. Nothing, not even Clint Eastwood's classic Dirty Harry, could keep his mind from wandering to Liz. He wondered what she was doing and how she was feeling.

~~~~

Liz and Darrin ate dinner at a Mexican restaurant, where they ignored the stares and whispers of the other diners. Later that evening, while Cohen speculated about where she was and what she was doing, Liz lay thrashing in ecstasy beneath Darrin's sweating body, in his cramped, dirty apartment.

~~~~

The jury gave up trying to reach a verdict after eleven p.m. and retired for the night. They were six to acquit, four to convict, and two undecided. They would reconvene at eight o'clock the next morning.

The following night the jurors were seven to acquit, two to convict, and three undecided.

Two days later, after grave concern the trial would end in a hung jury, a unanimous decision was finally reached.
~~~~

Chapter 13

"Have you reached a verdict in the matter of King County versus Elizabeth McGwire, Madam Forewoman?" The judge asked.

"We have, Your Honor," the bespectacled woman that looked like everyone's favorite grandmother answered.

"Please hand your verdict to the clerk."

She did so.

"Will the defendant please rise."

Looking anxious, and gripping Cohen's hand, Elizabeth rose from her seat and faced the jury.

"How say you?" Westerfield asked.

"We, the jury, find the defendant, Elizabeth McGwire, not guilty."

The courtroom erupted in bedlam. Reporters elbowed one another out of the way to run to record live reports and call the news into their editors. Television stations interrupted their regularly scheduled programming to bring the verdict into every home and business in America within moments of it being announced. Then they replayed clips from the highlights of the trial.

Cohen, Olin and Liz hugged each other and cried. Elizabeth pulled herself from Richard's embrace. She turned, expecting to find Darrin's waiting arms behind her.

True to his *I-couldn't-care-less* nature, Darrin wasn't even in the courtroom. He had once again overslept, and had no idea the jury had even reached a verdict.

Liz had left him countless messages on his answering machine that morning to advise him that the jury was back in, and would be announcing her fate shortly.

Pat Camden, in an uncharacteristic display of emotion, yelled as the forewoman read the verdict, "What? Are you people out of your mind! She's guilty dammit, guilty!" She was lead from the courtroom by red-faced coworkers.

The District Attorney held a press conference later in the day stressing King County's commitment to justice, so one shouldn't blame Ms. Camden for her passionate reaction.

The prosecutor's outburst would be splashed across newspapers and magazines for the next month. Late show hosts Letterman and Leno were presented with a rich source of material for their opening monologues.

Pat Camden—embarrassed and ashamed, avoided public scrutiny for months. As a final slap in the face, the District Attorney transferred her to white collar crimes.

Camden became obsessed with the fact that Elizabeth McGwire was not found guilty of the murder of her grandfather. Her husband, unable to stand her constant complaining, told her to get over it. The case was closed, move on. When she still held on to her obsession, unwilling—or perhaps unable to part with it, her husband, finding living with her unbearable, left and filed for divorce.

As if to rub salt in her wounds, to Camden's utter amazement, he married Liz's friend, Tiffany Sims. Immediately after their divorce was final, with the ink barely dry on the decree, Pat was once again the front-page story of check-stand tabloids. The headlines, this time screaming, *Camden Dumped* and *Woman Scorned.*

Her ex-husband and Ms. Sims profited nicely from a lucrative book deal about the trial.

~~~~

Patricia Camden never wavered in her belief that Elizabeth McGwire was guilty of first degree murder. The trial haunted her for the rest of her life. After her marriage fell apart she moved to Michigan, where she teamed with a retired police captain to open a successful private investigation office.

Throughout her life, Patricia Camden was scarred by the Elizabeth McGwire trial and its verdict of acquittal. The thin, red haired woman with the emerald green eyes haunted her dreams. She told her partner that someday she hoped to meet Theodore McGwire in heaven, so she could tell him she was sorry that his murder had gone unpunished. She had done the best she could. She hoped he knew that.

~~~~

Richard Cohen's practice continued to grow, representing high-profile clients in high-profile cases. He had twenty-seven straight victories before he and Olin finally lost a case.

A reputed mob-boss on trial for money laundering was found guilty. There were threats made on Richard's life, but fortunately the verdict was overturned on appeal and the man set free. Cohen and Olin breathed a sigh of relief, as they had visions of being taken for a one way ride if they didn't win that appeal.

Richard Cohen continued to date women with problems and continued to have predictable break-ups. Two years and four therapists later, he married Olin's eldest daughter, Jenny. She was twenty-one, Cohen forty-four. They had two children. Richard Cohen seemed to have finally recovered from his Rapunzel complex and found contentment.

Chapter 14

Six months later

With her grandfather's estate finally probated and the money released to her, Elizabeth adjusted to her new life in the mansion.

She and Mrs. Renfrew avoided each other as much as possible, and life gradually settled into a routine. Elizabeth's face disappeared from the gossip magazines, and she could once again go out in public without being stared at. Cohen called her numerous times after the trial ended. Liz never returned his phone calls, and Richard Cohen, a sadder but wiser man, finally realized he was out of her life forever.

Elizabeth McGwire remained as discontent as she had been during her trial. She and Darrin spent sporadic time together. She occupied her days buying lavish clothes and jewelry for herself and the man she loved. She rearranged the furniture continuously, but seemed never satisfied with their placement in the big, lonely house. Only the paintings remained unmoved. And still, Elizabeth felt they watched her with accusatory eyes, from their place high up on the walls.

She drank a nightly glass of wine or cognac, but rarely over-indulged anymore. She watched Mrs. Renfrew, accompanied by Rembrandt, pass by the living room window, with robotic precision, at precisely seven-thirty each night.

She wished she could sell the old memory-ridden house, and reside in a smaller and newer home, away from its haunting aura. She longed to escape the watchful eye of Mrs. Renfrew and the paintings. She was a prisoner of her grandfather's will—forced to remain in the mansion, and allow Mrs. Renfrew to reside there, undisturbed, until the housekeeper's death.

In quiet desperation, Elizabeth McGwire wondered how life could be so cold and empty, when seemingly one had everything they could ever need or want.

~~~~

It was, of course, Elizabeth's relationship with Darrin that still plagued her. Now that she had all the money they could ever need, she could not understand why he refused to marry her. He would not move into the mansion with her. He insisted on keeping his own dingy quarters half way across town. Elizabeth paid his rent, and as usual, he remained unemployed. She made no demands. When she cautiously brought up the subject of marriage, he grew surly and withdrawn.

It was in desperation, and in a state of utter hopelessness over their relationship, that Liz found herself at the door of Bella Luna on a gloomy and rain-sodden afternoon.

The pretty shop girl with the long, black hair greeted her warmly. Liz bent down to pet the black cat she had seen on her previous visits.

"Hello, Ms. McGwire, it's nice to see you," Gabriella smiled from behind the ancient counter.
~~~~

"Hi… um… I need to see Belda, if she is available," Liz stammered, looking nervously around the store.

"Are you able to wait a few moments? Belda is with a customer right now." Gabriella pointed to the tiny room in the corner. The door was closed, and Liz looked at it with frightened eyes.

"A customer? Like… Like me?" she asked.

"No, Ms. McGwire, not like yourself," Gabriella laughed, "We have many customers, each quite unique. Can you wait, or shall I have Belda phone you later?"

"No, I can wait. I will just have a look around."

Gabriella ushered her into a lofty, sepulchral book-lined room. "There are many books for you to browse through," she told her. "Also, there are items of interest in the back of the store, such as candles, decks of Tarot cards and numerous metaphysical items. We have much to keep you occupied while you wait. Can I offer you some tea?"

"Yes, thank you, tea would be nice," Elizabeth replied. She wondered if it would be the same kind Belda had given her on her previous visit. That seemed like a lifetime ago.

The girl disappeared. Liz glanced up to see the black cat staring down at her from atop a high shelf. She recoiled in horror from the cat's penetrating stare, and suddenly felt swallowed up in the dark aisles of books.

Was it her imagination, or did the light suddenly grow dim in this dusty book-laden room? She wondered if this could be an omen of impending misfortune.

Liz shivered as she turned and wandered to the back of the store, where the girl had indicated other items of occult interest were to be found.

The first item she inspected was an old, battered tin box with faded lettering. She cautiously opened the box, from which a fetid stench, evocative of a haunted graveyard arose. With a cry of revulsion, Liz dropped the damning piece and backed away.

Hideous and other-worldly items lined the walls. Sinister eyes seemed to stare malevolently from the corners. Terrified, Elizabeth ran to the front of the shop. Just as she was about to lose her resolve and flee, she heard Belda's voice. She watched as a famous actress raced from the tiny room that served as Belda's inner sanctum. The actress's skin was ashen, her eyes huge and frightened. Without so much as a glance at Elizabeth, she ran out the front door, sending the bell overhead to peal wildly.

"Why, Elizabeth," Belda smiled, obviously pleased to see the thin woman standing nervously by the door.

"Hello, Belda." Liz put her hand out for the old woman to take.

Liz looked toward the front door and asked, "Was that—"

The old woman cut her off. "Is Gabriella getting you something to drink?"

"Y… Yes."

"Excellent. Well, come into the office and tell me how things are going."

"Oh, okay." Elizabeth allowed herself to be ushered to a chair by the odd old woman—the source of her freedom and wealth, and at the same time, the cause of the horrendous hell she had been through.

The scent of the actress's perfume still lingered in the air. "That lady… Isn't she—"

"Elizabeth," Belda scolded in an icy voice that frightened her. "Should one of my customers see you leaving the store, how would you wish me to respond if they asked, 'Isn't that the woman who was in the news just a few short months ago?' Would you wish me to gossip and tell them who you are… And why you came?"

Liz shook her head violently, "No, of course not."

"Then do not think I would be so indiscreet as to identify another of my clients." Belda looked at her with stern eyes, hard as flint. "You forget you saw that woman, or anyone else you happen to glimpse in my store. Is that understood?"

"Of course. I'm sorry, that was very rude of me."

Her momentary outburst forgotten, Belda handed a steaming mug of tea to Elizabeth from a tray Gabriella had placed on the claw-foot table.

"So what brings you to Bella Luna today, dear?"

Liz sipped the tea with a disquieting sense of deja vu. It wasn't as soul-satisfying as the cup of tea she'd had on her previous visit. She suspected it was nothing more magical than a Lipton teabag. But it did help to steady her nerves.

"I need to purchase another potion." Elizabeth looked down, clearly embarrassed.

"I see." Belda gazed at her thoughtfully. "Some would say you are a glutton for punishment."

"You said there are potions that can make someone love you. Remember telling me that?"

"So, this is about your young man?"

Liz nodded, but wouldn't meet the woman's eyes.

"And you are quite sure that you want this young man to love you, Elizabeth?"

Liz answered vehemently, "Oh yes. Very sure."

"Are you willing to accept whatever consequences occur as a result of your obsession with this man? Are you sure this is really what you want?"

"Yes, Belda. I've loved Darrin for a long time. There is no one else for me. There never will be." The conviction in Elizabeth's voice was unmistakable.

Belda sighed, "Very well then. The cost will be the same as the first potion you purchased and the terms the same. Understood?"

Elizabeth nodded and rose from the chair. "Thank you, Belda. When shall I pick it up?"

"Tomorrow, around noon. We will need to meet for a few minutes. There are very specific instructions that must be followed to the letter, or it could result in irreparable consequences," Belda said gravely, looking at her through narrowed eyes. "Do you understand, Elizabeth? *To the letter.*"

Liz replied impatiently, thinking the old woman far too melodramatic, "Yes, I understand. Thanks, I will see you tomorrow."

She ran from the building anxious to be rid of this demonic bookstore and its strange occupants.

Gabriella watched her leave, then turned to Belda. "Well, what does she want this time? Surely it's not more money?"

"No, dear. This time she wants one of the few things money can't buy. Love."

"I wonder if he is a good man?" Gabriella asked.

"No. I don't believe he is," Belda replied in a tired voice.

Gabriella was silent for a few moments, then she asked the old woman, "How many times do you think she can play Russian roulette before she gets shot?"

The old woman shook her head. "Sadly, I believe this purchase may prove to be the fatal bullet."

Chapter 15

When Elizabeth arrived at Bella Luna to purchase the love potion that would magically transform Darrin into an ardent suitor for her hand in marriage, her eyes were swollen from crying.

She could not reach Darrin by phone the previous night. She drove by his apartment after midnight and saw not only his motorcycle, but an unfamiliar car parked in the space reserved for his apartment as well.

The next morning she called his apartment and a woman answered. When Liz asked to speak to Darrin, the woman mumbled, "He's in the shower."

Heartsick, Elizabeth hung up the phone.

When Darrin emerged from the steamy bathroom, he glanced at the message light on his answering machine. It wasn't blinking. "I thought I heard the phone ring. They didn't leave a message?"

"No, she didn't," Darla replied.

"She? How the hell do you know it was a she?"

"Because it was a woman's voice that asked for you," the bimbo answered, rolling her eyes.

"Oh shit! You answered it?"

"It rang, what was I supposed to do?" Darla sounded defensive and annoyed.

"Oh fuck! You stupid bitch! You should have let the machine pick up. It was probably my goddamn girlfriend," Darrin raved.

"What girlfriend? You never told me you had one."

"Shit! Just get dressed and get the hell outta here, will you, Diana." he yelled.

"It's Darla, you imbecile. You know she's a real lucky chick, that girlfriend of yours," she retorted sarcastically. She glared at him, as she gathered up her strewn clothing and headed into the bathroom.

~~~~

Gabriella led Elizabeth McGwire to the cozy corner office and told her Belda would be down momentarily. Liz declined the girl's offer of tea, and waited impatiently for the old woman to give her the potion she so desperately wanted.

When Belda entered the cramped little room, Liz shot up from her chair. "Where is it? Please Belda, I need it right away!"

Belda put a soothing hand on Elizabeth's shoulder. "Relax, dear, I have the potion right here." She held up a small vial that contained what appeared to be cut flowers in a pale lavender color.

"Please let me have it. Here's the cash," Liz cried. She looked longingly at the vial, as she desperately shoved a white envelope into the woman's arthritic fist.

"Just a moment, Elizabeth. Sit down and calm yourself. There are instructions that must be followed as I told you yesterday, so settle down and listen to me!"
~~~~

Elizabeth took a deep breath and sat on the edge of the chair. She eyed the bottle with open greed and then reluctantly dragged her eyes back to the old woman. “Alright, I’m calm. Now just tell me what the hell I have to do.”

Belda sighed, “You are sure you want to go through with this? Elizabeth, sometimes we think a man is—”

“Yes dammit. Quit asking me that,” Liz snarled, cutting her off. “You have your money. Now just tell me what I have to do so I can get out of here.”

Belda looked at her with ill-concealed contempt. “It’s very simple. You pour this into the young man’s drink. The beverage should be a cold one. It does not matter if it is alcoholic or not, just make sure he finishes the drink to the last drop. And when he does—and this is the most important part, so you better pay attention—make sure you are the first person he looks at once the drink with the potion is consumed. Do you understand, Elizabeth? You must be the very first person he lays eyes on when he finishes the drink. The first woman he sees, he will love unconditionally and completely for the rest of his life. Do you understand?”

“Yes, I do,” Elizabeth answered victoriously. She believed, at last, Darrin Perkins would finally be hers.

The old woman handed the vial to Liz, thinking, *you selfish, stupid woman.*

As Liz left the bookshop, Belda watched her through the dusty window with a feeling of abhorrence tinged with pity.

~~~~

“Dinner was great, babe. Thanks for having me over,” Darrin grinned.
~~~~

"Let's go in the living room. I'll get you another beer," Liz smiled in return.

"You sure you ain't mad at me about the cleaning lady answering the phone this morning?"

Elizabeth's eyes narrowed to slits, "Cleaning lady, huh? She sure doesn't do a very good job."

Darrin laughed uncomfortably. "I'll take that beer."

Liz went into the kitchen and pulled a beer from the refrigerator. She glanced around to make sure Darrin was still in the living room before uncapping the ale and pulling Belda's vial from the pocket of her slacks. Prying the tiny cork out, Elizabeth gagged at the putrid odor it released.

"Oh, gross," she whispered, "What the hell is in there?"

She hurriedly poured the contents into the opened bottle of beer, and watched in awe as the flowers disappeared and blended invisibly with the ale. She cautiously sniffed the beer. No rank odor remained.

"Here," Liz handed Darrin the bottle.

"Cheers, babe," he replied, putting the bottle to his lips.

Liz watched him closely. He saw her staring at him, and asked, "What's wrong? Is there something hanging from my nose?"

"No. What do you mean?" Liz answered, looking away.

"You're staring at me."

"Sorry," she mumbled.

He took a few more swallows from the bottle, then offered it to Liz. "You want a drink?"

"No!" She took a small jump backward, away from his outstretched hand.

He looked at her with a curious expression. "The bottle won't bite, babe. But I might if you ask nice," he laughed lecherously at his own joke.

When Liz didn't even crack a smile, just continued eyeballing him warily, Darrin commented, "You sure are acting weird tonight. You sure this isn't about the cleaning woman that picked up the phone this morning?"

"It's nothing. Just drink up like a good boy, will you."

Darrin laughed, "You trying to get me drunk, so you can take advantage of me, sweetheart?"

"Right. You bet," Liz answered with a look that Darrin, from past experience, instantly recognized as an invitation to love making. She told him to close the drapes.

He rose from the couch, holding the beer bottle loosely in his fist. Only a few sips remained. He walked to the front windows and looked out at the lawn.

As he reached up to draw the heavy curtains, Darrin took the final swig from the bottle and glanced at his watch. It was seven-thirty p.m.

From around the corner of the house, looking pathetically weary and careworn, Mrs. Renfrew and her faithful Rembrandt came into view. The aging housekeeper had gained even more weight since the trial, and she walked with deliberate slowness. She pushed her wind-blown, gray hair back from her temple and glanced at Darrin through the window. He was barely aware of a shrieking and hysterical Elizabeth McGwire behind him, as she frantically called his name, and screamed for him to turn around. He stood mesmerized, staring at the elderly woman. As if by some hellish magic, their eyes met…

PART II
What Martin Reynolds Did To Get Ahead

Each success only buys an admission ticket to a more difficult problem.
–Henry Kissinger

Each success buys a new pair of shoes.
–Sheila Reynolds

Chapter 1

Sheila Reynolds stood before the mahogany floor-length mirror that dominated the corner of their bedroom. The big four-poster bed was littered with dresses she had tried on and discarded in an effort to find the perfect one for the dinner she and Martin were attending that evening.

Her husband sat perched amid the sea of rejected evening wear. He balanced his laptop on his knees, checking the NASDAQ.

Sheila turned around in all her silver sequined splendor, and asked, "Marty, does this one make my butt look big?"

In the history of time, there has never been a diplomatic answer to this question. A wise man, Martin Reynolds knew this. The truth was, her backside in that dress reminded him of two huge disco-balls, circa the early 70's dance clubs.

"Well, hon, I liked the black one better," he offered tentatively.

"Which black one!" Sheila exploded, "I've tried on five of them."

Martin sighed. He went through this ordeal every time they attended one of these goddamn dinners.

The Manhattan law firm of Carson, August, Bench & Associates, his employer the last twelve years, had promoted another underling to partner. *Why in the hell,* Martin thought, *do those son of a bitches always pass me by?*

Though extremely out of character for Shelia Reynolds to ever pass up the opportunity to go shopping, she refused to buy a new dress to wear for these dreaded occasions, until it was Martin's promotion they would be celebrating. Hence, all of the dresses were a little tight. Sheila had gained weight since their purchase. Tailors had let a few of her favorites out at the seams, but even those inevitably grew more snug each time a promotion came within Martin's grasp and was once more dashed away.

When Martin told her she should just buy a new one, she adamantly refused. Sheila felt buying a new dress for one of these miserable functions was somehow admitting his defeat. She would rather suffer in an ill-fitting gown than concede that her husband was a failure.

Reynolds had been passed over for promotion seven times. He loathed these dinners almost as much as he hated bringing home the disappointing news to Sheila that once again the celebration dinner would not be in his honor. Sheila never took the news well. It inevitably resulted in an eating binge, Martin being the scapegoat for her added poundage. Sheila had been battling her weight problem for most of their married life. She was convinced if Martin could just make partner—complete with the raise and the bonus checks, they could move out of their cramped apartment, and the extra pounds she carted around would magically drop off, giving her the svelte build of a high fashion model.

Martin thought if his wife had just a little discipline and stopped eating everything that didn't eat her first she could probably lose the weight. He wisely never mentioned that theory to her.

This time the promotion was awarded to Clive Cheznik, a specialist in maritime law, and a man ten years younger than Reynolds. Cheznik had a pretty little blonde wife who never needed to ask if anything made her butt look big. It was a butt Martin found highly appealing.

Reynolds actually liked Clive Cheznik. He was a good lawyer and a pleasant man to be around. In a firm of over fifty lawyers, that was saying something.

What Martin found galling was that he had been with the firm four years longer than Cheznik, and had recently successfully litigated a tobacco lawsuit. He not only won a verdict in favor of their client—the tobacco company, but made the firm over half a million dollars in billable hours.

Reynolds had high hopes when the short nomination list was released last month with only three names on it. Surely the promotion would be his this time.

"Hello, earth to Martin." His wife was leaning over the bed and waving a hand in front of his face.

"Sorry, dear, I was woolgathering. What did you say?"

"I asked if this was the black one you liked?" She twirled in front of him. It was a chiffon number that was cut so low Martin thought no one would bother to look at Sheila's rear. The show was clearly in the front. It was a definite improvement over the sequined thing.

"Yes, that one is lovely," he nodded and closed the laptop with a snap. "Guess I better go get dressed." He rose from the bed with a heavy sigh.

Sheila placed a tentative hand on his arm. "Marty, the next time that list comes out with your name on it, I really think you should think about using that stuff you bought from the woman in Seattle. After all, we did pay an awful lot of money for it."

Martin cringed.

It had been two years since he had lost the partnership a fifth time and went into a bar to drown his woes. He drank one too many single-malt scotches, and bemoaned to a stranger the sad state of affairs about his missed promotion. He told the fellow that he was contemplating leaving the firm. The man commiserated with Martin, speaking of similar frustrations in his own career. He then slipped a business card from his wallet and slid it across the bar.

Casting a surreptitious glance sideways, the stranger whispered from the corner of his mouth, "This place can help. Ask for Belda." He then excused himself to use the restroom and never returned.

A tipsy and slightly unsteady Reynolds tucked the business card into his wallet, paid his tab, and hailed a cab home to the apartment in Queens he shared with his wife.

A week later, after the fifth bitter celebration dinner in another man's honor, Martin thumbed through his wallet and pulled out the card. He laid it on the desk in his tiny, windowless office and eyed it closely. The card read "Bella Luna Bookstore and Metaphysical Shop." It gave a Seattle address and phone number.

Martin's first reaction was to think this was some kind of psychic mumbo jumbo. He threw the card into the wastepaper basket at the side of his desk. Moments later his eyes were drawn back to it involuntarily. He gazed at the business card uncomfortably for a few seconds and fished it back out. What if the janitor found it and decided to gossip a little about how poor old Reynolds was now employing the help of a psychic to attain his elusive promotion? He had enough trouble without that. He stowed it away in his wallet, planning to send the stupid thing down the incinerator in their building that night. The card never made it to the incinerator, and many months later—after all the trouble began, Martin could never quite convince himself that holding on to it had merely been an oversight.

A few weeks later, the bitter seed of defeat Martin carried in his heart, had bloomed into something very near despair. On a Saturday afternoon when Sheila left for her bridge club, he walked up the street to purchase a Wall Street Journal and a coffee. As he opened his wallet to pay for his purchases, the business card slipped free and fluttered neatly to the ground at his feet. Martin stared at it, transfixed. He was jolted back to reality by the clerk clearing his throat and asking if he planned on standing there all day. Martin hastily apologized and placed a five dollar bill on the counter. He scooped up the fallen card, feeling an uncharacteristic blush creep up his cheeks. Not waiting for his change, he bundled the newspaper to his chest and walked quickly away. He sloshed burning coffee over his wrist and onto the business card, still clenched in his fist.

Martin locked himself in the apartment and sat down on the couch, pulling the phone onto his lap. He wiped the stained business card on his shirt with a slightly trembling hand. He stared at it for a long time, his despondency growing with each tick of the clock.

Finally, with a sigh, he lifted the receiver and dialed the phone number.

"Good afternoon, Bella Luna, how may I help you?" the pleasant female voice answered.

There was a drawn out pause as he hesitantly asked, "May I speak to Selma?"

The amused voice responded, "Do you mean Belda, sir?"

"Uh... Yes, sorry," Martin stuttered.

"One moment please."

Belda? What the hell kind of name is Belda? Martin wondered.

He was preparing to hang up, when the phone was picked up by an older woman.

"Hello, this is Belda. To whom am I speaking?"

Suddenly at the sound of that voice, all the saliva in Martin's mouth dried up and a sickening wave of fear coursed through his belly. He sat paralyzed, unable to speak.

After a few seconds, the woman asked, "Hello, is anyone there?"

With great effort, Martin cleared his throat. "My name is Martin. I was given your business card by... by..." He couldn't remember the man's name.

The woman ignored his discomfort. "You have a problem that perhaps I can help with?" she asked kindly.

"I have been passed over for promotion five times. I have been with the firm for over a decade, I am a good lawyer and I make them plenty of damn money, yet they never choose me! Never!" he exploded with fury he did not know he possessed.

"I understand, Mr. Reynolds, and I believe I can help you."

Did I tell her my last name? Martin wondered. He couldn't remember. From the moment she picked up the phone it was as if he had been transported from his pleasant living room, with the sun streaming through the windows, and entered some alternate darker, colder reality. He felt like a marionette in the hands of some evil puppeteer, speaking of things he had never intended discussing when he placed this call.

"How? How can you help me? How can anyone help me?" Martin's voice cracked with desperation.

"Trust me, Mr. Reynolds, I can," she replied in a soothing, yet chilly voice. "Why don't I turn you over to my assistant, Gabriella, and she can make an appointment for you. We can talk more then. Trust me, Mr. Reynolds, trust me."

"I… okay, I will," he replied in a dull, nearly drugged voice.

There was a click and the music was back in his ear. At the same moment whatever spell he had been under seemed to break and he pinched the bridge of his nose, feeling a dull headache throbbing at his temples. Later, he wondered why he didn't just hang up then. Instead, he waited docilely until her assistant picked up the phone and he made an appointment. He had ample vacation time accrued he could cash in to make the trip. The tricky part was what to tell Sheila.

Biting the bullet he told her the truth, and was stunned by her enthusiasm. "I'm thrilled that you are going to try it!" she cried ecstatically, "We need all the help we can get at this point."

Two weeks later, he found himself in a dusty, old bookshop half way around the country. The bookshop exuded an aura he found both unsettling and depressing.

From the moment the beautiful girl led him into the office where he met the strange old woman, he felt like he was in a trance.

The woman said she could mix up a blend of herbs that would somehow take his competitors for a promotion out of the running. She refused to be more specific than that, and in all honesty, Reynolds didn't ask many questions. Down deep in the darkest cavern of his heart, it was bitterly compelling to think of those in his way being cast aside like pieces in a chess game. There was only the tiniest twinge of guilt for using what he thought to be witchcraft to rid himself of his rivals. His only real fear was that this woman was giving him some type of undetectable poison and he would be committing murder.

Once she had allayed these concerns, the woman suggested putting her herbal remedy into their coffee, or a beverage. Reynolds didn't think this would be too difficult. There were many business lunches, many company parties. Slipping something into someone's glass wasn't complicated. In fact, Martin suspected it had probably been done at their Christmas parties when the executives were trying to score with the secretaries.

The price for these intriguing herbs was several thousand dollars. Martin found the woman's cool delivery of the terms much harder to accept than the price tag.

"What do you mean I die if I tell anyone?" he stammered, his eyes flying open in shock when Belda reached this point in her practiced summary of the terms.

"Just that, Mr. Reynolds. This must be a private transaction for obvious reasons," Belda replied.

"Well, I wouldn't tell anyone! Good lord, woman, they'd think I was crazy. But you threatened my life, madam!" Martin sputtered indignantly.

"Exactly so. I have my, ah… livelihood to consider. Accept my terms or leave my shop now, Mr. Reynolds, it's all the same to me." Her voice had turned to ice.

Martin took Belda's potion and paid her in cash. He hoped never to return.

That was two years ago, and the strange little bottle with the scarlet and brown leaves had remained locked in a metal box on the top shelf of his bedroom closet ever since.

~~~~

"We've been through this before, Sheila," Martin shifted uncomfortably from foot to foot, "It's probably all just nonsense anyway." He gave a dismissive wave of his hand.
~~~~

"You said the only reason you didn't try it this time was because you were sure they were going to chose you," she argued.

"We don't have time to talk about this right now. I have to get ready." His voice sounded weary. He closed the bathroom door on his wife's exasperated glare.

When he opened the closet to select his clothes for the miserable evening ahead, he took down the metal box and placed it on the nightstand. He opened the drawer in the stand and rummaged through it until he found the key. With slightly trembling fingers, he unlocked the box and opened it for the first time in over a year and a half. Martin looked at the small bottle lying innocently in the bottom and poked it. When he felt no heat, he lifted the vial out and held it under the light, examining it closely.

After a few moments the small cylinder began to grow warm and Martin hastily dropped it back into the box and slammed the lid shut.

That tiny bottle scared the hell out him. He had never forgotten the day he purchased it. That innocent looking little vial had burned a hole in the pocket of his trousers and blistered the skin of his thigh.

He didn't know if what was inside could actually make him a partner, but he felt it could damn well do something. He had been tempted on more than one occasion to pour the contents down the toilet and toss the bottle in the incinerator. Of course he never did—but nor did he ever follow the instructions the woman gave him, and stir it into anyone's cocktail either. Now, with his seventh miss at the partnership, he thought next year if he was nominated again, maybe he would. Just maybe.

Chapter 2

A crescendo of fragrances rose up and greeted them as Martin and Sheila entered the ballroom reserved for tonight's occasion. The smell of good food and expensive perfume mixed with the smell of fine Cuban cigars. Light strains from a string quartet spilled through the balcony doors. Dresses rustled, jewels sparkled, and everyone was turned out in their best splendor. An endless river of expensive liquor had loosened tongues and created a jovial atmosphere.

Upon stepping through the grand double doors, Martin was immediately clapped on the back hard enough to make him stumble. A hearty voice bellowed in his ear, "Hey, Marty! Always a bridesmaid and never a bride, huh, old boy!" Jack Calloway, the lawyer who beat him at partner two years before boomed a jovial laugh.

Martin forced a weak smile to his lips. "Sure seems that way doesn't it?"

Sheila bit her lip and looked away from the pained expression on her husband's face.

They made their way into the ballroom and drinks were thrust into their hands. Martin was dragged into a conversation about the tobacco case he just litigated, which inevitably segued into a conversation about how stunned everyone was that once again the partnership had eluded him. Sheila was enfolded into her own circle of friends from her bridge club and all the women clucked sympathetically to her about Martin's continued disappointment.

Martin spotted Clive Cheznik chatting quietly in the corner with two of the senior partners. His luscious wife was wearing a tight-fitting navy blue sheath that made Martin temporarily forget his anguish at being passed over again. He was eying the woman with open lust when Sheila reappeared at his side with a buffet plate heaped with food.

"Put your eyes back in your head," she snapped around a mouthful of shrimp cocktail.

Martin blushed to the roots of his hair and wrestled a guilty look off his face. He took his wife by the elbow and steered her to an unoccupied table in the corner of the room.

After making his way through the crowd, and the inevitable unwanted comments from his colleagues about how shocked everyone was that he hadn't made partner again, Martin tapped Clive on the back and offered his congratulations. Cheznik smiled sympathetically and shook his hand. He mumbled his thanks, along with the standard platitudes about next time being Martin's turn.

Glad to have the necessary amenities out of the way, and proud of himself for maintaining his composure in the face of Jack Calloway's oft repeated bridesmaid joke, Martin filled his own plate from the ample buffet table and rejoined his wife.

They smiled and raised their glasses along with everyone else when Mr. Bench, who only came out of retirement for these dinners, proposed a congratulatory toast to Clive Cheznik's success.

"How much longer do we have to stay?" Sheila asked out of the side of her mouth.

"Not long." Martin was as anxious to leave as she was.

"This dress is killing me," Sheila complained. She tried to adjust her girdle inconspicuously.

Martin bit his tongue against a nasty retort as he looked at the stack of empty dishes beside her. An argument with Sheila tonight was the last thing he needed.

Sheila excused herself to the ladies room and Martin nursed his drink.

When a shadow fell over the table, Martin looked up into the clear blue eyes of Carla Cheznik.

"May I join you for a moment?" she asked a little shyly.

He choked on his champagne.

Carla clapped him on the back. "Are you okay?" she asked, looking both worried and slightly amused.

He waved away her concern and stood up awkwardly to pull a chair out for her.

"Thank you, Martin."

"You must be proud of Clive," he mumbled and looked away.

Carla smiled sympathetically. "Listen, Martin, I wanted you to know that we are both very sorry it wasn't you they picked this year," she said earnestly. "I mean, believe it or not, we both thought you deserved it. Clive told me what an awesome job you did on that tobacco case. He said you should have made partner years ago,"

Martin was dumbfounded, and also very pleased. To have this beautiful woman saying such nice things to him almost made this night of pure hell bearable. Almost.

Just to have her talking to him at all was enough to send shivers down his spine. "Well, I really appreciate your saying that, Carla. It means a great deal." Reynolds grinned like a schoolboy.

Carla glanced around to make sure no one was in earshot. "Look, I heard something, and I thought maybe you should know."

"Oh?" he asked curiously.

"It might just be idle gossip. I heard it from Calloway's wife, so it might not even be true—" Carla picked up an empty wine glass from the table and mimed drinking it, "—if you know what I mean," she said conspiratorially and rolled her eyes.

Wanda Calloway was a heavy drinker, and an even heavier talker. She was the reigning gossip queen in their little corner of the world. Sheila played bridge with the woman and had told Martin she wasn't sure if you could believe half the stories that came out of Wanda's drunken mouth. She was always the source for who was stepping out on whose spouse, who was filing for divorce and who was having trouble meeting the American Express bill that month.

"Well, what did you hear?" Martin asked, a nervous twitch pulling at the corner of one eye.

"You know, I wouldn't even mention it if it didn't make a sick kind of sense." Carla plucked restlessly at the tablecloth.

Just then Sheila reappeared at the table, both of their coats over her arm. "Are you ready to go, dear?" she asked through gritted teeth.

Martin jumped from his chair, rapping his knee sharply against the table, and not succeeding in keeping the guilt out of his eyes this time. "Yes, yes all ready," he sputtered, taking Sheila's arm and bidding a hasty goodbye to Carla Cheznik.

"My congratulations to you and your husband," Sheila said, unable to keep the chill from her voice.

"Thanks," Carla replied, guilt flashing in her eyes as well. She quickly retreated to her husband's side.

Before they made their escape, they were waylaid at the exit door by Jack Calloway. He shouted boisterously, "Maybe next year you'll catch the bouquet, huh, Reynolds?"

As they undressed for bed, Sheila asked, "So what did the Barbie doll want? Just to rub it in, I suppose."

Martin, unsure why he was doing it, lied to his wife. "Yes, that's exactly what she was doing. Not a nice woman."

"Yeah, well the cute, skinny ones are always bitches," Sheila commented smugly, a satisfied smile settling on her lips.

~~~~

The glowing orange numbers on the clock read 4:07 a.m. when Martin conceded defeat in his battle for sleep. Sheila was a dark hump beside him under the covers, snoring softly in the shadows. Martin climbed quietly from the bed trying not to wake his wife. He donned an old, tattered terrycloth robe and tiptoed to the closet. Reaching up into the dark, he pulled the metal strong box from the shelf and carried it with him into the living room. He sat with it on his lap in the darkened house for several minutes. When the bottom of the box grew warm against his legs he set it aside and stared forlornly out the window.
~~~~

A ribbon of moonlight illuminated the deserted street. Martin felt like a lone traveler on insomnia's isolated highway. He desperately wanted to know what Carla Cheznik had been trying to tell him. Damn Sheila for coming back and making him react like a cat caught with his paw in the fishbowl. What could Carla have heard that would cause her to seek him out that way? Cause that guilty look in her eyes? And how was he ever going to find out now?

He jumped, inhaling a startled gasp. A man had appeared in the street several stories below. He wore a trench coat, and stood slightly outside the soft circular glow cast by the single streetlight. He beckoned Martin to come outside. This was New York, and in Martin's opinion, no one that was up to any good could possibly be standing in the middle of the road at this hour. Martin hastily closed the curtains and carried the box back to the bedroom closet.

Sleep would not come easily. Not for several weeks.

Chapter 3

Gabriella slammed the book *Alchemy for Witches* shut with a snap and rubbed her eyes. This book was a welcome distraction from studying for her mid-terms. She was now a junior at the University of Washington. A pile of textbooks littered the floor in front of her. She sat at the table in the little conference room of Bella Luna, where she often studied. Most of her nights were spent at Nicholas's apartment in the U District, which was much closer to school than her mother's home. She would go to classes in the morning and spend her afternoons at the bookstore, either working or studying. Nicholas took up all of her evenings now.

Their relationship had grown from the close friendship they shared to something much more over the last few months. Gabriella wondered if Belda knew she and Nicholas were lovers. She supposed the old woman did; it seemed she knew everything.

Gabby's interest in witchcraft developed over the years of her employment with Belda. The bookstore was a wellspring of knowledge on the subject, and Gabby never lacked for reading material when her schoolwork became overwhelming. She began practicing spells six months ago. So far none were successful.

Belda refused to teach her how to make the potions, so Gabriella tried to figure it out on her own. She found *Alchemy for Witches* little help.

Belda didn't think the art of witchcraft was a good distraction for the girl.

Belda spent the many years before Gabriella entered her life believing that when she died, her special talents would die with her. She was secretly delighted that Gabriella wanted to be groomed to take over. But that time was still a number of years away. Right now, Nicholas was a much better distraction for the girl, in Belda's opinion.

It was ironic Gabriella should wonder if the old woman knew of their romance. It was one of Belda's potions which created it, unbeknownst to either of them.

With a dull headache throbbing at her temples, Gabriella stretched her long legs, yawned and rose from the chair. She left her school books behind, and walked to the front of the store. There Nicholas and Belda had their heads bowed together in deep conversation.

"What are you two whispering about?" she asked.

Belda smiled, "Oh, just discussing the best course of action for a little problem we may have on the East Coast."

"What problem?" Gabriella's eyes narrowed in suspicion.

"A potion that was purchased two years ago and not used. Our client is preparing to use it now, and I'm not sure what might happen. No one has ever tried to use a potion that old. Nicholas was in New York this weekend as you know."

Gabriella sighed. "Ah, damage control. Did you get the potion back? Give him a fresh one?"

Nicholas shot an uneasy glance toward Belda. "Afraid not, babe. Belda just sent me there to remind the customer of the terms of his contract, should he choose to use the potion at this late date."

Gabriella cast a worried frown at Belda. "Are we going to have trouble?"

Belda looked out the window. "I have my concerns."

"Because of the potion being old?" the younger girl asked, her voice rising in alarm.

She tried to think back to what her books had said about old potions. Some went bad, she knew, but not all.

Belda gave her a knowing look, as if she knew exactly what Gabriella was thinking. "Because Mr. Reynolds is about to become an unstable and angry man," she replied, "and the potion may have… picked up on that."

"Shouldn't we have replaced the potion if it was expired, Belda?" Gabriella wondered.

"It's not expired, my dear. Just, well, a bit unpredictable at this point. Of course, that's half the fun." An obscene grin parted her lips, a hint of sheer madness gleamed in her eyes.

Chapter 4

Sheila was sullen and moody during the weekend that followed the dreadful celebration dinner for Clive Cheznik. She cancelled on her bridge club and did little except mope around the house—and eat and eat and eat.

Martin, lost in his own world, trying to puzzle out what Carla Cheznik could have possibly wanted to tell him, ignored her.

Monday morning Reynolds walked into the kitchen to find his wife banging the pots and pans around as she made breakfast.

Irritated, he asked, "What the hell is the matter?"

"Nothing," she grumbled and slammed a plate of fried eggs and bacon down in front of him.

"Fine, you don't want to tell me, then don't, but quit slamming things around like a two year old."

Martin blinked in surprise when Sheila broke down in tears and ran from the kitchen sobbing.

"Oh, hell," he groaned, and rose from the table.

She slammed the bedroom door, and when Martin tried the knob it was locked. He tapped on the door.

"Sheila, open up."

"Leave me alone," she bawled in a tear-choked voice.

"Sheila, honey, open the door." Martin was bewildered and a little nervous. He'd practically never seen his wife like this. *She's not,* Martin thought in sudden alarm, *pregnant or anything, is she?*

"Go away!"

"Please, Sheila, let me in. Talk to me," he pleaded, and tried in vain to turn the locked doorknob.

After several minutes of cajoling, Sheila finally unlocked the door and allowed Martin in. He sat beside her on the bed and stroked her arm with a soothing hand.

"What is it? Is it something I did?"

"It's us, Martin, both of us," she blubbered.

"What? I don't understand," Martin replied, confused.

"Don't you get it? We are a laughing stock. Everyone talks behind our backs. They all have more money than we do, they all live in nicer homes. Everyone in our circle has made partner except you, and I'm… I'm… fat! I'm a fat pig!" she wailed.

"No, honey! No. That's not true. No one is talking about us. These people are our friends, and you aren't fat, that's nonsense," Martin soothed.

"Then why would you rather be with Cheznik's wife than with me?" she sobbed.

Martin was dumbfounded. "Sheila, I don't want to be with Carla Cheznik! What in the world would give you an idea like that?"

"Well, look at her. She's skinny and she's pretty and your eyes pop out of your head every time you see her. And, you never look at me that way anymore, Martin. I'm… I'm…" her shoulders wracked with fresh sobs.

"Sweetie, listen to me. I don't want Clive Cheznik's skinny wife. I only want you. I want to make partner to make you happy. I don't care who has more money, or more clothes, or a better apartment than we do. I only want you to be happy, that's all." He pulled a handkerchief from his pocket and handed it to Sheila.

She dabbed at her eyes, then blew a mighty honk and sniffed. "Do you mean that?" she asked, looking intently into his eyes.

"Of course I do." He placed a reassuring arm around her shoulders.

"Then next time they put out that damn nominations list and your name is on it, use that bloody bottle in the closet, Martin! USE IT!" she screamed.

~~~~

The next few weeks were among the worst of Martin Reynolds's life. The misery began as he reached his office building in Manhattan, still worried about his wife's tearful breakdown that morning.

As he was stepping into the revolving door, fingers dug sharply into his shoulder. A dark figure dragged him around the corner of the building and into the alley behind. His briefcase fell from his hand and clattered into the gutter. Before he fully understood what was happening, he was face to face with a broad-shouldered, muscular young man with a twisted scar running up the left side of his face.

"I have no money!" Martin squawked in a frightened, breathy voice.

"I don't want your money, Reynolds," the man breathed, looking intently into Martin's terrified eyes.

"Oh, God! You aren't going to rape me are you?" the quivering man sobbed, looking desperately down the deserted alley.

Nicholas Aguilar grinned and shook his head. "Don't worry, Reynolds, you aren't my type."
~~~~

"Then what do you want?" Martin moaned, his voice little more than a glassy whisper.

"To remind you of the terms of a contract you entered into a couple of years ago in Seattle. Do you remember that?"

Martin's heart was hammering, his forehead broke out in slimy sweat. "Were you standing outside my apartment building the other night?"

"Yeah, I guess you were having a little trouble sleeping, huh? You should have come out and talked to me. We could have avoided all this unpleasantness." He loosened his grip on Martin's shoulder.

"The woman sent you?" Martin stammered.

"Who sent me isn't important, Reynolds. All I need you to do is tell me if you remember the terms of your contract?"

Martin nodded violently. "Yes, I know. I know not to tell anyone. Is that it? Is that what she is afraid of?"

Nicholas looked appraisingly at Martin for a long moment. Around them, the sounds of the city seemed strangely muted. Martin trembled as he waited for the tall young man to speak again.

"Fear isn't an emotion she's real familiar with," Nicholas said at last. "I am just here to remind you of the terms of your agreement, and to advise you to tell your wife those terms apply to her too. Or being afraid is something you are going to learn more about than you ever dreamed, Reynolds. You understand me?" Nicholas leaned in until his nose was bare inches from Martin's.

"What, do you mean my wife? She would never tell anyone, I swear."

Nicholas raised an eyebrow and didn't answer.

"Why have you come now?" Martin asked. "I've had that dreaded concoction for two years, and it will be at least another one before I have any reason to use it—if I ever do!"

Nicholas chuckled, "You might be surprised at just how soon that little bottle might come in handy. You just make sure the little woman stays quiet about it, and you do too, and you won't ever have to see me again. And believe me Reynolds, if you do see me again, you better have your affairs in order and your life insurance all paid up." Within seconds of voicing that final threat, Nicholas disappeared around the corner, a terrified Martin gawking after him.

Martin tried to leave the alley, but found that his legs had turned to rubber. He slid down the wall to the ground. It took ten minutes for his breathing to return to normal, and another ten before he felt steady enough to rise from the dirty cement and walk back around the corner.

His briefcase was gone, stolen during the confrontation with Belda's henchman. Fortunately he hadn't taken any files home with him. The most valuable items the thief got away with were Martin's cellphone and his Montblanc pen. At that moment Martin counted himself lucky that his briefcase had been the only casualty.

He tucked his shirt back in and straightened his tie, then crossed the street on shaking legs to a deli. He called in sick from a payphone.

Martin let himself into his apartment an hour later. "I've got an upset stomach," he told Sheila.

She put a hand to his forehead. "You look terribly pale. I hope this isn't because I was upset this morning. I know how you hate it when I get all weepy."

Martin shook his head. In a hesitant voice, he asked, "Uh, Sheila, you haven't told anybody about the… the thing from Seattle have you?"

She looked at him with alarm. "Oh jeez, Martin! No! People would think we were crazy. And, if it really did… I mean really *does* work, then I… Well, I don't even know what they would think then."

Martin nodded, relieved. "Okay, Sheila. Just make sure you never utter a word to anyone. It could be very dangerous for us, if anyone ever knew."

Suspicion bloomed in her eyes. "Why are you bringing this up now all of a sudden? That bottle has been in the closet for two years. It will be another year before you have to use it. So why now?"

"Never mind, Sheila, just don't ever tell. I have to go lie down. I don't feel good."

He escaped into their bedroom, undressed and climbed into bed. He lay there tossing and turning for two hours, contemplating throwing the vicious little cylinder down the incinerator. Twice he rose and opened the closet door. He couldn't even bring himself to touch the metal strong box that held the poison, let alone open it. He desperately wished he could sleep. Having gotten so little rest over the weekend, he thought he would be able to. But sleep never came. Not that morning, and not that night. Not for a long, long time.

~~~~

Within a matter of days the cold, steel fingers of insomnia gripped Martin's world like a vice, and he was operating on less than two hours of rest a night. In the wee hours of the morning, while all of New York slumbered peacefully in their beds, Martin sat up in his living room in the dark. He didn't dare open the curtains and look out into the gloom, lest the horrible stranger with the scar reappear.
~~~~

But as each sleepless day rolled by, he grew less concerned with being threatened again, as another matter overshadowed his thoughts entirely. His mind was plagued by Carla Cheznik's cryptic sentence the night of her husband's celebration dinner: "It made a sick kind of sense."

What? What, made a sick kind of sense? His overtaxed, sleep-deprived mind screamed.

Martin had nearly asked Clive Cheznik if he knew what his wife was trying to tell him, but lost his nerve.

He looked through the database on the computer at work and jotted down the Cheznik's home phone number. Several times he picked up the phone and began to dial it, before slamming the receiver back down in frustration. The worst part was he could feel eyes boring into his back when he walked down the halls. Could feel the snickers of his coworkers as he passed by. Was Sheila right? Were people laughing at him? He didn't know if it was sleep deprivation making him paranoid, or if it was true. The line between real and imagined grew gossamer thin.

Sheila had presented any number of remedies for his insomnia. Over the counter medications, liquor, warm milk, even rigorous sex—which though nice, did nothing to allay his fatigue or bring restful slumber. He finally made an appointment with the doctor and got a prescription for a sleep aid.

The pills worked. However, on the first night in over three weeks that Martin Reynolds finally found himself in the depths of slumber, a nightmare of monstrous proportions followed him there.

They were back at the party in Clive Cheznik's honor. Martin was sitting at the same table where Carla had approached him. He could hear the pleasant music coming from outside the balcony doors and smell the rich aromas of food and cigars.

He was nursing his drink when a shadow fell over the table. He looked up to find Carla Cheznik standing before him again. Only this time she was totally naked. Martin gawked in wonder at this glorious woman's body. The golden hair falling to her bare shoulders in gentle waves, the luscious curve of her full breasts, the smooth tanned flesh of her stomach.

Martin shot to his feet and tried to shrug off his suit coat to cover the woman's nakedness. He was stunned to find that he was wearing no coat to shrug out of. No coat, no shirt, no clothes whatsoever. He too, stood completely naked before her. And he was absolutely horrified to see that he was sporting the biggest erection of his life.

Carla pointed to his middle-age potbelly and shrieked, "Well, it makes a sick kind of sense, doesn't it?" She cackled vicious laughter.

Martin grabbed the tablecloth to cover himself, as the rest of the crowd, drawn by the woman's piercing laughter, gathered around her. They all stared and pointed at him right along with her.

Jack Calloway began taunting, "Always a bridesmaid and never a bride, huh, Reynolds."

Wanda Calloway whispered slyly, "He's got a thing for the Cheznik woman. Just look at that woody! It makes a sick kind of sense, don't you think?" She howled laughter like a banshee.

Martin turned around to see Sheila watching the whole spectacle, wide-eyed and horror-struck from a few feet away. She was wearing the silver sequined dress. The one that reminded him of those huge disco balls when he looked at her from behind. The seams were splitting. They made loud ripping noises that sounded to Martin like guttural yells of pain. She seemed to be gaining weight as he watched her. Her stomach chugged outward in lurches, her hips extended out to the sides in rolling layers of fat, turning her into not just a plump woman, but into an obscene and obese caricature of herself. She turned and ran, the dress falling in shiny tatters at her feet, her massive rear-end threatening the seams of her girdle. Then the girdle was splitting too, her elephantine hips growing too huge to be contained.

He watched in terror as she heaved out onto the balcony where the music was playing. With amazing agility, she shimmied up the railing. She looked back over her mammoth shoulder at Martin, and dove from the 30th floor.

A few seconds later he heard horns blaring from below, and a sickening splat that made his stomach lurch.

When Martin turned back to the jeering crowd he saw that Carla Cheznik was no longer naked. She was once again clothed in the lovely blue sheath. Martin however, was still completely naked, though his erection had withered and died from fright.

He woke up with a start and stuffed the sheet in his mouth to stifle the scream rising in his throat. His body was bathed in sweat and trembling uncontrollably.

The orange glowing numbers on the clock told him it was two-thirty in the morning. Sheila still slept peacefully beside him.

He rose from bed, the last threads of the dream still clinging to him like a cobweb inadvertently stumbled into.

He went into the bathroom and splashed water on his face, then shambled into the kitchen and made a cup of tea. He added a healthy shot of Courvoisier to help settle his jangling nerves.

He was drinking the tea and reliving the nightmare in his mind, when Sheila's voice cut through his reverie.

She was standing in the doorway, still half asleep. "Pills didn't work, huh?" she asked, her eyes concerned.

"I guess not," he lied. He couldn't bear to tell her about his dream, not with it ending in her suicide.

"Poor thing," Sheila squeezed his shoulder and pulled a cup from the cabinet over the sink.

"You don't have to stay up with me," Martin told her.

"I know, babe," she replied, pouring steaming water and instant hot chocolate into the mug. "But I want to."

They sat in companionable silence holding hands and sipping their drinks.

Once the last vestiges of the awful nightmare departed and his wife's warmth surrounded him, Martin found he was able to at last find dreamless sleep.

Chapter 5

It was two months after Clive Cheznik's promotion. On a blustery Monday morning, with clouds overhead threatening a storm, Martin arrived at work and found a memo on his desk.

> *Mandatory staff meeting. Conference room, 10:00 AM. Those whose presence is required in court may be excused. All others must attend.*

The air in the building felt thick with tension and no one seemed to know what was going on. An eerie and stifling silence blanketed the halls, causing heightened nerves and shortened tempers.

At the appointed hour everyone crowded into the conference room and faced the grim senior partners.

"We have some bad news," Miles Carson began. He cleared his throat. "There has been a death."

He waited while everyone tittered and gasped, then went on, "This morning I received a phone call from Wanda Calloway. Jack had a heart attack last night and he died at the hospital early this morning."

The room immediately erupted in conversation. A few of the secretaries started to cry. Martin's world turned gray and swimmy. He was overcome by a wave of dizziness. With a shaking hand, he poured some water from a glass carafe.

"We will let everyone know when the funeral will be, and we will be taking up a collection for Wanda. Flowers will be sent from the firm. Of course anyone that wants to do something on their own, I'm sure the family would appreciate it. Wanda has indicated she will take phone calls, but receive no visitors for the time being. Does anyone have any questions?" Finishing his prepared speech, Carson mopped his brow with a handkerchief.

There were no questions. Everyone was too stunned to ask any.

Once the room had settled down, Greer August announced, "There is a matter of business that has to be discussed. We know this will be a difficult time for everyone, and we will all grieve Jack's passing in our own way, but business must continue as usual. Jack left a caseload that has to be attended to. As such, the need to promote someone to partner to fill his slot will be taken care of right away. Therefore, the nominee list will be circulated this afternoon. We expect it to be a short list, and we will make our decision sometime next week. Thank you."

The room disbanded, but Martin remained at the conference table. He was too shaky to trust his legs to support him. He sat alone at the huge table trying to grasp what he had just heard. He drank another glass of water and held the cool glass to his forehead with one trembling hand. Finally, he rose on wobbly legs and returned to his office, locking himself inside. He phoned Sheila, but got their answering machine. He left a message for her to call him right away.

By the time she received it, she had already heard the news from one of the women in her bridge club. She sent a basket of fruit to Wanda Calloway, and called her to extend condolences and offer assistance with making the necessary arrangements.

The firm closed early and everyone went home in a state of shock.

As Martin was exiting the building, his thoughts on some distant horizon, he walked headlong into Clive Cheznik.

"Hey, you okay?" Cheznik asked. He took in Martin's ashen pallor and shaking hands.

"Just surprised. And saddened," Martin replied.

Clive clapped him on the back. "Yeah, we all are. Jack's really gonna be missed. No one knew how to liven up a party like he did." He wiped at tears that burned his eyes.

Martin felt unwanted tears sting his own eyes. He bid the other man a hasty farewell.

~~~~

The next few days took on a surrealistic quality for Martin. The short nomination list for partner was passed out, and not surprisingly his name appeared. There were three others as well: Mark Munson, a tax specialist; William Francis, a probate lawyer; and Rhonda Baldwin, part of a criminal defense team.

Martin paid little attention to the list as the funeral drew closer. He slammed the door on unwelcome thoughts about what the man with the scar had told him. He did not want to think
~~~~

about the stranger's dire prediction that the little bottle stored in the closet would come in handy sooner than he thought.

Sheila was tearful, and everyone was sad on the dark and blustery day they buried Jack Calloway.

It was after the service and back at the Calloway home when Carla Cheznik chose to finish the conversation she had begun with Martin all those months before.

The house was crowded with mourners. Martin, feeling claustrophobic, slipped outside to take a walk. He had only gone about twenty feet when he heard heels clopping behind him on the wet sidewalk.

Turning around, he saw Carla Cheznik jogging to catch up to him. She wore a modest black dress and low-heeled pumps.

Martin stopped and waited for her to reach his side.

"Do you mind a little company?" she asked hesitantly.

Martin smiled. "Not at all. In fact, I'd welcome it."

They started off together, heads bent against the battering wind, coats pulled tight around their shoulders. When they were out of earshot of the Calloway home, Martin said, "I feel as though maybe I owe you an apology."

Carla looked at him surprised. "An apology? What on earth for?"

"The night of Clive's promotion dinner, when my wife caught us talking… I… Well, I reacted like I was guilty of something… and I suppose maybe I was." He thrust his hands into his pockets.

Though Carla had been crying, her eyes danced with amusement at his confession. She looked at him slyly, and winked. "Impure thoughts, perhaps?"

Martin, stunned by her insight, smiled in return. "You knew?"

"Well, maybe just a little. I'm not blind you know. But my theory is that it's okay to look, just don't touch."

They both laughed. "You have my word, no touching." Martin said.

After a few moments, Carla asked, "Do you remember I started to tell you something that night, then ran off like the cat that ate the canary when Sheila walked up?"

Martin nodded rapidly. "Yes, and I wracked my brain and lost sleep for a month afterwards wondering what the hell it was."

Carla looked surprised. "I thought about calling you, but I didn't want to do anything that Sheila—or my husband—might have thought inappropriate."

Martin gave her an odd little grin. "I guess great minds think alike. I pulled your number from the company database, but couldn't bring myself to make the call."

She sighed. "You know it was probably nothing. And especially now with the woman's husband having just died, I feel a little guilty even bringing it up again. But I think you should know what Wanda said. I don't know that there is any merit to it, but I will tell you. You can decide if it's something you want to pursue. Just please don't tell anyone who you heard it from, okay? I didn't even tell Clive."

"You have my solemn vow," Martin promised. "Cross my heart."

They leaned against a tree at the far end of the block that offered minimal shelter from the howling wind.

Carla began, "The night of the dinner for Clive, several of us were talking. Don't be upset, but someone mentioned Sheila looked like she had gained weight. That was when Wanda blurted out something to the effect of, 'Well if the woman is going to go on an eating binge every time Martin gets passed over for promotion she will be as big as a house in a few years. They are *never* going to promote him. They never had any intention of promoting him.'

Well, I was curious, so I asked her if they never had any intention of promoting you why your name was always on the list." Carla paused here and looked at Martin to see how he was taking this.

He stood stone faced, waiting for her to go on.

"You see, Martin, she said they do it every year as a running joke between the partners, because everyone knows how badly Sheila wants you to become partner. There is this rumor that she won't even buy a new dress to wear to the celebration dinners until you get promoted. So, they put your name on the list, like to make fun of you—and mostly to make fun of your wife I think."

Martin stood red-faced watching the traffic go by, trying to absorb what he just heard. "What are you saying? They put my name on the list because they find it funny that my wife and I get disappointed every time? Do they also get their jollies by dangling scraps of meat in front of hungry dogs?"

Carla placed her hand on his arm. "I'm sorry. Maybe I shouldn't have told you. After all, Wanda is a lu… well, a pretty heavy drinker, and maybe you can't believe a word she says. Most people don't. But if it is true, it's just so incredibly cruel that you had a right to know. I mean after all the years of service you have put in at that firm, I guess I thought it was unfair of me not to say something. Please don't be mad at me."

Martin looked at her with sad and angry eyes. "Carla, I am not mad at you. I am grateful that you were honest with me. I feel like I have a made a friend. I appreciate that you came to me with this." He had balled his hands into fists. He forced himself to unclench them when he felt his nails digging into his palms. "I see what you meant now when you said it made a sick kind of sense. I don't think anyone else has ever been up for partnership seven times and never gotten it."

"Clive says not. Like I told you, I didn't tell him what Wanda said, but we did talk about how many times you have lost out. He said no one else ever got nominated that many times without making partner. It is awfully weird," Carla commented.

"Let's go back." Martin took her elbow. "They will wonder where we are." They started walking back in the direction of the Calloway home.

Almost as an afterthought, Carla mentioned, "It's not all of them, Martin—just the seniors, August and Carson. The ones that do the list,"

Martin stopped and turned to look at her, "Is that what Wanda said?"

Carla nodded. "Yes, I guess Moira August plays bridge with Sheila. She tells Greer how anxious Sheila gets every time the list comes out with your name on it."

"I see," Martin replied. He was suddenly very weary. So tired, he could lie down right there on the dirty sidewalk, close his eyes and fall asleep.

He impulsively reached out to hug Carla and kiss her cheek. "Thank you. You have given me a great deal to think about." Martin escorted her back up the steps to the grieving widow's house.

Chapter 6

Martin couldn't tell Sheila. She would be devastated. He was heartbroken to think she had been right the day she sat crying on their bed and telling him they were a laughing stock. The same day a menacing stranger appeared out of nowhere, threatening his life and telling him the potion would soon be coming in handy.

He had to find out the truth. It was Thursday, and the announcement of who would be made new partner was scheduled for the following week. Martin wished the senior partners had announced what day they planned to reveal their choice. The only information they had divulged was that it would be sometime during the coming week. That gave him only a tiny window of time to find out if what Carla told him was true. He needed to know before the weekend.

The following day Martin told Sheila he needed to work late. He stayed in his office until 8:30 p.m., when the janitor usually showed up. He had seen the man over the last twelve years, but didn't think they had exchanged more than three dozen words in all that time. Martin reasoned that if anyone knew what went on behind closed doors, it was the person who emptied the trash.

Martin heard the hum of a vacuum cleaner start up down the hallway. He walked to the edge of the carpeted hall. Tony the janitor had earphones jammed against his skull. As he vacuumed, he gyrated his hips and snapped his fingers to a tune only he could hear.

Martin waited apprehensively for the man to look up from his work. His attempts at conversation were drowned out by the music blaring in the janitor's ears and the noisy rumble of the vacuum.

When Tony saw Martin out of the corner of his eye, he pulled the headphones off and toggled the switch on the vacuum. "Evening, Mr. Reynolds. Something I can do for you?"

"I wondered if I might have a word with you," Martin replied awkwardly.

Tony looked at him with a quizzical expression. "Uh, yeah. I guess so." He spun the volume control down on his iPod and leaned against a desk. "What's on your mind?"

"This is a tough question for me to ask, Tony, and I only ask you because I honestly don't know who else might have the information I need. If you don't want to answer—or you can't, I will completely understand. The only thing I would request is that you not tell anyone I asked you," Reynolds trudged on, growing more nervous by the second.

"Ask me what?" Tony wore a blank expression.

"Have you ever seen anything about the partner's nomination list?"

"Seen anything? Like in the garbage?"

Martin nodded. "The garbage, or maybe on someone's desk? Or heard anyone talking or joking about the list?" Martin pulled a folded hundred dollar bill from his pocket and held it out between two fingers.

The janitor looked longingly at the bill, as a dog might eye an offered biscuit from his master's hand.

"You mean anything that might say who they was gonna promote?" he answered, never taking his eyes from the bill in Martin's outstretched hand.

"Yes, Tony. Or who they weren't. Is the nomination fixed somehow? Maybe there is someone on that list they never intend on making partner. Not ever."

"I don't want to lose my job." Tony wrung his hands nervously.

"No one would ever know where I heard it from." Reynolds thrust the bill into the janitor's fist. "Is there anything you know?"

The bill disappeared into Tony's gray jumpsuit as he glanced up the hallway. "Yeah, there is something."

Martin paled. "Please, Tony, tell me what you know. I have spent a lot of years with this firm and I have made them a lot of money. If there is something you have seen or heard, then please tell me."

"Do you remember the last promotion? That Cheznik dude?" Tony asked.

Martin nodded. "Of course."

"Well, one night just before they announced they was gonna make Cheznik partner, Carson was in his office. The door was open and he didn't see me standin' outside. There was someone in the office with him, but I couldn't see who. Carson said somethin' like, 'yeah, poor old Reynolds think we gonna give it to him again.' And then they both laughed. I didn't hear no more, 'cause I was afraid they'd come out and know I overheard, so I went down the hall." He watched Reynolds for some reaction.

Martin stared at the janitor, numb with fury. “Anything else,” he growled.

“No, man. Like I said I got the hell outta there after I heard them laugh. I didn’t want to get in no trouble for eavesdropping. I got a kid to feed. I need this job.”

A wave of rage welled up in Martin Reynolds’s gut. His stomach churned. He used his hand to stifle an acidic belch rising in his chest.

Martin thanked the janitor and left. He went to the same bar, where long ago, a man had slipped a business card to him and whispered the name “Belda.”

He sat in a corner booth drinking scotch after scotch, finishing one before the waitress could set the next on his table. His head felt as though it were full of furious, buzzing wasps. A headache zigzagged across his forehead. All the fiery wrath of hell burned in his heart. The time had come to open the metal box in the closet.

Chapter 7

Belda sat alone in the darkened bookstore. The "Closed" sign hung in the window and the doors were locked against the outside world. She sat in the little conference room where Gabriella studied, and Belda met with unhappy and desperate people willing to pay any price to alter the course of their destinies. Eros was asleep on the chair beside her.

The room was nearly devoid of light. The only illumination provided by a single black candle, flickering on the little round table. It threw dancing shadows against the walls in the gloom.

The table was covered in a purple cloth with a gold parallelogram in the center. On the parallelogram was the candle, a crudely made plump doll that vaguely resembled a woman, two playing cards—the queen of clubs and the ace of spades—a single cashew, and a scattering of dried, pungent herbs.

Belda's eyes were closed as she chanted unintelligible words. Guttural moans escaped her lips. Her gnarled hands stretched out before her, hovering over the table and moving in lazy circles above the motley array of items on the purple cloth.

When she completed the spell, Belda's eyes fluttered open and stared off in the distance. A small smile played at the corners of her mouth. After several minutes her eyes began to clear and she reached over and stroked her sleeping cat. "Remember, Eros, loose lips sink ships. And in Mrs. Reynolds's case, that's a pretty accurate description." She barked a sinister cackle, and rose from the chair to put away the malevolent and damning items on the table.

~~~~

It was Saturday and Sheila was getting ready to go to her bridge game.

"I really wish you wouldn't go today," Martin grumbled.

"Why on earth not?" she asked him. "You usually like your Saturdays to yourself."

"Just don't say anything about the promotion or the list, okay? Don't tell anyone how much you hope it's me this time. Nothing like that, alright?"

"What do you care what I tell the girls? They all know I want you to be partner. We've talked about it for years now."

Martin shook his head in frustration. "Never mind, just forget it."

A worried look settled on Sheila's plump face. "Marty is this about getting nominated for the partnership because Jack died? If it is, that isn't your fault."

Now that Jack was safely buried, all of Sheila's energy was channeled into reminding Martin that he promised to use the sinister potion from Seattle the next time the opportunity arose.

Martin erupted in anger. "No!" he spat with uncharacteristic venom. "It's about getting the partnership because of that poison that's been sitting in the closet for two years! Maybe I should just
~~~~

quit the damn firm and go work somewhere else. Someplace where my hard work would be appreciated."

"Look," she said, taking his hand, "If you start over at another firm now it will be years before you are even eligible to become partner, Martin. The promotion was sure to be yours this time anyway. The stuff in the closet is just, well… It's just sort of extra insurance, that's all."

He looked away uncomfortably. Sheila would never know the dirty little secret he uncovered thanks to Carla Cheznik.

Sheila asked, "How are you going to slip the other nominees that potion? There's so little time!"

"I don't know yet." He closed his eyes against a headache forming at his temples.

"Martin, you promised me this time you would use the stuff. You promised!" she yelled vehemently.

He stormed from the room, calling over his shoulder, "Just go play bridge, Sheila." And slammed the bedroom door behind him.

~~~~

Sheila had just won her second trick in a row. She took a sip from her third glass of chardonnay. She was working her way through a giant bowl of mixed nuts with a sincere commitment to reach the bottom.

The conversation turned to Martin's nomination, as it inevitably did during her Saturday afternoons with the bridge club.

Wanda Calloway was absent. The rumor floating around was that she had remained nose-deep in a bottle of Southern Comfort since Jack's passing. Moira August was also not present, which left the few women that Sheila could truly trust and call her friends sitting around the card table with her.
~~~~

Carol Afton, whose husband joined the firm around the same time as Martin, and had been partner for at least six years, asked, "So, is Martin optimistic, Sheil? Does he think the goose is finally gonna lay that golden egg?"

Giddy from her winning hands and the wine, Sheila replied, "Oh, Carol, this time it's in the bag."

Sandy Werner, who was one of the few women in the club that wasn't the wife of a lawyer with the firm, remarked, "Sweetie, not to burst your bubble, but you say that every year."

Sheila gave an offended little sniff. "Well, this time it's guaranteed. Martin has a little trick up his—"

When she didn't finish, the other women looked up from their cards. Sheila's head cocked sideways, a flush starting at her throat. Her face bore the startled expression of someone just told a bit of unexpected news. Her mouth was working open and closed, but no words came out.

"Sheila, what's wro—" Carol started to ask.

Sheila suddenly began clawing at her throat with one hand. She knocked her wine glass and a spray of playing cards to the floor with the other.

She was scratching at her throat and rolling her eyes theatrically.

Karen Winston, yet another partner's wife, sprinted across the room, her own game forgotten. She yelled, "Jesus Christ, call 911! She's choking!" Karen wrenched Sheila from her chair and pulled her to a standing position to administer the Heimlich maneuver.

Sandy raced to the phone and dialed 911.

~~~~
~~~~

While Martin's wife was choking on a wayward nut, he sat in his kitchen trying to figure out how he was going to transfer what lived in the dreaded bottle in his closet into the stomachs of his rivals.

Sheila was right. If he quit and went to work for another law firm, he would be eligible for retirement before he was eligible for partner. The humiliation it would cause Sheila was more than Martin could live with. Everyone would know why he'd left the firm. Always a bridesmaid and never a bride, in the infamous words of the dearly departed Jack Calloway.

Besides that, Martin was angry. Angrier than he had ever been in his entire life. Angrier than he knew he was capable of being. The wasps were still buzzing inside his skull. He had been played for a fool and betrayed by a company he gave his heart and soul to for over a dozen years.

Once the decision was made, Martin knew he had to act quickly. The announcement of who had been selected could be as soon as Monday. That gave him the weekend, and if he was lucky, Monday morning to get this dastardly deed done.

He went to the phone and opened the little phone book sitting on the desk by the living room window.

Mark Munson had done the Reynolds's taxes for the last three years. They were friendly with each other and had socialized on a few odd occasions. Though Mark might be a little surprised by Martin calling, an invitation to join him for a beer would raise no suspicions.

Martin began to dial the number when a voice screamed in his head, *How? How will it work? What if it hurts them? What if it's poison?*

He slammed down the receiver. "It's too late to worry about that now," he told the voice. "If it hurts them, it's on Carson and August's head, not mine. Besides, the old woman swore it wasn't poison."

Martin cleared his throat and dialed the number. "Probably isn't even home," he mumbled.

On the third ring a little girl answered the phone. Martin asked to speak to Mark.

The phone was dropped with a clunk, and the girl yelled, "Daddy, telephone."

After a moment Martin heard the sound of approaching footsteps. Mark came on the line a few seconds later.

As Martin extended the invitation to meet for a beer, he was relieved to hear his voice sound steady and natural.

Mark replied, "Well, we are going away for the weekend, but I have an hour or two before we have to leave the kids with Cheryl's mom. Sure, Martin, I'd love to have a beer."

Had Martin left his house even one minute later, he wouldn't have missed the frantic phone call from Sandy Werner, to tell him his wife had been rushed to Mount Sinai.

One minute later and the first domino that fell in a long and hellish series might have been avoided.

Martin Reynolds and Mark Munson lived only a few blocks apart, and they agreed to meet at a sports bar located half way between both of their buildings. Both men walked out of their respective front doors practically the moment they hung up the phone. Twenty minutes later they were perched comfortably on barstools, nursing draft beers, talking shop, and watching a muted baseball game on a television mounted above the bar.

A tearful Sandy Werner was left to deliver her devastating news to Martin's answering machine.

Martin had taken the hateful little bottle out of the metal box and wrapped it in a thick gauze bandage found in their medicine chest. He figured if it was going to burn him, at least it would have more layers to go through. Oddly, the bottle never warmed in his pocket.

Martin wondered briefly if the vile mix hadn't finally lost its juice.

When Mark excused himself to the men's room, Martin gingerly reached into his pocket and unwound the gauze. He glanced around to make sure no one was watching him. Hunching his back over the bar, he pried the little cork out of the bottle. Soup from the devil's kitchen could not have smelled more foul. Martin nearly gagged. His eyes watered as the bitter odor attacked his senses. He hurriedly tipped the vial, tapping a few dry leaves into Mark's beer glass. Martin replaced the little cork and shoved the cylinder back into his pocket, watching wide-eyed as Mark's ale began to fizz and smoke. The effect lasted only a second before the beer returned to normal. Martin blinked his smarting eyes and swiped at them with the backs of his hands.

Mark emerged from the restroom and glanced at his watch. He downed the remainder of his beer in two large swallows and shrugged into his jacket.

"So where are you guys headed?" Martin asked.

"Clive Cheznik and his wife invited us to a condo they own on Long Island for the weekend. Just going to play a little golf. Not exactly a major vacation, but it will be a nice break for Cheryl from the kids. Her mom is taking them."

Martin felt a sudden weight in his chest, as though he just swallowed a barbell. His stomach cramped up and he broke out in a slimy coat of sweat. He fought the urge to tell Mark everything and scream at him not to go. Beg him to cancel the trip.

Running late and his mind on the eighteen holes that lay ahead, Mark Munson didn't notice the color drain from Martin's face, or the sheen of sweat that suddenly erupted on his forehead.

He thanked Martin when he picked up the tab, and they agreed to get together again soon.

Each man wished the other luck in his quest for the partnership.

Martin watched as his rival walked down the street in the direction of an uncertain fate.

Chapter 8

Martin let himself in his front door barely in time to make it to the bathroom. His stomach had clenched up uncontrollably as he jogged home. He was unbuckling his pants as he ran through his living room toward the bathroom, where a bout of explosive diarrhea left him pale and shaking.

Martin rose on watery legs and flushed the toilet. He left his pants on the bathroom floor. After washing his hands and splashing cold water onto his face, he walked into his bedroom and flopped onto the bed.

The answering machine's flashing red light went unnoticed in the living room.

Oh God! What have I done? he wondered.

As Martin watched Mark Munson turn his back and start down the street, a feeling of such horrific and impending doom washed over him, that he was forced to grab a telephone pole for support. His legs had turned to jelly, and it was only his increasingly worrisome bowels which forced him to peel himself from that pole and run home.

Not my fault! The interior voice shrieked. *Whatever happens, blame it on August and Carson, those bastards!*

He rolled onto his side and sobbed. Unable to shake that sick feeling of dread, Martin fell asleep.

An unknown amount of time later, he was awakened by the incessant ringing of the telephone. He rolled away from its shrill sound, clamping a pillow over his head to drown out the noise. Still half asleep, he thought he heard a frantic female shrieking into his answering machine out in the living room, but decided it was his overwrought imagination. He dropped off to sleep again.

When the phone shrilled again ten minutes later, he reached out without opening his eyes and fumbled the receiver off the bedside table. "H'lo," he mumbled.

"Martin! Oh thank God I reached you!" a woman sobbed into his ear.

"Huh? Who is it?" he slurred.

"It's Sandy. Sandy Werner. Oh, oh, God, Martin it's so awful, I, I, I…"

Martin stared at the phone and tried to clear his muzzy head. There was the sound of a scuffle on the other end of the line as someone yanked the phone from a hysterical Sandy's hand.

Another female came on the line. "Martin, is that you?"

"Yeah, me. What the hell is going on?" he muttered.

"It's Karen Winston. We are at Mount Sinai with Sheila. There's been an accident."

Martin's guilty conscience conjured up Mark Munson at the sound of the word accident. Still struggling to find his way back to the land of the fully conscious, he asked, "Oh no. Is it the Munsons?"

There was a long pause on the other end of the line. "Um, Martin, are you alright?"

"Just tell me if Mark is alright," he hollered.

"I don't know what you are talking about, Martin. I am trying to tell you that Sheila choked and we are at the hospital with her. I tried to do the Heimlich on her, but I couldn't get my arms all the way around… I mean I couldn't get it dislodged," Karen started to cry. "She wasn't breathing by the time the ambulance got there. You have to come down right away!"

"Sheila? Sheila choked?" Martin asked, horribly confused and uncomprehending.

"Yes, Martin, she choked on a goddamn cashew. She is at Mount Sinai, and the doctors don't know if she sustained brain damage from the lack of air. She wasn't breathing for several minutes, and they don't know if—"

"What do you mean she wasn't breathing? My God! She's not—"

"No!" Karen cried. "The paramedics dislodged the damn thing, but she is still unconscious. They can't wake her up."

Martin's mind felt as though it had been spun in some malevolent spider's web. He struggled desperately to shake free from the deadly threads, but remained stuck fast. At any moment some repulsive and huge spider—a black widow maybe—was going to appear and suck the very breath from his lungs.

Guilt weighed like a stone against his heart. Somehow the vile herbs he had dropped into Mark's beer caused Sheila to choke. With the pained sigh of an ailing old man, he found his feet and climbed from the bed.

~~~~

By the time the taxi dropped Martin at Mount Sinai, Sheila had regained consciousness. She was confused and remembered little of
~~~~

the events that led up to waking in the hospital with a roaring headache, difficulty swallowing and chest pain.

When Martin entered her hospital room, she looked up at him with dazed eyes. “Did I have a heart attack, Marty? No one will tell me anything.”

He pulled a hard plastic chair to the side of the bed and took her hand. “No, Sheil, you choked.”

“Choked?” she cried, alarmed.

“Yes. Don’t you remember? You were eating some nuts and one of them got stuck in your throat.”

“I don’t remember anything, except winning a couple of hands in a row, and then waking up here.”

A doctor walked in the room carrying a chart. “How are we feeling?” he asked.

“We feel like shit, thank you very much,” Sheila snapped.

Amused, he said, “I need to run a few tests. Just want to make sure all the wires are connected properly. Mr. Reynolds, why don’t you go tell your wife’s friends she is awake now. They are waiting in the lobby and are quite worried about her.”

“What do you mean the wires are connected properly?” Sheila asked, alarmed.

“Mrs. Reynolds, you were without oxygen for a few minutes before the aid crew cleared your airway and there is always the danger of minor brain damage. We just want to make sure—”

Sheila cut him off with a shriek. “Brain damage! What the hell?”

Martin fluttered nervously next to her bed. “Honey, simmer down. Let the doctor look at you.”

Sheila started to cry. “Marty, don’t leave. Please, you know I hate doctors. I hate hospitals, I hate all this! Nothing is wrong with me. I’m fine, just let me go home.” She dissolved into tears.

Martin turned toward the doctor. "Could you come back in a few minutes?"

When the doctor hesitated, he said, "Please?"

The doctor slowly nodded his head. "Okay. But the tests have to be done before we are released."

"We won't get up and run away, Doctor Sensitive," Sheila snapped through her tears.

The doctor's pleasant expression turned to a sour frown as he marched from the room.

"Martin, don't let them touch me!" Sheila grabbed Martin's hand with panicky tightness and squeezed hard enough to grind the bones.

"Hon, you heard the man. They have to run a few tests before they will let you out of here. The sooner you let them do it, the sooner WE can take you home." He grinned at her to see if she got the joke.

She offered a small smile in return and her hand eased up a little. "I wish I could remember what happened."

"The important thing is that you are alright." Martin patted her shoulder.

"This is all very embarrassing," Sheila said forlornly.

"Sheila, there is nothing to be embarrassed about. You should be relieved you are going to be okay. Now, can I go get the doctor back in here so he can do his tests?"

Sheila sighed. "Yeah, just tell him to make it fast. I want to go home."

Martin walked into the antiseptic hallway in search of the doctor. Around the corner in a depressing waiting room with yellow walls, Sandy Werner and Karen Winston sat discussing the events of the day in hushed tones.

The doctor had told them Sheila was awake and probably out of danger.

Sandy Werner, with uncharacteristic cattiness, sniped, "Well if she hadn't been so busy gloating about Martin's—quote—unquote—'in the bag' promotion, maybe she wouldn't have swallowed the damn cashew wrong."

When Karen didn't respond, Sandy added, "She's certainly had enough practice chewing to be able to navigate one damn nut down her—"

"Stop it, Sandy." Karen Winston cut her off. "I don't want to hear your insults. Sheila is my friend."

Shocked at Karen's harsh reaction, Sandy bristled. "Well, crap Karen, you couldn't even get your arms around her to—"

Standing just out of sight, Martin heard the exchange. He came barreling around the corner, glaring at Sandy Werner and cutting her off mid-sentence.

"My wife nearly died! What's the matter with you? How can you sit here, practically right outside of her hospital room, and talk about her like that? Why don't you just get the hell out of here!"

A red-faced Sandy, rose from the chair stammering an apology. A moment later she fled the hospital.

Karen walked up to Martin and put an arm around his shoulder, "I'm so sorry, Martin. You didn't need to hear that garbage. Sandy is just upset. When she gets upset, she gets stupid and shoots her mouth off. She really was just terrified like the rest of us. Is Sheila okay?"

Martin exhaled a long sigh. "Yeah, I think so. The doctors need to run some tests, but it looks like she is out of the woods."

"Well, thank God. She scared the hell out of us." Karen blew a sigh of relief.

"What did Sandy mean Sheila was gloating about my promotion?" he asked, a worried frown falling like a shadow over his face. "They haven't announced anything yet."

"Oh, Sheila was talking about the partnership when she choked. She's sure you are going to get it this time."

"What the hell was she saying?" Martin asked, his voice rising.

Karen looked away uncomfortably. "Nothing, Martin. She just has a lot of faith in you. It was nothing to get upset about."

Martin wanted to press her about what exactly Sheila said, but he could see that Karen was growing increasingly agitated with the grilling questions he was firing at her.

"Why don't you go on home, Karen. I appreciate all you did. Sheila should be released soon, so you don't need to hang around."

Karen looked at him doubtfully. "Are you sure? I could stay if—"

"No," Martin replied firmly. "She's fine now. Really."

"You'll call if you need anything?"

Martin nodded.

Karen brushed a polite kiss in the air an inch from his cheek and went home.

The hospital released Sheila an hour later, having determined that she sustained no permanent damage.

She was wheeled from the room by an orderly, as the doctor chided, "We were very lucky, Mrs. Reynolds. We will want to be more careful when we chew our food in the future."

Sheila gave Martin a *God help me* look and rolled her eyes.

By the time they arrived home the answering machine was bursting with calls. News of Sheila's choking had spread like wildfire.

"Well that didn't take long to travel the grapevine, did it?" Sheila asked, disgusted.

When Martin didn't answer she turned to see him gazing out the window. "Martin? Marty?"

When he turned to her his eyes remained distant. "What, dear? I'm sorry."

"Where did you go?"

"Nowhere. Just thinking about how glad I am that you are okay. Can I get you anything?"

"Well, maybe a sandwich. I'm a bit hungry."

~~~~

Martin spent the rest of the weekend jumping at shadows.

On Sunday, Sheila asked him, "So, have you figured out how you are going to get the stuff into their drinks yet?"

Martin closed his eyes. "I already took care of one of them." He shuddered at his choice of words.

"What? When? Why didn't you tell me!" Sheila cried.

"Yesterday. While you were at your bridge club—or maybe the hospital. I guess, I really don't know which," he answered forlornly.

"Well, for chrissakes, Marty, which one?"

"I called Mike Munson and asked him to meet me for a beer. I did it at the bar when he was in the men's."

"Oh my God! Did he suspect anything? What did it do? Did he get sick or anything?" She was dancing foot to foot in her excitement.

"No. Nothing. I hope… I hope it doesn't hurt him," he said quietly.

Sheila shrugged. "It won't. It will just do something so he doesn't get the partnership, that's all. I just hope the stuff works. What about the other two?"
~~~~

"We'll see."

"What do you mean *we'll see*? You need a plan. We have to think of something."

"Sheila!" he roared, "Let me worry about it. I have no idea what opportunity the morning will bring to conclude this nasty deed—if it brings one at all. Now get off my back about it, will you!" He slammed himself into their bedroom.

Martin didn't sleep all that long, miserable night. He lay awake listening to Sheila snore, afraid to even rise from the bed and sit in the living room.

He had briefly dozed, and dreamt that the white and bloated corpse of Mark Munson was standing out in the street below his living room window, beckoning him down. He didn't even need to stifle a scream as he jerked awake. These days, on the rare occasions when sleep found him, it never came alone. The nightmares were always riding shotgun.

Chapter 9

A bleary-eyed Martin rode the subway to work on Monday. He had nearly convinced himself that police officers would be waiting at his office to arrest him for poisoning Mike Munson. He pictured himself arriving at the office and being thrown against the wall by a burly detective, while a pair of uniformed officers slapped handcuffs on him and read him his rights. He could see all his co-workers clustered in a tight circle, wide-eyed and jostling each other to get a better view of his arrest. Sheila's bridge club would have enough gossip to last them into the new millennium.

Martin was so sure the authorities would be waiting for him with handcuffs in one hand, and a Miranda warning in the other, that when he arrived at his office he stood outside on the sidewalk for several minutes trying to get his breathing under control. He steeled himself to walk inside the building.

Once in the elevator, he leaned against the railing and mopped perspiration from his brow. When Martin reached the opaque glass doors leading to the firm, a wave of dizziness washed over him. He stood for several moments, head bowed, perspiration dripping from his face, one clammy hand clutching the door handle. After what felt like an eternity the vertigo passed. Resigned to whatever fate awaited him on the other side of the door, Martin Reynolds marched inside.

He thought he might be hallucinating when he stood at the threshold and saw no police officers waiting for him. The receptionist greeted him, as did all the other people he passed in the halls on the way to his office. Nothing appeared out of the ordinary or amiss. He hadn't seen Mark Munson, but this wasn't unusual since they worked in completely different divisions. The tax section was one floor below the one Martin worked on. Sometimes he wouldn't see Mark for weeks at a time.

Gradually his thrumming nerves began to settle. There were no ominous memos left upon his desk summoning him to the conference room. If anything had happened to the Munsons over the weekend, surely the partners would have heard about it by now. They would have called an impromptu meeting to relay the grim news to the rest of the firm.

No memo also meant that the announcement of who would be made partner was probably not going to be made today.

Unwelcome words whispered from his mind, *This gives me at least through the afternoon to figure out how to finish the job.* Martin was furious at himself for entertaining such thoughts. After the fright he just suffered, he would do well to just throw the damn stuff away and forget this fiendish errand.

But time heals, and by ten o'clock Martin's courage reasserted itself. He slipped into the lunch room. Seeing it unoccupied, he closed the door behind him. Glancing surreptitiously around the vacant room, he grabbed two mugs from a rack. With a hand that trembled only slightly, he poured each one full of coffee and reached into his pocket.

He unwrapped the gauze-swaddled vial and tipped it over one of the cups. Once again, the acrid smell assaulted his nostrils and burned his eyes. The coffee bubbled and flared a deep ruby for barely a second before returning to normal. He added cream and sugar to one cup, and left the other black. Drawing a deep breath for courage, Martin flung open the door to the lunch room and started down the hallway toward the group of offices that housed the criminal defense division of Carson, August, Bench and Associates.

~~~~

Rhonda Baldwin was an attractive woman in her early forties. She was a well liked, well respected lawyer. She never over-billed her clients and she tried not to defend those she honestly believed were guilty—much to the chagrin of her fellow defense council.

Martin barely knew the woman. They crossed paths enough to say hello in the hallways or in the elevator, but had never held a conversation longer than the length of time it took to ride down twenty-nine floors. He occasionally heard her deep and sexy laughter resonating down the corridor, and was always grateful for the distraction. Rhonda's voice was silkier than any midnight-disc jockey. Her laugh never failed to send a few shivers down Martin's spine.

Rhonda wasn't surprised that her name was on the nomination list for partner this time. She was one of only six female attorneys the firm employed. Two years ago Carol Hodges's name had been on the list. The year before that, Doreen Gilbert's. The last female to have actually received the partnership, however, was over five years before. This year it was either nominate a woman or nominate a black, Rhonda figured. Had the firm employed a
~~~~

black woman, that's the name that would have been on the list, thus achieving the height of political correctness. The senior partners were nothing if not politically correct.

Rhonda held no illusion that it would be her name called when the envelope was opened. Political correctness extended only so far within the walls of Carson, August, Bench and Associates.

~~~~

Rhonda was dictating a brief for a pro-bono client on death row, when a light tapping at her office door interrupted her chain of thought.

She clicked off the tape recorder, and called, "Come in."

Martin elbowed open the door and poked his head inside. "Am I disturbing you?"

Rhonda smiled and beckoned him inside. "Ah, my arch rival. Come to gloat prematurely, have you?"

Martin's laugh boomed a little too loud to ring true. "No, no, of course not. Actually," he said, handing a cup of coffee to her across the desk, "I came to offer a good luck toast. I hope you take it with cream and sugar."

"Well, how very civilized of you, Martin. But you know they are never going to give it to the token female on the list. Nonetheless, I appreciate the gesture." Rhonda raised her cup to his in a mock-toast then tilted it to her lips.

The credenza against the back wall was lined with photographs of a little girl with long, curly red hair. She smiled at the camera from a half a dozen assorted frames.

Martin sat across the desk from Rhonda and sipped his coffee. He nodded toward the pictures. "Very pretty little girl. How old is she?"

A sunny smile lit Rhonda's face. "Seven. Going on nineteen, of course. Do you have any kids, Martin?"
~~~~

He shook his head. "Every year Sheila and I talk about it, and every year we come up with a hundred different excuses to wait one more year."

Rhonda barked her smoky laugh. Even under these strange circumstances it sent a pleasant shiver down Martin's back.

She said, "I wasn't given that luxury. Jenny was an unexpected surprise. Her daddy took off on his Harley the day I told him I was pregnant, and I never heard from him again. Rumor has it he's a bouncer at a biker bar somewhere in Newark."

A guilty flush rose up Martin's cheeks as he watched Rhonda drink heartily from her coffee cup. His eyes moved to the empty ring finger on her left hand.

"I didn't know you were single," he remarked. "For some reason I always thought there was a Mr. Baldwin somewhere."

"There is," she grinned. "My father."

Seeing the flush rise on Martin's cheeks, Rhonda took his reaction for the mistaken assumption that she was married. She quickly said, "Hey, don't worry about it. That's what happens in a firm this size. I think it shows tremendous form that you even knew which office was mine. You can't be expected to know my marital status too."

Martin forced a weak smile to his lips. "I guess I should let you get back to work. Good luck to you, Rhonda."

She raised her hand in a wave, "Yes, well, like I said, I doubt I will be given the keys to the executive washroom this time around, but I really appreciate the gesture, Martin. Thanks for the coffee and good luck to you too."

Martin felt the same sickening cramps that attacked him outside the bar yesterday grip his stomach the moment he stepped out of Rhonda's office. He sprinted to the men's room and locked himself into a stall. Dropping his pants, he doubled over in pain and wrapped his arms around his middle. After passing noisy and pungent wind, gradually the pain eased up, and he was able to catch his breath. He wondered if his stomach would ever feel right again.

Martin returned to his desk. He tried to keep his mind on work, but it was impossible.

One thought kept resonating in his mind over and over again. *She's single. She's a single mother.*

Martin didn't know why the fact that the woman had no spouse should bother him so much, but it did. It rolled a guilty stone against his heart he thought he might never dislodge. Somehow putting the old witch's potion into Rhonda Baldwin's coffee seemed worse than pouring it in Mark Munson's beer. Much worse.

But why? He asked himself. *What's the difference?*

The answer hit him seconds later. *Because Mark has a wife. Someone to raise the kids just in case anything should ever happen to him. All Rhonda has is a missing biker, presumed to be somewhere in New Jersey.*

"No!" he cried out loud.

A secretary happening by gasped. She peered suspiciously at Martin through the open door of his office. "What's wrong?" she aked.

"N... Nothing. I just realized I... um... forgot to file a motion. Missed the deadline," he stammered.

The secretary gave him a final baleful look. She rolled her eyes, and shook her head. "Lawyers," she muttered under her breath.

Martin contemplated leaving early. He could claim he was ill and discovered that wouldn't be a lie. He closed his office door and called Sheila.

"She's a single mother," he said miserably, after telling her about delivering the potion to Rhonda.

"So what? What does that have to do with anything?" Sheila sounded unconcerned.

"What if… What if it does something to her? What if it hurts her?"

"Oh for crying out loud, Marty! Did you hear that Mark Munson was rushed to the hospital, or that he died suddenly over the weekend?"

"No," Martin reluctantly admitted, "But still, something could happen."

"That crazy biddy in Seattle couldn't have sold you something that was going to kill somebody, Marty," Sheila responded reasonably, "that isn't legal."

"Oh hell, Sheila!" Martin exploded. "You think she cares about legal? She sent her goon to remind me not to open my mouth or they'd kill me. Is that legal?"

This was the first Sheila had heard about Martin's encounter in the alley with Nicholas Aguilar.

"What?" she cried, alarmed.

"Do you remember the day I came home sick a couple of months ago? The day you got so upset because you thought everyone was laughing behind our backs because I wasn't partner?"

"What about it?" she asked suspiciously.

"I wasn't sick. That morning as I was walking in the door to work, some crazy grabbed me and hauled me into the alley behind the building. He threatened me. Said if I ever told anyone about that miserable bottle of God-knows-what that I bought from that hag, he'd kill me." Martin paused then quietly added, "He said he'd kill you too. I hate to remind you that you nearly died this weekend, Sheila. Legal has nothing to do with this."

Sheila gasped. "Oh my god, Martin! Why didn't you tell me?"

"How could I tell you? And what does it matter anyway at this point? I've already given it to two out of three of the people on that goddamn list. There is no turning back anymore."

"No," Sheila replied in a soft voice, "I guess we're in too deep now. You might as well finish it."

"Should I? Shouldn't we wait and see if it does anything to Mark or Rhonda before I try and slip it to William Francis too?"

"No!" Sheila hissed. "No, Martin. Don't you dare wimp out on me now! Like you said, there is no turning back. Finish it. We'll deal with the consequences later."

"Thanks, dear. That's a real comfort."

"Martin, you are being ridiculous. If anything had happened to Mark Munson you would have heard something by now. You know how fast bad news travels in that place. It's probably like you said all along—it was wasted money and won't change a thing. Just finish it. Finish it, Martin," she insisted.

"You realize that I don't even know who William Francis is, don't you, Sheila? I have never worked a case with him. I couldn't even pick him out of a crowd. The probate section is on the 31st floor. I've never even gone up there for anything."

"You can look him up in the roster. Use the same ploy on him that you did on the Baldwin woman. Just bring a cup of coffee and offer your good wishes."

Martin hung up the phone with a headache pounding at his temples.

She doesn't care who we hurt in the process, he thought. *Nothing else matters to that woman except my becoming a partner. If I do that, the woman could die happy—and in her mind, thin.*

Martin shuddered. "Oh, Christ!" he moaned under his breath. He was suddenly gripped by an overwhelming urge to get out of the building.

She's probably right, anyway. Damn stinky leaves probably came from that crazy bitch's back yard and have no more power than a potted plant.

But he knew that wasn't true. A potted plant wouldn't grow so hot it blistered your skin. It wouldn't grow so hot that it needed its own metal strong box to keep it from burning down the closet. And it wouldn't make a cup of coffee or a schooner of beer change color and smoke either.

Who am I kidding?

Martin sighed wearily and rose from his desk. He went across the street to the deli and ordered a sandwich that he didn't really want. While he waited for his number to be called, he took a seat at one of the few empty tables in the crowded restaurant. He sat nursing a soda out of a paper cup.

Moments later a good looking man in his mid thirties, wearing an exquisitely tailored suit approached Martin's table. He looked vaguely familiar, but Martin couldn't place him.

"Hello," the man said, extending his hand, "You're Martin Reynolds, aren't you?"

Martin allowed his hand to be shaken. His eyes grew watchful, his tone wary. "That's right. Who wants to know?"

"I'm Bill Francis," the man replied, growing uneasy at Martin's terse reaction. "I just wanted to say good luck," he finished hurriedly and started to turn away.

"Wait!" Martin called. "Hey, I'm sorry. I'm a little touchy today."

The other man relaxed a little and smiled. "Well, it's a tense week for all of us on that list. Lousy to get nominated for partner because someone died. Hell, I don't even know if I could fill Jack Calloway's shoes. I didn't know him personally, but the guy was something of a legend."

"Hey, have you eaten? Why don't you join me." Martin forced a smile to his lips.

Bill Francis hesitated. "I don't want to bother you."

"No. You're not," Martin answered.

When the man still didn't sit down, Martin waved a hand toward the empty chair. "Really. You aren't bothering me. It's good to meet you."

Bill Francis sat down. "Well, I wouldn't want people to think you were fraternizing with the enemy or anything."

Martin laughed. "We aren't enemies, Bill, but if you don't mind my saying so, you look awfully young to be up for partner. How long have you been with the firm? I don't get up to probate much."

"Five years," Bill replied, unable to hide the arrogant confidence from his voice. "I'm your classic overachiever. First in my class—Harvard of course. Deans list and top three when I took the bar. Come to think of it, I guess if anyone could fill Calloway's shoes, I could, right?" He laughed at his own joke.

Martin smiled, but said nothing. He was relieved to find that the more Bill Francis talked, the less he liked him. Maybe that would make it easier.

A voice over the loud speaker, announced, "Number twenty-seven, your order is ready."

The young lawyer looked at his receipt. "That's me. I'll be right back."

Martin wasted no time. He reached into his pocket and dumped half of the remaining contents of the vial into the beverage cup the man had left sitting on the table. One thin tendril of smoke curled lazily out of the drink. Then, without warning, the soda began to leak out of two small, smoldering holes that materialized in the sides of the paper cup.

By the time Bill returned to the table with a huge sandwich and a salad, Martin was mopping the remainder of his drink up with a napkin.

"What happened?" Bill asked when he saw Martin wiping up the puddle of soda.

"Uh… Your drink sprung a leak," he stammered.

A few minutes later Martin's number was called. He was relieved to see his legs were steady as he rose to get his lunch, and further pleased to see his appetite had returned.

When Bill rose to replace his drink, Martin grabbed the little glass bottle from his pocket one final time. He dumped the remaining contents onto the other man's salad. The vile herbs glowed a brilliant emerald green for the briefest moment, and one thin tendril of smoke twisted lazily up from the plate. Then, the smoke and the herbs vanished, as if the salad had absorbed them.

William Francis was a braggart and an arrogant, vain man. He spent the better part of the forty-five minutes he shared with Martin telling stories about all the secretaries in the building he had slept with, and where he had his suits custom made.

He implied that his pending promotion to partner would help pay for the new Porsche he just bought. It was clear that he didn't think Martin had a prayer at being promoted over him, nor any "chick" as he referred to Rhonda Baldwin.

No cramps attacked Martin's stomach this time, and no guilty stone rolled against his heart.

It was done. All done.

The two men exchanged farewells in the elevator. Martin was relieved to be away from him. He thought Bill Francis had been right about one thing: he was a young Jack Calloway in training, alright. Same big mouth—same small mind.

Martin didn't see the younger man's skin had broken out in a thin sheen of sweat, his vision had grown blurry, and his hands were shaking as he stepped out of the elevator on the 31st floor.

William Francis, a man who had never taken one sick day in five years with the firm, went home ill twenty minutes later. He thought it was the sandwich.

When Martin called Sheila after returning to his office, she said, "See, it was meant to be. The little shit fell right in your lap. You didn't even have to go find him."

"It sure seems that way, doesn't it. So what do I do now, Sheila?"

"What do you mean, what do you do? You wait. We will know by the end of the week if we got our money's worth."

By 4:00 that afternoon Martin was feeling almost normal again. He disposed of the vile little cylinder that had plagued his life for the past two years by flushing it down the toilet after lunch. The relief he felt at being shut of the miserable bottle's contents was enormous.

He passed Rhonda Baldwin in the hallway twice that afternoon, and she looked perfectly fine and healthy. This went a long way in putting Martin's mind at ease.

Martin was able to enjoy the relief he felt late that afternoon for a full thirty minutes.

After 4:30 p.m., Martin Reynolds would never feel good about anything again for the rest of his life.

Chapter 10

Martin finished dictating all his correspondence and popped the tape out of the hand held recorder he used.

He shared his secretary with two other attorneys, one of which was Clive Cheznik. He walked the tape down the hallway to Deanna Capswell's office, only to find her looking even more harried than usual. She was talking on the phone with a very annoyed client.

"No, Mr. Wilson, he's not avoiding you. Mr. Cheznik hasn't been in all day, so he hasn't gotten your messages yet," she said through gritted teeth.

Martin froze in his tracks just inside the doorway of Deanna's office. His heart began thudding heavily in his chest.

"Yes, Mr. Wilson, I will have him call you first thing tomorrow morning."

Deanna saw Martin leaning against the door and waved him in impatiently with her hand. Hanging up the phone she rolled her eyes at Martin. "I am going to kill Clive when I see him."

"Where is he?"

"I don't know. He never showed up today." She was clearly angry.

"Did he call in sick?" Martin asked through dry lips.

"No, and there is no answer at his house all day. He was due in court this morning, so he has not only a bunch of pissed off, neglected clients, but a pretty angry judge to contend with tomorrow as well."

All the color drained from Martin's face. He stumbled back to his office, dictation tape still clamped in his fist, and slammed the door. He fell into his desk chair and put his head between his knees to try and fight off the urge to pass out. The world had gone gray before his eyes, and white spots were exploding before them. With shaking hands and shallow breath, he thumbed the Rolodex on his desk. He found Mark Munson's extension and punched the numbers on the phone.

A female picked up the phone, sounding as harried as the overworked Deanna.

"Mark Munson's office," she answered in a clipped tone.

"Can I talk to Mark?" Martin said. It came out barely above a whisper. The secretary had to ask him to repeat himself.

When he did, she replied, "He isn't in. Can I take a message?"

"Was he in today at all?" Martin asked, his voice squeaking.

"Who's calling please?" the secretary asked, a guarded tone entering her voice.

"Martin Reynolds, from litigation upstairs," he managed.

"Oh sorry, Martin, I didn't recognize your voice. He hasn't been in today."

"Is… Is he sick?"

"I'm really not sure. He didn't call in. That's not like him, but he was going away for the weekend. Maybe he got delayed or something. He didn't have a real full schedule today, so he probably just decided to take a long weekend. I just wish he would have told me."

Martin mumbled his thanks and hung up. He stomach had been rolling since he fled Deanna's office. He knew he wasn't going to have time to make it to the men's room before he threw up. He couldn't even get up off the chair, let alone make his legs carry him. He yanked the wastebasket over and vomited until his stomach was clenching with dry heaves. He drew his handkerchief across his mouth with shaking fingers and fought back the hysteria trying to overtake him. He went back to the Rolodex and found Mark's home phone number. His fingers were trembling so badly, he misdialed twice before finally punching in the right digits.

After four rings, a mechanical voice answered, "The voice mailbox of the party you are calling is full. Please try your call again later."

Fear, cold and icy, stole through Martin's chest. His throat closed and he felt like he couldn't breathe. He fell from his desk chair and lay in the fetal position beneath his desk. He remained there for the next two hours.

~~~~

A worried Sheila left numerous messages on Martin's voicemail wondering where he was. She called his secretary, who went down the hall to check on him. Receiving no answer when she knocked, Deanna opened his office door. All she saw was an empty office chair. Martin was under the desk tucked out of sight. She wrinkled her nose at the foul smell rising from Martin's garbage can, and decided to leave that for the janitor.

Tony arrived around 7:00 to vacuum Matin's office.
~~~~

When Martin heard the vacuum in the hallway drawing closer, he clutched the side of the desk and pulled himself up. He sat down in his chair and raked his fingers through his hair.

Tony opened the door. Seeing Martin, a guilty flush rose in his cheeks. He switched off the vacuum cleaner.

Martin tried to work his face into something of a smile, but failed.

Tony looked down the hall guiltily. Leaving the vacuum outside the office, he came in and shut the door behind him.

"Mr. Reynolds. I gotta talk to you. I been hoping to run into you."

Martin looked at him through haunted eyes and said nothing.

Tony appeared not to notice. He reached into his pocket and pulled out a folded bill.

He slid it across Martin's desk. "I can't keep this. It's the money you gave me, and I can't keep it because I lied to you." He looked away quickly and waited for Martin to respond.

Martin stared transfixed at the folded hundred dollar bill. He looked up at the janitor. "Lied? You lied?" he whispered.

"Yeah. I'm sorry. I just… You know, you was holding out that bill and I needed money. I got a kid to feed, and I figured if I took the money I gotta give you something for it, and so I made up that story about Carson laughing at you."

"Made it up?" Martin's voice cracked.

"I'm sorry, man, really. I mean I'm giving you back your money, so no harm done, right?"

"No harm… Oh my God! Why? Why, Tony?"

"I just told you. I needed the money." He looked away shamefacedly.

"Why are you telling me this now?"

"Well, that's the thing. I figured you wouldn't get promoted again. I mean you never do, right? So I figured you would be mad at them anyway, so what's the difference. But, shit, guess what? This time they picked you!" Tony cried.

Martin's eyes flew open. "What? What did you say?"

The janitor reached into the pocket of his overalls and pulled out a folded piece of paper. He handed it to Martin. "They picked you, man. I found a copy of this memo they are putting out in the morning. It's you. You got it!"

Martin snatched the paper from his hand.

It was dated for tomorrow and came from the desk of Greer August. Martin read the words 'It is with great pleasure that we announce…' The rest was blurred by his tears.

Tony shifted nervously from foot to foot. "Listen, I don't want you to think I only came clean with you about this because you got promoted. That ain't it. I truly felt guilty, man. It's been bugging me ever since I told you that shit. That bill," he pointed at the hundred lying on the desk, "it's the same one you gave me. I been carrying it around. I never spent it or nothing."

When Martin didn't reply, he said, "Hey, you ain't gonna get me in trouble for this are you? I mean I did the right thing and all, so—"

"Get out!" Martin shrieked in a broken voice, spraying spittle onto his desk. "Get out, you miserable fuck, get out!"

Tony stumbled backwards toward the door. The look in Martin's eyes terrified him more than his venomous outburst. He threw open the door and fled down the hallway.

Martin put his face in his hands and sobbed. When the phone on his desk rang he reached out with a blind hand, knowing it was Sheila.

"Yes?" he breathed into the phone.

Sheila was crying, "Marty? Thank God! I've been so worried. Are you alright?"

"No. No Sheila. I think something happened to Mark Munson… And to Clive Cheznik."

Sheila sniffled into the phone. "Oh, Marty! You haven't seen the news yet have you?"

"Why? What now?" he cried.

"Their car, Marty. Their car… It went off the Long Island Expressway last night."

"No! Sheila, no!"

"Everyone inside was killed. They identified the bodies today by dental records. The car… It burned and they didn't know who was in it, and…" Sheila broke down weeping. "Marty we have to take it back! We have to take it back!"

Dull pain throbbed at Martin's temples. An acid belch rose in his gut and tears streamed down his face.

"Sheila," he responded quietly, "We can't take this back." And he hung up the phone.

Chapter 11

It was after midnight when Martin let himself into his apartment. Sheila ran to the front door as soon as she heard his key turn in the lock. She threw her arms around his neck.

"Where have you been?" She buried her face against his neck. Her eyes were puffy and red from crying. "I've been sick worrying about you."

He gently pushed her away and walked into the kitchen. He poured himself a glass of whiskey. His breath smelled as though he already had a few before finding his way home.

"I needed to be alone," he said, and sat heavily in a chair at the kitchen table.

Sheila sat down next to him and took his hand. "Marty, listen to me. This isn't our fault. It was just an accident. It's awful. I know that, but it is just a coincidence. That's all, just a horrible coincidence."

The dead voice of Carla Cheznik whispered in his ear. "It makes a sick kind of sense though, doesn't it?"

He shuddered and drained his glass with a grimace.

~~~~

The next day was one of the worst in the firm's history, and by far the worst day of Martin Reynolds's life.

Martin stared around him at the crowded conference room. Tears were flowing. Shocked and saddened faces surrounded him. He was getting furtive glances from everyone. Some looked at him with a mixture of pity and horror; others with outright suspicion.

Sheila sat up with him until she passed out on the couch at dawn. She nearly had him convinced that the accident was just a nasty coincidence. That was until he arrived at work the following morning and found a memo on his desk. Not the memo he had been expecting, but one that had been hastily printed just that morning by Carson's tearful secretary, summoning everyone to the conference room for a devastating and completely unfathomable announcement.

Mark Munson, Clive Cheznik and their spouses killed in a car crash over the weekend. William Francis found dead in his bed early that morning from a massive brain hemorrhage. And Rhonda Baldwin quitting the firm unexpectedly and giving no notice. She left a hurried message on Carson's voicemail early that morning, saying something about her child's father appearing on her doorstep after a seven year absence, and asking her to move to Schenectady so they could be a family.

Bench, who had crawled from the comfortable cocoon of his retirement, announced the horrible news himself about Clive, Mark and Bill. He looked like a shell of the hail and hearty man that had toasted Clive Cheznik's promotion just two months before.

Almost as an afterthought he announced Rhonda's sudden departure.
~~~~

And as an even smaller afterthought he announced Martin's promotion in a distracted and distant voice.

Carson quickly added, "Ironically, the decision to promote Martin Reynolds was made before this, uh... tragic chain of events. You should all know that." He looked at Reynolds and said, "Martin, I want you to know we had already decided... We..." his voice broke and he couldn't finish. He couldn't quite bring himself to offer any congratulations. Nor could anyone else. And Martin was grateful for that. He would have screamed and fled if anyone had tried.

After the grim news was imparted, Martin hurried from the building. As he exited he caught a voice from a few feet behind him whispering, "If I didn't know better I'd think he killed the competition."

Martin broke into a run and nearly jogged in front of a speeding cab as he crossed the street against the light.

He never noticed the taxi's driver as he blared the horn, screamed an obscenity, and raised his middle finger. Martin stumbled up the sidewalk toward the subway.

~~~~

Hours later, Miles Carson and Greer August stood at the window of Carson's huge corner office, overlooking Manhattan and sharing a good scotch. They discussed the unspeakable events of the day.

"Maybe we should have promoted him years ago? Maybe we jinxed him." A forlorn August remarked.

Carson rolled his eyes, "That's absurd, Greer. We were giving it to him this time, remember? There was no need for anyone else to be..."

"Eliminated?" August finished for him.
~~~~

"I liked Cheznik. I'm really going to miss that boy," Carson sighed.

"Everyone liked Cheznik. Everyone liked Mrs. Cheznik too."

Carson nodded, "Beautiful woman, what a shame."

August turned to Carson, and asked him incredulously, "And what about Rhonda? Talk about senseless! I can't believe the woman walked out on her clients like that. She treated them like they were her children, for chrissakes! Did you ever know her to do something this impulsive? Didn't that guy dump her when he found out she was pregnant?"

Carson shrugged, "Apparently the torch must have never gone out." He went to the cabinet to pour them another drink.

~~~~

Perhaps Rhonda's torch never did burn out, but had anyone asked her—even the day before, what she would have done if the bum, whose only contribution to her daughter's life had been the donation of his sperm one hot July night, ever showed up again, she would have told them she'd slam the door in his face with no hesitation at all. And had her long gone ex-boyfriend been asked if he ever thought about Rhonda, or the child he never knew, he would have answered, "Who's Rhonda?"

Ain't love a funny thing sometimes?

~~~~

The partners closed the firm for the remainder of the week right after the gruesome announcements were made. They wanted to give everyone time to deal with the magnitude of the loss, and to make it through two double funerals and one single one.

The clients, even the larger ones, were all quite understanding. Judges willingly rescheduled trials and court appearances. They gave continuances, even at great inconvenience to themselves.

The firm of Carson, August, Bench and Associates was a hot topic in New York's legal community for months to come. It was nearly impossible to believe that in a single day three lawyers from the same firm could have died.

In the weeks that followed, five lawyers quit because they thought the firm was cursed—or more accurately they thought Martin Reynolds was.

Once Sheila's bridge club had sufficiently recovered from the shock, tongues wagged. Sheila was conspicuously absent from the bridge club, giving her fellow members ample opportunity to say all the things about her she feared they had been saying all along.

"Well, Sheila finally got her wish. Wonder why she isn't here to gloat."

"Sheila must be so humiliated."

"I wonder if Sheila will finally buy a new dress for the celebration dinner?"

"Hell, I wonder if she will even be able to show her face at it."

"Poor old Martin. Passed over for promotion seven, count them, seven times! The only way he could get the partnership was by some freak of nature, some monstrous coincidence too huge to be ignored."

"You don't suppose he had anything to do with it do you?"

Martin Reynolds's legend would forever be that he had made partner only because everyone he was up against suddenly and inexplicably died or disappeared. The fact that the decision was made prior to the tragedies was never mentioned. It wouldn't make for nearly as good gossip.

To Sheila's credit, in the first two weeks following the tragedies, she couldn't have cared less what anyone said. Sheila was living in a private and guilty hell that only her husband understood.

~~~~

After Martin and Sheila left the graveside service for the Munsons, they went to their bank and withdrew their small savings. They took half of it and had a bank check drawn and made payable to Frieda Carol, the maternal grandmother, and now legal guardian of Mark and Cheryl Munson's two children. They opened up a trust account in the name of the two children and deposited the other half of their meager savings in there. They mailed the passbook, along with the bank check, anonymously to Mrs. Carol. Then they went home and held each other until dark.

Many hours later, in the gloom of their living room, neither of them able to sleep, Sheila wondered, "We aren't evil people, Martin. Are we?"

Martin was quiet for so long she didn't think he was going to answer. Finally he replied, "We are if greed is the same thing as evil."

"Am I greedy, Martin? Was it so greedy to want you to be successful? To want us to have the same things as all our friends?"

"I don't think wanting those things is what makes us greedy, Sheila. I think what we were willing to do to get them does."

She gripped his shoulder, tears coursing down her cheeks, "But we didn't know," she cried. "We didn't know what it would do!"
~~~~

Once again Martin didn't answer. Many minutes later, he said, "That's the point, Sheila. I didn't know what it would do, and I gave it to them anyway. I guess that makes me a monster."

He rose from the couch and padded silently into their bedroom and shut the door. The sound of Sheila's sobs followed him.

Chapter 12

After a few weeks, once the shock had worn off—and the bodies had all been buried, things simmered down at the firm. Work was getting caught up, new attorneys interviewed to replace those which were lost. The general air of sadness and depression began to lift. It looked like life at Carson, August, Bench and Associates would go on.

Everyone was recovering except for Martin, who went through his days in a drug-induced haze.

As partner, he was discreetly moved to a larger office; one with a window. His caseload was being handled mostly by two legal assistants. The senior partners knew that Martin's concentration was shot. He could barely dictate a letter into his hand-held tape recorder, let alone appear in court, or write a brief or a pleading. He was nervous and jumpy, despite the prescription tranquilizers he took. He slunk down the halls, head bowed, body pressed against the wall, as if he could make himself disappear if he just clung to it closely enough.

They were giving him time to recover. No one was going to push Martin. Not anymore. Not about anything. Martin had become scary. Bad things happened to people that got in Martin's way, was the consensus, and no one wanted to go there. Martin was only spoken of in the hushed tones reserved for the devil himself, and well out of his earshot.

He had lost weight. Despite the tranquilizers, haunting dreams still followed him into sleep. Horrific, invasive dreams of bodies locked inside burning cars. Carla Cheznik's corpse smiling at him through a mouthful of squirming insects and graveyard dirt. Always repeating the same phrase over and over: "It all makes a sick kind of sense now, Martin. It all makes sense to me now." And she always wore the lovely blue sheath she had worn the night of her husband's celebration dinner. Only now it was moldering, gritty and stiff with dirt. Even with the tranquilizers he would wake up sweating and gasping for breath, while Sheila slept in her own drug induced and blessedly dreamless slumber beside him.

~~~~

Martin was splashing water on his face one afternoon in the men's room, when Greer August walked in. He looked at Martin's drawn features and blank eyes. Martin lost in his guilty world, barely noticed the senior partner's critical gaze. "Martin, lets talk."

"Huh?" Martin looked from his haggard reflection in the mirror to August.

"Martin, I think it's time we celebrate your promotion. I wanted to wait a respectful amount of time after the… After what happened, but I think we all need to move on—especially you. I am going to plan the celebration dinner for two weeks from Saturday."

Martin stared at him speechless. August clapped him on the back, "Now that ought to make Sheila happy, shouldn't it? It will do you both a world of good."
~~~~

Martin stammered, “Greer, I don’t think that’s appropriate. Not under the circumstances.”

“Nonsense,” August overrode him. “What wouldn’t be appropriate would be to treat your promotion any different than anyone else’s. It’s settled, now you tell Sheila to go pick out the most expensive dress she can find, you hear?”

~~~~

Sheila decided to go back to her bridge club the Saturday after August approached Martin in the bathroom.

“Look, Martin,” she said, “If they are trying to get over this thing and move on, then we should too. I am not going to hide my face any longer. No one knows about the stuff from Seattle, and no one ever will. Everyone just thinks it was an ugly coincidence. For all we know, maybe it was. I don’t want to talk about it ever again. I wish you would find a way to get over this, Martin. We can’t bring them back. We can’t walk into the police station and confess to a crime that we didn’t really even commit.”

For the next two weeks Martin struggled with his demons for everything he was worth. For Sheila, he was willing to try and put it behind him. And had it not been for the damn dreams, he might have even won the battle.

~~~~

On the eve before his celebration dinner Martin left work early. Before departing, he left an envelope with some documents inside on the middle of his desk blotter. It was addressed to Greer August and marked *Personal and Confidential.*

He walked from the building and took a cab to the airport. There he rented a car and drove to the cemetery where Clive and Carla Cheznik had been laid to rest. He put flowers on their graves, where no grass would grow until the following spring. He sat quietly for an hour having a conversation with the deceased couple. He felt peaceful when he left.

Next, he drove forty miles to another boneyard. There he did the same thing by Mark and Cheryl Munson's grave. He told them of the gift he and Sheila had bestowed on their children, and asked for their forgiveness.

William Francis had been flown home to Texas to be buried in the family plot, so Martin stopped at a church and lit a candle for him.

~~~~

Sheila was relieved to see Martin acting more normal when he arrived home Friday night. She knew nothing of where he had gone that day, or about the errands he had attended to. There were still dark circles under his eyes, but she thought those eyes looked a little less tortured, and hoped that meant he was finally beginning to heal.

They went out to a nice supper and made love. Martin slept dreamlessly and druglessly for the first night in longer than he could remember. Sheila was starting to believe that maybe—just maybe, Martin had finally found somewhere to bury this inside his heart. Somewhere where it would stop killing him little by little, and let him live the rest of his life free of the shame and guilt over what he had done. What *they* had done.

In a way she was right. Martin had found a way.
~~~~

Chapter 13

Sheila Reynolds stood before the mahogany floor-length mirror that dominated the corner of their bedroom. The big four-poster bed was littered with dresses that she had tried on and discarded in an effort to find the perfect one. She needed to look her best for the dinner she and Martin were attending that evening.

Each dress was brand new and purchased over the last two days. One from just about every boutique in Manhattan. She giggled like a schoolgirl as she tried each one on and twirled in front of Martin.

"So which one?" she asked happily.

Martin looked at his wife with great affection and kissed her cheek, "I like the black one."

"Which black one?" she cried, "I have four of them." She sifted through the sea of discarded evening wear on the bed, picked one out and held it up in front of her. "This one?"

"Perfect," he said, rising from the bed. "I guess I should go get ready too."

Sheila threw her arms around his neck. "I knew we would get through this, Martin. I knew we would." She kissed him lustily on the mouth. "Your tux is hanging in the closet."

Martin walked to the closet and glanced for a moment up to the top shelf. The strong box had been thrown down the incinerator chute the month before. No trace remained of the little bottle, what it contained, or of an old withered woman in Seattle and a bookstore called Bella Luna. It was all gone. Just like Clive and Carla Cheznik, Mark and Cheryl Munson, William Francis—and in some ways worst of all—Rhonda Baldwin and her seven year old daughter.

Martin carried his tuxedo to the bathroom and showered and dressed for the evening ahead.

~~~~

A crescendo of fragrances rose up and greeted Martin and Sheila as they walked through the doors of the ballroom that had been reserved for tonight's occasion. The smell of good food and expensive perfume mixed with the smell of fine Cuban cigars. Light strains from a string quartet spilled through the balcony doors. Dresses rustled, jewels sparkled, and everyone was turned out in their best splendor. An endless river of expensive liquor had loosened tongues and created a cheerful, if a bit subdued atmosphere.

There was no Jack Calloway to slap Martin on the back. There was no one to joke about always being a bridesmaid. Martin's day had come. Everyone congratulated him. Sheila was enfolded into her group of friends. She was the star of the party. Bench made the champagne toast and everyone drank. It was a lovely evening.
~~~~

Several hours later as it drew to a close, Sheila excused herself to the restroom. Martin politely thanked Carson, August and Bench for all they had done, and for making the evening such a special event, for himself, and especially for his wife.

Martin removed his suit jacket and hung it carefully over the back of his chair. He checked the creases in his trousers. He calmly walked out to the balcony and past the string quartet as they did a lively version of La Cuceracha. He climbed over the railing and jumped thirty stories to his death.

~~~~

Sheila was right. Martin had found a place in his heart to put it. He couldn't live with it, so he chose to die with it.

The documents he left on his desk on his way out of the office the day before were his last will and testament. He made sure Sheila was taken care of. The rest was split between the trust account for Mark Munson's children, and another he had opened in the name of Rhonda Baldwin's daughter. His last request was that Greer have one of the firm's private detectives find her and give it to her.

~~~~

Finally, Martin had found peace. And there were no more bad dreams.

PART III
What Stormie Banks Did For Eternal Youth

Rarely do great beauty and great virtue dwell together.
–Petrarch

Who needs virtue when you have great beauty?
–Stormie Banks

Chapter 1

Academy award-winning actress Stormie Banks lay drunk and limp in the backyard of her twelve-million-dollar Hollywood Hills home. The heady scent of Night Blooming Jasmine filled the air.

She reached blindly beside her in search of the glass that held her sixth—or maybe it was her seventh vodka tonic of the evening? She couldn't quite remember.

Stormie watched the moonlight glimmer softly off the pool water. It was nearly midnight, but few stars could penetrate the light pollution of Hollywood Hills.

Few stars, Stormie Banks thought, through an alcoholic haze. *But I'm one of them.* She giggled.

The giggling jostled her hand. One long, crimson fingernail knocked the crystal glass over, spilling ice cubes and alcohol onto the cement.

"Aw, shit," Stormie grumbled, swinging her legs off the chair. She stumbled toward the back door and tripped over Franklin, the Mastiff Travis had brought to their marriage five years before.

"Sorry, Frank," Stormie soothed. She patted the dog's head.

A tickling on her cheek alerted Stormie that the bandage from her latest facelift was dangling loose again. It simply wouldn't stay on the sutures behind her right ear. Stormie reached up to reaffix it. When the bandage continued to flap askew like the shutter of a haunted house, revealing the horrors that lay beneath, she ripped it off. She inhaled sharply as her nails grazed the still-tender flesh.

Stormie reached the French doors off the patio.

"Aw, shit," she mumbled again, rattling the handles violently up and down. She must have locked the doors by mistake.

With a weary sigh, she backed up a few feet to see if there was a light on upstairs. If so, Travis might still be awake.

A thin ribbon of light shone from the bathroom window.

"Travis," Stormie slurred. She aimed her breathy whisper toward the back of the house. "Travis, le' me in. Locked my ass out."

Receiving no response, she yelled, "Goddammit, Travis, open the fuckin' back door!"

Franklin barked once, as if to say, *Shush, you'll wake the whole neighborhood.* He looked a little embarrassed for his mistress.

"I know, baby," Stormie commiserated, kneeling down beside the dog. She slung one arm companionably around him. "I'm all fucked up tonight."

"TRAAAAAVIS," she bawled again. Franklin cringed away from the noise.

A side gate opened quietly on well-oiled hinges. A sleepy woman with disheveled brown hair stepped into the yard. She surveyed the scene. Spotting Stormie, she pulled her knee-length peach robe tighter about her and approached. She extended a hand to help her employer up off the ground.

"Stormie, Travis isn't home," she said. "He's in Tennessee at the Opry, remember?"

Stormie peered through puffy and bloodshot eyes at her housekeeper. Carolyn Hewitt and her husband lived in a small guest house at the rear of the sprawling property. “Really? When did he leave?” she asked, a confused furrow knitting her brow.

“Two days ago.” Carolyn hoisted Stormie off the ground. The discarded bandage clung to Stormie’s left heel.

Carolyn withdrew a leather cord from around her neck. On the end dangled a key, which she used to let them in. Franklin followed at their heels.

Carolyn guided Stormie by the elbow through the darkened house, maneuvering her around the throw rugs, and past the glass-fronted cabinet where Stormie’s awards for stage and film glimmered under soft light, at one point catching her as she skidded on the polished marble floor.

She stopped at the foot of the elegant, curved stairway off the main hallway. “Can you make it upstairs, or you want me to help you?”

Stormie looked doubtfully at the stairs as they doubled, then tripled before her bleary eyes. “Hmm… maybe you’d better come along for moral support, Carolyn. I’m not feeling so well.”

With the heavy sigh of a woman forced to embark on a distasteful task yet again, Carolyn looped an arm around Stormie’s waist. She helped her up the steps and deposited her on the big sleigh bed that dominated the master bedroom. With a groan of disgust, she plucked the bandage from Stormie’s foot.

As Carolyn was turning to leave, Stormie asked, “Hey, Carolyn, you aren’t sleeping with Travis, are you?”

“No, dear.” Carolyn turned off the light, saying softly, “Sweet dreams.” She glanced back briefly at the already comatose figure on the bed before descending the staircase and returning home.

Chapter 2

Fifty-four years earlier.

Stormie Banks was born Stella Burkowitz in Mishawaka, Indiana. She arrived in Hollywood on a Greyhound bus at the age of nineteen. She came seeking fame, fortune, and a new name. She was tall and willowy, with long, sinewy legs. Her most striking features were dark gray, oval eyes framed by thick, black lashes. She had golden blonde hair and a pure, radiant face.

Unfortunately for her, her face fell just short of beautiful by a nose that betrayed her ethnicity. She also had a chest flatter than a thirteen-year-old boy's.

Full of hope and promise, Stella went to rent a room from a cranky old woman in North Hollywood. The whole house smelled like Bengay and the woman looked like a mummy hauled through the streets of Mexico on Day of the Dead.

"I heard you had a place available," Stella held out fifty dollars. "I brought my deposit."

The landlady grabbed the money with the admonishment, "No boys, no booze, and no music."

Stella promptly found employment as a waitress at Art's Deli on Ventura Boulevard in Studio City—the hangout of television casting people, producers, and directors.

Stella then began to search for an agent. She met with dozens of rejections. She was told she was too Jewish, too flat-chested, had the wrong look, and needed head shots.

Undaunted, Stella sought a professional photographer to remedy the only thing on that annoying list that she could.

Head shots were expensive, so Stella slept with the photographer to pay for them. It wasn't so bad; she thought he was kind of cute.

Of course, the pictures didn't change the chest, the nose, or the look. Stella continued down the path of perpetual rejection, until finally, after she broke down in tears of frustration in her office, a woman agreed to represent her. The woman ran a talent agency from a seedy little office above a Mexican market in Harlem, but she would do.

After trying out for numerous commercials, Stella landed her first role in a thirty-second ad for a diaper delivery service. The star of the commercial was an eight-month-old baby who received twenty seconds more airtime than Stella. But the commercial earned Stella a Screen Actors Guild card and enough money to take care of the problematic nose, so she thought she was well on her way to stardom.

She slept with the photographer again for new pictures after the bandage came off, and left the seedy agent above the Mexican market for one slightly higher on the food chain in West L.A.

In the next two years, Stella was cast in only one part: a two-word walk-on in a soap opera.

Eventually, Stella moved into a new apartment, so she didn't have to live by the "no boys, booze, or music" rule. She didn't much care either way about booze or music, but boys were the only balm she had for her failed acting endeavors.

She quit her job at Art's Deli and took one at the Brown Derby.

After three years, when Stella was on the verge of giving up and going home to Indiana, she met a man named Roger. He took one look at her and observed that the key to opening the door in Hollywood was boobs. "All the beautiful starlets have them in great supply," he told her.

Not long after, Stella boldly approached Dr. Herbert Katz, the plastic surgeon who had done such a fine job on her nose. She embarrassed herself by offering to sleep with him in exchange for new breasts.

Happily married, and feeling sorry for the girl, Dr. Katz politely declined the trade, but agreed to let her pay out the procedure on a monthly basis.

Once she went from an A cup to a D, things changed. Unfortunately, Stella was still forced to trade sex for small and unmemorable roles, but at least she was getting some film credits under her belt—along with a minor sexually transmitted disease from the director of a low budget indy film.

Having struggled for three years in Hollywood, and suffering back problems from the heavy trays at the Brown Derby, Stella gritted her teeth and accepted whatever paltry bones were thrown her way… at whatever cost to her remaining dignity.

Stella's first big break came when she was offered a supporting role by ABC, in a dramatic movie of the week. This was a legitimate part in a movie, based on her screen test and not on her overlarge breasts or willingness to hit the casting couch. It was from this movie that she met her first husband, George Banks. He was the producer.

On their third date, as the filming was wrapping up, Stella told George she wanted a new stage name. He suggested the name Stormie, because her eyes looked like a raging storm, and Banks, because it was his last name. He proposed at the same time and they flew to Vegas that very night to make it legal.

It wasn't long after the marriage that Stormie Banks became a household name. Her marriage to the well-known producer, infamous playboy, and confirmed bachelor only boosted her notoriety. This was the first time of hundreds that Stormie found herself splashed all over the tabloids.

She proved to have talent, sex appeal, and chemistry with the men she costarred with. Maybe too much chemistry, because a few years later Stormie made headlines again when she divorced George Banks and married her costar in a major motion picture—a picture that secured Stormie her first of six Academy Awards.

Eighteen months after her second marriage, Stormie was in Rome shooting an epic drama for Warner Brothers. There, she met an Italian opera singer named Antonio. She divorced the actor to marry him. This third union lasted only six weeks. It ended during a heated argument in Barcelona, when Antonio suspended Stormie over an open hotel room window ten stories high, threatening to drop her onto the cobblestone path below.

In deep despair over the breakup of her short-lived third marriage, Stormie had a brief affair with a married stand-up comedian in Los Angeles. The affair resulted in pregnancy, threats from a jealous wife, and another year of front-page news. Nine months later, Stormie's only child was born. She named the baby girl Heather.

Tired of the publicity and of reporters jumping from behind every bush, and wanting to give Heather some stability, Stormie became a recluse.

In her thirties now, a little older and a little wiser, she discreetly settled into her fourth marriage. Marvin Gaines was a studio executive. He was considerably older, and had been a friend and confidant for many years. The thought of bringing up her daughter alone in Hollywood was frightening. Marvin was a kind and gentle man who loved her dearly. For Stormie, it was a marriage based on practicality and desperation much more than love.

It was a pleasant surprise when she discovered, within a year of the wedding, that she had fallen hopelessly in love with Marvin.

Stormie spent the next decade and a half raising her daughter and enjoying her marriage. She acted little, only choosing the choicest roles in the largest motion pictures. During those years, scripts arrived at her front door by the dozen. Famous screenwriters created roles specifically for Stormie, only to have her turn them down because she didn't like the film, or didn't want to take time away from her family. During those years, she disappointed many producers, directors, and screen writers. Hers was the most sought-after face in Hollywood, but Stormie reserved most of her time for her daughter and husband; her career came second.

Heather was seventeen and away at boarding school when Stormie found her husband lying in the circular driveway of their Beverly Hills home. He had died of a heart attack.

During all her years in Hollywood, where booze and drugs were both readily available and the numbing agent of choice for those in the fast lane, Stormie had avoided temptation. Her drug had first been men, later her career, finally her family.

After Marvin's funeral, she succumbed to the numbing bliss of alcohol in grand style. She didn't want to date and she didn't want to act. All she wanted to do was drink. She drank enough the first year Marvin was gone to make up for all the decades she'd worked clean and sober.

In Stormie's humble estimation, Marvin Gaines had walked on water. Fourteen years of living with his extraordinary kindness, respect, and love for both her and Heather had made the common man pale in comparison. Stormie eventually tried to date, but no one could fill Marvin's shoes—no matter how famous, how rich, or how handsome he might be.

Finding no solace in companionship, Stormie tried to throw herself back into her work. She was stunned to find that once she turned forty, she wasn't in the same demand. The roles were still offered, but more reluctantly, and they were different. Lower budget films, supporting parts instead of leading ones, and far less money than she had been making before.

Stormie revisited her old friend Dr. Katz for a tummy-tuck, a butt-lift, Botox injections, collagen treatments, and the first of many face-lifts, confident this would breathe life back into her flagging career.

Stormie sold the Beverly Hills house, because Marvin's ghost haunted every corner, and bought one in Hollywood Hills. Meanwhile, her drinking continued to escalate.

Her first stint in rehab came when she was found face-down in the pool of her new home.

Stormie snuck out of the facility after the fourth day and went on a bender. Intoxicated to the point of falling down, she knocked on a stranger's door and asked if she could borrow the family's car. The man of the house, star-struck enough to give Stormie his firstborn if she had asked for it, produced the keys to his five-year-old Chevy Lumina without argument.

He later sold his story to the *National Enquirer* for an undisclosed sum.

Stormie smashed the car into someone's garage a few blocks away and went back into the tabloid spotlight with a DUI conviction. She checked into the Betty Ford Center for a full thirty days.

Stormie's sobriety lasted for six months, until the unthinkable happened. She did a screen test and was turned down for a part. The director told her the pure and hellish truth was that there wasn't enough theatrical makeup in the Western Hemisphere to make her look thirty again.

Never since her first Academy Award had Stormie been turned down for anything. The pain and devastation was nearly tantamount to finding Marvin dead in the driveway.

The following morning after this most debilitating of all rejections, Stormie made an appointment with Dr. Katz again. He insisted there was no more surgery he could possibly perform to make her look any younger. Her file was seven inches thick and had its own drawer.

He told her, "Short of locating the fountain of youth, you are stuck with the face you have, Stella." He patted her shoulder, and added softly, "None of us stays young forever."

After the humiliation of losing a role to a younger, fresher actress, and after drying out again in another high-priced treatment center, Stormie launched herself into charity work. She joined foundations, recorded public-service announcements for the homeless, AIDS victims, and animal rights organizations. She made appearances, attended charity dinners—all in a vain attempt to find some meaning in her life.

It was during one such dinner that she first met country singer Travis Bullock. Travis was ten years her junior. He was on the downhill slope of an extremely successful twenty-year singing career that had begun in his teens, and had now dwindled down to recycling old songs on greatest hits CDs. There was also the occasional appearance at the Grand Ole Opry.

When they met, Travis was in the middle of a divorce from his first wife. He and Stormie were cordial. The chemistry didn't come until they ran into each other two years later, at a benefit for endangered species.

The couple dated only briefly before being married in a civil ceremony at the courthouse. Travis moved to Hollywood to be with his bride.

Travis had three children from his first marriage. Two hated Stormie instantly, and one—the one with no money and no job—found her and the twelve-million-dollar mansion tolerable.

Stormie married Travis for much the same reasons he married her. Both were lonely, and on the verge of being has-beens. They had a mutual respect for each other's station in life. And, most importantly, Travis made her laugh. Laughter had been in short supply since Marvin died.

Chapter 3

Stormie awoke with a hangover and a hungry dog licking her face.

"Franklin, quit it. You got worse breath than I do." She pushed the dog away and tried to sit up. The room spun. Nausea rolled through her stomach like a tsunami. With a groan, she lay back down. She fumbled open the drawer next to the bed and pulled out a half-empty bottle of Absolut Vodka.

Stormie tilted the bottle and took a healthy swig. She stifled a belch behind her hand and swung her legs over the side of the bed.

"Ah, much better. Nothing like a little hair of the dog that bit you."

Franklin hopped off the bed and ran to wait by the bedroom door, wagging his tail hopefully.

Stormie stumbled out of her bedroom, holding the vodka bottle to her forehead. She squeezed her eyes shut against the morning sunlight, and navigated her way down the stairs by touch and stubbed toe. Franklin pressed himself against her leg, herding her toward his bag of food.

Half on autopilot, Stormie scooped out dry kibbles for him and poured them more-or-less into his bowl. When Franklin kept looking at her and wagging his tail, she put down the vodka bottle and opened a can of smelly dog food that did nothing to improve her nausea. This she scooped in the general direction of the kibble.

She carried Franklin's water bowl to the sink. The splash of cold water on her hands helped Stormie pry her eyelids apart a little more. She gave Franklin his water and scratched behind his ears as he attacked his breakfast.

Stormie reached again for the vodka bottle, hesitated, and made herself coffee instead. She popped three aspirin and then settled herself at the counter to drink coffee and read a script.

The script had arrived yesterday by courier. So far, Stormie liked it.

It was a romantic comedy set in Manhattan. The female lead was a sassy advertising executive who fell in love with a garbage man. The character was light and funny, and Stormie was flattered the studio had sent it. It had been a long time since anyone had considered her for a role like this.

Stormie was studying the script when Travis arrived home with his brother in tow.

There was no love lost between Connor Bullock and Stormie. Many years before, when Travis announced his engagement, his brother, had asked, "Where the hell did you find her? The clearance rack in hell?"

"Connor," Stormie spat upon seeing him. "If you're here, who's running Hell?"

He smirked at his sister-in-law. "Donald Trump, of course. You just surprised to see me, Stormie, or didja go and get your eyes lifted again?"

Stormie elbowed past him outside and went to her husband's side. Travis finished paying the limo driver and claimed his suitcase from the trunk.

He kissed her cheek. "Hey, sweet thing. I missed you."

"Why didn't you tell me you were coming home today? I could have picked you up from the airport."

The annoyed frown that crossed Travis's normally pleasant face lingered for only a moment. "I did, hon. I left you the itinerary on the fridge and I called last night and left the flight info on the answering machine. Where were you?"

Stormie averted her eyes. "I must have been in the shower or something. Didn't check the machine."

Travis didn't reply. He was accustomed to his wife's drinking binges, and knew they got worse when he wasn't home to monitor her.

"So, how was Nashville?" Stormie asked, anxious to change the subject.

"Hot. But the shows went well and we raised a lot of money for the homeless."

Franklin, hearing his master's voice, came bounding around the corner, paws slipping on the waxed tile flooring.

Travis bent down to greet him. Stormie and Connor took the opportunity to glare at each other across the foyer.

"What's he doing here?" Stormie asked coldly, nodding at Connor's scowling face.

The annoyed frown stayed a little longer this time, as Travis replied, "I told you Connor was coming to visit for a few days. We're looking at a restaurant in L.A. we might buy."

"You mean a titty bar? Or do they call those restaurants in the South?" Stormie snapped sarcastically.

Travis sighed and didn't answer.

"I got a script from Warner's yesterday," Stormie said hastily, wanting to smooth over the bumpy start. "I like it,"

"Yeah? Is it the part of Chucky in *Child's Play XV*, or whatever the hell number they're up to?" Connor drawled, lighting a cigarette. "You'd be just about perfect for that one, Storm."

"Connor Bullock, you light that thing in my house and I am going to put it out on your left testicle. Now why don't you run along outside with Franklin, and let me talk to my husband?" She shot a look of pure loathing at him.

Connor opened his mouth to retort, and then promptly slammed it shut as Travis looked at him sharply and shook his head. You didn't want to cross Travis when it came to Stormie.

Connor had learned that lesson the hard way on Christmas two years before.

After Connor had voiced some insulting and thoughtless remark regarding Stormie's numerous plastic surgeries, Travis had propelled him out the front door and down the steps. He crashed on his ass. Seconds later, an upstairs window was thrown open and his half-zipped suitcase tossed out. A wayward pair of boxer shorts floated down, parachute-like, and landed on the grass a few feet away.

Travis thrust his face out the window into the crisp December wind. His voice was eerily calm. "You don't ever insult my wife or use that kind of language in front of my stepdaughter again, or you can forget you got a brother anymore, Connor. Don't plan on setting foot in my house again until you have apologized proper to both of them for your disgusting behavior."

Connor held up his hands. "Whoa, Travis, man, hold up a second there, I was just…"

That's as far as he'd got before Travis cut him off with, "Now, I am going to go downstairs and press that little button that activates the gate at the edge of the driveway. I am going to leave it open for thirty seconds, so I suggest you start running or you can sleep on the grass tonight. I am gonna call you a cab; you can meet it at the corner. Merry Christmas, Connor."

The window then slammed shut. A few seconds later Connor heard the electric whine of the big wrought iron gate purr to life. He rose from the damp cement, scooped up his wayward boxers and zipped his suitcase. He jogged down the long driveway—his luggage banging against his leg. The gate was already trundling shut by the time he reached it. He squeezed through bare seconds before it clanged home with a bang.

Connor's suitcase remained trapped between the gate and the metal post. He pulled with all his might, but the valise would not budge.

With a sigh of resignation, Connor looked up into the security camera mounted to the post and pressed the intercom button directly below it. The security light winked on and Connor pointed to the suitcase. The camera, mounted on a gooseneck, swung around in the direction Connor indicated and fixed on the gate. The whir of the electric motor whined briefly to life. The gate slid back just far enough to release the suitcase and then slammed shut again with utter finality, the light in the security camera going dark.

The brothers hadn't spoken for two months. It took Connor that long to realize his brother was serious, and to swallow his pride enough to *apologize proper,* as Travis had put it, to Stormie and Heather. Connor learned his lesson about insulting the lady of the manor.

Now, with an offended sniff, Connor turned on his heel and walked out the back door.

"So tell me about the script, darlin'." Travis opened the refrigerator to retrieve a can of beer.

"It's a romantic comedy set in New York. I really like it!" She couldn't hide the enthusiasm from her voice. "I haven't done anything like it in such a long time."

Travis smiled. "Honey, that's great. What's it about?"

"It's hilarious! It's about a high-powered advertising executive in Manhattan who falls in love with a garbage man. She convinces him to pretend he's a doctor when he meets her family."

Travis's laugh held a false note that Stormie missed. "Hmm… Is that right? So what's the character's name?"

"Ashley Evans. How yuppie is that?" Stormie laughed.

"Well, hon, it's good to hear you so excited about a project. It's been too long since anything's made you smile."

Stormie grinned and latched herself onto his arm, resting her chin on his shoulder. "Will you come with me to New York for filming?"

"Guess that depends on if we buy us that restaurant," Travis answered gently. "When do they start shooting?"

"In about two months."

"Well, we'll see then," Travis looked at Stormie with troubled eyes.

"What?"

"You want me to go 'cause you're afraid your drinking's gonna screw you up if I'm not there, right?"

"No," she replied softly, hurt flashing in her eyes. "I want you to go because I like when you're with me, and I would miss you."

"I wish I knew when you was actin' and when you was tellin' the truth," he sighed. He shook her off, turned on his heel, and went to join his brother.

Stormie closed her eyes and rummaged in the cabinet for some more aspirin. She hated it when Travis was unhappy with her.

Once she gulped down the aspirin and began to feel a little better, she peeked her head out the back door. "Hey, hon? Will you run lines with me? I have to read a scene with an actor they're testing for the male lead."

Travis rose from the chaise lounge and stretched his long legs. "Sure, baby. I'd like to see the script."

Connor rose from the adjacent chair. "Guess I'll go on upstairs and take a shower. Wash the road dust off."

With a supreme effort at civility, Stormie offered, "I'll make you boys a good dinner tonight when I get home from the studio."

Stormie didn't like to cook. She only did it on rare occasions. Usually when she had angered Travis and wanted to make amends.

Touched, Travis chuckled. "Darlin, ain't you sweet. I always said if Victoria's Secret and Betty Crocker had an affair, you'd be their love-child."

Connor snorted. "Really? I always thought of her more as Goldie Hawn meets Godzilla."

Before Travis could say anything, Connor disappeared up the staircase and into the safety of the guestroom. Sometimes, he just couldn't resist.

~~~~

After Stormie left for the studio, Travis shook his head in disgust. He didn't like it, and he couldn't understand why in the world they wanted Stormie for the lead. He was pretty sure the only reason she was so excited about the script was because the lead character was clearly a very young woman.
~~~~

Young and stupid, in Travis's humble opinion. There was a time when Stormie would have thrown such a ridiculous piece of fluff in the garbage without a second glance—but that was before she became obsessed with aging. The studio asking her to star in this low-budget piece of crap was validation that she retained the kiss of youth.

Travis glanced at the inlaid oak display cabinet mounted on the back wall of the living room. Stormie's Oscars were on the top shelf. Next to each one was a three-by-five silver Tiffany frame engraved with the date and the name of the winning film. Each frame held an embossed card with Stormie's name in elegant, scrolled letters. These had been taken from the envelopes when the winner was announced. The second shelf held Stormie's Golden Globes, and the bottom shelf her People's Choice Awards.

Travis's wife was a Hollywood legend. She had starred in extraordinary films, many that would remain classics for decades. Why, he wondered, would she want to embarrass herself by starring in a poorly written, low-budget movie with shallow and unremarkable characters?

The obvious answer made his chest constrict. Anything to prove she wasn't getting older. He could just imagine what the critics would do to her with this one.

Stormie had visited Dr. Katz so many times in the last three years that she resembled a living waxwork. The backs of her ears were a landscape of scars from countless facelifts. Her public appearances were rare these days, and Travis was glad for it; every time she stepped out of the shadows launched a new media barrage.

Last year, Stormie had guest starred on ER. For the following two weeks she proved a rich source of material for every late-night talk show host's monologue on network TV. Comparisons between her and Michael Jackson were not uncommon. The transformations in the celebrities' looks were equally disquieting.

Travis wished Stormie could find a way to be comfortable with who she was. She worked out with a personal trainer four times a week. Her body was probably in better shape than most women half her age. Travis thought his wife was a lovely woman, beautiful in fact—at least she had been before the last few times she'd gone beneath the plastic surgeon's blade. She was fifty-four years old and easily looked ten years younger. But she wasn't twenty-five anymore… and for the life of him, Travis couldn't understand why she wanted to be.

~~~~

The lobby of casting director Glenda Michael's office was eerily quiet and tense. Stormie sat on one end of the room pretending to study a script. Hollywood newcomer, Kyra Hastings, sat on the other.

Kyra won an Academy Award for best supporting actress in the first motion picture she had ever been cast in. At twenty-three, she was fast becoming a valuable commodity in Hollywood. She was easy to work with, talented, and had not yet been around long enough to become demanding and temperamental. Like Stormie, she was tall and blonde with classic good looks. But unlike Stormie, she possessed a perfect little Patrician nose that had never been acquainted with a surgeon's knife. The press had taken to calling Kyra *The Next Stormie Banks.*

The tension between the two women was palpable. Stormie's jealousy wafted across the room like a draft.

When Stormie first read Kyra's nickname, she had fumed to Travis. "What the hell do they mean *the next one?* What exactly is
~~~~

wrong with the current Stormie Banks? They don't need another me. I am still perfectly capable of learning my lines and dressing myself."

"Honey, it's a compliment," Travis had soothed.

"Compliment my ass. They're insinuating that I am over the hill. They're looking for my replacement."

Travis wisely didn't respond.

Glenda's assistant poked her head out a half open door. "Stormie, come on in; we're ready for you."

With a final baleful glare in Kyra's direction, she rose and walked into the office.

The producer, director, three casting people, and the potential leading man were all seated around the room in overstuffed chairs and a leather sofa.

Glenda smiled at Stormie. "I guess you know almost everyone, except Scott Rutherford." she gestured toward the good-looking young actor.

He rose and took Stormie's hand, "It's a pleasure, Stormie, I'm a huge fan."

She smiled warmly and they took their places in front of the video camera that had been set up for Scott Rutherford's screen test.

"Okay, we are going to start reading from page twenty-two where Sophie's line begins 'Carl, we need to talk.' Do you see that, Stormie?"

Stormie flipped her script to the page and ran a finger down until she came to the line in question.

Sophie was the role of the lead character's mother. This scene was between her and Carl, her daughter's trash-collecting boyfriend.

Stormie looked at the script. A puzzled frown crossed her taut features. "Glenda, I'm confused. Ashley isn't in this scene, so why are you having me read from it?"

Glenda raised her eyebrows as an uncomfortable hush fell over the room. The others all found something interesting to study on their feet.

Glenda, looking around for support and finding none, answered in a soft, comforting tone. "Well, sweetie, your role is Sophie, of course, not Ashley. Now, if we can just start..."

A flush bloomed in Stormie's cheeks. "Glenda, what the hell are you saying?" she gritted her teeth against barely controlled rage.

"Umm... Stormie, I thought you read the script," Glenda faltered. She fiddled with her own script, her eyes flickering to it when she couldn't bear to keep eye contact any longer.

Glenda cleared her throat. "Ashley is a girl in her twenties. We cast Kyra Hastings for the role. She is going to read a scene with Scott when you are done; that's why she's here. I thought you understood we wanted you for the role of Sophie, her mother."

Stormie exploded like a firecracker in the midnight sky. "Her mother? I am supposed to play a grown woman's mother?" she screeched in a banshee's voice.

Throats began clearing as an embarrassed tension flooded the room.

"Umm, Stormie, dear, you *are* a grown woman's mother. Isn't your daughter Heather at Harvard now?"

Stormie rose abruptly from the chair and threw the script across the room. It hit Glenda Michaels square in the face with an audible smack.

Glenda recoiled. A second later, she shot up from her chair, furious. "Oh, for the love of God, Stormie," she snarled, "you can't be serious! How the hell could you have possibly thought we were casting you as Ashley?"

Scott Rutherford scooted his chair back from the table, wedging himself halfway behind a potted plant. The fronds trembled as he lowered them to hide his face.

Stormie stood trembling. Tears spilled down her tight cheeks, cutting lines into her makeup. "Who do you people think you are? I am not old enough to be that slut's mother. Do you hear me? The world doesn't need the next Stormie Banks when I am still right here!" she roared.

No one said anything. When they all just looked at her with a mixture of pity and disgust, Stormie fled from the office. Vision blurred by tears, she collided with a table and sent it crashing end over end. She swore and kicked it, then bolted for the elevators.

Chapter 4

Stormie didn't know what time it was. She had passed out after drinking a bottle and a half of Absolut straight from the bottle. She was slumped in the front seat of her car, on a dead-end residential street. Angry, gray clouds drew together overhead. The air was thick and damp, signaling a brewing storm. The grisly afternoon replayed itself in Stormie's mind. Her head was pounding more from embarrassment and shame, than vodka. When she'd left Glenda Michael's office, Stormie drove directly to Dr. Katz and berated his secretary in front of a room full of patients. The poor secretary finally broke down and pulled the doctor out of his current appointment.

Dr. Katz sat across his desk, exasperated, shaking his head.

Stormie held up a small mirror and ran her finger underneath her eye. "See, Herb, just a little right here? If you could just—"

The doctor cut her off. "I told you, no! Absolutely not, Stella! Not one more procedure. No!"

"But, Herb," she cried, "if you could just make these little lines here..."

"Dammit, Stella! I said no. Listen to me. You have a sickness. I looked this up the last time you came in here insisting on another completely unnecessary procedure—one that, against my better judgment, I performed."

"What are you talking about? What sickness?"

Dr. Katz reached behind him and pulled a thick hardback book from a shelf behind his desk and began rapidly flipping pages. Finding the passage he wanted, he turned the book toward Stormie.

"Read this, right here," he cried, jabbing his finger savagely halfway down the page.

With apprehensive eyes Stormie began reading.

> Body Dysmorphic Disorder (BDD) / Dysmorphophobia This disorder has also been nicknamed "Imagined Ugliness Syndrome." Sufferers of BDD have an irrational preoccupation with a perceived body defect, either present in themselves or in others—the latter being dysmorphophobia-by-proxy. BDD sufferers cannot accept that their fears of their perceived body defect are out of all proportion, and frequently seek plastic surgery and/or other measures in an attempt to rectify the perceived problem.

Stormie slammed the book shut and slid it back across the desk, shaking was with rage. "Tell me something, Herb. Is it my imagination that I am not a young girl anymore? Is it my imagination that I don't look like I did when I first came into your office with a bigger nose than tits? Am I dreaming that?"

"Why do you think you should look twenty years old, Stella? You aren't, and no miracle of modern medicine can make you. For a woman of your age, you are remarkably well preserved, and God knows you have spent enough money on that body of yours that you ought to be. But for chrissakes, you don't want me, you want the fountain of youth! I suggest you take your money and use it to invest in a good psychiatrist, because I really can't help you anymore, Stella. Now if you will excuse me, I have patients waiting." With that, Dr. Katz stalked from the room and slammed the door.

Shaken and crying, Stormie stared after him in disbelief.

She left Dr. Katz's office and drove blindly to the nearest liquor store. It bore the charming name *Liquor to Go-go.* Tears streamed down her face as she pulled into the parking lot.

She never noticed the tabloid photographer lurking behind the bush. His eyes lit up when he saw her. He immediately lifted his camera and snapped a picture of Stormie emerging from the liquor store, cracking the first bottle open before she was even back in the car. That picture would be all over the tabloids in twenty-four hours.

Stormie drove down a quiet, tree-lined residential street and parked her Mercedes GL450. She drank until she passed out.

Two empty bottles lay on the seat beside her. The third, half full, tipped over in her lap and soaked vodka through her pants.

The sun was setting. The last of the day's light bled from the sky as Stormie hunted around for the vodka's cap. When she couldn't find it, she opened the window and poured the remaining contents into the street.

As vodka splashed onto the curb, a girl approached the car.

"Excuse me," the girl said shyly, "may I have your autograph? I've seen all of your movies and I just love you, Miss Banks." The girl didn't seem to find it strange that a superstar was parked at the dead-end of a middle-class neighborhood, pouring booze onto the road.

Stormie looked at the girl through bloodshot, swollen eyes. "Sure, honey. You got something to write on?"

The girl handed her a scrap of paper and a pencil.

"What's your name?" Stormie asked.

"Melissa."

Stormie scribbled something on the paper and handed it back. "Here you go, Melissa."

"Thank you, Miss Banks." As the girl turned to leave, she dropped a white business card in the window. It landed on Stormie's lap.

"Hey, you dropped this," Stormie called after the girl, plucking the card from her drenched pants. Stormie blinked and looked around the deserted street, where just a moment ago the girl had been standing.

"What the hell?" she whispered to herself. She glanced at the business card. She rubbed her eyes, trying to make her hazy vision focus on the small print.

Bella Luna Bookstore and Metaphysical Shop
Seattle, WA

She turned it over. Written on the back in neat block lettering were the words,

Miss Banks,

I saw you parked there for hours. I know something is wrong. Call this store and ask for Belda. She can fix anything. I promise.

Your greatest fan,
Melissa

Stormie barked a rueful laugh. "Thanks, Melissa, that's just what I need now; a psychic."

Adopting a falsetto voice, she said in a quavering tone, "Ooh, Stormie, I do not predict much frontal nudity required in your future contracts."

Stormie tossed the card onto the seat beside her and yanked down the visor. Looking into the mirror, she grimaced. Her eyes were swollen, red, and caked with dried mascara. Tear tracks cut through her makeup in harsh streaks.

"Oh God, thank you for not letting my greatest fan have a camera with her," she sighed wearily. She tugged her handbag onto her lap and searched for her makeup. Using the visor mirror, she fixed her makeup as best she could.

Once satisfied, Stormie put the Mercedes in gear and pulled away from the curb.

~~~~

When Stormie returned home the house stood empty. There was a note on the counter from Travis advising her that he and Connor had waited for her until after seven. They had gotten too hungry and decided to go have dinner at Mr. Cecil's on Pico.

Stormie was glad to be alone. She wasn't ready to see Travis yet—and even on a good day, she was never much prepared to do battle with Connor. She took three aspirin from the cabinet and washed them down with vodka.

Stormie poured another drink and took it into the backyard. Travis had moved the patio furniture into the garage in anticipation of the coming storm, so Stormie lay down on the grass and allowed the rain to soak her. Her clothes reeked of vodka. She felt
~~~~

like only the rain could cleanse this miserable day from her worn-out body.

Franklin sat inside the open doorway, looking at his mistress curiously. She passed in and out of consciousness for the next two hours. She heard the phone ringing inside the house, but felt too spent to get up and answer it.

Travis and Conner arrived home to find her still on the grass, unconscious, her clothes drenched and her body shivering. Travis lifted her from the sodden ground and carried her inside. "Connor, go fetch some towels from the downstairs toilet," he ordered.

"Shit, Travis, what's she done now?" Connor shifted nervously from foot to foot. He thought his sister-in-law looked dead.

"Just go get some towels. And for once, keep your trap shut. I mean it," Travis growled. He brushed Stormie's wet hair from her face. "Baby, can you hear me?"

She moaned something unintelligible, but didn't open her eyes. As Travis laid her gently on the couch, Connor returned with the towels from the powder room. Travis grabbed one and wiped his wife's damp face, while Connor threw another over her trembling body like a blanket. Travis slapped Stormie's face gently a few times, trying to rouse her.

"Stormie? Honey, wake up."

A deep, guttural groan escaped from between Stormie's chattering teeth.

"I think she's gonna be sick," Travis said. "Go get a waste-basket, Connor."

"Travis, what…"

"Now!" he yelled, lifting Stormie to a sitting position.

Connor returned with the basket. Travis leaned his wife's head forward and put the wastebasket between her knees.

As Stormie began retching, he called to his brother, "Go upstairs. Let me deal with this."

Connor turned on his heel and began ascending the stairs. "Come on, Franklin," he said. "This ain't no place for children."

Apparently agreeing with that assessment, the dog followed him.

When Stormie finished heaving and spitting the foul taste into the steaming trashcan, Travis handed her a can of ginger ale, then went upstairs for her terrycloth bathrobe and thick socks.

"So, what the hell happened?" he asked, struggling to keep the anger from his voice. He helped her peel off her wet clothing. Her fingers were too stiff and numb to do much good, and he ended up batting them away and finishing the job himself. Then he wrapped her in the bathrobe and pulled the socks onto her feet.

"What do you mean? I just had a few drinks, that's all. Guess I overdid it."

"Don't bullshit me. I come home, find you passed out in the rain—all after you go to the studio about the first part you have wanted in years. And you tell me that's it? You just drank too much? What kind of an idiot do you think I am? Now tell me what the fuck happened to set you off."

Stormie sighed heavily. She set her soda down and curled her feet beneath her before looking at Travis. Tears brimmed over her lashes.

"I had it wrong," she was fighting to keep her voice steady. "They didn't want me to play Ashley. They wanted me for the part of her mother, Sophie. I misunderstood when they sent over the script. They just assumed I would know which role I was being offered, so they didn't specify."

Travis exhaled a loud breath, his irritation replaced by concern over his wife's embarrassment. "Oh shit. I'm sorry, honey. So what happened?"

"Before or after I threw the script in Glenda Michael's face?"

Travis winced. "You didn't?"

"Yeah, I did. And if memory serves me, I think I knocked over a table in the lobby during my grand exit and hit Kyra Hastings's foot with it." A cheerless smile played at the corners of her lips as she remembered the absurdity of it all.

"So where did you go? Not to a bar, I hope? More tabloid fodder."

"No, of course not. *Liquor to Go-go* on Hollywood Boulevard."

Travis frowned. "Then where?"

"Just drove until I found a quiet street, parked at the end of it, and drank until I passed out. Some girl came up to the window and asked for my autograph when I woke up." Tears spilled from her eyes again. "Gosh, Travis, don't I just make you so proud of me sometimes?"

He pulled her into his arms. "I'm always proud of you, Stormie. Just wish you'd do your hysterical drinking at home, that's all."

"Well, I did the rest of it at home. I was in the backyard drowning, but I was home."

"Inside with the doors locked next time, okay?"

"You aren't mad at me?"

Travis shook his head. "No. I'm just sorry you got embarrassed like that. And I wish you had the sense not to drive when you're all liquored-up. I thought that script was the worst thing I'd ever seen, by the way."

"Oh, I forgot the best part," Stormie said.

"There's more?" Travis's lips drew down in a worried frown.

"I went to Katz's office and made a scene in the waiting room until his secretary schlepped him out of an examine room to talk to me."

Travis's eyes narrowed. "Oh lord, Stormie. What now? What the hell are you doing to yourself this time? Hell, the incision ain't even healed over from the last thing you did."

"Not to worry, dear. I'm not doing anything. Katz won't touch me anymore. He whipped out some medical dictionary and told me that I have some sort of syndrome or something."

"Syndrome?"

"Yeah, Body Dysmorph something or other. A fancy name for low self-esteem. Can you imagine? Me with low self-esteem. I don't know about you, but I find that very amusing. At least I will when I get over this hangover. Anyway, Katz says I need to see a shrink."

"I'm glad he said he won't perform anymore surgeries. Christ, Stormie, what are you trying to do to yourself? This insanity has to stop. I think he's right, maybe you ought to go talk to someone."

She pulled away from him violently. "Don't you understand, Travis?" she yelled. "I am all washed up. Finished! I can play the new Stormie Banks mother, or I can do fuckin' guest spots on sitcoms, but that's it. My star has officially fallen. I'm just a drunk joke in Hollywood now. No one wants to see an aging fifty-year-old bag doing any love scenes on the big screen these days."

Travis sighed, exasperated. "Stormie, you are a beautiful woman. In fact, I think you'd be even more beautiful if you stopped messin' with your looks all the time. You have a beautiful body, a beautiful face, and a cabinet full of Academy Awards. You've got a star on Hollywood Boulevard, more money than you could ever spend in a lifetime, and a beautiful daughter who's on the dean's list at Harvard. Not to mention a husband that loves you. Why ain't that enough? It's more than most people find in a lifetime. So tell me why the hell it ain't enough for you?"

She gave a scornful laugh. "Right, Travis. And when you see some gorgeous young thing walk by with smooth skin and a tight little ass wiggling in your direction—like that bimbo Kyra Hastings, for instance—you tell me that doesn't turn you on? Big news, fella, I don't have a twenty-year-old ass anymore."

Travis looked at her with a mixture of pity and wonderment. "You think I want a twenty-year-old ass?"

"Don't you? Doesn't every man?"

"If I wanted a twenty-year-old ass, I would have married a twenty year old, Stormie. I don't know what to say to you anymore. I don't think anyone can help you. If I find the portrait of Dorian Gray at a yard sale, I'll be sure and pick it up for you. Short of that, you are stuck growing older, just like the rest of us, so you'd better figure out a way to live with it. Do you know what the press would do to you if they got a hold of today's stunt? It would be breaking out of rehab and driving that guy's car into someone's garage all over again. You don't need that kind of publicity. And frankly, neither do I."

Chapter 5

Travis grabbed the ringing telephone just as the answering machine clicked on.

"Hello? Hello?" he said over the beep of the machine.

"Travis, is that you?" Heather's voice crackled with static over the long-distance line.

"Heather? Hey, sweet girl, how yah doin'?"

"I think we have a bad connection, Travis. I'm on my cell phone and I can barely hear you. Is Mom okay?"

"Well, she had a tough week, sugar, but I think she'll be alright once the dust settles."

"I saw the picture of her walking out the liquor store," Heather fumed. "It was all over the magazines. I wish those vultures would leave her alone already."

"Oh, Heather, she don't want to be left alone. Once a drama queen, always a drama queen. You know your momma."

"Yeah," she sighed. "I do."

"So what about you? How are things at Harvard?"

Heather laughed. "Would you believe me if I told you I was in love?"

"In love? Well, darlin', that's wonderful. Who's the guy and how big is he? I need to know in case he does you wrong and I gotta whoop his ass."

Heather giggled. "He's a fourth year student here. And please, Travis, don't open up any cans of whoop-ass just yet."

Travis laughed. "Okay, honey, but if he ever makes you cry, I'm on the first plane out there."

"I know, big guy. You're my hero." She rolled her eyes theatrically. "Is Mom home?"

"No, but you can probably reach her on her cell phone."

"As bad as our connection is, I don't think I want to try it. Can you tell her I will be home two days before Thanksgiving?"

"Sure. Do you need us to pick you up from the airport?"

"No, we'll rent a car."

"We? You bringin' your fella with you?"

"Yeah," she said hesitantly. "Is that okay? I really want you and Mom to meet him."

"Honey, it's fine. We're happy to have him. I'll let your momma know."

Inside, Travis worried about Heather's new boyfriend meeting Stormie now, on the heels of her latest catastrophe. *Well,* he figured, *what better test of true love than meeting the infamous Stormie Banks?*

"How did you meet him? In class?" Travis asked, raising his voice over the line's increasing static.

"No, not in class. It's a long story. I'll tell you all about it when I get there. I think I'm losing you, Travis. I'm driving in the trees."

"Okay, darlin'. We'll see you the twenty-second. Love you."

"Love you too, Travis, and tell Mom I love—"

And the line went dead.

As Travis replaced the receiver he bent and patted Franklin on the head. "Don't worry, she woulda sent her love to you too, if we hadn't gotten disconnected."

He tried to reach Stormie on her cell phone. Hearing about Heather's visit was sure to cheer her up.

~~~~

Stormie tried. She really tried. She even made an appointment with a psychiatrist. The therapist spent the hour reciting all of her favorite lines from Stormie's old movies. She asked for Stormie's autograph at the end of the session.

After that bitter encounter, Stormie sat in her car trying to fight the urge to drink. A thin sweat broke out on her forehead. Her heart pounded wildly in her chest.

The fountain of youth and a portrait of Dorian Gray; those are what Katz and Travis think I need. *Old!* she thought sullenly. *They think I'm old, dammit, and they are right!* She pounded her hands on the steering wheel in frustration.

"What if I'm not ready to be old? What if I'm not ready to be put out to pasture?" she screamed to the passing cars. "What if I'm not ready to play the part of the fucking mother? What if I'm not? What then? Do I retire? Do I take the fucking guest spots on primetime and be grateful when they run one of my old movies on cable? Is that what I am supposed to do? Well I won't!" She slammed the steering wheel again, her vision filling with blood. "They can't just get rid of me like an old plow horse! They can't treat me like that. I can still act! And I am still damn good at it!"

She drummed her hands on the steering wheel until they were red and throbbing. Finally, she pulled herself together enough to
~~~~

drive home. Travis had told her she couldn't do her hysterical drinking on the road anymore, so she would get home before obliterating the pain. She'd go home and do her drinking inside. With the doors locked, just like her husband wanted.

As Stormie wound through the familiar streets, her cell phone jangled. As she reached for it, her hand brushed the business card the young fan had dropped in her lap.

Stormie let the phone ring and picked up the card to examine it. She read the message again.

"So this Belda can fix anything, can she?" Stormie laughed as she guided the Mercedes home. "Anything? Well, let's see about that."

She grabbed her cell phone and punched in the number on the card.

A male voice answered. "Bella Luna, Nicholas speaking."

"I'd like to speak to Belda please," Stormie replied. She was suddenly sure that the man on the other end was going to say, *I'm sorry there is no one here by that name.* Instead, he said, "She's with a client right now. Can I take a message?"

"Let me ask you something, Nicholas."

His voice grew wary, "What's that?"

"Can she make me a star again?"

There was a pause as the man considered her question. Stormie was stunned into silence when he responded cautiously, "Yes, ma'am, she probably can."

Stormie hung up the phone and tossed it onto the seat beside her as though it were suddenly too hot to hold. She pulled into her driveway and headed inside for a drink.

Chapter 6

Travis was folding clothes and packing them neatly into a suitcase laid out on the bed. "Babe, I really wish you'd come with me," he said.

Stormie lay stretched out on the big bed, watching him pack. "No, I need to get things ready for Heather's visit. So, what else did she say about this new boyfriend of hers?"

"Not much. Just that he's a fourth year law student at Harvard. I guess she'll fill us in on the details when she gets here."

"Must be serious if she's bringing him home."

Travis stopped packing and turned to his wife. "Now, you better behave when they get here, Stormie. I got the impression she's really sweet on this boy."

"What's that supposed to mean? You think I'm going to make a scene?"

Travis took her hand and kissed it. "Wouldn't be the first time, honey. Remember when she brought home that rock musician?"

"Oh Christ, Travis! He made a bigger scene than I did!" she laughed.

"Yeah. He pulled me aside and asked me, man to man, how much I thought he could get for your panties on eBay. Wanted to know if it would be enough to buy a new amp."

"So there. I reserve the right to make a scene if this guy wants to hock my delicates on the internet. Fair enough?"

"I suppose," he laughed, "But maybe we'll like this one."

"Let's hope so. When will you be home?"

"The day before Heather arrives. And, honey, Connor and Cal are coming for the holiday."

"And I'm not supposed to drink? What, are you crazy?"

Travis smiled. "I thought you liked my son."

"I do. It's Connor I can't stand."

"Seriously, you gonna be okay with me away this week? I know that whole thing with Glenda Michaels and the tabloid picture shook you up."

Stormie shrugged. "Wasn't the first Kodak moment of me splashed all over the news. Probably won't be the last."

"Well, I'll keep the cell phone with me during the day, and call you to check in every evening before I hit the stage."

"What's the charity du jour this week, the homeless? Wild Kingdom?"

"This one's for the inner-city kids."

"Travis, I married a saint. We are a match made in heaven, the sinner and the saint."

He looked at her levelly. "Honey, are you sure you're okay? I can cancel if…"

Stormie cut him off. "Quit worrying about me, Travis. You act like I never saw my face on the front of the *National Enquirer* before. I'm fine. I'll keep myself busy getting ready for Heather's visit. I'll shop, get my nails done, and plan the Thanksgiving day feast with Carolyn. All nice and therapeutic."

Travis sighed. "Okay, hon." But his eyes betrayed his worry.

Travis loaded his valise into the back of the Mercedes and climbed into the driver's side. As he waited for Stormie to lock the front door, he spotted the white business card on the passenger seat. Curious, he picked it up. His eyes flashed with disquiet as he thought about a desperate and drunk Stormie calling some psychic hotline in Seattle and being rooked into spending thousands of dollars.

Travis pulled out his wallet and tucked the card into one of the small plastic windows. The other windows held pictures of his kids and a clipping from the *Hollywood Reporter* about the day he and Stormie were married. The article included a cheesy picture of the smiling couple, who were cutting the cake at their reception.

~~~~

When Stormie returned to the empty, too quiet house after dropping Travis off at the airport, the message light was blinking on the answering machine. Sarah Stewart, an old friend and fellow actress of the same vintage as Stormie, had called to say hello. She and Stormie had starred together in a film back in the early 1980s. They had remained close friends ever since.

The only time their friendship had nearly been ripped asunder was when Stormie bought her Hollywood Hills mansion. Sarah and her husband had put in an offer on the same house. When Stormie found out from the realtor that her friend had also made an offer, she substantially raised her own bid to insure that it would be accepted. When Sarah found out, she was furious. The rift between the two women took over two years to repair.

Stormie took the cordless telephone into the backyard and sat under the covered patio, watching light rain patter softly into lush foliage. She called Sarah and they spoke about their husbands and
~~~~

children. The conversation drifted toward what roles they were currently working and what ones they were considering.

Sarah's present gig was a recurring role on a sitcom as the mother-in-law.

Stormie laughed out loud, "Oh Christ, Sarah, the mother-in-law? That's worse than the mother. How long are you going to keep that up?"

Sarah laughed with her, not in the least bit offended. "Probably awhile, since no one's asked me to guest-star on Baywatch lately. Hell, the cameraman would need to back halfway out of the room in order to get my jiggling boobs in the same shot as my face. Damn things are down around my waist now."

"You know Herb Katz could take care of that in a single afternoon?" Stormie commented.

Sarah was the same age as Stormie, but she had never succumbed to the pressures of Hollywood, and retained all her original parts. She embraced her fifties with a calm serenity that Stormie envied. Sarah's world these days was entirely centered around her family. Her first grandchild had just turned two, and his presence in the universe made Hollywood and its demands nonexistent to Sarah.

Sarah answered, "Naw, I think I'll leave 'em where they are. If I moved them, I'd be afraid Rob wouldn't know where to find them anymore."

Finally, the conversation turned toward what happened to Stormie in Glenda Michael's office.

"I really don't blame you for hurling the script at the bitch, Stormie," Sarah commiserated. "What a slap in the face to be offered the role of the little twit's mother. I mean, especially after she just got the starring role in the remake of *Golden Sunset*."

Stormie froze. The color drained from her face. *Golden Sunset* was the film she had won her second Academy Award for, and her most critically acclaimed role.

"What remake?" Stormie gasped.

"Oh my God! You mean you haven't heard?"

"What remake?" Stormie screamed.

"MGM is doing a remake of *Golden Sunset.* They hired Kyra Hastings to recreate your role as Desiree."

Stormie felt like the air was knocked from her lungs. Her hands balled into fists and she forced herself to unclench them.

"When the hell did this happen?" Her voice was tight with barely controlled fury. She was angry enough to burst into flames.

"It was all over the industry two weeks ago. I thought for sure you heard. When Rob told me, I nearly picked up the phone and called you, but I figured you wouldn't want to talk about it," Sarah said sympathetically.

Rob was Rob Evans, Sarah's husband, and producer of several hit sitcoms, including the one his wife had her recurring mother-in-law role on.

"I have to go," Stormie breathed into the phone. She was losing her battle to keep the water from boiling over.

"Oh… okay, Sweetie. Hey, I am really sorry to spring it on you like that. I honestly thought you would have heard by now."

"Goodbye, Sarah." Stormie threw the phone in the pool and let out a blood-curdling scream.

Franklin cringed in the doorway.

She stalked to the bar, muttering obscenities under her breath. She started to fix a drink, but abruptly changed her mind. She went barreling out to the garage and savagely flung open the Mercedes' passenger door. When her eyes didn't immediately spot the business card from the bookstore in Seattle, she felt around on the seat for it.

It was gone. She searched under the seats, between them, through the glove box, and on the floor. In her frenzy to find the card, she didn't hear herself muttering repeated obscenities, or notice snapping off one of her fingernails. The card had vanished. It never crossed her mind that Travis might have seen it, let alone taken it.

She went back inside and dumped the contents of her handbag all over the kitchen counter.

"Where the hell did I put the goddamn thing?" she spat.

The card was nowhere to be found. Stormie wracked her brain and couldn't come up with the name of the store. *Bell something*, she thought. Suddenly it seemed very important to get in touch with that bookstore again.

She returned to the bar in the dining room to pour herself that drink. She spied her cell phone, sitting plugged into the charger on the desk. She left the drink, still untouched, and pulled the phone from its cradle. She scrolled down to *recently placed calls.*

There it was—a phone number with a 206 area code. The only long distance call she had made from her cell phone all week.

She wrote down the number on a pad of paper, then went back for her drink and downed it in two large gulps. Running one unsteady hand across her mouth, Stormie desperately tried to control the venomous anger coursing through her veins.

How could they do this to me? Anyone but her. Anyone but the next fucking Stormie Banks! Her outraged mind cried.

She needed to get control of herself. She snatched the cell phone from the desk and punched in the number with shaking fingers.

"Good afternoon, Bella Luna, how may I help you?" A melodic female voice answered.

"May I speak to Belda, please?" Stormie asked, her shaking voice betraying her emotional state.

"Who's calling, please?" the girl replied.

"I would rather not say. I… I'm well known and… I was given her card, and I can be in the Seattle area tomorrow. I wondered if she could see me."

The girl's pleasant, professional demeanor never wavered, "It appears we have an opening at nine a.m. That is an hour before the store opens for business. If you are concerned about discretion that may be the best time to avoid a store full of customers. Will that time work for you?"

Relieved, Stormie replied, "Thank you. I am grateful for your understanding."

"Do you have our address, Miss…?"

"Banks. Sto… it's… I'm…"

Sensing her discomfort, the girl interjected, "I have you down for nine o'clock, Ms. Banks." She wished her a good day and disconnected.

Stormie turned on the computer and booked a round trip ticket on Delta, and a limousine to meet her flight when she landed at Sea Tac airport. She didn't dare do this through her travel agent and risk Travis finding out. She could leave tonight and be back before he returned on Monday.

She stuffed an over-night bag with cosmetics and a change of clothes and hurried to the airport.

All of this was done on autopilot. Stormie had slipped into a dimension far from Hollywood Hills upon hearing the news of who would be starring in the role she had made famous so many years before. She was now driven by murderous rage and desperation.

Her last conscious thought had taken place before she hung up the phone with Sarah. Everything that followed felt like a dream.

One thought repeating in her mind from the moment she hung up the phone: *I must stop her. She can't. I must stop her. She can't.*

~~~~

The first-class section of Delta Flight 310 from Burbank International Airport to Sea-Tac was less than half full, for which Stormie was grateful. She had a row to herself. Behind her, a weary businessman fell into a coma-like doze the moment he sat down.

Stormie immediately ordered a double vodka martini and spent the duration of the flight asking herself the same question over and over. *Just what the hell am I doing exactly?* The only answer her tormented mind could offer was the mantra *I must stop her. She can't.*

One way or another, she wasn't going to let Kyra Hastings get away with this. She was going to stop her.

Upon arriving in Seattle, Stormie instructed the driver to take her to the Four Seasons. The hotel was full, but her fame could still buy her way into an over-booked hotel.

Stormie locked herself into the suite, called room service, and ordered a Caesar salad and double vodka martini. She wasn't hungry, but knew better than to keep drinking without eating something.

On impulse, she asked, "Is there any way I could get a bottle of Absolut sent up?"

"Yes, Ms. Banks. I'm sure I can get one from the bar."

Stormie didn't think the little splits from the minibar would be enough to get her through the night.
~~~~

She changed into the thick, plush terrycloth robe provided by the hotel, then sat on the edge of the deep marble bath and examined the array of bath salts. Choosing lavender, she started the water and added the salts to the steaming tub before returning to the living room.

Stormie always tried to stay at a Four Seasons when she was out of town. She loved the large airy suites, the plush king-sized beds, and more than anything, the heated towel racks in the bathrooms. The Four Seasons might not be quite as luxurious as her home, but it was the next best thing.

When room service arrived, Stormie handed the star-struck young man a ten dollar bill and asked him if he'd ever heard of Bella Luna bookstore.

He hadn't.

After soaking in the tub and drinking all of the martini and a third of the bottle of Absolut, Stormie nibbled halfheartedly at the salad.

When the telephone beside the bed jangled, she jumped, sloshing vodka all down the front of her robe.

"Aw, shit! No one knows I'm here, who the hell could that be?" she asked the empty room, her voice slurred. Cautiously, she picked up the receiver.

"Yes?"

"Ms. Banks?"

"Who is this?"

"This is Dominique. I'm the concierge downstairs. Alex, the room service waiter said you inquired about Bella Luna Bookstore. I have some information for you."

She exhaled a loud sigh of relief. "Have you been there?" she asked, relaxing on the bed.

"I purchased a birthday gift for a friend there a few months ago. It's a rather large store, rows and rows of books on just about every subject of the supernatural you can imagine. The clerk was quite helpful. My friend is interested in reading Tarot cards. I purchased her a deck of cards and a book. Was there something specific you needed from there? Perhaps I could order it for you to save you the trip. It's really quite a dreary place."

"Are you familiar with someone there named Belda?"

"I think the young lady that assisted me was named Gwyneth or Gabby, something like that."

There was a pause. The concierge lowered his voice to a conspiratorial whisper. "Do you wish me to make a discreet inquiry into the store, or this Belda person?"

Stormie laughed, trying to make light of the offer. She had done just what she was hoping not to do—drawn attention to herself. She wasn't even entirely certain what she was doing here.

"Thank you, Dominique. That's very kind of you, but not necessary. A friend asked me to stop in and say hello to Belda if she still works there, that's all."

"As you wish, Ms. Banks. But if I can assist you any further don't hesitate to ask."

Stormie hurried off the phone. She smiled a little at the conversation. One of the first observations she'd made when she'd became famous was that people became enthusiastic about playing a role in your life any way they could. Offers of assistance came not only from hotel employees, but also gardeners, pharmacists, and clerks at the bakery. It was kind of funny. When you were famous, everyone thought your life was one big conspiracy. She chuckled until her internal voice asked, *Speaking of conspiracies, just what are you doing here exactly?*

She pushed the voice away and unscrewed the top of the vodka bottle.

~~~~

Dominique had been right. The place was dreary. Downright gloomy, in fact. The closed sign hung in the window, but when Stormie tried the door, the knob turned easily. A melodic little bell overhead shivered as she walked in.

Rows upon rows of bookcases filled the enormous store, stretching further than Stormie could see. A rickety staircase spiraled up one side, presumably leading to yet more bookcases. The only light came from the sun, fighting its way first through Seattle clouds, then through the shop's opaque glass door. Stormie peered around owlishly, looking for signs of life.

"Hello?" she called. She felt swallowed up by the silence. "Is anyone here?"

A black cat appeared at her ankles. She bent and picked him up.

"You must be Belda. You're going to turn into a witch in a puff of smoke like in the old Bewitched TV show, right?" Stormie held the purring cat against her bosom and scratched under his chin.

"I see you have met Eros," a pleasant voice called from the top of the rickety staircase.

Stormie put the cat down and walked to the edge of the steps, squinting up into the darkness. "Are you Belda?"

"Yes, Ms. Banks. Welcome to Bella Luna. Can I offer you some tea?"

"Actually, coffee, if you have it."

"I'm sorry, dear, but I don't."
~~~~

The woman remained shrouded in shadows at the top of the stairs. She sounded amused when she added, "You might find my tea very helpful for a headache."

"Just what makes you think I have a headache?" Stormie asked, far more sharply than she had intended.

"Call it a lucky guess. Now, can I interest you in that tea?"

Stormie sighed. So, this Belda knew she had a hangover. It was no secret she had a drinking problem. Just pick up last week's *National Enquirer*, with its front cover of her clutching a half open bottle of Absolut in her fist. You didn't have to be psychic to figure out she spent most mornings with a headache these days.

"Sure. The tea would be great."

"There is a little office against the far left wall where I meet with my customers. Why don't you get settled in there? I will be down in a few moments."

Stormie walked in the direction the woman had indicated. She stopped at one of the towering shelves and pulled a thick, leather-bound book down. The title was, *White Magic in a Dark World.* She flipped to the contents page. There were spells for love, spells for money, spells for success, and spells for revenge. She raised her eyebrows, suppressing a giggle.

Again the thought, *Exactly what the hell am I doing here?* raced across her mind. The answer came at once—*Stop her. She can't.*

Replacing the book on the shelf, Stormie found the office and stepped into the gloom. It took a few moments for her eyes to adjust to the dimly lit space. The strong aroma of incense wafted over from the shelves.

Stormie took in the surroundings and sat down. The cat jumped into her lap and began purring contentedly. Stormie stroked him absently, glancing at the few items on the small, round, claw-foot table next to her.

Everything was disappointingly normal. A few books, letter opener, a small mirror, and a stapler.

"Where's the crystal ball?" she asked the cat.

"Oh, I don't employ anything so cliché," the woman responded from the doorway. Stormie jumped and the startled cat jumped from her lap.

"You scared me."

"My apologies, dear. I didn't mean to sneak up on you." She set a tray with two steaming mugs on the table.

Belda settled into a chair. She handed Stormie one of the mugs. Her hand, Stormie noted, was misshapen. More striking were Belda's eyes. Those eyes looked almost preternatural, as if Belda were half spirit.

Stormie shifted uncomfortably, hoping *she* would never look so old.

"So, Ms. Banks, what brings you to Seattle—and specifically to Bella Luna?"

Stormie barked a hollow laugh and sipped the tea. "That's a good question. I'm not sure myself. I was given your card. I called the shop and spoke to one of your employees—Nicholas, I think his name was."

Belda gave an encouraging nod. "Go on."

"Are you some kind of a miracle worker? Is that it?"

"Miracle isn't the word I would use. Sometimes I can evoke the desired effect from a situation. For a fee, of course."

Stormie offered a humorless smile. "Of course. So is that the politically correct way of saying you're a witch, or what?"

"I prefer to think of myself as an alchemist," the woman bristled. Clearly she didn't care much for the term 'witch.'

"Sorry. No offense intended."

"Ms. Banks, what is it that you hope I can achieve for you?"

"Well, I asked your employee if you could make me a star again. He seemed to think you could."

There—it was out. Stormie felt her cheeks burn with the confession. She lowered her eyes to the ground, waiting for the weird old woman to laugh in her face.

Belda didn't laugh. She only looked at her for a long, thoughtful moment.

"If I'm not mistaken, you are still considered a star. You have one of the most famous faces in America. Perhaps you could be more specific."

She certainly isn't going to make this easy, Stormie thought. She blurted out, "I thought they wanted me for that horrible, low budget, piece-of-shit movie. But they wanted *her*—that… that miserable little…" She pulled in a long, shuddering breath and drank greedily from the steaming mug of tea. "I'm sorry. I know I am not making any sense."

Belda shrugged and smiled kindly. "Take your time."

Stormie placed the tea back on the table and began again. "It was a movie. A really stupid movie, and I thought they wanted me to star in it. Instead, they offered me the part of the mother of the star. The mother, for chrissakes! Then, to add insult to injury, the girl they chose to star in this movie is also starring in a remake of a movie I did twenty years ago."

"And whom did they cast in the role you wanted for yourself, Ms. Banks?"

"Kyra Hastings!" Stormie spat the name like a bitter taste from her mouth. "The little bitch the press is calling the next me." She was annoyed to realize that tears had brimmed over her eyes. She took a vicious swipe at them with the back of one trembling hand.

"Do you think if Miss Hastings were out of the picture—no pun intended—they would have offered you the leading role instead of that of her mother?"

Stormie paused, a brief war raging in her head—sanity versus complete insanity. Insanity emerged victorious. She answered, "Well… I… I don't know."

"Or," Belda wondered, "would they have offered it to another younger actress?"

Stormie could not face the unlovely truth. She knew the answer—so did the old woman, obviously. But here Stormie Banks and reality parted company.

With downcast eyes, she muttered, "Maybe they would have offered it to me if there were no Kyra Hastings. It's possible."

Sudden insane light flooded her eyes. In a stronger voice, she remarked, "After all, this is Hollywood we are talking about. The place where reality and fantasy trade places every day. Maybe if the world had never heard of the new Stormie Banks, they wouldn't be in such a hurry to get rid of the old one."

Stormie's tormented mind grasped onto this thought like a drowning man reaches for a life raft. Maybe they would have offered her the role of Ashley in *A Manhattan Love Story*. Maybe MGM would have dusted off the role of Desiree in *Golden Sunset* and given that one to her as well. In fact, they probably would have, she decided. If only the world had never heard those two ugly words—Kyra Hastings.

Sitting in this dark, smoky room, this seemed not only possible, it seemed likely.

Belda broke into her dark reverie. "So what is your desire, Ms. Banks? For the leading role in this love story, or to see what would happen if there were no Kyra Hastings to offer the part to?"

"Nothing would make me happier than if there were no Kyra Hastings—but there is. So what can you do about it?"

"First, I need to know what you want. Do you want there simply to be no Ms. Hastings in Hollywood? Or do you just want her not to have the role of Ashley in this movie? There is a big difference."

"Even without that ridiculous role, the bitch is still starring in *Golden Sunset*—and that is even worse! She's a thorn in my side. I hate her," Stormie spat.

"Do you want her to go away?" Belda asked, her eyes peering at her client with an intense, sinister glow.

"Yes," Stormie whispered. "I want her to go away."

Belda quoted her fee for making Kyra Hastings disappear. Stormie pulled out her checkbook without hesitation.

By ten o'clock that night, Stormie was back in Los Angeles. She went to bed sober for the first time in two months.

~~~~

"Nicholas, you will need to run an errand in Los Angeles." Belda handed him an envelope stuffed with cash, and a small bottle stuffed with bitter herbs.

He thumbed through the bills and whistled under his breath. "The actress?"

"Indeed. She has paid for a service that would be dangerous to perform herself. Unfortunately, she has made it no secret she is unhappy with a rival. Should anything unexpectedly happen to this rival, it could raise undue suspicion of our client."

Nicholas grimaced. "Who is the rival and exactly what is this little bottle of sunshine going to do to her?" he asked.
~~~~

"Her name is Kyra Hastings, and what our client paid for is between us."

Nicholas gasped. "Kyra Hastings? Oh man, what a shame. She's a hottie."

Gabriella, standing at the cash register, adding up the day's receipts, turned a flaming gaze on Nicholas. "Excuse me?"

"Not as hot as you, babe," he amended quickly.

"She should be given this potion as soon as possible," Belda said.

"Can't it wait until after the holidays? Doesn't seem right to do it before Christmas. I mean, her family and all."

"Nicholas, you are so sure that what's in that bottle is going to harm the girl. Do you think me that sinister?"

Nicholas turned red and looked away uncomfortably.

Gabriella stopped working and looked up, alarm showing in her eyes.

"No. Of course not," Nicholas replied, "I'll take care of it this weekend."

"Having an attack of conscience after all these years?" Belda asked, her eyes probing into his.

He shook his head. "I'm sorry. I shouldn't have said anything. I will make sure it's handled right away." He shifted nervously from foot to foot, keeping his eyes on his shoes.

Belda kept her penetrating stare on him a moment longer. "I'll leave you two lovebirds to lock up. I'm going up to bed. Come along, Eros."

Still holding their breath, Nicholas and Gabriella watched the old woman negotiate her careful way up the staircase, the cat close at her heels. They didn't say anything until they heard the door close behind her.

"What's the matter with you, Nicholas? You don't want to make her mad at you. You know what happens to people that anger her," Gabriella hissed.

He put a reassuring arm around her waist and kissed her temple. "Sorry, Gabby, I know. I just thought maybe we could give the poor girl through Christmas."

"She didn't say what was going to happen to Kyra Hastings, Nicholas. You don't always have to assume the worst. For all you know, she will be just fine."

"You will have to forgive me if I doubt that. No one who drinks her little message in a bottle ever ends up *just fine.*"

Gabriella placed her hand over his mouth. "Stop it now. I want *you* around for the holidays a lot more than I do Kyra Hastings, understand? Ours is not to question, and it certainly isn't to philosophize about what she does. You know better."

Nicholas nodded, but his eyes remained troubled. "Hurry up and finish the books. I'm hungry and I guess I have a plane to catch tomorrow."

"Alright… but Nicholas?"

"Yeah?"

"I don't want to discuss this any further. Even after we leave here tonight. It's not safe; you know that."

Yes, he knew that. Belda had a way of knowing things, whether she was in the room or not. He'd be wise to keep his mouth shut and just do his job. Kyra Hastings was no one to him. He'd find her, slip her the mickey, and be back home with Gabriella the next day, several thousand dollars richer. For that kind of reward, Belda deserved his silence and respect—if not his trust.

Chapter 7

Stormie nervously checked her appearance in the mirror every five minutes. She could hear the sounds of a ball-game drifting out of the den. The afternoon had been punctuated with male voices hollering obscenities as their team continued to lose.

Heather and her new boyfriend were due any minute. Stormie didn't know how Travis could be so calm. She was a wreck, wondering what kind of character her daughter was going to present for her approval this time. When Stormie looked up at the security camera mounted in the kitchen, she saw the spear-tipped, wrought iron gate gliding open. A non-descript Chevy rental car swung into the driveway. Stormie caught a glimpse of a dark-haired male behind the wheel before the car swung out of view of the camera.

Stormie did a final check in the mirror, and smoothed her hair down. She strode to the front door, calling over her shoulder in the direction of the den, "Travis, they're here!"

Travis joined his wife in the foyer and watched Heather leap from the passenger seat of the Chevrolet. She ran up the steps to her waiting mother's embrace. Then Travis lifted Heather off the ground in a bear hug.

"Sweetheart, you look beautiful! Stormie, doesn't she just look beautiful?" he cried.

"Absolutely gorgeous!" Stormie agreed merrily, craning her head over her daughter's shoulder to get a look at the tall young man emerging from the rental car.

He stood uncertainly at the bottom of the steps, looking up at the embracing trio.

Travis cleared his throat and pointed.

Heather spun around. "Oh my God! Sorry, Dan! Come on up, they won't bite." Out of the corner of her mouth she whispered to her mother, "You won't, will you, Mom?"

Her boyfriend took a couple hesitant steps toward the porch and stopped.

Heather grabbed his hand, pulling him the rest of the way onto the porch.

"Mom, Travis, I'd like you to meet Daniel Holliman. Dan, these are my folks."

Stormie took in the young man's appearance. Tall, at least six feet, slender, with an unruly shock of wavy brown hair and big, brown eyes, framed in scholarly horn-rims. He wore a neatly pressed blue button-down shirt and Dockers.

"Pleased to meet you," he mumbled, clearly embarrassed by Heather's mother's open appraisal of him.

Stormie and Travis exchanged small, approving smiles that Heather noticed and grinned at.

"So where's Connor?" Heather asked over her shoulder, as she dragged Dan into the house. "I want Dan to meet him."

"He's in the den with Cal, watching the Patriots get annihilated," Travis answered.

"Cal's here too? Oh cool! I haven't seen him in ages." Heather dashed for the den, dragging her nervous boyfriend behind her.

He nearly ran into her when she stopped short.

"Franklin, baby dog!" She squealed, letting go of Dan's hand long enough to roll around and wrestle with the dog for a few minutes.

Stormie and Travis watched from the door. "You like him, don't you?" Stormie asked under her breath.

Travis nodded, "Poor thing's a little overwhelmed, but he seems like a good sort. I don't think he'll be pulling me aside and asking me how much your drawers will go for on eBay, anyhow."

"Did you catch the rental car?"

"Yeah," Travis smiled. "A nice sensible Chevy for a nice sensible boy, and clearly not trying to impress the movie star mother."

Dan was accosted by the men and herded into the den, where he was forced to endure the last quarter of the Patriots' brutal beating. Stormie and Heather slipped out to go shopping and have lunch.

When they returned a few hours later, laden with packages from Rodeo Drive, the men were companionably sprawled in the den, open bottles of Heineken on the coffee table before them.

Heather was relieved to see that Dan was clearly enjoying himself and looked far more relaxed than when she had left him.

When he saw Heather peek her head into the den, Dan smiled and rose to join her. "Need some help with the bags?" he asked, planting a kiss on the corner of her mouth.

"Thanks. How did it go with the cowboy clan in there?" she asked, hooking a thumb back toward the den.

"They are great, Heather. Connor is a hoot and your step-dad seems like a pretty cool guy."

"Oh, he's the best. What about Cal?" Heather arched one eyebrow in amusement.

Dan grinned. "He's an interesting one."

"True, but relatively harmless."

"Seriously, I really like them."

"I'm glad, but you haven't gotten to know Mom yet. Might want to reserve your judgment on the Bullock clan 'til you do."

~~~~

The night before Thanksgiving, Heather and Dan were out visiting with some of Heather's old friends from high school. Travis, Connor, and Cal were playing poker at the dining room table.

Dealing the cards, Travis asked his son if he had found work yet.

At twenty-one, Calvin Bullock had yet to find a career path that suited him. He still lived at home with his mother and her current boyfriend. Every now and then he would take a job, only to discover a few days later that he didn't care for it, and quit. Cal had not inherited his father's musical talent. He had no idea what he wanted to do when he grew up—should that day ever come.

"No, Daddy, I'm not workin', but I am thinkin' I might like to go back to school."

Connor coughed back a snort of laughter. He didn't want to spend another holiday thrown on his ass outside, and he knew from experience that Travis could be just as sensitive about his kids as he was about his wife.

"School? What for?" Travis asked, his curiosity peaked.

"It's a school right in Abilene, not too far from the house," Cal replied, vaguely.
~~~~

"What kind of school, son? What do they teach?"

The card game ceased as Travis looked levelly at his son across the table. This was a kid that had barely finished high school and seemed for all intents and purposes allergic to anything even remotely academic.

Cal cleared his throat. "It's called The Amazing AJ's Academy of Magic and Illusionary Arts."

Connor, unable to control the snort this time, downed his beer in a single draught and excused himself to the bathroom.

A thunderstruck Travis didn't notice his departure. "It's called what?"

"It's a magician school, Daddy." Cal was turning red at the tips of his ears and around the collar of his sweatshirt.

Travis blinked a few times and took a swallow of his beer. "Is that right? When did you become interested in becoming a magician, son?"

Cal grew even more uncomfortable. "I don't know. A while ago." He tugged at the collar of his sweatshirt as if it had suddenly tightened around his throat.

"Why magic?"

"Because I got a friend, and she's going to start school there in January. I think it'd be neat."

"A girlfriend?" Travis asked suspiciously.

"Yeah, kinda."

"Have you told your momma?"

Cal nodded. He lowered his head and muttered, "She won't give me the tuition."

"Tuition, huh?" Travis looked doubtful.

"Well, yeah, Daddy. It's a school; you gotta pay tuition."

"And how much is this tuition?"

Cal began playing restlessly with the stack of poker chips on the table. "It's for the whole two years."

"That don't answer my question, Calvin. How much?"

"Twenty-five thousand dollars." When he saw the look on his father's face, he hastened to add, "But it includes everything—all your books and supplies, the cape, the wand, the whole works."

"For twenty-five grand, it ought to include the woman in the leotard and the saw to cut her in half," a stunned Travis declared.

Cal looked earnestly at his father. "Daddy, this is what I want to do. Did Grandpa laugh at you when you traded your first motorcycle for a Fender guitar?"

That gave Travis pause. Not only had his father laughed at him, he'd called him three kinds of fool and told him the only audience he'd ever be singing to would be standing in the unemployment line right next to him.

"Tell me something, son," Travis replied, "Is this something you really want to do, or are you just doin' it for this girl?"

"I really want to do this. Maybe I'd be good at it."

Travis nodded thoughtfully. "Let me think about it."

"Thanks, Daddy. If I'm gonna do this, I need the money by December tenth. School starts the first week of January."

Travis nodded. He grabbed the deck of cards and started to shuffle.

~~~~

Later that night, Travis lay beside Stormie. In the darkened room he asked, "Is *illusionary* even a word, for chrissakes, or did this Amazing AJ character just make that up?"
~~~~

"I think it's a word. We're going to give him the money, aren't we?" She rose on one elbow and looked at her husband.

That's why he loved her. Everything was *we.* It was never *me* or *you.* From the day they'd gotten married, all bank accounts and children were commingled. The thought of a prenuptial agreement had never crossed her mind. Travis was wealthy, but Stormie was a millionaire several times over. None of that mattered. When she'd married Travis, she was in it for better or worse until death did them part.

"I don't think it's legitimate. I'm not gonna shell out a bundle of cash to someone that probably don't even run a real school. I'd feel a lot better about this if it was David Copperfield's school and not AJ's. You know what I mean?"

"Why don't you take a trip to Texas and check the place out?" Stormie laid her head on her husband's chest.

"I think that'd hurt the boy's feelings. It wasn't easy for him to ask me. If he thinks I don't trust him, that's gonna make it even worse than not giving him the money."

Stormie threw the covers back and flipped on the light by the bed. She took Travis's hand. "Come on."

"Where are we goin'?"

"To Google the Amazing AJ."

They sat together in front of the glowing computer monitor, reading the school's colorful webpage.

"Satisfied?" Stormie asked.

"What if he's just doing it for the girl?"

"Since when is love such a terrible motivation?" Stormie asked, taking his hand again.

"Love is a dandy motivation—it's lust that ain't."

"You can't have one without the other. Besides, Travis, it wouldn't matter if this was Le Cordon Bleu and Cal wanted to be a

French chef. Without something to motivate him, he wouldn't make it past the appetizer semester, and it wouldn't be the school's fault. You see what I mean?"

"Yeah. This girl's lit a fire in his belly, and while it's burnin', he might have some chance at finally gettin' a little direction."

"Exactly," she smiled, reaching into the desk drawer and pulling out the checkbook.

Chapter 8

The rich smells of cooking filled the house Thanksgiving morning. Stormie was out for a walk with Franklin and her daughter's new boyfriend. Cal was still asleep. Travis, Connor, and Heather stood in the kitchen, drinking coffee and trying not to nibble on the forbidden platters of food until Stormie and Dan returned.

The recycled picture of Stormie exiting the liquor store and cracking open the bottle of vodka once again graced the cover of some Hollywood gossip rag. Connor had picked up a copy the night before and left it lying on the counter. Not even that dampened Stormie's holiday cheer.

Travis nodded at the magazine. "Connor, throw that damn thing away."

"Can I ask you somethin'?"

"What?" Travis asked warily. He knew his brother and he knew that tone.

"I just wondered, did Michael Jackson and Stormie select the same nose from a catalogue or somethin'?" He tapped the photo of

Stormie on the cover of the magazine. "I could swear they got the exact same one."

Heather stifled a giggle. She loved her mother dearly and hated the repeated plastic surgeries she had put herself through, but sometimes you just had to laugh at the absurdity of it.

"Connor, knock it off," Travis grumbled. He worked his jaw, desperately trying to hold back the laughter that was threatening to pour out. He almost won the battle—would have, in fact, if he hadn't shifted his eyes to Heather's face and seen an identical expression of suffering mirrored in her eyes. Once their eyes met, the war between heart and funny bone was over, with funny bone emerging the winner. They both busted out laughing, Travis spitting coffee.

"Damn you, Connor," Travis muttered, stalking from the kitchen, still laughing.

"Why do you hate my mother, Connor?" Heather's voice carried an amused lilt to it.

"Oh, sweetie, I don't hate your momma at all. She can't be all bad, 'cause look at how good you turned out."

"Flattery will get you everywhere," Heather smiled, stealing a deviled egg from a plate and shoving it in Connor's mouth.

As she did so, he grabbed her left hand. His fingers pinched the thin band of gold on her ring finger. He reached under her hand to the palm side and turned the ring over, revealing a small, tasteful diamond. "What's this you're hiding?"

Heather hesitated.

"Spill the beans, little girl. Did that boy ask you to marry him?"

She had kept this secret inside so long that it was bursting to come out. She nodded enthusiastically. "Yeah!" she gushed. "In fact, right now he's asking Mom for permission. That's why he asked her to go for the walk. Dan's so old-fashioned! Isn't that the sweetest thing?"

Connor checked his watch. "How long have they been gone? If they ain't back in ten minutes, I'd say there's a real high likelihood your momma done killed that boy, and we'll need to get our story straight before we alert the authorities."

Heather punched Connor in the arm. "Connor!" she shrieked. "Aren't you even happy for me?"

"Hell, yes I'm happy for you, girl." He pulled her into a hug. "I'm just worried for your fella, is all."

"Oh quit it. Mom likes him." After a pause she added, "Doesn't she?"

Fifteen minutes later, Dan and Stormie stepped through the kitchen door shrugging out of their jackets. Dan bent down and released Franklin from his leash. The dog trotted to his master, looking for food. Travis reached under the plastic of one of the platters, his eyes never leaving his wife's, and absently handed a deviled egg to the dog.

Heather was biting her lip and staring nervously at her mother, trying to read her expression. Her eyes shifted restlessly from Stormie to Dan. The silence in the room drew out like a blade.

Finally Heather could take it no longer. "Oh God, Mother, you didn't say no did you?"

Stormie gazed at her daughter with calm eyes. "I told him he needs to ask Travis too." She turned to Dan. "Well, what are you waiting for?"

Heather looked as though she was going to faint.

Connor took her hand and gave it a reassuring pat.

Travis winked at his wife and turned toward the shaking young man. "Speak up, boy. You got something to say?"

Dan fiddled nervously with his glasses. He opened his mouth to speak but only a croak came out. He cleared his throat and tried again. "Sir, I would like to ask your permission to marry Heather. I love her very much and will do everything I can to make her happy."

Travis looked at the young man for a few seconds, but didn't speak. He turned to Heather. Stormie was enjoying this show immensely.

"Heather, you want to marry this guy?"

She nodded enthusiastically, twisting the ring on her finger nervously.

Travis turned back toward Dan. "Alright then, Dan Holliman, welcome to the family." He put his hand out for the very relieved young man to shake.

~~~~

A glorious turkey steamed on its platter by Travis's right side. Travis held a carving knife in one hand and a fork in the other. To the oohs, awes, and stomach growls of his family, he set to work on the bird.

As Travis sliced, the rest began passing: celery, mashed turnip, rolls, creamed onions, cranberry sauce, mashed potatoes, stuffing… all beautifully prepared and as aromatically irresistible as the turkey.

"So how did you meet?" Travis asked, when he had finished slicing. "Heather said you two didn't meet at school."

"That's right," Dan replied around a mouthful of stuffing.

Heather was happy to see how comfortable he was with everyone. She knew how overwhelming her mother could be. She
~~~~

was relieved that her mother hadn't been drinking very much during their stay. Heather genuinely thought Stormie liked Dan, and much to her relief, her future husband was not the least bit star-struck by her famous mother. She nodded to Dan to tell the story.

"It's a pretty funny story, actually," he grinned at Heather with affection. "I was walking past a construction site by the school one afternoon last spring. Out of nowhere, I hear a girl scream 'look out!' and I'm shoved off the sidewalk, and there is—as you would say, Connor—a whole bunch of woman right on top of me."

"That'd be me!" Heather smiled coyly.

"Anyway, then I hear this crash and next thing I know, we are both covered in white paint and some guy is shouting down from a scaffold, 'Hey, kid, you alright? Damn paint can flew right outta my hand.' If Heather hadn't seen it coming and knocked me out of the way, the thing would have brained me! It missed by maybe half a foot."

Heather picked up the story there. "I saw the can fall and just thought, *Oh my God! That guy is gonna get creamed,* and I dove to push him out of the way. I lost my balance and landed right on top of him. It took me two weeks to wash the paint out of my hair. But, as they say, the rest is history."

"And I walked away from it with a ruined pair of pants, a skinned knee, and the love of my life," Dan replied, "instead of a concussion."

They beamed at each other across the table.

Cal rolled his eyes. "Dang, that's the stupidest thing I ever heard."

Heather looked at him tolerantly. "What's stupid? The fact that I didn't let the paint can brain my future husband?"

"No, the fact that you didn't sue the moron that dropped the paint, sugar."

Heather shrugged. "We didn't think about that; we were too busy falling in love."

"And you call yourself a lawyer," he teased.

The festive feeling in the house remained throughout the day. The meal was consumed, and the men were in the den, feet propped up, screaming obscenities at the Packers. Stormie and Heather stayed in the kitchen, putting away leftovers and sharing a glass of wine.

"Have you set a date?" Stormie asked.

"Yes. May fifteenth. Dan is from Boston, and all his people are there, so we aren't sure if we should get married in Massachusetts or here. We want to do whatever is easiest for the family."

"If you had your choice, where would you want to get married, sweetheart?"

"Truthfully?"

Stormie nodded.

"Right here in the backyard. I love this house, and it's certainly big enough for the reception. Besides, I think Dan's family would get a kick out of seeing their baby married at a movie star's mansion, yah know?" she giggled.

"Guess you can take the girl out of Hollywood, but you can't take Hollywood outta the girl." Stormie hugged her daughter.

~~~~

Stormie couldn't sleep. Glancing at the clock and seeing the dial settled at half past two, she rose and donned a robe. Travis was a lump in the shadows, snoring softly.
~~~~

Stormie tiptoed down the stairs, not wanting to wake any of the guests. In the kitchen, she put the teakettle up to boil, then walked into the living room.

There was the inlaid wood case that held her many awards for theatre and film. Above it was a recessed light in the ceiling that illuminated the case in a soft glow. Stormie felt along the wall for the switch and smiled when the case was bathed in the mellow light.

After pouring a cup of tea and adding a healthy shot of Remy Martin from the bar, Stormie returned to the living room and opened up the case. She carefully lifted down one of the small Tiffany frames that held the cards bearing her name. This one had been removed from the envelope just after Kirk Douglas said, "And the winner is..."

Her mind wandered back thirty years to that night. She remembered the dress she'd worn, one that had earned her a place on Mackie's top ten best-dressed list the following week. She remembered the emeralds that encircled her throat, on loan from Cartier. She remembered the indescribable feeling of exhilaration as she climbed the stairs of the Dorothy Chandler Pavilion to accept the award.

Stormie lovingly caressed the frame. As she did so a troubled frown creased her brow. She pulled the small frame right up in front of her eyes, but in the darkened living room, she couldn't be sure of what she was actually seeing. She carried it into the kitchen. Underneath the fluorescent lights, she examined it again.

"Oh no," she breathed quietly, tears stinging her eyes. She turned the frame over and pried up the clasps with her finger nails, then lifted the back off. She removed the card from inside and stared at it in horror. A single tear splashed on the glass of the frame.

"What are you doin' up? Poisoning my breakfast for tomorrow?" a sleepy voice asked from behind her.

Stormie wiped at her streaming eyes, and turned around startled. Connor was standing in the doorway. His hair was sleep-tousled and he wore an old bathrobe.

Seeing that Stormie was upset, he stood uncertainly, not wanting to intrude. "Sorry," he muttered. "You okay?"

Stormie shrugged. "You couldn't sleep either?"

Connor walked into the kitchen and leaned against the counter next to her. "What you got there?" he nodded at what she held in her hand.

Tears filled Stormie's eyes again. "This is the card that was in the envelope that announced the winner of the first Oscar I ever won."

"The one you keep in the cabinet with the statues, right?"

She nodded and held it out to him, "Look at it," she sniffed.

He held it in his hand, unsure what it was that made her so sad. Finally he asked, "What am I looking for?"

"It's turning yellow," she sobbed. "It's getting old and brittle, just like me."

Connor smoothed the card and placed it carefully back into the frame. He replaced the backing and handed it back to Stormie. He poured himself a cup of tea from the simmering kettle and sat down at the kitchen table.

Stormie stood with her back to him, nursing her own tea. Finally, she turned. "You want some brandy in that?"

She handed him the open bottle of Remy Martin without waiting for a response and sat down across from him.

"Thanks," he tilted a healthy belt into his cup. "Stormie, listen. You and I, we haven't always gotten on real well. But you make my brother happy. And the truth is, I think you are a good woman. I don't really understand why you want to stay young forever, and I am not sure Travis does either. Don't you think there is some beauty in becoming… oh hell, I don't know, older, seasoned, wiser, something like that?"

"This coming from the man who only dates twenty-year-old strippers," she shook her head. "When your life's blood takes place in front of a camera, Connor, youth is the most important thing."

"I get that, girl, but people retire. Even show biz folks. They find new life's blood, if that's what you call it. They find it in their spouses, in their kids, in planning those kid's weddings. In watchin' them graduate from law school even. Those are things you can take pride in," he patted her shoulder. "That beautiful girl and that serious looking young buck she brought home to meet you that are asleep upstairs."

"What if I'm not ready to be a has-been?" she sighed miserably.

"Stormie, you done good—both in your career, and where it really matters—with Heather. You raised an intelligent daughter who's gonna marry a guy that's crazy about her. They are both going to be Harvard graduates and lawyers. Hell, you ought to be doin' handsprings out the back door when you look at that kid of yours. You raised her in Hollywood, and she ain't shallow, she ain't materialistic, and she ain't stupid. You did that. You ask me, that's plenty more to be proud of than some copper statues hangin' in the living room."

"Gold," Stormie smiled at Connor through her tears.

"Pardon me?"

"They are gold, you ass, not copper."

Connor threw his head back and laughed. "I made you feel better, admit it."

"You know, Connor, once in a great, great while, you actually seem almost human."

"Why, thank you, darlin', that's the nicest thing you done ever said to me."

Stormie smiled. "I would have never hated you in the first place if you hadn't asked Travis if he found me on the clearance rack in hell, you know."

"Well, that was my mistake, Storm. At the time, I didn't know hell don't even have a clearance rack. I found that out later from Trump."

Stormie chuckled and shook her head thoughtfully. "Maybe you're right, Connor. I mean, about what I should be proud of in my golden years. I'll think about that. But if you ever tell anyone I said you might be right about anything, I swear I'll deny it, and I *will* poison your breakfast. And that's a promise."

Chapter 9

Stormie and Travis rode back from the airport in silence, both lost in their own thoughts, and feeling a little melancholy. The Chevy was back at Avis and Heather and Dan were on their flight to Cambridge. Conner and Cal had left the night before.

Travis broke through Stormie's reverie with, "The house is sure gonna seem quiet with everyone gone."

She nodded. "We're like empty nesters. Want to get a Winnebago?"

"Honey, two days on the road without a five-star hotel and you'd be filin' for divorce."

She laughed. "You know me too well. Guess there's always Christmas."

A frown settled over Travis's face.

"What is it?" she asked.

"Didn't Heather tell you? They are spendin' Christmas with his people in Boston. They ain't comin' to L.A."

Stormie's face fell. "No. She didn't tell me. Guess she didn't want to hurt my feelings. I suppose this is how it's going to be from now on. Having to divide the holidays between the families."

"At least he's a good boy, Storm. He'll make her a fine husband, I think."

"She wants to get married at our house."

Travis raised an eyebrow. "How does Mr. Middle Class America feel about that?"

"I don't know. I guess they will talk about it and let us know. I hope he's okay with it, though. It's something she really wants."

"Well, hon, I get the feeling that boy would do just about anything to put a smile on Heather's face, so if she wants to marry at the house, then my guess is that's where they'll marry."

"I hope you're right. I am going to be pissed off if she's already not getting her way."

Travis laughed. "Not a chance in hell, babe. She's still your daughter."

"Can we stop at the liquor store?"

"It's a little early in the day, ain't it?" Travis snapped.

"Who said I was going to drink it now?" Stormie snapped right back.

Travis knew better then to push the issue. Her drinking was a subject Stormie was very sensitive about. She knew she had a problem and didn't need anyone else—least of all her husband, reminding her. To say anything further would have been to provoke an argument that he wasn't in the mood for. If anything would increase the drinking she was already planning to do today, fighting with Travis was it.

Travis silently guided the Mercedes to the liquor store and left her in the car while he went inside to buy the vodka. The last thing they needed was another tabloid photographer hiding in the bushes to smear Stormie all over the papers again.

~~~~

It wasn't as bad as he'd expected. At least not yet. She only had two drinks and was currently in the kitchen fixing them some leftovers for dinner. If she was eating, that was a good sign. When his wife got down to the serious drinking, she never ate.

Stormie carried two laden plates into the den and switched the television to the evening news.

She was only listening with half an ear until the newscaster intoned, "In local news, there are still no clues in the bizarre disappearance of actress Kyra Hastings."

Behind the anchor was a studio shot of Kyra, smiling her thousand megawatt smile. "Hastings was last seen Friday night leaving a nightclub with an unidentified man that police are interested in questioning. He hasn't come forward and no one at the bar was able to give police a description. Hastings's car was still in the parking lot of the popular Hollywood nightspot the following morning, but the actress hasn't been seen."

Stormie voiced a startled squawk. Her plate slipped off her lap, tumbling to the floor and spilling food everywhere.

Travis jumped up, setting his own plate aside. "Honey, what's wrong?"

Stormie had nearly forgotten about her visit to Seattle, what with the holiday and Heather's big news. The two days she spent in Seattle carried such a dreamlike quality that she had nearly convinced herself that that was exactly what it had been; a dream. She hadn't picked up a newspaper or watched the television in over a week. Hearing the report of Kyra's disappearance sent a nasty jolt of fear down her spine.

"Did you know about this?" she cried.
~~~~

"About Kyra Hastings? Yeah, I heard about it a few days ago." He bent down to help Stormie clean up the fallen food. "You didn't know?"

"No! I haven't seen the news since before Heather arrived. Oh my God!"

"She probably ran off with some guy to Mexico or something. I'm sure she'll turn up."

Stormie finished cleaning up the spilled food, then took the bottle of Absolut upstairs to their bedroom and locked the door. She dialed directory assistance and got the phone number for Bella Luna. *What have I done?* she thought. She was shaking uncontrollably and her teeth were chattering.

"Good evening, Bella Luna, how may I help you?"

Stormie recognized the pleasant, female voice from her last call.

"I need to talk to Belda," Stormie gasped into the receiver. "It's an emergency."

"Who's calling pl—"

"None of your goddamn business! Put her on the phone!" Stormie shrieked.

In the same professional, clipped tone, the girl responded, "Just a moment please."

There was a click. Piped-in elevator music drifted into Stormie's ear. *Oh God! Oh dear God, what have I done?* the voice in her head shouted.

What felt like hours later, the phone was finally picked up.

"This is Belda. To whom am I speaking?" the woman was clearly annoyed. She did not like having her help yelled at, apparently.

"This is Stormie Banks. What did you do to that girl? What did you do?" she cried.

"Ms. Banks, calm yourself."

"Calm myself? Are you crazy? She's gone! It's all over the goddamn news!" Stormie sputtered.

"Ms. Banks, you paid for a service and the service was rendered. Did you not tell me in those exact words that you wanted Ms. Hastings to disappear?"

"Okay, fine. I changed my mind. Bring her back, and keep the damn money. Just bring the little twit back!"

"I'm afraid that's not possible," Belda replied regretfully.

"Why not?" Stormie whispered, "Is she…" she swallowed hard. "Is she dead?"

"I can't answer that question."

"Why the hell not?"

"Because, Ms. Banks, I do not know. How it works is you tell me what you want, and I mix up a blend of ingredients. This particular blend caused the person that ingested it to disappear. Once the mixture leaves my hand and enters the body of the intended party, it takes over from there. I have no more control over it. It is—as they say—out of my hands."

"Oh this is just great. Just fucking great! How the hell did you get her to take it? How did you even find her?"

"Ms. Banks, that is what you paid me to do."

"Well, can I pay you to mix up another little blend of crap to bring her back?" Stormie was frightened half out of her mind.

"You could, but I'm afraid I don't know where she is. Perhaps you should have thought this through a little more carefully before consulting me."

"Please, you have got to listen to me. When I was in Seattle, I wasn't thinking clearly… I… I had been drinking… um, drinking a lot… and the whole thing, it didn't even seem real. It was… I don't know… It was like being in a movie or something. I didn't understand what I was doing."

"Ms. Banks, the check you wrote me was real enough. The deed you paid for is now done. It doesn't necessarily mean the girl is in jeopardy. It just means she is no longer a problem to you, and that the desired effect has been achieved."

"You mean she's okay? She's not hurt, or dead, or something?"

"As I told you, I do not know. But I would remind you that she could as easily be in good health as any other alternative. She's just not in Hollywood anymore."

"Can this be traced back to me?"

"Of course not. A large part of what you paid for was discretion. However, Ms. Banks, I would advise you to speak of this to no one. Not now and not ever. Should you do that, I would have no choice but to… well, to make you disappear." She chuckled at her own joke.

"What?" Stormie shuddered. She was terrified. "What are you saying?"

"You know what I am saying, Ms. Banks. You are many things, but naïve is not one of them. I would advise you to quit worrying about this. It's today's news; tomorrow, it will be history. Don't concern yourself with it any further. When we last spoke, that girl was a nettle in your side—an annoying problem that you wanted to go away. Now it has. So enjoy whatever good fortune you receive as a result of it, and forget you were ever even peripherally involved."

"How? How do I forget? How do I ever sleep again? How do I cope?"

"The same way you cope with everything else, Ms. Banks. In the bottom of a bottle, I would suspect. Good day."

The phone went dead in Stormie's ear.

Stormie sat for several moments, shaking violently. The receiver remained clutched in one white-knuckled hand at the side of her head. She didn't hang up until the phone began buzzing in her ear.

Belda was convinced she would deal with her remorse by drinking, but Stormie wasn't so sure. She doubted there was enough vodka in the western hemisphere to even begin to wash this wretched stain off her conscience.

Chapter 10

Belda had been accurate in her prediction; the fervor surrounding Kyra Hastings disappearance died down quickly. By week two, it was a one-paragraph blurb buried in the back of the *LA Times*, with no photograph of the famous face. The tiny column stated, in essence: nothing new to report; she's still missing.

Shortly after that, the news carried no mention of the actress's disappearance at all. Stormie was finally able to stop holding her breath.

Travis was leaving again, this time for Las Vegas to help Connor with something to do with his club. Stormie was offered a guest spot as a mob wife on the Sopranos and was anxious to return to work. She was also asked to present an award at this year's Oscars. Her life had finally returned to normal.

After Kyra disappeared, Stormie went to the doctor for a tranquilizer prescription. Travis never knew his wife had replaced booze with pills, he only knew she wasn't drinking as much as he'd feared she would once Heather had left. Stormie was distant and preoccupied, but he was accustomed to her erratic mood swings, and had anticipated as much.

After the new year, Kyra Hastings stopped consuming Stormie's every waking thought. Back in the part of her heart that Stormie didn't like to think about, a small voice began wondering what they might do with Kyra's pending projects.

The question was answered in a small article in the *Hollywood Reporter* in early February. It indicated that the studios were suspending shooting until resolution of the police investigation into her disappearance. The roles were not being recast.

At least, not yet, the evil little voice said from Stormie's heart.

Stormie finally believed no one was going to be able to tie her to this, and was naturally extremely relieved. She also marveled at what the woman in Seattle was capable of. It was remarkable. *What might another fifty grand buy?* she wondered. *Or a hundred and fifty, for that matter?*

True, the woman had insulted her. The bitch had chosen the one subject that Stormie didn't need thrown in her face. But hadn't that snide comment also helped her get control of her drinking? Hadn't she stopped pouring the booze down her throat because of that old woman's confidence that Stormie would drown her anxiety in vodka? The answer was yes. And maybe for that, Stormie could forgive the old biddy's attitude and think of her as a genie in a bottle. But this genie might be good for a lot more than just three wishes. If the money was right, she could be good for as many as Stormie needed. She was sure of that.

~~~~

As winter gave way to spring, the public's memory of Kyra Hastings grew more and more dim. Stormie had convinced herself
~~~~

that once the studios gave up on the girl ever returning and began recasting her parts, they would call her to recreate the role of Desiree in *Golden Sunset.* A role she had once brought to life with such style and flair. She had won an Academy Award the first time, so why not twice for the same role?

It wasn't until this grand illusion came crashing down around her that Stormie fled back to the comfort of her bottle.

The story was in Variety, the trade's gossip rag. The studios had indeed given up on Kyra's return, just as Stormie knew they eventually would. They had recast the roles. Kirsten Dunst would be Desiree. Stormie read the article over and over, growing more angry each time.

"How could they do this to me?" she fumed to Travis.

"Do what, honey? You didn't honestly think they were going to cast you as Desiree again, did you?"

"With Kyra Hastings gone, why not?" she screamed.

Travis shook his head, bewildered. "You know, I really thought you were over this whole obsession with being young again. For cryin' out loud, Stormie, you shot that movie when you were half the age you are now. Do we have to go through this again? Next thing you'll be calling Katz and telling him to—"

"What are you saying, Travis? I couldn't pull it off? I'm too old to pull it off, is that it?"

For the first time in his entire married life to the infamous Stormie Banks, Travis didn't even try to appease her on the subject of her lost youth. He replied simply, "Yep. That's what I'm sayin'." He rose and walked from the room, leaving Stormie staring after him, her eyes blazing with hurt and fury.

Stormie spent the rest of the day and night drinking. The bitter confrontation with Travis took place around four o'clock in the afternoon. Stormie locked herself in their bedroom and sucked Absolut straight from the bottle until she passed out.

Somewhere around one o'clock in the morning, Travis broke the door down and found her on the floor, choking on her own vomit. He roused her enough to get her airway clear and called 911. She was admitted to Cedars of Lebanon Hospital with alcohol poisoning.

Thanks to an emergency room nurse, Stormie once again made headlines. Headlines embarrassing to herself, her husband, and her daughter.

During one tearful phone conversation with Travis, Heather cried, "Why does she do this? Why does she do it to herself and why does she do it to us?"

Travis had no answer. He had asked himself the same question a thousand times.

Stormie refused to go into a treatment center. She swore to Travis she would never do anything like that again. She had scared the hell out of herself this time.

Depression settled around Stormie like a rain-soaked cloak. All the same relentless voices in her head clamored on and on about getting old. All the same resentment toward younger actresses. The stubborn refusal to take a single role that didn't cast her as a young leading lady.

Not that there were many parts to refuse now. Since word of her hospital stay had surfaced, the scripts had dried up, and the Academy of Motion Picture Arts and Sciences had diplomatically withdrawn their invitation for her to present at this year's Oscars.

Stormie tried valiantly to stay away from the vodka, settling instead for another prescription for tranquilizers. They made her drowsy and she slept twelve, and sometimes fourteen hours a day. Travis didn't know what to do for her anymore. She was inconsolable. Even a weekend visit from Heather did nothing to brighten her spirits.

~~~~

Three weeks after Stormie's release from the hospital, the telephone rang in the wee hours of the morning.

Travis reached over his drugged wife's sleeping body and fumbled the receiver to his ear. "'Lo?"

"Travis, it's Marsha," his tearful ex-wife cried into the phone. "Something terrible has happened. Cal is in the hospital."

He snapped fully awake and fumbled for the light switch. "What happened?" His voice was strained with worry.

"There was a fire at the magic school. They were doing some kind of show and something went wrong. The whole building burned to the ground! Cal saved three people, but he... he..." She burst into tears and couldn't finish.

"Oh Jesus, Marsha, he's not...?"

Stormie had begun to stir next to him.

"No, no... I'm sorry Travis," she sobbed. "He's not dead. He has third degree burns on his right arm and he suffered smoke inhalation. Travis, they say he needs a skin graft. Can you come right away?"

"Of course. I'll be on a plane first thing tomorrow. Can I talk to him?"

Stormie sat up and stared at her husband with huge, frightened eyes. She mouthed, "What is it?"

Travis shook his head and returned his attention to his ex-wife.

"No, he's asleep now. They have him on painkillers and sedatives. Please, Travis, just get out here."

He offered a few words of comfort and reassurance to Marsha, then hung up and told Stormie what happened.
~~~~

"I'll go with you," she replied immediately.

He shook his head. "No. Marsha is a mess, and the last thing she needs is to see you right now."

Stormie began to protest, but knew it was in vain. When Travis made up his mind about something, it couldn't be changed. Besides, he was probably right. She didn't want to make things worse than they already were. Things had been terribly strained between her and Travis since she had been released from the hospital.

"Go back to sleep. I'm gonna go downstairs and try to find a flight on the internet."

Stormie threw the covers off and climbed out of bed, stumbling a little as she found her feet. "You're not dealing with this alone, Travis. Maybe I haven't been much good to you lately, but I'm still your wife, so don't shut me out. I'll come downstairs with you and make some coffee."

He nodded. "Okay. I'm sorry, I just thought…"

She shook her head. "Nothing to be sorry about. I love you, Travis, and I love Cal."

~~~~

"How long do you think you'll stay?" Stormie asked Travis, when he phoned the next evening from Texas.

"At least a couple weeks. He's doing pretty well, considering, but I need to be there for the skin graft."

"Was anyone else hurt?"

"Not as badly as my son. There were three people trapped behind the stage when a seven-foot board caught fire and fell over. Cal had already run from the building, but he went back in and shoved the board away so they could get out. That's how he
~~~~

burned his arm," Travis's voice was tinged with pride. "The others suffered some smoke inhalation, but they would have died if he hadn't gone back in. The local newspaper is calling my boy a hero. I'll bring back the article for you to read."

"Like father, like son," Stormie said.

"What about you?" Travis asked.

"What about me?"

"How are you doin'?"

"I'm fine. Tired."

"You takin' the tranquilizers?" he wondered.

"No, I told you I was going to stop while you were gone." Her voice grew tense.

"You haven't been drinking, have you?"

"Don't start, Travis," she snapped and immediately regretted it. She added miserably, "I'm sorry, hon."

"I'll call you tomorrow." His voice had grown chilly.

She started to say, "Give my love to—" But the line went dead in her ear.

She hung up the phone and walked into the bathroom to take a shower. She felt like crying for snapping at Travis when he was going through such hell.

Stormie turned on the hot water in the shower and automatically reached for the bottle of pills sitting next to the sink. She pulled her hand back just before it touched the bottle.

"Old habits die hard," she mumbled. She stripped out of her clothes and looked at herself critically in the mirror. She turned around, appraising her naked body in the full-length mirror as the bathroom filled with steam.

"God, look at me. Little fuckin' wonder I wasn't on MGM's wish list to play Desiree again. Little fuckin' wonder." She grabbed the bottle of tranquilizers with one violent swipe of her hand and dry-swallowed two. She glared at her harsh reflection in the mirror one final time, and said to her steam-blurred image, "What the fuck are you looking at, old lady?"

Stormie stood under the hot spray of the shower for twenty minutes, tears pouring down her face. She slid slowly down the wall until she was sitting on the floor. "I can't go on like this," she wept. "I just can't do it anymore."

As the water finally ran cold, Stormie pulled herself up from the wet tiles. After drying off with a towel and donning a robe, she sat on the bed with the bottle of pills in her hand. She wondered how many it would take to kill her.

Stormie shook a handful of the little blue pills into her palm and looked at them thoughtfully. She thought about what the media had done to her after she drank herself into the hospital. The only thing that stopped her from swallowing the pills was her fear of botching the job and ending up spattered yet again across the headlines. She knew Travis would never forgive her if he had to listen to the likes of Conan and Letterman make fun of her all over again.

Stormie threw the pills against the wall and fell sobbing to the floor. "So what do I do? What the hell do I do?" she screamed.

After a while, she slept. She awoke when the day had grown dark, and knew what she needed to do. The answer to her problems lay in Seattle.

Chapter 11

Stormie sat ramrod straight in a hard plastic chair at LAX and waited two hours for the next flight to Seattle. She ignored the stares and whispers of the people milling around the airport when they recognized her.

An employee of the airline approached her once and asked if she wouldn't be more comfortable waiting for her flight in the VIP lounge.

She barked a harsh laugh that sounded half mad, and snapped, "I don't feel very VIP today."

Once the plane landed in Seattle, Stormie climbed into a taxi. She arrived at Bella Luna just as a young couple were locking the doors and turning the *Open* sign over to *Closed.* The young woman was beautiful, with long, straight black hair flowing halfway down her slender back. Nicholas eyed Stormie expressionlessly.

"I'm sorry, we just closed," the young woman remarked, as she turned toward the woman climbing out of the cab.

Nicholas stepped in front of Gabriella. "Gabby, unlock the door," he put his hand over hers and guided the key back toward the lock.

"But Belda—" she began.

"Unlock it now," he commanded, reaching for the famous actress's elbow to help her from the cab.

Stormie's hair was uncombed. She wore no makeup, and dark shadows tinged the skin below her eyes a pale blue. Never in her entire adult life had she gone out in public looking as she did today. Whatever the media frenzy might make of this, she couldn't care less.

Gabriella's heart fluttered in her chest like the wings of a small bird. She fumbled the key back into the lock and managed to get the door open. Nicholas guided the disheveled actress inside and led her back to Belda's small office. He lit several candles.

"Gabriella," he said quietly, "make Ms. Banks some tea."

Too flustered to argue, Gabriella muttered, "Christ, I didn't even recognize her!" and turned to do as Nicholas asked.

"You just sit right here," Nicholas soothed, settling Stormie into a chair. "Everything's going to be alright." He patted her hand and quietly left the room, closing the door softly behind him. He then ran for the staircase.

Stormie didn't speak. She couldn't speak. She sat with military erectness, just as she had at the airport, waiting. Silent tears slid down her cheeks.

Several minutes later, the old woman opened the door. She entered in a warm breeze of incense and perfume that smelled vaguely familiar to Stormie.

Sitting down in the chair opposite the actress, Belda took Stormie's hand and enfolded it in her own arthritic fingers.

"I made a mistake," Stormie said, robot-like, a few moments later. She stared straight ahead as if she were in a daze.

"I know that, my dear. Do you know now what it is you really wanted when you came to see me before?"

"Yes, I do."

"It had nothing to do with the Hastings woman, did it? She was just a symptom of the real problem."

"I want to be young. That's all I want. I just want to be young again."

"You're certain of this?"

"I've never been more sure of anything in my life," her voice cracked with emotion.

"Very well," Belda answered softly. "Wait here." She rose from her chair and left the movie star sitting alone in the candle-lit room.

When Belda emerged from the office, Gabriella and Nicholas were waiting huddled by the counter, looking at her with anxious eyes.

Gabriella took the old woman's arm, "I'm sorry, Belda, she didn't have an appointment, and I didn't recognize her looking like that. We didn't want to wake you, but—"

"It's fine, Gabriella, dear," Belda cut her off. "We will allow Ms. Bank's oversight of not scheduling this meeting to slide. She is rather upset, I'm afraid."

"Yeah, no kidding," Nicholas replied. "Is everything okay? Do you need us to stay?"

"Everything is quite fine. Gabriella, would you be kind enough to book Ms. Banks a suite at the Four Seasons, and call a limousine service to pick her up here in about two hours, please? Then you may both go home."

"Of course," Gabriella replied, turning toward the phone.

"Thank you, dear. You both have a pleasant evening." The old woman turned and started up the stairs.

"What about her?" Nicholas asked, hooking a thumb toward the closed office door.

"Ms. Banks is waiting for a potion."

"Tonight? You are making her a potion now?" Nicholas asked incredulously. "Don't you need a few days?"

"Well, of course, under normal circumstances it is best for me to have a bit more time. I will have to be careful to make sure I don't forget anything—especially for a spell of this magnitude. But I believe this situation is a bit of an emergency for Ms. Banks, and she is a very valuable client. So I will make an exception and hope for the best." Belda shrugged, put one arthritic claw on the banister, and began her careful climb upstairs.

Gabriella and Nicholas exchanged an uneasy glance.

Nicholas mouthed, "Hope for the best?"

Gabriella felt the hairs on the back of her neck rise.

~~~~

Later that evening, snuggled on the couch and listening to Barry White, Nicholas said, "Can I ask you something?"

"Hmmm?" a sleepy Gabriella murmured.

"Do you think Belda is going insane?"

Gabriella gasped and struggled out of his embrace. "Nicholas! Don't ever say that out loud! Are you mad? If she knew you thought such a thing, God only knows what she would do!"

"Calm down, Gabby. She needs me, she isn't going to hurt me. I just worry lately. She didn't used to take chances. Sometimes I get scared that if she goes down, we go with her."
~~~~

Gabriella leapt from the couch and spun around as though someone were behind her wielding a bludgeon. She shrieked, “Stop it, Nicholas! You don’t know what she is capable of! Stop talking like this. If you don’t, she’ll kill you! Do you understand that she demands complete loyalty? Don’t overestimate your usefulness. That could be a deadly mistake.”

Nicholas stared at the woman he loved. The wild-eyed and fearful expression he saw on her beautiful face hurt his heart. “You’re probably right. I’m sorry, babe,” he soothed, taking her hand and pulling her back onto the couch. “I won’t bring it up again.”

“Promise?” she leaned her head on his shoulder.

“Promise. What do you suppose she’s mixing up for Stormie Banks?”

He felt Gabriella shudder against him. “I have no idea. Frankly, that woman scares me more than Belda ever could.”

“Why is that, Gab?” he asked, honestly curious.

“Her sense of entitlement. Her very stature in life. She shows up out of nowhere and demands Belda drop everything and take care of her. She has no idea how careful each potion has to be, and that forcing Belda to mix one up this very evening, with no time to check her work, could be extremely dangerous.”

“Force Belda? Honey, no one forces Belda to do anything. Belda thrives on this kind of drama as much as that actress does. Besides, she wouldn’t have agreed to make her something if she didn’t think she could do it right.” Nicholas brushed Gabriella’s hair back from her brow.

But Nicholas wondered. And he couldn’t push away the worry that was gnawing at his mind. He had a bad feeling about this actress. *Hope for the best*, Belda had said.

Yes, he had a very bad feeling indeed.

~~~~

Stormie didn't know how long she waited for the old woman to return. She may have dozed. The candles that had been burning when Belda left the tiny room were extinguished now, and the room was pitch black. From a high shelf, Stormie heard purring and looked up to see Eros's glowing green eyes.

When Belda returned to the tiny office, she carried an oil lamp in one gnarled hand, and a small glass cylinder in the other. The lamp cast a dim blue glow about the room. Shadows danced around Belda as she sat down across from Stormie, and set the items down on the table between them.

When their eyes met, Stormie's blood ran cold. In this eerie light, the woman looked utterly insane. Stormie thought for the briefest of seconds, *And she thinks the same thing about me.*

Stormie reached out for the bottle, but the old woman snatched it away with uncanny speed and dexterity.

"Not so fast, Ms. Banks. We have a few things to discuss first."

Stormie closed her eyes and sighed. "How much?"

"We'll get to the financial aspect in a moment. First, there are more important things."

"Such as?" Stormie eyed the woman cautiously.

"That garbage you have been taking. The little blue pills," Belda said, her voice dripping contempt.

Stormie grimaced. "You know about the tranquilizers?"

"I know a great many things, Ms. Banks."

"You don't care much for modern remedies, I take it."

"Those are no remedy; they are merely another crutch, like your vodka. They need to be out of your system completely before you ingest this. Your body must be completely free of all toxins,
~~~~

including alcohol, or something could go wrong. Horribly wrong. Do you understand?"

Stormie shuddered. "What could happen?" The daze that had shrouded her, that had carried her from Los Angeles to Seattle on this hellish errand, was beginning to loosen its fiendish grip. She was growing frightened.

"Best case scenario, the mixture simply wouldn't work. Worst case, death or disfigurement."

Stormie gasped. She stared at the old woman, horrified and speechless.

Belda appeared not to notice. She instructed, "Pour the mixture into a drink. Anything but liquor will do fine. It can be either hot or cold, and you will need around eight ounces. If the beverage you choose changes color once the blend is added—I never know from potion to potion if it will—allow the color to return to normal before you drink it. Once the mixture dissolves completely, consume the entire beverage. And I must tell you something else. I am not used to putting anything together this quickly. I am hoping I didn't make any errors in the blend."

Stormie stared at her. "And what if you did… make an error? What happens to me then?"

Belda held the glass vial up to the oil lamp. Something dark and thick swirled inside. "In life," Belda replied, "we take chances and hope for the best. For what it's worth, I have been doing this for many years, and I have rarely made mistakes. However, if you find you don't wish to drink the potion, that's entirely up to you. You could dump it down a garbage disposal, or leave right now without it and I wouldn't charge you a penny. The choice is yours, Ms. Banks."

Stormie said hastily, "I want it. Believe me, I do. It's worth the risk."

"Very well. The final rule is simple. You are never to tell anyone about this. If you do, I'll kill you."

Stormie jumped. "What?" She began shaking uncontrollably. She felt like the temperature in the room just dropped twenty degrees and an arctic wind blasted her skin. Termite-like creeps crawled up her legs and over her back.

"My discretion is as important as yours, Ms. Banks. Just remember that and we will get along fine. There is only one last thing."

"What's that?" a terrified Stormie whispered through chattering teeth.

"There is no refund. Regardless of the outcome."

"I suspected as much. May I have it now?" Stormie swallowed hard, trying to clear the lump from her throat. She desperately wanted to get out of this creepy place and out from under this strange old sorceress's penetrating stare.

Belda pressed the glass into her waiting palm and wrapped her claw-like hand around Stormie's fingers. "Good luck, Ms. Banks. I hope you find what you are looking for."

The price was quoted. As Stormie wrote out the check with trembling fingers, Belda said, "A limo will be waiting outside to deliver you to the Four Seasons."

Stormie jumped. "I forgot to make a reservation."

"Yes, I am aware of that. It's been taken care of. I suggest that upon arrival to your suite, you phone your housekeeper and ask her to feed your dog and take him for a walk."

Stormie handed Belda the check. "You are a scary woman, Belda. Did anyone ever tell you that?"

Belda smiled benignly. "Not to my face. However, I will not punish you for such impudence, Ms. Banks."

"Why is that, Belda?"

"Because I really enjoyed *Golden Sunset.*"

Chapter 12

Safely locked in her suite at the Four Seasons, Stormie phoned Carolyn and instructed her to take care of Franklin. She offered no explanation of where she was, or why she had left without feeding the dog or making arrangements for his care. Carolyn didn't ask. Stormie's eccentricities weren't new to her.

Next, Stormie called room service and ordered dinner. When the girl taking her order asked what she would like to drink, she began by force of habit, "A double Absolut marti—" then abruptly changed it to, "uh, no, I mean a Diet Coke. Just a Diet Coke."

Stormie changed into the big plush robe the hotel provided, and lay down on the bed. In her hand, she held the little glass vial from Bella Luna, and wondered how something so small could cost so much. The old woman had charged her well into six figures for this little gem.

The vial was only the length of Stormie's pinkie, and twice as wide. The glass was slightly cloudy, but Stormie could see that the liquid inside was dark and viscous.

Stormie wedged a fingernail under the vial's cork and pried it off. A faint aroma rose into the air: mild, not unpleasant, and vaguely familiar.

The potion itself, now that she could see it properly, looked like freshly mown grass stuffed into a blender. There were even little *bits* left in it, solid spots darker than the rest.

Stormie recorked the bottle. She wondered what the potion that forced Kyra Hastings's untimely departure from Hollywood had looked like.

Stormie spoke to the bottle. "You are my last chance. If you can't bring back the youth I've lost, then I give up. My next headline will be my last. It will be my obituary."

Deep inside the vial, the potion began to pulse a dull red as if it had heard her plea. Heat burned her fingers through the glass.

Stormie's eyes flew open, and she dropped the cylinder to the floor. "What the hell?" she breathed in awe. She stuck her searing fingers into her mouth.

Thankfully, the glass vial had not broken when she dropped it, and the cork remained firm. Stormie bent down, examining the strange little bottle where it lay. The glowing brick color was fading.

When room service knocked at the door a moment later, Stormie nearly screamed. She cinched her robe tightly around her waist and caught her breath before walking out to the suite's foyer. "Who is it?"

"Room service," a voice on the other side of the closed door responded.

"Just leave it outside, please."

Stormie left the potion on the floor, too afraid to pick it up. In her entire life, she had never needed a drink as badly as she did right now. She was grateful she had left the tranquilizers behind in California, or she would have been popping a couple right now, Belda's dire warning or not.

Stormie ate a little of the dinner she'd ordered, her eyes never leaving the ominous little vial.

Sleep didn't come easily. Not without pills or booze to lull her, and certainly not with that strange potion on the floor next to the bed. Finally, as the sun was breaking in the east, Stormie drifted off for a few hours.

When she woke, she tore a piece of hotel stationary from the pad on the desk and slid the small vial onto it. She treated it like a dead insect; her fingers never making direct contact with the glass. Stormie just couldn't bring herself to touch it, although the strange contents were once again the color of freshly cut grass.

Stormie wondered briefly if the violent red color she witnessed beneath the glass the night before had been an illusion brought on by the lateness of the hour and the strangeness of the errand which had brought her here.

No, she decided. It hadn't been. She was not given to hallucinations even when in the deepest depths of drunkenness. Stormie had no reason to think she would fall prey to one while completely sober.

She sat on the bed and dialed the concierge's desk. "Is Dominique working?" she enquired of the man that answered.

Stormie was placed on hold for a moment before the cultured voice she remembered from her last visit answered, "Hello, this is Dominique."

"Hi, this is Stormie Banks in room 802."

"Ms. Banks," he cooed indulgently, "what a pleasure to have you staying with us again. How may I assist you?"

"Can you book me a flight back to Los Angeles tonight?"

"Of course. First class?"

"Yes. You can use the credit card number you have on file for me at the front desk."

"I will take care of that right now and have the itinerary for you shortly."

"Thank you, Dominique."

Stormie had no intention of drinking Belda's potion in a hotel room at the Four Seasons in Seattle. If anything was to go—as Belda had put it—*horribly wrong,* she didn't want to be found by the hotel staff in a strange city. She would rather do this in her own home and have Travis clean up the mess, both publicly and privately. Lord knew it wouldn't be the first time he'd be standing on the horizon with a broom to tidy up after her.

The only consolation was that this most certainly would be the last mess he would ever have to sweep up in his famous wife's destructive wake.

~~~~

Traffic was light when Stormie drove home from the airport. For the first time in the last twenty-four hours, she thought about someone other than herself. She wondered how Cal was doing. She wondered if Travis had tried to phone her. She had kept her cellphone turned off while in Seattle.

Throwing her keys on the counter, she pet Franklin and picked up the mail Carolyn had left on the counter. Stormie looked longingly at the bar, but dragged her eyes away and went to the refrigerator for a can of soda instead.

Travis had left a message. Cal was feeling better, the skin graft was scheduled for the beginning of the week, and he missed her.
~~~~

Fortunately, Travis sounded preoccupied. She didn't think he would ask where she'd been when they next spoke.

Stormie fed Franklin and took him for a walk.

That evening, the dog seemed quite agitated and was acting strangely. He followed her around the house and whined nervously. When Stormie let him sleep on the bed with her, he stayed glued to her side all night. She didn't know what had gotten into him. He was normally the most easygoing animal. Maybe he missed Travis? Surely the dog couldn't be sensing what she was planning on doing the next morning, or what was going to happen when she did. How could Franklin possibly know, when Stormie herself had no clue that the life she had been leading for the last thirty years was about to end?

Chapter 13

In the morning, Franklin was more nervous than ever. He refused to eat, even when Stormie offered him his favorite flavor of canned dog food, and whined pitifully at Stormie from his place by her feet.

"Franklin, what's the matter, honey? You miss Daddy?" She scratched behind his ears and retrieved a Milk Bone from the pantry. Franklin sniffed that most beloved of treats only once and then completely ignored it.

Stormie poured herself a second cup of coffee and left it sitting on the sink. She rummaged in her purse until she found the small glass vial lying in the Four Seasons' stationary at the bottom.

Stormie carefully removed the bottle from the paper. Her heart was pounding with excitement, her breath coming in shallow little gasps of anticipation.

If that woman could make Kyra Hastings vanish, how hard could it be to make me young again? she mused.

Stormie pulled a small hand mirror from her cosmetic bag and blew a kiss goodbye to the face staring back at her.

Carrying the potion in one hand and her coffee cup and compact mirror in the other, Stormie walked out the French doors and into the backyard.

Franklin followed her, barking.

Stormie sat on a lounge chair and set her coffee cup down next to her. "Franklin, shush! What's gotten into you, boy? Now be a good dog and go lie down; Mommy's busy."

Franklin wandered toward the grass like a drunken sailor. He stopped a few feet away, threw his head back, and howled woefully.

A cold finger of ice ran up Stormie's back. The hair on her arms stood up. "Okay, that's enough. Come on, Franklin. Back in the house." She took him by the collar and led him back inside, closing the French doors on his pitiful whines.

Franklin sat with his nose pressed against the glass, yelping inconsolably.

Stormie sat back down on the lounge chair and pulled the little cork from the very expensive vial that held all her hopes and dreams for the future. The smell was much stronger now: sharp and acidic. It assaulted her nostrils. Stormie held the tiny bottle at arm's length, and cried, "Whew!" Her eyes burned and watered.

The glass once again grew warm in Stormie's hand. The dull red glow pulsed ominously inside.

Before it grew too hot to hold, Stormie dumped the contents into her coffee. It glooped out in a single blob, splashing coffee onto Stormie's hand. She absently licked the spill off, watching the liquid closely. Almost immediately, the beverage turned bright Halloween orange, and then faded to a dull, bloody red. Small tendrils of smoke curled up, carrying the acrid, bitter odor with them.

Stormie blinked and rubbed at her stinging eyes. When she drew her hands away, the coffee had returned to normal. She sniffed it cautiously, but smelled only the rich aroma of French Roast.

Franklin was jumping at the doors, scratching to get out, barking frantically.

Stormie ignored him. She lifted the cup to her lips and swallowed its contents in three large gulps.

Nothing happened. She waited a few minutes, picked up the compact mirror, and examined her face. No change.

"Oh, I bet that bitch is having a good laugh at me now," she stewed. "A good laugh all the way to the bank. God, what an idiot I am."

Franklin was going insane behind the doors, trying to break through with his paws.

Stormie rose from the chaise to let him out. As she did so, a wave of vertigo overcame her. She collapsed back onto the chair in a graceless heap.

Stormie felt her eyelids grow heavy. Franklin's frantic yapping grew more distant, until it was only a dim sound coming from someplace far away.

And then there was nothing but darkness.

Chapter 14

“Oh my God, Rob, there is a woman floating in the pool!” actress Sarah Stewart screamed to her husband. She scooped up her grandson and ran back inside the French doors of their Hollywood Hills home. Sarah had been babysitting all afternoon, and had just walked out back with the toddler to splash around in the pool.

Her husband appeared beside her, squinted in the direction of the pool, and then charged past her and dove into the water.

Sarah ran into the house for the phone and called 911. She yelled to the operator, “Please hurry! There is a woman dead in our pool!” Then she returned to watch her husband wrestle the stranger out of the water.

Rob Evans grabbed the hem of an oddly outdated cotton, floral-print dress. He looped an arm around the waist of the tall, thin girl and pulled her toward the shallow end. He turned her over and hauled her out of the pool by her shoulders.

“Is she dead?” Sarah called anxiously. The baby began to cry.

“I don’t know,” Rob panted, winded by the exertion. “Sarah, get the baby inside.”

Sarah hovered at the back door, uncertain whether she should leave her husband alone.

Rob checked the girl for a pulse. It was there, but thready and weak. He brushed long, blonde hair from her face and pounded the girl's chest, trying to expel the water from her lungs.

Sarah heard the distant wail of a siren and ran back inside. She pressed the button that would open the spear-tipped, wrought iron gate at the head of their driveway.

By the time the aid crew arrived, the girl had coughed up the water she'd swallowed and was regaining consciousness. Rob saw a straw handbag next to the pool. He picked it up and looked inside. His wife had handed their grandson over to their housekeeper and rejoined him.

"Who the hell is she?" Sarah wondered.

"That's what I'm looking for." Rob extracted a wallet from the bag. He opened it up and found an Indiana driver's license.

"This must be a fake; look at the date," he whispered to his wife.

They exchanged an uneasy glance.

Meanwhile, the aid crew had rushed to the girl's side.

"What are you doing?" the girl asked blearily, when the medic began to examine her. "Why are you in my yard? I never said you could come in. What is happening?" she batted the medic's hands away. "Stop it! Stop touching me. I'm going to call my husband!"

"We just need to get you to a hospital—"

"A hospital? I don't need any hospital, I'm fine. Don't you know who I am? Get your hands off me!"

"Miss—"

"No!"

The medic shook his head and approached Sarah and Rob instead. "Do you know her?"

"No, we've never seen her before. How the hell did she get into our backyard?"

"She claims she lives here. Maybe we'd better get the police out here." The medic shot a wary glance at the soaking young girl Rob Evans had fished out of his pool.

"Is she going to be alright?" Sarah asked, thinking of lawsuits.

"I think she may have sustained a head injury when she fell in," the medic replied. "She's extremely confused and is refusing to let us take her to the hospital."

The girl was blinking stupidly and looking around the backyard. She looked up at Sarah. Her eyes flew open in shock. "Sarah, what the hell are you doing here?"

"Oh shit," Rob breathed under his breath. "She's a stalker. Didn't this just happen to Meg Ryan? Some nutcase showed up at her house claiming to be her husband or something?"

Sarah responded to the girl in that patient, *everything-is-going-to-be-just-fine* tone reserved exclusively for the severely insane. "Uh, I am here because this is my home. You fell in our pool."

The girl looked at her like she was crazy. "No, Sarah, this is my house. I just got up to let Franklin out. I must have fallen and hit my head or something. Why are you and Rob here, and what the hell happened to my patio furniture? Who changed it?"

Rob closed her wallet and placed it back in the purse. He whispered to the medic to call the police. The medic told him they were already on their way.

Rob knelt down next to the girl. She looked like she was barely out of her teens. "We have never met you before and we don't know why you came here, but if you go away quietly we won't press any charges."

"Press charges for what? Rob, what is going on here?"

"Miss, how did you get into our backyard?"

"Why are you calling me 'miss' like I'm some stranger? I have known you for over twenty years! And this is my backyard, not yours! *You* are at *my* house!" She looked around in absolute bewilderment.

"Young lady, is there someone we can call? Your parents maybe?" he asked.

The girl rose unsteadily to her feet. She looked at Sarah pleadingly, "Remember, Sarah, we didn't talk for two years because you and Rob wanted this house too. Remember how mad you were at me when I raised my offer fifty grand to make sure I got it?"

Rob and Sarah exchanged another uncomfortable glance and then looked at the young girl with a mixture of pity and fear.

"I mean the patio furniture is wrong, but... Hey, wait a second. Is this someone's idea of a joke?" the girl cried, an edge of hysteria creeping into her voice. "Is there a hidden camera somewhere? Because let me tell you, it's not funny." Sarah cleared her throat. "Um, do you want to put on a robe and get out of that wet dress? I can have Carolyn put it in the dryer for you, okay?" The girl was beginning to scare the bejesus out of her. She wanted to calm her down until the police arrived and hauled her crazy butt out of here.

The girl stood swaying from side to side. "Carolyn is off today," she muttered, and began to swoon.

One of the medics strode over and put a supportive arm around her waist. He led her to a padded chair and eased her down.

"I really think you should let us take you to the hospital and let them check you out."

"No. Please, would you all just get out of here and let me lie down. God, I need a drink."

"Miss, where do you live?" the medic asked patiently.

"For the last time, I live here, you idiot!" she exploded.

Sarah looked uncertainly at her husband, who just shrugged and twirled his finger around his ear in the age-old gesture signifying madness.

Sarah took the girl by the hand and helped her up. "Come on, let's get you out of that dress."

The girl nearly collapsed again when she entered the house. Her eyes flew open wide at the furnishings. "What did you do?" she hissed in a breathy whisper.

Sarah backed away from her and called, "Carolyn, get down here."

The housekeeper descended the stairs quickly.

The girl stared at her balefully. "So you're in on this too? You can start looking for another job, Carolyn," she spat. "Where the hell is Franklin? He was having a fit and I need to make sure he's okay."

The housekeeper's jaw dropped. She looked at Sarah and mouthed, "Who's Franklin?"

Sarah took her elbow and whispered, "She's completely crazy. Just humor her until the police arrive." She turned back toward the girl. "Sweetie, Carolyn is just going to dry your dress, okay? She doesn't want to hurt you. No one does."

The girl looked down at her wet dress for the first time and gasped, "Oh my God! I haven't seen this old thing in…" She stopped suddenly, and looked up at the two women staring fearfully at her. A deep and palpable dread began to envelope her in its steely embrace. She stood shaking. All the color drained from her face. She passed out just as two uniformed officers entered the house.

After hearing the story from Rob Evans, the officers approached the girl. The medics had roused her. She was settled back into the chair in the backyard.

"Miss Burkowitz? I'm Officer Ortiz and this is Officer Cole," he said in a soft, comforting tone.

"What did you call me?" She looked at him through narrowed eyes.

"Is that not your real name? Your driver's license is obviously a forgery. Or a joke—I mean, given the date and all."

The girl stared at him. The dawning horror of what that old crazy bitch in Seattle might have done was beginning to sink in with steel teeth. It left her mute with terror. *She couldn't have pulled this off. No way. I am NOT Stella again.*

The girl looked at the officer and tried to clear her head. Her breath was coming in short little gasps and the world started to swim in front of her once more.

"I think I'm going to faint," she moaned.

Officer Cole took her hand. "Here, put your head down between your knees. We think you sustained a head injury when you fell in the water. You really ought to let the medics take you to the hospital where someone can take a look at you. You might have a concussion."

When the swimmy feeling passed enough that she could sit up straight, the girl replied desperately, "I can't go to the hospital. If I end up in the tabloids again, Travis is going to kill me."

The officers exchanged a nervous glance. Ortiz sighed. "Okay, here's the deal, Stella. These nice people aren't going to press charges for trespassing as long as you give them your word that you won't come back here ever again. They think you are a fan that just got a little overzealous. In their line of work, that happens sometimes. You don't have any drugs in your purse, so there isn't much we can hold you on if they don't want to press charges. So Officer Cole and I are going to put on our report that you were let off with a warning. Now, if you don't want to go to the hospital and get checked out, we will give you a lift somewhere, but we need to leave the property now, okay? And I need your word that you aren't going to come back here again. If you do, we are going to have to arrest you, understand?"

She needed to get somewhere where she could think. Panic gnawed at the corner of her mind like a feral rat. What it appeared had happened to her was just too awful to contemplate. What the old woman must have done was completely impossible. If Stormie Banks had gone back in time, why was everyone else still in the present? And how exactly did Sarah and Rob end up owning her house?

The girl employed the best of her theatrical training to act humble and apologetic. She made up a story about staying with a friend who was working late. She didn't have a key to the apartment. She asked the officers to drop her off at Plummer Park, promising to wait there until her friend could come pick her up.

They were reluctant to leave her, but eventually agreed because there was nothing more they could do. With Rob Evans and Sarah Stewart refusing to press charges, it was a victimless crime. They couldn't book her.

With an admonishment to stay out of trouble, the policemen let the girl out of the patrol car at the west entrance to the park and watched her walk down the path.

"You don't think she's dangerous, do you?" Cole asked, still watching the girl.

"Nah. Just some kooky kid with a sixties fetish. Did you get a load of the dress and the purse?"

"How do you suppose she shimmied over those spears on the fence into their yard without getting impaled on them?" Ortiz wondered.

"God takes care of fools and drunks. Isn't that what they say?"

"I don't think she's a fool."

"Maybe not, but she's seriously messed up," Cole observed.

"Did you see the driver's license? You ever seen a forgery like that? Why would anyone forge a date back thirty years? Can't very well arrest her for fake ID, when she couldn't even use it to buy a bus ticket."

"What was that she said about ending up in the tabloids again?" Cole shook his head.

"Hell if I know. She's a real wack-job."

"Well, she's not our problem anymore—unless she decides to go swimming in somebody's pool again."

~~~~

The girl sat down on a bench and rummaged through the purse she carried. She found the driver's license and stared at it. Only after several minutes, and with great effort, did she pull her eyes away.

Further inspection of the wallet revealed her high school student identification card, a couple hundred dollars in small bills, some change, a pair of cat's-eye sunglasses with small rhinestones set in the frames, a comb, and a makeup bag with a jumble of cosmetics the stores hadn't carried in at least twenty-five years. The exact same belongings she had brought with her on a Greyhound bus over thirty years before. The only thing missing was the set of mismatched luggage she had brought her clothes in. Two cheap suitcases full of pedal pushers and sweaters that she could probably make a fortune on if she sold them to a vintage clothing shop today.

What the hell did that bitch do? The girl wondered incredulously.

The straw purse had large, pink fabric flowers glued to the side. She flipped the handbag upside down violently onto the
~~~~

bench, tearing one of the flowers. She pawed through the strewn contents. No credit cards, no ATM card, no keys, no ID bearing the name she'd woken up with this morning, no cellphone. Nothing. Not a single remnant of Stormie Banks.

The coppery taste of fear coated her throat. She stuffed everything back into the straw purse and rose to find a drinking fountain. She located one just outside the public bathroom. She drank greedily, then stepped into the ladies room. She lay the ridiculous floral purse on the floor and warily approached the cracked and rusted mirror. Seeing the pale, distorted reflection of a ghost staring back at her from the glass, she screamed and fell back against the wall, banging her back on the air dryer. She slid to the floor, gasping for breath. She shrieked, "No, no, no, no!" and whipped her head wildly back and forth. "This isn't happening!"

It took the girl several minutes to peel herself from the wall and steel herself for another inspection. This time, she gripped the edge of the sink with one sweaty palm and pulled the long, straight blonde hair back from her face with the other. No, not *her* face. No plastic surgeon's blade had ever been anywhere near this face. This face was the one she had carried with her to Los Angeles when she had been nineteen. It was unlined, youthful, disturbing, and most unwelcome.

Hysterical laughter began to bubble up from the girl's throat. She jammed a fist against her lips to gag the insane peals of laughter trying to escape. She ran her fingers over the bridge of her nose. Her original nose. A considerably larger one than the one she'd woken up with. One she had paid very good money to get rid of a long, long time ago.

"Oh, that crazy old crone! What the fuck has she done to me?" she wailed to the deserted bathroom.

Breath whistling in and out of her throat, heart hammering in her ears, she swallowed hard and pulled the bodice of her dress out with two trembling fingers. When last she looked, a plum colored, Victoria's Secret demi-cup bra supported her ample bosom. Now, as she stared down the front of her dress, she saw a white cotton stretchy thing. The delicate little swells of her breasts barely filled the comically small bra.

"Penney's," she cackled crazily. "I bought this at J.C. Penney in nineteen fucking sixty-seven."

Tears poured from her eyes. She didn't know if the hysterical wails pouring from her lips were laughs or cries. She let go of the front of her dress with a grimace and stumbled into one of the filthy stalls, sure she was going to pass out. She sat down hard on the toilet seat and folded her arms across her narrow chest, clutching her elbows and sobbing.

"This isn't what I meant!" she screamed. Her voice echoed off the tiles in the deserted bathroom. She screamed even louder, "This isn't what I meant, you crazy old fuck, and you know it! You sick bitch! You knew what I meant and this fucking wasn't it! You did this on purpose, you fucking miserable hag!"

And then she did pass out. She listed sideways off the toilet, her head rapping sharply against the toilet paper dispenser.

The girl had no idea how much time had elapsed when gentle hands shook her shoulders and she began to rouse. A soothing, grandmotherly voice told her not to worry, the paramedics were coming.

That brought her fully awake. All she needed now was for the same two that treated her at Sarah and Rob's house (*My house, mine, mine, mine!)* to show up and find her like this in the damn john. Fighting a wave of nausea, she climbed unsteadily to her feet.

"Where's my bag?" she asked the old woman.

"Everything spilled out. I cleaned it all up and put it on the sink," the woman answered, concern showing in her pale eyes. "Maybe you should sit d—"

The girl shook her head vigorously. She grabbed her purse off the sink and ran from the bathroom, just as wailing sirens pulled into the parking lot. She fled from the park without looking back.

~~~~

When her legs were nearly unable to support her and a cramp pulsed painfully in her calf, Stella Burkowitz stumbled through the doors of a Burger King in Hollywood. The moment the rich, greasy aroma of fried food greeted her, she realized she was starving. She ordered a hamburger and fries, ignoring the curious glances cast her way. She was used to being ogled in public, although for entirely different reasons than the current ones. She slid into a corner booth, where she ate greedily and drank a large soda.

Once Stella ate and got her nerves under control, she knew what she needed to do. She would call Travis and have him wire her some money. She wouldn't have to explain her appearance to him. Not yet anyway. She prayed he would accept "I'll explain later," when he asked why she couldn't withdraw money from their account herself. There was no lie convincing enough to keep him from booking passage on the next plane home. And that was the one thing she knew must not happen. Not until she figured out how the hell Sarah and Rob had ended up in possession of their house.

It never entered her mind that she would have no identification as Stormie Banks to produce at the Western Union office when she went to claim the cash her husband sent. It also never occurred to her that Sarah and Rob might not be the only people who wouldn't remember her.

Stella's mind was set on one thing: boarding a plane to Seattle and making that insane old bag fix this disaster.
~~~~

Stella took a ten dollar bill from the straw purse and traded it for a roll of quarters at the counter. She then walked a half mile to a Chevron station and locked herself into a phone booth. She plugged in two of the quarters and dialed Travis's cell phone number. A mechanical voice answered, "The wireless phone number you have dialed is not in service at this time."

"Oh that's just great. Perfect fucking day for the cellphone to die," she groaned.

Stella didn't know what hospital Cal was in and didn't know Travis's ex-wife's phone number. That information was in the phonebook in the den of what used to be her house.

That thought turned on the panic again. She took a few deep breaths, telling herself that if she didn't stay calm, she was never going to get out of this.

Stella dialed the phone number to Heather's apartment in Cambridge. Another mechanical voice told her to deposit four dollars and fifty cents for three minutes. She did so, praying Heather would be home. The phone was answered on the second ring by Heather's roommate Karen.

"Hi Karen, is Heather there?" Stella asked, clutching the phone cord between two white knuckles.

"Who?"

"Heather. Your roommate!" she responded through gritted teeth.

"Umm... I think you have the wrong number. There is nobody here by that name," the girl replied.

"Is this Karen Talbot?"

"Yes, but I don't have a roommate named Heather. My roommate's name is Michelle. You have the wrong number."

The phone went dead in her ear. Sweat broke out on Stella's brow, a pulse hammered at her temples. Panic nibbled at the corner of her mind again. Stella willed herself to stop it. The phone began to slide from her sweaty fist. Her ears were ringing and she could feel her heart trying to pound out of her chest.

She dialed 411. "I need the phone number for the registrar's office at Harvard Law School in Cambridge Massachusetts."

Stella scribbled the number on the shelf with a chewed down pencil found on the floor of the booth. She dialed the number and was told again to deposit four dollars and fifty cents.

"Shit!" she screamed. She slammed the phone down and walked over to the attendant at the service station. "Do you have a roll of quarters I can buy?"

The teenager leered at her openly. She turned her head away, unable to believe a boy that was young enough to be her son was eyeing her with such brazen lust, while he fished in the cash register for the quarters. When she returned to the phone booth, an old woman had locked herself in. It was fifteen minutes before she emerged.

Stella Burkowitz was shaking so badly, she dropped two quarters to the ground as she tried to shove them into the coin slot. Finally, the call was connected.

"Registrar's Office, Peggy speaking."

She cleared her throat and did her best to keep her voice calm. "Yes. I am looking for Heather Banks. She is a third-year student there. Can someone get a message to her? I don't know what class she is in right now."

"Just a sec," Peggy answered, and Stella heard the clacking of a keyboard in the background. "I'm sorry, what did you say the last name was?"

"Banks. B-A-N-K-S."

"I don't show a student registered by that name."

Stella swallowed hard, and her throat clicked. "Do you have a Daniel Holliman registered? He's graduating this year."

There was a pause at the other end of the line, and this time no clacking of computer keys.

"Hello?" she said when the girl didn't respond.

In a soft voice, the girl replied, "I had a class with Dan last year. He… he was involved in an accident this past spring."

Stella shut her eyes. "What kind of accident?" she whispered.

"It was really freaky. He was walking by a construction site when someone dropped a can of paint from a really high scaffolding. It crushed his skull. He's been dead for nearly a year."

When she heard the sharp intake of breath from the other end of the phone, Peggy stammered, "I'm really sorry you had to find out this way. Was he a friend?"

The mechanical voice broke back through the line with "Please deposit another three dollars."

Stella slammed the phone down and fell to her knees sobbing. She was startled by someone pounding on the door to the phone booth. A gruff looking man yelled through the glass, "You gonna be in there all day, or what?"

Stella fled the booth, leaving the unused quarters behind on the shelf.

Chapter 15

Stella Burkowitz didn't know how long she walked. She asked directions twice and both times ended up completely lost and nowhere near her destination. Finally, as the sun was sinking in the pastel sky, she walked through the dirty glass doors to the Greyhound station. The eyes staring out from her exhausted face were glazed and glassy. She bumped into a homeless man who snapped, "Watch where you're going, girlie." She never even heard him as she approached the counter.

The clerk asked, "Can I help you?"

"I need a ticket to Seattle."

"When are you traveling?"

"Immediately," she answered, "I want to go tonight."

"First bus to Seattle doesn't leave until tomorrow morning at six," he replied. "Do you want a ticket for that one?"

When she didn't answer, he looked up from his computer screen. He saw a disheveled blonde teenager staring at him with murderous rage. The wild look in her eyes caused him to back up a few steps.

With a huge effort, Stella stopped herself from reaching over the counter and strangling the clerk. “Yes, that’s fine.”

Moving one cautious step closer, he said, “That’s $53.70 with tax.” He took the cash she slid across the counter, careful not to let their hands touch. He didn’t think insanity was contagious, but you could never be too careful.

~~~~

Stella drank several cups of coffee in a vain effort to stay awake. A battle she eventually lost. Nestled into a hard metal chair bolted to the ground, she awoke just as they announced the boarding of her bus. She shoved a fat woman leaning on her shoulder away. She narrowly escaped a thin rivulet of drool that slipped from the corner of the woman’s slack mouth.

Stella climbed the steps to the coach and settled into a seat at the extreme rear. Her back was stiff, her mind reeling. She stared out the window as the bus pulled from the terminal, thinking, *That old bitch is going to fix this, or I am going to kill her with my bare hands. How in bloody hell did she do this?*

As the light ran away from the day, California gave way to Oregon. Stella slept occasionally. When the bus stopped, she disembarked with the rest of the bleary-eyed passengers and bought food from her rapidly dwindling roll of cash. She ignored the attempts at conversation from the other passengers. She still couldn’t believe any of this was happening. She couldn’t believe when she’d woken up the previous morning she had a beautiful home, a bank account full of cash, and a body thirty years older. She sincerely hoped this was just some ghoulish nightmare from which she would soon wake. Maybe it had been brought on by too much vodka.
~~~~

The worst part of this nightmare was Heather. All she wanted was to hear her daughter's voice, see her daughter's smile, and know that Heather was safe. Why didn't she live with Karen Talbot? Why wasn't she registered in school? Where was she? And how was it even possible that her fiancé had been dead for nearly a year? Did that old crazy bitch in Seattle do something to her daughter?

Oregon gave way to Washington, and five hours later the coach swung into the Seattle terminal.

~~~~

Belda saw a customer through the glass door, under the tinkling little bell. She turned to Gabriella. "I need you to do something for me, dear."

"Okay." Gabriella looked at her, a ghost of unease in her eyes.

"Page Nicholas and tell him to come to the store right away."

"What's wrong?" Gabriella's eyes opened wide in alarm.

"Do as I ask, my dear," the woman replied, strain evident in her voice.

Gabriella picked up the phone and punched in the number of Nicholas's pager.

~~~~

By the time Stella reached the bookstore, she was winded, her feet covered in blisters, and her hair a snarled corona framing her gaunt, pale face.

The door crashed open, the bell screaming in angry protest.

When Gabriella saw the girl, she jumped and squawked.

"Where is she?" the girl snarled.

With an effort, Gabriella stopped herself from staring at the wild-eyed vagabond standing in the doorway. "She's waiting for you in the office," Gabriella stammered. She pointed.

The girl stalked to the office and slammed the door behind her.

Belda sat peacefully in her chair. She looked up at the frightening girl and clearly recognized her. In Bella Luna nothing had changed. Even the book Stormie Banks had pulled from the shelf on her first visit remained slightly askew.

How had her world been completely changed, when this one remained exactly as she remembered it? Stormie Banks wondered.

A pleasant smile lit Belda's face as she looked upon Stella. "Well, my goodness," she remarked. "It worked even better than I anticipated. Just look at you!"

"Yes, you insane old hag. Look at me!" the girl spat.

The smile slid from Belda's face. "Sit down, Stella. You sound most ungrateful." She pointed to the opposite chair.

"Don't you call me that! I am Stormie Banks!" the girl shrieked.

"Not anymore. Now sit or this meeting is over," the old woman replied firmly. "After all, you can't afford my time anymore."

The girl's eyes were blazing, but she dropped into the chair.

"Now, I assume you traveled all this way because you have some questions about your newfound youth?" Belda asked pleasantly.

"Where's my daughter? What have you done to her?"

"You don't have a daughter, Stella. You are only nineteen years old. Heather didn't come along until Stormie Banks was nearly thirty."

Tears stung Stella's eyes. She batted them away with trembling fingers. "You killed my daughter! And you killed her fiancé!" she sobbed.

"You aren't listening to me. I killed no one. I simply took you back to nineteen—an age before you had any children. Heather Banks has not been born, so she was not there to knock poor Dan Holliman out of the way when that paint can fell. You didn't think you could be young again without any impact on anyone else's life did you? Everything we do affects those around us."

"No," Stella spat. "You never said anything to me about hurting Heather or Dan or anyone else. This was about *me,* just me. It wasn't supposed to involve other people."

"Maybe the problem is that you were only thinking about yourself when you showed up here after closing time and asked me for that potion."

"Oh, spare me the sermon. I paid you a fortune."

Belda sighed as if the conversation had grown tiresome. "Yes, you did. And I did exactly what you paid me to do."

"I did not pay you to screw up my life. This—" she pointed at her body with loathing—"is not what I paid you for."

"You wanted to be young again. You never specified how young, so I just picked an age. I thought it romantic to send you back to the age you were when you first arrived in Hollywood. I can see you don't agree."

Stella stared at her in horror. "I want my daughter back," she gasped. "You can't do this. Travis won't let you get away with it."

"Ah yes, Travis. Well, I don't really follow the gossip, but I believe he married about a year ago. Stormie Banks wasn't there for him to meet, so he took up with some young girl in Vegas who worked in his brother's club."

"What are you saying? You erased my entire past? How? How could you do that?"

"I erased Stormie Banks's past. Yours is still very much intact, Stella. All nineteen short years spent in a small town in Indiana."

"What about Travis? What about everyone I know? What did you do to them?"

"Their lives are exactly as they would have been without Stormie Banks."

Stella launched at the old woman, hands curled into claws. She saw a lightning quick movement from the corner of her eye before she was grabbed from behind. Her arm was twisted painfully behind her back, restraining her.

The crazy old bitch sat placidly before her. Belda didn't flinch. She looked at Stella sympathetically, and said in her calm, serene tone, "Nicholas, show our guest out."

The girl screamed in fury and tried to twist out of Nicholas's grasp. He tightened his grip on her arm, yanking it even higher. She screeched in pain.

He whispered in her ear, "Just take it easy. I don't want to hurt you."

Her breath was coming in rasping little sobs, tears coursed down her cheeks. She stopped struggling against him.

"Now are you going to behave?" he asked, loosening his grip a little.

She nodded.

"Okay." He turned her so she was facing him. Clamping his hand on her wrist, he pulled her toward the door. "Let's go take a walk."

The whole way, Stella's murderous eyes marked the old woman. She whispered, "I'll get you."

Nicholas led her past a worried Gabriella, toward the front door. Gabriella watched anxiously from the window, ringing her hands.

Nicholas led the girl down the block. After he was sure the girl had calmed down enough to listen to him, he pulled an envelope from the pocket of his jeans. "Take this." He pushed it into her hands.

"What is it?"

"It's some money. You will need some clothes and a place to stay. There's also a plane ticket in there to Los Angeles, if you want to go back, and a current driver's license."

She tried to push the envelope back. "No. You don't understand. I'm not staying like this. I have everything I need back in California. I just need that crazy old bitch to change everything back."

He sighed. "You still don't get it, do you? That actress with the big house in California is gone. You don't have anything except your youth. That's all you paid for."

She looked at him thunderstruck. "How? Tell me how the hell did she do this to me?"

"I don't know how. Truly, I don't."

"What did she think? That I would just forget my whole life and accept this?"

"You will forget." Nicholas said with assurance.

Stella gasped, "No, I never will! I have thirty years of memories in my heart. Not even that old crone can take those."

"You underestimate her even now?"

Stella looked at Nicholas with pleading eyes. "Please, just stop this insanity and tell me what I have to do to get my life back."

Nicholas shifted uncomfortably. God, he hated this. He had seen the consequences of Belda's handy work many times. He had often cleaned up the messes left in the wake of her potions, but this was by far the worst. Even he didn't understand how she had managed this one. "You can't."

"I'll pay her! I'll give her anything she wants!" the girl cried in despair.

"You don't have that kind of money. You are just a nineteen-year-old kid now, fresh off a bus from Indiana. I'm sorry."

"I'll kill her," she breathed.

"No. You won't. She'd know you were coming and she'd kill you first."

Her eyes bored holes into him. She hissed, "Don't you realize she already has?"

Chapter 16

The old bitch had given her five thousand dollars. A fraction of what Stormie had paid for that nightmare in a bottle.

When Nicholas put her in the cab, Stella was so despondent she could barely speak.

There was a liquor store on the corner by the motel, but the clerk wouldn't sell her a bottle of Absolut because she wasn't twenty-one.

~~~~

Stella used the plane ticket the old woman had so thoughtfully provided her. Coach seating, of course. Upon returning to Los Angeles, she went to the library. She didn't understand how Belda could have simply erased the last thirty years of her life. What about her films? Her husbands? Could the woman alter history and change the lives of so many people?

Stella sat at a computer and searched the internet for information on who had won her Oscars, starred in her movies, and
~~~~

married her husbands. She was most curious about *Golden Sunset.* She grimaced when she saw Lauren Bacall had played Desiree. She hadn't won an Oscar for the performance. That year, the award went to Louise Fletcher in *One Flew Over the Cuckoo's Nest.* Stella felt some relief at this.

Stella looked up what had become of her eradicated history. Tears poured down her face. Her first husband had never married. He died in a car crash in 1981. He had been drunk. She remembered that George had been a heavy drinker. He'd joined Alcoholics Anonymous at her urging a year after they were married and quit drinking.

She didn't much care about what had become of her second and third spouses, but she looked them up anyway. She wasn't ready to look up Marvin or especially Travis. That sick bitch in Seattle said Travis was married to someone else. How in the world could that be?

Finally, though, Stella had to know.

Marvin had married a screenwriter. It was she who had found him dead in the driveway on the same date that Stormie had found him there in a different lifetime.

Finally, she looked up Travis. The date of his divorce from Marsha was the same, but he hadn't remarried until less than a year ago. She found a few photos from the wedding. The girl was a twenty-six-year-old stripper with flame-red hair. She had been employed at Conner's Las Vegas club. She and Travis had only known each other two weeks when they were married.

God, Travis. How lonely and desperate you must have been to marry that tart, Stella thought as she ran her fingers over his picture on the monitor.

When she couldn't take any more, Stella left the library. Daylight had drained from the day. She needed to find somewhere to stay. She purchased a copy of the *LA Times* and *The Hollywood Reporter*. She tucked herself into a corner booth at a diner and began flipping through *The Reporter*. A full page ad announced the opening of Kyra Hastings's new movie.

She's back! Stella thought. Then she realized that, with Stormie Banks life erased, there had never been a potion to make her disappear. "Good for you, honey," she mumbled. "None of this was your fault anyway."

She flipped open the *Times* and began thumbing through the pages looking for the classifieds. She froze as her eyes fell on a small article buried in the back of the national news section.

BLAZE KILLS THREE IN TEXAS FIRE

Her eyes scanned the article. It was about the fire at the magic school Travis's son had been involved in.

"No!" she cried. "Cal saved those people!" A few diners looked up from their meals, and the waitress walked up to her table. "Miss, is everything okay?"

She looked at the waitress, tears streaming from her eyes again. She grabbed a napkin off the table. "Fine, sorry," she muttered. The waitress walked back toward the kitchen, casting concerned glances over her shoulder.

Jesus, did I do that too? Travis must not have given him the money to go to the school. The bodies just keep piling up, she thought miserably.

Heartbroken, Stella walked for hours. She tried to make some sense out of what had happened to her life, and to the lives of everyone she loved. She couldn't believe how many people had been affected by this insane somersault in history.

She had thought she wanted to be young again. Stella now realized, belatedly, how selfish she had been. And that the last thing she wanted to do was grow up all over again. Now that it was too late, she knew how truly blessed her life had been.

How could she go on without Heather and Travis? How could she live with herself, knowing what she had done to them and others by her self-centeredness?

It was like mourning the dead. Worse, mourning those you have killed with your own black heart.

The woman who would never be Stormie Banks found a cheap motel and purchased a room for the night. She went to bed certain she would die in her sleep, choking on her sorrow.

Chapter 17

"Travis, honey, I'm going to the mall. I'll be back later. Don't forget to go pick up the dry cleaning and something for supper."

"Okay, Tanna," Travis sighed. His wife wiggled out the door on four-inch stilettos.

He'd been married to her for nine months. The last six had been just about the most miserable of his entire life. Sex, Travis discovered, when it was the only thing carrying a relationship, had a very short shelf life. Tanna was the same age as his eldest child. He didn't know what had possessed him to marry her. The only excuse he could offer was that he hadn't been thinking with the big head at the time. He had been lonely, and man could she do some amazing things around a strobe-lit pole.

This past summer, he'd been spending a lot of time in Vegas with Connor because he had been bored and had nothing better to do. Several nights in a row, he'd watched Tanna dance at his brother's club.

Travis had been drinking more than he should have, but even sober Tanna was sure pretty. His last clear memory of that time was buying her dinner and somehow ending up at The Chapel of the Bells at the end of the strip, and standing before an Elvis impersonator who was also an ordained minister. To this day, he was unsure how he'd gotten there. There was no pre-nup.

With heavy footsteps, Travis walked into the kitchen and sat down to read the paper. This was a morning ritual he was unable to perform until Tanna left the vicinity. If he dared read during breakfast, she would whine about him ignoring her. When Tanna was in the house, every single ounce of his attention had to be focused on her exclusively. Hence, he'd missed his newspaper on many a morning these last several months.

Travis unfolded the paper and frowned. The front page headline was about a fire at an obscure institution of higher learning called *The Amazing AJ's School of Magic.* Travis recognized that name. Not long ago, his son had begged him to pay for his tuition to attend the Amazing AJ's school. Now three people were dead.

"Thank God I said no," he said to Franklin, who was lying at his feet. "The boy probably would have gotten killed!"

Cal had been seeing some girl who was starting classes at the magic school. He had wanted to go there with her. Travis felt like living proof of what happened when you let some young thing with a nice ass turn your head. He'd be damned if he was going to let his son make the same mistake he did and wind up in a similar purgatory.

Travis folded the paper and climbed the stairs to the bedroom he shared with his new bride. Franklin followed him. He took his wallet from the top of the dresser to look for the dry cleaning ticket. If he didn't do as Tanna asked, she'd pout. When she pouted, he had to fight the strong urge to put his fist right through the middle of that pout. He'd never wanted to hit a woman until he met Tanna. Come to think of it, he'd never wanted to hit anyone until he met her. She made his first wife look like Mother Theresa.

He sat down on the bed and started going through the wallet. Where was the damn ticket? He couldn't find it.

Travis reached behind a photograph of his children and felt back there. No dry cleaning ticket, but a folded magazine article he didn't recognize was stuffed behind the picture. He pulled it out, a puzzled expression crossing his face. "What's this?" he muttered as he unfolded it. A white business card fluttered out of the middle and landed face down on the floor at his feet. He ignored the card and stared thoughtfully at the article.

"What the fuck?" he cried. The dog looked up briefly, then put his head back down on his paws to snooze. The article had been torn from an old edition of the *Hollywood Reporter*. The date across the top said, August 14, 1996. Over five years old. Headlined in bold was,

SCREEN LEGEND STORMIE BANKS WEDS COUNTRY CROONER TRAVIS BULLOCK

Travis stared at it in shock. There was a photo of him and a very pretty blonde cutting a wedding cake together and smiling happily into the camera.

"What the hell is this?" he asked the sleeping dog. He had never posed for this photograph, never seen this woman, so how had the picture ended up in a back issue of the *Hollywood Reporter*? How had it ended up in his wallet, for that matter?

Travis had never heard of anyone named Stormie Banks, yet the picture in the article caused such a deep feeling of loss and despair to well up in his heart that his vision was momentarily blurred by tears.

Travis read the article. It said he was this woman's fifth husband, and she his second wife.

None of it made any sense. He didn't know who Stormie Banks was or how many times she'd been married, but his second wife was a former stripper named Tanna Marie Shaw… even though he wished things were otherwise. He felt like he was losing his mind.

With shaking hands, Travis went to the phone and called David Genesee, a friend who worked in the publishing industry.

"Hey, man. I need a favor," Travis said, when David came on the line.

"Sure, Travis, what's up?"

"I need a back issue of the *Hollywood Reporter*. One from 1996. Can you do that?"

"Probably. What do you need it for?" David wondered.

"I think someone's playin' a really nasty prank on me. I can't explain right now."

"What date do you need?"

Travis told him. David promised to do his best to get him a copy. David phoned an hour later to say it would be sent to his home via overnight mail the next day. Travis thanked him and hung up.

Travis lay on the bed, reading the article over and over again, trying to figure out where the thing came from and why looking at the woman paralyzed him with longing.

Travis bent down and retrieved the business card that had fallen out when he'd plucked the folded article from his wallet. Bella Luna Bookstore and Metaphysical Shop. He examined the card, then turned it over and read the hand-written message on the back. It was to Ms. Banks from Melissa, her greatest fan.

"Stormie Banks," he said out loud, shaking his head. "Who the hell are you?"

At the mention of that name, Franklin looked up at his master and barked.

~~~~

Travis stood across the counter from his buddy, Ken Sharp, the owner of Photo World. Ken studied the picture in the article with a magnifying glass.

"So did someone superimpose my picture in there with that woman? Is that how this was done?" Travis asked.

"The photo isn't a fake, Travis." Ken frowned. "If it is, it's the best damn fake I've ever seen. But having attended your first wedding, and knowing that you didn't even have a cake at your second, I don't know what else it could be. I gotta tell you, buddy, this seriously blows my mind."

"I feel like I just woke up in an episode of the fuckin' *Twilight Zone*," Travis grumbled.

"Just being married to Tanna could cause that," Ken commented.

Travis shot him a look and he mumbled, "Sorry. So, let me get this straight. You found this in your wallet?"

"Yep. I was looking for a dry cleaning stub and there it was. You think this is Tanna's idea of some kind of joke?"

"Tanna?" Ken laughed. "Well, I don't claim to understand the mind of a teenager, but hell, Travis, what would be the point? And honestly, the young Mrs. Bullock really isn't this imaginative."

"I called Dave Genesee. He's getting me a back copy of the *Hollywood Reporter* this supposedly came from."
~~~~

Ken nodded. "Good idea, Travis. If it were me, I'd certainly want to verify the authenticity of an article about a wedding I never had, to a woman I never met, complete with a picture I never posed for. You bet."

"Okay, Einstein, then what would you do?"

"You said a business card fell out of the article when you found it?"

Travis reached into his back pocket and extracted the card.

Ken donned reading glasses and inspected it. "What I'd do is take a trip to Seattle, and find this store and this Belda person. Maybe she can shed some light on this."

Travis grimaced. "Just what I want to do. Get more people involved in this craziness. Strangers, no less."

~~~~

The woman who used to be a middle-aged movie star and was now just a lonely, anonymous girl, sat on a barstool in a dark, seedy tavern in West Hollywood nursing a glass of cheap wine. The bartender hadn't carded her. When the scraggly looking guy next to her offered to buy her another glass, she accepted. They made small talk for a while and then she leaned in close and laid one long, elegant, unlined hand on the man's leg.

"I'm looking for something," she whispered in his ear.

"Well, you found me, baby," he responded.

"Actually, I need to purchase something. Maybe you can help me."

The man looked around uneasily. He didn't want to disappoint this pretty young thing by saying no to whatever it was she was after, thereby ruining his chances at getting in her skirt, but he
~~~~

didn't want to get arrested by a vice cop for soliciting a prostitute either. Better to tread lightly until he knew what she wanted.

"What do you want to buy?" he asked.

"A gun," she breathed into his ear. "For protection," she added hastily.

"So go to a gun shop," he responded coldly, draining his beer and rising from the barstool.

"Wait!" She put a restraining hand on his arm.

He looked at her with disgust. "Hey, I was just looking for a good time. I'm not interested in helping you blow away your old man, or whatever you're trying to do."

"I told you. It's for protection. If I go to a gun store, I have to apply for a concealed weapons permit and wait thirty days before I can get it."

"So if it's just for protection, why can't you wait thirty days?" he asked, putting one haunch back down on the barstool.

Stella wrote her own script and acted it beautifully, complete with tears. "There is this man. He has been threatening me and I am scared for my life," she sobbed theatrically.

"An ex-boyfriend?"

She nodded. "Yes, and he's threatened to kill me. I've gone to the police, but they won't help me." She mopped a hand across her brow, showing just the right amount of misery, and down the man's other haunch went back onto the barstool.

He sat thinking for a minute. "Maybe I can turn you onto someone that could help," he said finally. He took a coaster from the bar and asked the bartender for a pen. He wrote down a number.

Handing it to her, he said, "Ask for Marty. Tell him you're a friend of Skeeter."

She thanked him, tucked the coaster in her purse, and left without a backward glance.

~~~~

"Dang it, Travis, you've been moping around here all day," Tanna pouted. "You're no fun."

He got up from the sofa and went toward the front door.

"Where are you going now?" his irate wife called after him.

"To check the mail."

"You just checked it five minutes ago. You know it doesn't come this early. What are you waiting for?"

Travis groaned. "Tanna, why don't you go shopping?"

She had bought enough outfits to clothe a medium-sized village in the brief time they had been married. But Travis had found that shopping was the only way to get her out of the house, so he unlimbered his credit card on a nearly daily basis.

The pout faded. "Okay." She brightened at once. "Hey, Sugar, let's go dancing tonight."

"You go. Go with your friends, Tanna. I'm not in the mood," he grumbled. He walked out the front door and sat on the steps, waiting for the mailman and thinking about a woman he'd never known. A woman named Stormie Banks.

The front door opened and Tanna sashayed out, purse slung over her shoulder, car keys dangling from one long, crimson fingernail. "Call me on my cellphone when you cheer up, you grouch." She slid behind the wheel of her new Jaguar.

When the mail truck pulled up, Travis leapt to his feet. The mailman handed him an overnight envelope and turned a clipboard toward him to sign.
~~~~

Travis sat back down on the steps and ripped open the envelope. Thumbing through the five year old issue of the *Hollywood Reporter*, he stopped abruptly at page 9. That was the page number in the bottom right corner of the article he'd found folded up in his wallet. The corresponding page in the issue he now held in his hand featured an interview with Bruce Willis about his latest movie and an advertisement for a West Hollywood courier service. That was all.

Travis was utterly bewildered. He had been holding onto some thin shred of hope that the whole thing had been a bizarre publicity stunt of some kind. He dropped the magazine back into the envelope and rose from the steps. When he walked inside, he went straight for the telephone and called his travel agent.

~~~~

"I'm a friend of Skeeter," Stella whispered into the telephone. She proceeded to tell the voice at the other end of the line what she wanted. A price was quoted. Her hands were sweating. She wiped them on the threadbare coverlet of the bed in her motel room.

"Meet me behind Morgan's pub tomorrow afternoon at four."

"How will I know you?" she asked breathlessly.

"You won't. I'll know you." The line went dead.

~~~~

Travis tossed and turned all night. When sleep finally claimed him, he dreamt of the woman in the photograph.

She was standing at the end of a dark tunnel, screaming, "Travis, bring me back! Please bring me back!"

He tried to reach her, but the faster he approached, the further she slipped away. As she faded out of sight, her final cries were, "Where's Heather? Where's Franklin? Travis, please, you have to find them!"

He woke up tangled in the sheets, sweating. He glanced over at Tanna, afraid he had woken her. She slept soundly beside him. Poor thing was exhausted from a laborious day at the mall.

His mind recalled the frightening dream with vivid clarity. The woman had sounded so frantic and afraid. Travis didn't know anybody named Heather, and wondered how his dog had become mixed up in that crazy dream. The nightmare left him unable to find sleep again that night.

As dawn was breaking, Travis went downstairs. He scribbled a hasty note to his wife and tossed a change of clothes and some toiletries into an overnight bag. Ken was waiting for him outside, bleary-eyed and tired.

"Sorry I woke you up so early. I don't know how long I'll be gone, and I didn't want to leave my truck at the airport."

"No sweat, man. You'll let me know what you find out?"

"Yeah," Travis grunted. "*If* I find anything. I don't even know what the hell I'm looking for."

His friend left him at the airport, promising to check on his child bride and make sure she kept his dog fed while he was away.

Nearly half a day later, Travis landed in Seattle. As he disembarked the plane, he realized he was scared to death. He couldn't place where the fear came from, but it was everywhere. It wrapped him in its tight embrace, and clung to him like a wet sheet.

The dream of the mysterious woman had repeated itself on the plane and increased his disquiet and unease.

Travis hailed a taxicab and read the driver the address of Bella Luna from the business card.

When he was deposited at the door, Travis stood paralyzed. He stared at the front of the store. He didn't want to go in there. He had never been so frightened in his entire life.

When the rain began to fall, Travis reached out a shaking hand and slowly opened the door to the bookstore.

The little bell overhead shivered. A beautiful girl with long black hair was standing behind the counter. She looked up at him with a smile that froze halfway to her lips. Then it drained from her face, taking all the color from her rosy cheeks with it.

Travis stood uncertainly as the girl struggled to regain her composure.

"C-Can I help you?" she stuttered.

He closed the door behind him. "I am looking for someone named Belda," he answered. "Is she here?"

The girl was chewing her lip nervously. Travis couldn't tell if she was a nervous fan, or if the terror trailing him from the airplane was catching. Women had been reacting strangely to him ever since his face graced his first album cover.

She cleared her throat and looked around the deserted store as if she were looking for someone to help her. "I… oh boy… umm…"

"Honey, do you want an autograph or somethin'?" he asked, trying to ease her discomfort and get on with his business here.

"No, I'm sorry, we just never thought you'd… you'd…" the girl stammered.

"Excuse me?"

Gabriella recovered herself. She walked around the counter and took his arm. "Come with me, please. You can wait in the office for Belda." She led him to a little room in the side of the store and shut the door behind him. Then she bolted for the stairs, taking them two at a time. She pounded on the door to Belda's small apartment.

When Belda opened the door, Gabriella charged into her tidy little living room. "He's here," she cried.

The old woman took her by the shoulders, "Who, my dear? What has you so upset?"

"That actress's husband. The one that you… you know…"

Belda's eyes widened in alarm. For just a moment, Gabriella saw a look on the woman's clear, unlined face that she had never seen there before. Pure, naked terror.

Belda clutched Gabriella's hand in her own gnarled claw and whispered, "I forgot something in the potion. I knew it!"

Gabriella gasped. "Forgot what?"

The old woman's eyes turned instantly hard as flint. Her mouth pulled itself into a severe line. "Page Nicholas immediately. I will go down and speak to our visitor and find out what I omitted."

Oh yes, she had forgotten something. She'd known it all along. It had been nagging at her since the moment she'd folded the potion into Stormie Banks's waiting hand. She had thrown that brew together in record time while the actress waited downstairs for it. Belda had worked quickly and carelessly, and now, after all these years, the unthinkable had happened. She made a mistake. One that could destroy her.

What part of Stormie Banks's life did she miss? For the first time that Belda could remember, she was truly afraid.

~~~~

"Hello, Mr. Bullock. How may I help you?"

Travis stood up from the chair. "Good afternoon, ma'am." He reached to shake the woman's arthritic hand.
~~~~

She looked deeply into his eyes. Seeing no accusation there, she relaxed a little. "May I offer you some tea?"

"No, thank you." He shifted nervously from foot to foot.

"Please, sit down, Mr. Bullock, and tell me why you have come to see me."

Travis reached into his pocket and removed the folded article. When he handed it to the woman, her face turned pale as parchment.

"Ma'am, this may sound crazy, but I never posed for that picture and I ain't never seen that woman before."

Belda swallowed over a lump in her throat. All the spittle in her mouth dried up. "So why have you come here, Mr. Bullock? Why do you think I can help you?"

Travis reached into his pocket and handed the woman the business card. "Turn it over and read the back."

The woman's hand was shaking so badly she dropped the card into her lap when she tried to turn it over.

Travis watched her curiously. "I found that with the article. The note on the back is written to the woman in that photo. I thought maybe you could help me figure out who she is and just what the hell is goin' on."

Belda waved the card at him. "You say you found this? Where? Where did you find it?" Her voice rose shrilly.

"In my wallet with the article. I can tell by your reaction you know something about this. Ma'am, do you know that woman? Do you know Stormie Banks?"

She now knew what she'd forgotten: a single ingredient that took care of tiny details. *Oh,* she thought miserably, *it's always the little things that come back to haunt us. The devil is indeed in the details.* Just one tiny pinch and this whole nightmare would have been avoided.

For the first time in her very long life, Belda didn't know what to do. She rose quickly to her feet. "Mr. Bullock, excuse me a moment. You may not want any tea, but I do. I will be back shortly."

Belda closed the door behind her and leaned against it, wheezing. Gabriella, who had been waiting just outside the office, stared at the old woman's ashen face. Their eyes met. Together, they walked wordlessly toward the back of the store.

"Did you call Nicholas?" Belda asked.

"He's on his way. And I closed the shop. What happened?" Gabriella cried. Seeing Belda afraid was almost as terrifying as seeing her angry.

"I missed something," Belda gasped, wringing her hands. "Something very, very small but terribly important."

"Can it be fixed?" Gabriella looked sick with worry.

"It's too late. This man—he must be eliminated. Nicholas will have to—"

"No!" Gabriella thundered, grabbing the woman's arm. "You can't kill an innocent man, Belda! And you can't make Nicholas clean this mess up! That's not fair!" Tears stung her eyes.

"I must think, I need time," the old woman cried helplessly.

"Can't you bring back that woman's life? Can't you undo it?"

"I don't know. It may be too late,"

"What do you mean too late?" Gabriella sobbed.

"Stormie Banks may already be dead," the old woman moaned. "She may have killed herself."

~~~~

The girl who used to be Stormie Banks lay on the narrow bed in her motel room, staring up at the stained ceiling. It wasn't that she wanted to kill herself. It was that she had accepted what happened,
~~~~

and death now seemed the only option. She could live without the money and the fame. But she couldn't live without Heather. And she couldn't live with the knowledge that it was her own selfishness that had stolen her daughter's life… and consequently the life of the man Heather had been going to marry. Compounding the guilt were the three people who died in the fire in Texas. Travis's son was supposed to have been there to save them, just as Heather was supposed to save Dan. But somehow, without Stormie, everyone's fate had changed.

Stella felt like her world had become some psychotic version of *It's A Wonderful Life*—except that she wasn't going to get the chance to see things turn out right.

How could she live in a world without Heather? How could she live in a world where her husband didn't know who she was, didn't know the history they had shared?

She couldn't. No one could be that strong.

Every direction her mind turned, searching for solace, Stella only found more pain. Around every corner, in every shadow, was a reminder of something lost that could never be regained.

She hadn't known that her desire to be youthful again could erase the entire life she had built, nor that it would impact the lives of so many other people. What she thought Belda would give her was a brand new body and face. Those were all she'd expected to change.

Not her history, not everybody else's life. Who in their right mind would want to be nineteen again? Stormie had a lifetime of beautiful memories. In the blink of an eye, it was replaced by what?

A young, skinny body, with no boobs and a big nose. That wasn't a fair trade.

Stella wanted to kill that insane old bitch who'd done this to her. But in her secret heart, Stella knew the woman was no more responsible than Kyra Hastings had been. The woman possessed a bizarre gift. Or maybe it was more curse than gift. But she never sought out Stormie. Like all of the old woman's clients, Stormie went to her. Granted, most of Belda's customers probably didn't fully understand the devil they were entering into an unholy pact with, but still they came, and still they wrote their checks. And with few exceptions, they drank her terrifying potions.

A woman named Stormie Banks had asked to be young again. The request was taken literally and maliciously, but no one forced that foul tonic down her throat. Stormie Banks knew there was no one to blame but herself for the reincarnation of Stella Burkowitz. That was a far more bitter pill to swallow than Belda's potion could ever be.

Stella would take responsibility for this, just as she had every other mistake she'd made during her long and colorful lifetime. And she would do the only thing she could to fix it.

Kill the girl and hopefully, in death, be able to forget the woman.

~~~~

"Forgive me, Mr. Bullock. My assistant is attending to the tea. I have asked her to prepare a cup for you as well. Some say our tea helps the weary traveler shake off the miles." Belda, having regained her composure, sat down.

"That's right kind of you, ma'am," Travis replied. He knew the article from the *Hollywood Reporter* had rattled the old woman nearly as much as it rattled him, and he wasn't going to leave here until he found out what she knew.
~~~~

"Now then, you were asking me if I recognized the woman in the photograph with you," Bella sighed. She looked sympathetically at the confused man sitting across from her.

"Do you?"

"Let me ask you something first, before I tell you what I know—and, Mr. Bullock, I will tell you everything I can. My assistant has pointed out that I owe you that much."

Travis shifted uneasily in his chair. The old woman was staring at him, her wide gray eyes haunted. The cold sheet of fear tightened around his shoulders again.

There was a tap at the door. Gabriella stepped in, carrying a tray with two steaming mugs. She set it on the table between Belda and Travis and quietly walked out, closing the door behind her.

Travis did not want the tea, but his polite Southern upbringing was too inbred for him to resist the offered cup. He picked it up from the tray and sipped. It was some kind of herbal tea, soothing like chamomile, but with an unfamiliar sharp edge. "So," he asked, "what's your question?"

"When you look at that photograph, do you feel anything? Something like a sensation of some buried memory trying to uproot from your subconscious? Or does it evoke an emotion you wouldn't expect?"

Travis thought about the overwhelming heartache and deep sense of loss and emptiness he felt when he'd first looked at the woman in the picture.

"It makes me feel like someone died and I'm grieving," he said, shaking his head. He couldn't believe he was sitting in a psychic's quarters, baring his soul this way. But he needed answers, and this woman held them.

Belda nodded, as if she expected this. "Mr. Bullock, I run a service. Ms. Banks was one of my clients."

"Where did this photo and the article come from?"

She held up a hand. "One thing at a time. First, you must realize that you are not going to believe a word of the story I am about to tell you. Second, you should know that to protect myself and my associates, it was necessary to insure that you would not remember this conversation after tonight." She nodded toward the near empty mug he was bringing to his lips.

Travis barked an incredulous laugh. "Spare me the hoodoo, lady. I'm not going to pay you a dime. I just want to know who this woman is, where this article came from, and what you have to do with it." But he lowered the mug to the table before drinking the last few swallows.

"Very well," Belda replied. She proceeded to tell him the story of Stormie Banks.

Belda talked for the better part of an hour. When she finished, Travis's jaw was slack and his eyes held the look of someone who'd just survived a plane crash. His mind rejected this ridiculous, farfetched tale, but an ocean of conflicting emotions churned in his heart. The story was crazy, yet every word rang true in his soul.

"Bring her back!" Travis cried, not having any control over what he was saying. "For the love of God, woman, bring her back to me!"

Belda reached over and patted his arm with one misshapen hand. "I will try, Mr. Bullock. I promise you we will do everything we can. I only hope it isn't too late."

Chapter 18

The girl who used to be a famous woman rose in the morning and left the motel room. She was anxious for this day to be over—for the pain to be over.

Stella bought a huge breakfast, forcing herself to eat nearly every bite. Then she hitched a ride to Hollywood's Walk of Fame. She didn't want to do this. It would only add to her agony, but curiosity forced her. She simply must see whose star now lay where hers used to be. Had to see whose handprints were now permanently set into the cement where hers once were.

Stella remembered the day nearly twenty years ago, when Stormie Banks was forever immortalized in cement. But that was a thin and gossamer memory now, no more substantial than the dust on an antique in the attic.

When Stella awoke that morning, she was horrified to find that all her memories of being Stormie Banks carried this blurry and frail quality, as though they could be blown away with a single breath. The most devastating of all was that she couldn't quite remember the details of Heather's face. Stella had no photographs to remind her. This somehow felt like the final insult.

Stella had purchased one of Travis's compact discs from a music store the day before. The picture of Travis from the cover, she tucked into the side of the mirror in her motel room. At least she had something to keep his face alive in her mind, if only an old publicity photo. But all the history and all the years they spent as husband and wife were melting like butter left in the hot sun.

Stella believed no pain could ever be as excruciating as losing Heather and Travis. She was wrong. Losing the memories of the life they shared together was so much worse.

~~~~

Belda pressed the small bottle containing the ingredients to reincarnate Stormie Banks into Nicholas's palm. "You have your plane ticket?" she asked anxiously.

He nodded and shoved the vial into his pants' pocket.

"You have the address of the motel?"

"Yes, Belda, I have everything," Nicholas grumbled, unable to keep the surly edge from his voice. He had fulfilled similar errands countless times over the years. He wasn't about to fail now, when Belda was actually going to reverse one of her deeds.

"There isn't much time." Belda was nervous, her face pale and gaunt. "I worked on that potion all night."

"You're sure you didn't leave anything out?" Gabriella asked. She meant no impudence by it, she was just concerned. All three of them were.

"It will be fine as long as Nicholas reaches her in time," Belda replied.

The strain was evident around Nicholas's eyes. Belda hadn't been the only one awake all night. He knew the challenge lay not only in finding Stella Burkowitz still alive, but in convincing her to
~~~~

swallow another nightmare in a bottle from the woman who had destroyed her entire life with the last one.

"I better get going," Nicholas said.

Gabriella kissed him firmly on the lips. "You'll call as soon as there is news?"

He promised he would, then turned toward Belda. "Try not to worry. I'll do the best I can to get us out of this."

~~~~

Stella was twenty minutes early for her appointment behind Morgan's Pub. She walked around the block a few times, trying to hold onto what little memory of Heather still clung to the rapidly unraveling fabric of her mind. She wanted Heather's face to be the last one she saw as she pulled the trigger. With each hour that passed, it took more and more concentration to see the face of the girl who had been her only child.

At five minutes to four, Stella rounded the corner behind the pub and came face to face with a tall, thin boy in his early twenties. His hair was long and unkempt, a shadow of stubble trying desperately to become a goatee circled his mouth. It looked more like dirt than hair.

He eyed the tall, blonde girl before him appreciatively.

"Are you…?" she began cautiously.

"I'm anyone you want me to be, beautiful," he smirked, his eyes running busily over the landscape of her hips.

Stella pulled the envelope with the cash from her purse and held it out to him.

"You know," he purred, his eyes never leaving her body, "if you wanted to save a little of your cash, we could maybe work
~~~~

something out in trade for the piece." He reached a hand toward her hip.

She deftly side-stepped his advance. "I've got the money, so give me the gun. Don't cause me any grief, okay sport?"

"Aww, is that any way to talk to a guy like me?"

She rolled her eyes. The longer her attention was occupied with this idiot, the harder it would be to recapture Heather in her mind. "Look, I don't have much time. I can't play games with you. You quoted me a price, and it's all here, so let's conclude our business with a minimum of unpleasantness, alright?"

She thrust the envelope into his hands.

"You sound just like my mother, you know that?"

She offered a humorless smile. "That doesn't surprise me. Now give me the gun."

He cast a furtive glance up the alley, while extracting a small, snub-nose pistol from the pocket of his jacket. He handed it to the girl and she stuffed it in her purse.

"Thanks." She turned to walk away.

"Hey," the kid called.

She looked back to see him holding out a small cardboard box sealed with electrical tape. "You'll need this."

She took a cautious step back. "What is it?"

"The bullets, beautiful."

She looked doubtfully at the box. "Um… Do you think you could load it for me?"

The scraggly kid held his hand out for the pistol. "If you blow your head off by mistake, it ain't my fault."

Stella dug the gun out of her purse and handed it back to him. When it was loaded, he showed her how to disengage the safety. She thanked him and hurried out of the alley.

~~~~

The plane touched down at LAX twenty minutes late. It took another precious thirty minutes for Nicholas to find a taxi. By the time it pulled out of the airport and into rush-hour traffic, his heart was banging hard against the wall of his chest and his hands were sweating.

Traffic was snarled chaos stretched out before him on the interstate. "Can't you go any faster?" he snapped at the driver.

The driver shot him an irritated look in the rearview mirror. "Not without wings, buddy."

~~~~

Stella needed a bottle of liquid courage to help her conclude her final bit of business in Hollywood. Since she'd become nineteen again, liquor store clerks always asked for ID. Sobriety just wasn't an option anymore, so she waited in the parking lot of the liquor store near the motel and watched the cars come and go. A man who appeared to be in his mid-thirties pulled up in a Porsche. As he climbed from his sports car, she stepped in front of him.

"Excuse me," she said demurely, casting her best coy smile.

He looked at her inquisitively.

"I lost my driver's license, and I wondered if you would do me a little favor?" She licked her lips suggestively.

"I'm not buying you any booze," he said flatly, not even the ghost of a smile crossing his stern features.

She wasn't used to men behaving like that. Usually she could get them to do anything she wanted. Tears sprang to her eyes.

"Sorry." He wrestled past her and stalked into the store.

She shook her head in frustration. Her memories were melting with frightening speed. She had to hurry. She waited for the creep in the Porsche to leave. When the store was busy, with the clerks preoccupied, she wandered over to the wall with the vodka. Funny, she didn't even remember which brand she used to drink. She plucked the closest bottle from the shelf without looking at the label and jammed it into her bag. Stormie would have appreciated the irony—it was a bottle of Absolut. She hurried out of the store, sure a restraining hand was going to fall on her shoulder.

Once in the parking lot, she looked behind her and breathed a sigh of relief. No one had borne witness to the single act of thievery Stella Burkowitz had ever committed.

She ran back to the motel and locked herself in the room.

~~~~

"Looks like there's an accident up ahead," the bored taxi driver commented.

Nicholas slapped his leg in frustration. "Is there another route? This is really an emergency," he complained through gritted teeth.

The driver shrugged. "At this point, walking might be faster." He eyed the gridlocked mess in front of him.

Nicholas threw a twenty dollar bill over the seat and climbed out of the cab, into the middle of the congested freeway.

~~~~

Stella changed into satin lounge pajamas. She purchased them yesterday. They were similar to a pair Travis had given her a few years ago. They cost over two hundred dollars at a little boutique on Sunset. She wouldn't need to watch her pennies much longer; the pajamas were a final indulgence.

As she put them on now, she couldn't quite remember why she had liked them so much, or why they were what she wanted to be wearing when she ended this hell. But that didn't matter now. They were pretty, and felt cool and smooth against her skin.

Stella drank deeply from the bottle and grimaced. The alcohol burned her throat. She began to cough uncontrollably, a scarlet flush creeping up her neck and cheeks. It tasted like she'd just gulped liquid fire. She thought, *I used to drink this shit? It tastes like battery acid!*

Stella took a pen and writing paper from the small desk in the corner of the room.

She wrote, *I am married to Travis Bullock and I have a daughter named Heather.* Looking at the words helped remind her of why she was doing this, of who she had once been. Yet the words looked alien and confusing

Stella pulled the picture of Travis off the mirror and held it in her hand.

She took a final swallow from the bottle, then put it on the table and replaced the cap.

She pulled the gun to her.

~~~~

Nicholas ran over fifteen blocks without stopping. His side was a throbbing stitch, his breath a wheezing gasp, puffing from his throat in harsh blasts. He could see the piercing neon sign of the motel now; a welcome beacon, only a block ahead. He plunged into traffic against the light. An air-horn blared less than two feet
~~~~

from his head. He screamed and leapt out of the way, losing his balance and falling headlong into the damp gutter.

The trucker shook a fist at him, and snarled, "Watch out, you crazy fuck!"

Nicholas climbed to his feet and took off running down the street. He was nearly there.

~~~~

Stella stared at the picture of Travis. She opened the bottle of vodka and took another deep swig. It went down the wrong pipe and her throat constricted. She waited for another coughing jag to pass and her eyes to stop watering. The booze was beginning to make her nauseous. She drew in a few shuddering breaths and set the bottle on the nightstand.

I really can't believe I ever enjoyed drinking that. It's horrid! Must have been an acquired taste, she thought dully.

She lay down on the bed and looked at the scribbled words on the hotel paper. She began to cry again. They didn't make any sense. The names of her husband and daughter looked more unfamiliar with each glance. After a while, she looked at the gun lying beside her on the bed. It took her a minute to remember why she'd bought it. She picked it up and thumbed off the safety.

~~~~

Nicholas raced into the motel's dingy office, wet feet slipping on the linoleum. The startled clerk looked up from the paperback he was reading and took in the sweating man with the untucked shirt, muddy pants, and hair sticking up in all directions. His first thought was to reach for the phone and dial 911, but the gun the man pointed in his direction drove that thought from his mind.

"We don't have any money," the clerk squawked. "The safe is locked and only the owner has the combination."

Nicholas was gasping for breath. "Tall girl, about eighteen, long blonde hair, real skinny. What room?"

The guy looked momentarily puzzled, his eyes riveted to the gun held in this wild man's unsteady grasp.

Nicholas was just about to voice a further threat, when the clerk's eyes cleared and his memory reengaged. "Room 210, upstairs," he squeaked.

"Call the police and I'll kill you. Call anyone and I'll kill you," Nicholas panted, backing toward the door.

The guy bobbed his head up and down. "Sure thing. Right, no problem," he whimpered.

Nicholas didn't like something he saw in the clerk's face. He had to hurry, but having the cops scream up the sidewalk in five minutes wasn't going to help matters.

"You believe me?" He stopped in the doorway, training the pistol on the shaking young man.

"Yes, yes. I swear I won't call anyone," he choked.

"If I so much as see a black and white drive by—if I so much as hear a siren wail in the distance, you're dead. I can be back down here in five seconds flat." Nicholas shot a final baleful stare at the quivering clerk and then bolted for the stairs to the second floor.

~~~~

There was a line in a movie once. She couldn't remember what movie. Couldn't even remember if it was a movie she'd been in. The line was *So long, cruel world.* She slurred that line now, as she
~~~~

raised the gun to her temple. Her hand was steady. The relief already coursing through her veins solidified her decision. She felt oddly at peace now, even though she couldn't quite remember why it was she wanted to die. There was no fear.

~~~~

Nicholas pounded up the steps, breath raging in and out. He skidded to a stop in front of room 210.

He banged on the door, shouting, "Stormie! Stormie Banks, open up!"

The words were half way out of his mouth when he heard the gun go off with a deafening roar. He yelled a tortured, "No!" and sagged against the railing.

~~~~

Stella Burkowitz raised the gun to her head, curling her finger around the trigger. She closed her eyes.

As she was about to pull the trigger, a furious hammering on the door startled her so badly, her hand jolted back and the gun went off. The bullet tore a piece of plaster from the wall behind her. She heard a voice outside screaming a name that brought everything crashing back. All the unspooling memories flooded instantly home.

Stella dropped the smoking gun onto the nightstand and cautiously approached the door. "Who's there?" she breathed, barely above a whisper.

Nicholas found his feet and leaned against the door. "Stormie? Are you okay?"

"You know my name?" Her voice shook with wonder.

"It's Nicholas from Seattle. I'm here to help you. Please let me in."

She gasped. "What do you want? Haven't you people done enough damage? Can't you let me die in peace?" Her voice was choked with emotion.

"If you open the door, I can fix everything. I can make it the way it was before. Before you ever came to Belda in the first place. Please, Stormie, open the door!" he begged.

"I don't believe you," she sobbed, tears streaming down her face.

"Your husband knows, Stormie. He is in Seattle right now. Belda missed something in the potion she gave you and your husband is trying to find you."

"Travis?" she asked, breathless. "Travis remembers me?"

"Sort of. It's hard to explain. It doesn't matter now, because Belda has to fix this—or she has to kill Travis too. Do you want that?"

"You're lying! Travis doesn't remember me because that miserable old witch you work for erased me. Why are you doing this to me now? Why can't you just stop?" She collapsed against the door.

"Stormie, give me just five minutes. If I can't fix it in five minutes, you can shoot me too. Okay?"

She didn't respond. He heard only silence for several moments and was about to call out to her again, when he heard the bolt turn. A moment later, her tearstained face appeared in the doorway.

He breathed a deep sigh of relief when he looked in her eyes and saw a faint glimmer of hope.

Chapter 19

"Stormie, wake up, hon. The caterer is gonna be here any minute." A warm hand lightly shook her shoulder.

Stormie opened her eyes. A headache pulsed at her temples, and she felt a terrible sense of confusion. She turned her head on the pillow.

"Travis!" she shrieked, a sunny smile breaking out on her face. She threw her arms around him, jamming her breasts hard against his chest.

"Whoa," he said, returning the embrace. She looked in stunned amazement down at her chest. "Oh God!" she screamed. "My boobs!"

Travis looked at her, puzzled. "You just now noticing them?" he asked, taking one and giving it a gentle squeeze.

Stormie's eyes sparkled with amazement. She jumped from the bed and stood in front of the full-length mirror in the corner of the room. She ran her hands over her face and squealed.

Travis was looking at her, worried. "Honey, maybe you drank too much last night at the rehearsal dinner or somethin'. You're acting weird."

"Rehearsal dinner!" she exclaimed.

Travis rose from the bed and took his wife by the elbow. "Sit down, babe." He led her to the edge of the bed and sat beside her. "Today is Heather's wedding, remember?" he explained patiently. "We got a caterer due in an hour, a florist due in two, and a cake being delivered in two and a half. Then we got a nervous groom and a whole mess of future in-laws comin' to the house. Any of this ringing a bell?"

"Where is Heather?" she cried.

"Down the hall in her bedroom. Storm, you are scarin' me. I know it ain't everyday your only baby gets hitched, but you are acting really weird. What's gotten into you?"

She started to weep and he pulled her to him. "Honey, what is it? Is it the wedding? He's a good boy. He'll take fine care of her."

Stormie shook her head. "It's not the wedding. I had a… God, I don't know. It must have been a dream or something," she sobbed. "I dreamt I lost everything. You and Heather, my life, everything! It was all gone and I was… I was someone else. I wasn't me anymore. Where is Franklin? Is he alright?"

A ghost of unease drifted through Travis's heart. He felt the hairs on the back of his neck rise up.

Travis took his wife in his arms. He had a disquieting moment of déjà vu as he recalled having a nightmare himself. The details were hazy, but it had had something to do with Seattle. That's all he could remember.

"Franklin is downstairs, honey. He's fine. You know somethin'? I had a pretty bad dream too. I can't remember much, but it was awful." He shook his head. "Must have been the Moroccan Beef, huh?"

"Yes, I suppose so." She sounded utterly unconvinced.

"Well, we got us a wedding to pull off, so go wake up our girl." Travis released her from his embrace.

Stormie threw a robe over her shoulders. She stopped for just a moment to stare again at herself in the mirror before running down the hallway and throwing open the door to Heather's room. She burst into tears when Heather cracked open one sleepy eye and yawned.

"Mother!" Heather cried. "You promised not to do this. Now you are going to make me cry."

"I can't help it," Stormie wailed, launching herself onto the bed and pulling Heather into her arms.

"Mom, this is supposed to be the happiest day of my life. Now quit crying." Heather laughed, her own tears spilling down her face.

Stormie sniffed. "I got news for you baby; it's the happiest day of mine, too!"

"Oh, Mom," Heather bawled.

"Okay, okay, sorry. I just feel a little bit like Scrooge at the end of a Christmas Carol. Or Tiny Tim. You know, God bless us, every one!"

"Mom, that's the weirdest thing you have ever said, but I'm sure Dan would appreciate it just the same." Heather smiled.

"Oh my God! Dan! Is Dan okay?" The tears were falling again.

Heather's eyes narrowed in suspicion. "What do you mean *okay*? He was fine when I left him at the hotel last night with his parents after the rehearsal. I don't know if he's gotten cold feet and run off sometime between then and now, however. Maybe we should call the hotel and make sure he's still there." She was only half kidding.

Stormie dabbed at her eyes with the sleeve of her robe. "I'm sorry, baby. I guess I just can't believe this is really happening."

Heather hugged her mother. "As Connor said during his toast last night, you must have done something right to raise an angel like me."

They both laughed. Stormie took Heather's hand and together they walked downstairs.

Epilogue

One year later.

Stormie Banks smiled to her peers in the packed auditorium. She cleared her throat softly, leaning toward the microphone on the podium.

"And the Oscar for leading actress in a dramatic role goes to—" she slid the card with the embossed letters from the envelope—"Kyra Hastings for *Golden Sunset*!"

The audience erupted in applause as the theme song to *Golden Sunset* filled the loudspeakers. Kyra jumped from her chair, stopped briefly to hug her date and then ran up the steps to the podium.

Stormie offered her a warm hug. She murmured, "Congratulations," into the crying girl's ear.

She stepped back, to allow Kyra to recite her acceptance speech.

~~~~
~~~~

The little bell above the door to Bella Luna Bookstore and Metaphysical Shop jangled lightly as a well-dressed woman entered the store. Gabriella looked up from the books she was shelving.

"Good afternoon." She smiled at the customer.

The woman didn't smile back. She hunched her shoulders and hurried over to where Gabriella stood. She looked around once, to make sure no one could overhear what she was saying and then whispered into the girl's ear, "I'm looking for Belda. Someone told me she could help me."

Gabriella took the woman's elbow and began leading her to the small office in the corner. "Well, Belda has retired, but I'm sure that I could assist you with whatever your problem may be," she said, a glow lighting her eyes. "Have a seat right here. Can I offer you some tea?"

~~~~

Stormie unwrapped the Tiffany frame she just picked up from the engraver. She had instructed them to engrave it in exactly the same way as the half dozen she had made for her awards cabinet over the years. This one bore the date of the last Academy Awards and the name of a film in elegant script.

Stormie undid the fasteners and pulled the back off. She carefully placed a card into the frame behind the glass and replaced the backing. The card was the one she had taken with her from the stage, after announcing the name written on it as the Best Actress winner. She ran her hands lightly over the engraved date at the bottom, and the words, *Golden Sunset.*
~~~~

Stormie placed the frame and a handwritten note into a box and sealed it shut. The box was addressed to Kyra Hastings. The note inside read:

Dear Kyra,

Congratulations on being awarded the most prestigious recognition in our industry for your outstanding performance as Desiree in the remake of Golden Sunset. I thought perhaps you might like to keep this on the shelf beside your Oscar as a souvenir of that magical evening. Wishing you continued success in your career.

Best wishes,
Stormie Banks

About the Author

Krystal Lawrence works as a commercial voice over artist and media actress. She lives in Washington where she is working on the sequal to her successful novel, *Risen*.

Visit the author website:
http://www.darksidestories.com

CPSIA information can be obtained at www.ICGtesting.com
Printed in the USA
LVOW08*0946090114

368735LV00002B/260/P

9 781939 927453